SUSAN MALLERY

Already Home

MIRA®

ISBN-13: 978-1-61129-455-2

ALREADY HOME

Printed in U.S.A.

To Mike. You are always where I find home. I love you.

Already Home

One

"What do you think?" Jenna Stevens asked, doing her best to sound confident. When faced with something scary, like a big dog or a really bad decision, it was important not to show fear.

"I love it," her mother said. "Truly, it's amazing." Beth squeezed her daughter's shoulders. "I'm so proud of you, honey."

Proud? Proud was good. Proud implied an accomplishment. The only problem was Jenna couldn't claim one. She'd acted on impulse.

As a rule, she could respect a good impulse purchase. There were times when life sucked and a woman needed to buy a pair of shoes or a skirt or even a lipstick she didn't need just to prove she could. To show the world she wasn't defeated.

Only Jenna hadn't bought any of those things, mostly because she wasn't much of a shopper. But she'd sure stepped out of her comfort zone recently. Had she done it with a too-expensive handbag? If only. Instead she'd impulsively signed a three-year lease on retail space in a town where she hadn't lived in nearly ten years. As if she knew anything about retail. Oh, sure, she shopped on occasion, but that wasn't exactly the same as running a business. Just like being a chef didn't mean she knew squat about running a kitchen store.

"Breathe," her mother told her. "You have to breathe."

Apparently she'd shattered the illusion of courage by hyperventilating.

"Maybe not," Jenna murmured. "If I stop breathing and go into intensive care, the management company might let me out of my lease. There has to be a clause about a near death experience, don't you think?"

"Is there?"

Jenna turned from staring at the front of her new business and pressed her head into her mother's shoulder. Something of a trick considering Beth was a good six inches shorter and Jenna was wearing heels.

"I didn't read the lease," she admitted, her voice slightly muffled.

She braced herself for the chiding. She'd been raised to read *everything* before signing it. Even a greeting card. She deserved to be yelled at.

Her mother sighed and patted her back. "We won't tell your father."

"Thank you."

Jenna straightened. They stood in the parking lot in front of the space she'd rented. Right now it was just an empty storefront, but in a few short weeks, it would be her new business.

"Fifty percent of all new businesses fail," Jenna whispered.

Her mother laughed. "That's my little ray of sunshine.

Come on. I'll buy you a latte. We'll sit, we'll talk, we'll plan ways to have your soon-to-be ex-husband tortured. I'm sure your father knows a guy."

Despite the fear and the panic swirling in her stomach, the sense of impending doom and a life that bordered on pathetic, Jenna smiled. "Mom, Dad's a banker. Men who run banks don't know guys."

"Your father is very resourceful."

He was also a physically fit, active man who enjoyed plenty of outdoor activities. If Marshall Stevens wanted something physical to happen to Jenna's ex, he would do it himself.

"I'm just so angry at Aaron," Beth said, leading the way to her SUV. "That cheating, lying you-know-what."

The "you-know-what" was, of course, a stand-in for bastard. Or possibly sonofabitch. Either way, Beth didn't believe in swearing.

She was a traditional kind of woman. She put on makeup before leaving the house, always brought a casserole in a covered dish when there was a death in someone's family and never, ever had a cocktail before five. All things Jenna loved about her.

She knew people who thought traditions were stupid and a waste of time, but for Jenna, they were the warm, comforting glue that held her family together. She could count on her parents to be what they'd always been. Today, that was more important than ever.

They got into her mother's SUV, a late-model gas guzzler, and drove toward the closest Starbucks.

"I'll never forgive him," Beth announced. "I suppose I could accept it if he decided that your relationship wasn't working. Not every marriage lasts. It's the cheating that makes him a weasel. I swear, if my daddy was still alive, he would go after Aaron with a shotgun and I wouldn't stop him."

Some days Jenna wouldn't have stopped him, either. But her anger at her ex wasn't about the other women, although the thought of them didn't make her happy. What made her lie awake at night, questioning herself and every decision she'd ever made, was the other ways Aaron had hurt her.

The cheating simply gave her an easy excuse to say why the marriage had failed.

They pulled into the Starbucks parking lot. Her mother turned to her. "You get anything you want. Venti, syrup, whipped cream." Beth wrinkled her nose. "I won't even mention how resentful I am that you're as skinny as a string bean and I'm stuck with thighs that hate me. That's how much I love you."

Jenna laughed, then leaned across the console and hugged her mother. "I love you, too, Mom. Thank you."

"I haven't bought the coffee yet."

The thank-you wasn't about the drink, but then her mother already knew that.

"I'm glad you're home," Beth told her as she climbed out of the SUV. "This is where you belong. Real people live in Texas, not in Los Angeles. All those Hollywood types." She sniffed. "Is there anyone normal in the city?"

"A few, but they never go out at night." Jenna linked arms with her. "I'm glad I'm home, too."

Jenna couldn't quite escape the feeling that going back to look at her store was like returning to the scene of the crime. But it had to be done, and someone, probably her, needed to get her business started.

Despite having spent the past couple of weeks getting things ready for the grand opening, every time she pulled into the parking lot and stared at the space she'd rented, she couldn't bring herself to believe it.

Three months ago she'd been in Los Angeles. Her husband had walked into their tiny bathroom while she'd been brushing her teeth and had announced he was leaving her for another woman. He was in love and he was leaving.

What Jenna remembered most was standing in that cramped space wondering when she was supposed to spit. At what point in that kind of confession was it polite or expected for her to lean over the sink, spit and rinse?

She'd been unable to speak with all that toothpaste in her mouth, so she'd stood there like an idiot. Eventually Aaron had walked out, leaving her stunned, emotionally shattered and with toothpaste dribbling down her chin.

Later they'd talked. Or he'd talked, explaining all the reasons the breakup was her fault. She realized now that that was Aaron's thing. Taking whatever was good and strong in a person and systematically destroying it. On the outside, he was pure charm, all dark good looks and an easy smile. On the inside, he was the devil. Or at the very least, an evil minion.

She supposed she could have fought for her marriage, but a part of her had been relieved to have a reason to leave. So she'd packed up everything she owned and had returned to Georgetown, Texas.

She'd been lost, so going home had made sense. As much as anything could, under the circumstances.

She was grateful her parents had never asked why she didn't try to get a job in a restaurant. She'd been a professional chef for nearly a decade. It was what she knew. Or it had been. Today, cooking anything seemed impossible.

Oh, sure, she could throw together something easy. A bisque, a dozen or so pasta dishes, a savory tart, prime rib.

The basics. But to creatively cook? To take new flavors and blend them into something so good it was almost magic? That had been lost.

It was as if her culinary soul had been stolen. As much as she wanted to blame Aaron—and a case could be made that he was guilty of theft—she'd been the one not standing guard, not protecting what mattered most of all. She'd been the one to let him berate her, mock her and claim her best ideas as his own. She'd let herself begin to doubt her abilities, her imaginative self, and now she was just someone who had once known how to cook.

The killer was, no one knew. Not that she wanted to talk about it or have people feel sorry for her—she didn't. On the outside, she was as good as she'd ever been. It wasn't as if she'd lost her actual skills. But the thing she'd loved best—the spark of creating—was gone. And she didn't know how to get it back, much less articulate the problem to anyone else.

She tried to tell herself that opening a cooking store was a grand adventure. It was her new destiny. She would pass on her skills to others, share the wealth, so to speak. And if she didn't want to use that as inspiration, she had three years of lease payments to worry about. If she couldn't perk her mood with self-help, then she would get real with fear. Whatever worked.

At least the location was great, she thought, staring at the big windows and glass front door. Old Town was a thriving part of Georgetown, and her store was in the middle of it. To the right of her space was a yarn store called Only Ewe. To the left was an insurance agency and beyond that, a beauty salon.

Old Town itself—a series of square blocks—was a combination of business and retail with some residential areas.

There were restaurants, boutiques and a couple of banks. Foot traffic was high, and Jenna was hoping that impulse buying was also a part of everyday life.

As she got out of her car and studied her store, she told herself she could do this. She could be successful with her new business. She'd never been a big believer in "fake it until you make it," but maybe now was the time to explore a new philosophy. After all, like it or not, the store was opening. The sign would be delivered early next week. The final deliveries of her inventory would arrive two days after that. Then it was just a matter of getting everything in place and opening the doors.

She was waiting to see how well she did before spending money on advertising. Grate Expectations would sell high-quality kitchen supplies with expert instruction. She would demonstrate, offer cooking classes and give the people in town the chance to learn the secrets of professional chefs. There didn't seem to be any competition for this kind of business in the nearby communities.

As she pulled out her key to the store, she heard a car door slam. She turned and saw a dark-haired woman walking toward her.

"Hi," the woman called. "Jenna?"

"Yes. You must be Violet."

They'd spoken on the phone. Violet had been one of nearly a dozen calls she'd had about the job she'd posted in the paper. Of the potential applicants, Violet had had the most experience, not to mention the most normal personality.

Now Jenna took in the short, spiky hair, the dark eyeliner and thick lashes. Violet's beige lace T-shirt covered a deep purple tank top. Her skirt was layered and also purple. Dozens of necklaces hung down in various lengths, while an equal number of bracelets clinked on her left arm. High-heeled ankle boots completed the outfit.

She looked to be in her mid-to-late twenties. Humor and curiosity sparkled in her brown eyes and her smile was friendly.

"Great location," Violet said as Jenna wrestled with the door. "Very upscale. You'll get a lot of walk-in traffic. Especially if you're cooking. People will follow the smell."

They went inside. Jenna turned on the lights, then glanced around at the chaos.

She saw shelves against the walls and freestanding racks in the middle of the main room. A newly installed kitchen setup gleamed from one side. The desk for the cash register was in place. Boxes were stacked nearly five feet high. Unpacking was going to take days.

Daunting didn't begin to describe it, but Jenna didn't care. Hard work was exactly what she was looking for. If she was exhausted, she wouldn't have as much time to think. Besides, this was America. According to legend, all that stood between her and success was a little hard work. Fortunately, the ability to do what needed doing had always been one of her strongest attributes.

"Nice," Violet said, walking around. "The high ceilings are great. Some of the places around here have a second floor, so the ceilings are lower." She headed for the kitchen area, set down her purse and tugged on her sleeves. As she pulled up the lace, Jenna caught sight of a tattoo of flowers on the inside of her wrist.

Violet wasn't anything like Jenna had imagined. She'd pictured someone older. Someone more...conservative. But Violet had energy and an engaging smile. The pixie cut gelled to a fashion-forward mess suited her, as did the Goth-inspired makeup. Violet looked both fun and approachable.

Ten years of working in restaurant kitchens had taught Jenna to trust her gut when it came to hiring. For all his telling her that she didn't know what she was talking about, Aaron had listened to her gut, too.

"You enjoy working with the public?" Jenna asked.

She knew that was going to be the most difficult area for her. She was used to being behind the scenes, not dealing with the front of the house. Ordering, organizing, working under pressure—those were easy. But smiling in the face of harried customers? Not so much.

"Most days," Violet said with a laugh. "I think the difference between a place like this and, say, a big-box store is branding. You go to a retail chain with certain expectations. Sometimes it's price or convenience. But making a special trip to your store requires a little more thought. Customers have to want to come here."

She ran her hands across the stainless steel counters by the stove.

"I think the key to success is to give customers an experience they can't get anywhere else. Not only different products, but personalized service. You have to make them want to come back." Violet smiled again, her eyes dancing with excitement. "I do love a good challenge."

"Good thing—because we're going to have that here."

Violet faced her. "Maybe not. What's the competition? I don't think there are any other places like this in the area, but I didn't do the research."

Jenna stared at her. Research? She did her best not to wince. Right. Because most people had a plan when they opened a store. They checked out the area, ran the numbers, worked on a profit and loss statement. Things Jenna would have done had she been opening a restaurant.

"We're going to offer something unique here," Jenna said. "Neighborhoods like that."

"You've owned retail stores before?" Violet asked.

"Not exactly. I'm a sous chef."

"Oh, wow. That's great." Violet moved to the open area in front of the sink and held her arms open wide. "We could set up cooking stations here. People love to get their hands dirty. With that big oven and the six burners, they can all be cooking and baking together. People would kill to get real tips from someone like you."

Jenna shook her head. "I wasn't going to have the customers cook. I'll be doing demonstrations. Showing techniques for different dishes."

Violet's arms dropped to her side. "That would be good, too," she said with measurably less enthusiasm. "Will you have prepared the dishes in advance so they get to sample what you're doing?"

"Of course."

"That's nice." She walked toward the boxes and read the labels. "So you've never exactly run a store before?"

"No."

Violet bit down on her lower lip. "Are you hiring a manager?"

"I'll be the manager. At least for now." Jenna squared her shoulders. It was time to get to the interview. "I'm looking for someone to work full-time with me. We'll be open six days a week. I'd prefer you take your second day off on Monday through Thursday. I'm guessing Friday and Saturday will be busiest. I'm going to offer different kinds of cooking classes. Classic recipes, easy to make, foods that can be frozen and served days or weeks later."

Stuff she could do in her sleep.

A part of her whispered it might be fun to experiment a

little. To have customers surprise her with ingredients and then come up with something on the fly. She could—

Without wanting to, she remembered experimenting with bread pudding as an appetizer rather than a dessert. Using savory flavors, chilies and spices rather than sugar. Aaron had grabbed one of her samples before she could taste it herself. He'd taken one bite and quickly spit it back into his hand.

Then he'd patted her on the back and said, "It's good that you try."

As if she were some kid who'd made a mud pie. Some kid who had trouble learning and needed a lot of praise.

She didn't know which had been worse—the rest of the kitchen staff watching, or the fact that when she'd tasted her creation later, it had been delicious. But she hadn't trusted herself enough to give it to anyone else to try.

No. She wouldn't be experimenting anytime soon. The reality of that thought made her sad. No, sad wasn't the right word. It broke her heart.

"I want someone who can grow into the manager position quickly," she said before she could stop herself.

"I would be interested in that," Violet told her, looking pleased with the information.

Jenna pressed her lips together. If she wasn't managing the store, she would have plenty of time on her hands. Time to figure out how to find that lost part of herself.

Violet glanced around. "Are you going to sell the foods themselves? The various ingredients?"

"No, why?"

"You need something for the people to buy. Either a gadget or a pan. Cookware doesn't exactly break or go out of style. If you don't offer the customers a reason to buy, they won't. They'll come in, get the recipes and tips, then leave. That means no money for you."

"I see." Jenna hadn't thought that part through. "I'll work something out. Maybe charge a fee for the classes. Why don't you tell me about your current job?"

Fifteen minutes later Violet had run through her work experience. She had two letters of recommendation and an easy way about her. Jenna knew her own personality tended toward the control freak end of the spectrum. Violet seemed like a nice balance.

"Why are you looking to make a change?" Jenna asked.

"I like what I do," Violet told her. "But corporate America isn't my thing. I want to be part of a community. I've been in Austin a couple of years but I still feel like I'm settling in." She waved her hand at the shelves. "This is going to be a challenge and that's what I'm looking for. If you're sure there's a chance that I'll be considered for the manager position, then I'm interested."

Jenna was relieved. She'd already checked Violet's references and had been impressed with what she'd been told. At this point someone who knew what retail was all about would be a big help. "When could you start?"

"Next week. Tuesday."

"Perfect."

The front door opened and a blonde woman in her late twenties walked in.

"Hi. I'm Robyn. I own the yarn store next door. Thought I'd come say hi and welcome you to the neighborhood."

Violet moved toward her, smiling and holding out her hand. "I'm Violet Green," she said. "I know. Crazy name. I think my mother was deep into medication when she gave birth. Anyway, this is Jenna Stevens. She owns the store."

"Nice to meet you," Jenna said, thinking Robyn looked familiar. Georgetown was small enough that they'd probably gone to the same school, although in different grades. Robyn looked a few years younger.

Robyn looked around. "Great space. It's so light and bright. You're going to love it here. I'm hoping we'll be able to share customers." She wrinkled her nose. "I was terrified an auto parts store would move in next door. Not that I don't love my car, but not a lot of guys are interested in knitting."

Violet laughed. "I've been in your place before. It's beautiful. I love all the yarn."

"Do you knit?" Robyn asked.

"No, but I'd like to learn."

"We'll be starting a beginner class in a few weeks. If you're interested."

"Thanks."

Jenna found herself feeling shy and awkward. She reminded herself it was simple conversation. She could handle that. But the truth was, she hadn't been out in the "girl world" for years. Most of the people in the kitchens where she'd worked had been guys. While Aaron had always had a pack of friends hanging around, she'd had more trouble finding women to relate to. When she'd lived here before, she'd had a lot of friends. She promised herself she would call them soon.

"I'm going to be doing a lot of cooking here," she forced herself to say. "I can bring by samples."

Robyn smiled. "This is why you're going to be my favorite neighbor. I can already tell. When do you open?"

Jenna gave her the date.

"Let me know if there's anything I can do to help," Robyn told them both. "Even if you just want to pop over and have some coffee to get away from the craziness."

"Thanks," Violet said. "We will."

Robyn ducked out. Violet closed the door behind her and laughed.

"What an adventure. I can't wait."

Jenna thought about how she'd spent the past couple of months feeling like a total failure. This was a new beginning for her. A chance to prove herself.

"I can't wait, either," she murmured. This time, everything was going to be different.

Jenna arrived at her new rented townhouse a little after six. After pulling into the garage, she climbed the stairs to the main floor, only to find her father squinting at a power drill. He checked the mark on the wall, then carefully drove in three screws.

She waited until the drill was silent.

"Hi, Dad."

He turned and grinned at her. "Hey, kid. Your shelves are just about done. Give me a sec and you can help me put the brackets in place."

The shelves were decorative metal with hooks for all her pots and lids. While the townhouse had plenty of room for the average cook, Jenna traveled with a lot of cookbooks, notes and equipment. Extra storage space was required.

Her dad winked at her. "I checked with your landlord, to make sure adding the shelving was okay."

"I'll bet that was a tough conversation."

"He saw my side of things."

As the man who owned the entire complex was a close friend of her dad's, she wasn't surprised.

Marshall put down his drill and held out his arms. "You okay, Jenna?"

She stepped into his embrace and allowed herself to get lost in her father's familiar strength. "I will be."

"I'm sorry Aaron turned out to be such a jerk."

"Me, too. I wanted what you and Mom have." Growing up, she hadn't thought it was too much to ask. Now, looking back at her failed years with her ex-husband, she knew finding the right man wasn't as easy as it looked.

"You'll get there," her dad told her. "But do me a favor, kid. This time fall for a Texas boy."

She grinned. "You think they're that much better?"

"I know they are."

"What if he's an Aggie?" she asked in a mock whisper. Her father had gone to the University of Texas. Aggies— those who graduated from Texas A&M—were the enemy.

"Better an Aggie than someone from California."

She laughed. "I'll do my best."

"That's my girl." He kissed the top of her head and released her.

She stepped back and watched him finish putting up her shelves.

Maybe this wasn't exactly where she'd thought she would be at nearly thirty-two, but she could still make it okay. She'd failed at her marriage. People did that and recovered. Many of them thrived. She could thrive, as well. She could figure out how to make starting over the best thing that ever happened to her.

Two

Violet parked in front of Jenna's store and turned off her car engine. She still had a couple of sips left of her coffee. Based on the stacks of boxes she'd seen during her interview, she would need all the caffeine she could get to keep her energy going during the unpacking phase. Getting a store up and running was a lot of work.

She could see someone moving around inside and guessed Jenna had arrived before her. Enthusiasm was important, she thought, wondering if she'd made a huge mistake, quitting a job she'd had for nearly two years to work for someone with no retail experience.

The potential upside was that if the store was successful, and Violet made manager, she would enjoy being responsible for things running smoothly. The downside was Jenna didn't have any experience and some of her ideas were a little strange.

Still, Violet's gut had told her this was a good move, and

she'd learned to listen to her gut. Except when it came to men, it had never let her down. On the guy front, her gut was a total failure, but she was okay with that. It wasn't as if she was looking for a relationship. Career now, she told herself. Men, whenever.

She swallowed the last of her coffee, then got out of her car and headed for the front door. Jenna straightened at her knock and hurried to let her in.

"You're here. Thank God. I'm drowning in boxes. I made a diagram so we'd know where to put everything. What I didn't count on was the packing material. How is it possible that after I empty a box, there's more material to stuff in it than will fit? Is that a retail thing?" Jenna paused and laughed.

"Sorry," she said and shook her head. "I'm a little wired. I've been here since four this morning and I've had the coffee to prove it. Let me start over. Hi. Welcome. How are things?"

"Good. For what it's worth, you're right about the packing material. Somehow while it's on the floor it multiplies or something."

"That explains the mess."

Jenna gestured to what had been an open space the last time Violet had seen it. Now it was a maze of boxes and shelves. Whatever free floor space had been there before was now filled with open containers overflowing with paper and cardboard.

By contrast, Jenna looked cool and unruffled. She wore a white chef's coat over black pants. Black clogs covered her feet. She'd pulled her dark red hair back into a ponytail. Her green eyes were bright, her full mouth smiling, her skin perfect, despite the lack of makeup and probable lack of sleep.

She looked like a model dressing like a chef for a photo shoot, but more *Town and Country* than *Cosmo.*

Violet had dressed for comfort and physical labor. She'd pulled a long-sleeved T-shirt over jeans and had worn scuffed ankle boots. Despite the fact that she wore the more practical clothes, she felt as if she'd misread the invitation and had shown up in shorts for a fancy dress ball.

"Here's my diagram," Jenna said, pointing at several sheets of paper tacked to the wall. "Obviously the kitchen is in back. I ordered a few new things for that and they'll go in the cupboards under the counters. I'm organizing everything else by function. Pots and pans together, bakeware. You get the idea."

She quickly went through the layout.

"A woman with a plan," Violet said. "Why don't I take some of this trash out to the Dumpster? Most of it can go in the recycling bins."

"Great. I've been avoiding the boxes of ceramic bowls. I can't begin to imagine how many layers of packing material are in those. With you here, I think I can be brave."

They worked for the next couple of hours. Together they wrestled the impressively large mixers into place. Jenna did her share of ripping up cardboard and stacking supplies, which surprised Violet. A lot of bosses were more into gesturing about how the work should be done than actually participating.

Despite the physical labor, Jenna didn't break a sweat. Violet felt distinctively damp, but rather than be annoyed, she told herself she would have to accept the fact that her new boss was one of those perfect people. Perfectly organized, perfectly disciplined, perfectly elegant in every situation. Violet had always meant to be perfect...one day. But somewhere during her life journey, she'd made an imperfect turn and never recovered.

Around ten-thirty, they took a break. Jenna had already stocked the small refrigerator under the counter with diet Snapple and handed out a bottle of unsweetened tea. They sank onto the floor.

Jenna stared around at the piles of merchandise. "It's going to get better, right? If it's not, it's okay to lie to me and say it is."

Violet uncapped her bottle and took a drink. "It's going to be great. You'll see. In the future, the boxes will only arrive a few at a time. That makes it easier."

"I hope so. The worst I've had to deal with in a restaurant is finding out the beef I ordered hadn't been butchered."

Violet stared at her. "As in it was still a cow?"

"Practically. I had to prepare all the steaks myself. Let me just say, making tomahawks all afternoon strains the wrist."

Violet must have looked blank because Jenna added, "It's rib eye steak with a frenched rib bone."

"Right." As if that made anything more clear, Violet thought. "Does being able to cut your own steaks make you more or less popular with the guys?"

Jenna grinned. "It was important to prove myself in the kitchen. A little butchering can go a long way." Her smile faded. "I was always better at that than Aaron. Probably another reason why things didn't work out." She stared at her Snapple for a second, before raising her head. "I'm in the middle of a divorce. Paperwork is signed. We're waiting out the time."

A divorce. Violet hadn't seen that one coming. "I'm sorry," she said automatically. "Do you miss him?"

Jenna shrugged. "You'd think I would." She paused, as if thinking. "I miss what used to be good. When we worked together. In the past year or so, I couldn't do anything right. Or so he said."

Jenna stopped talking abruptly, as if she hadn't meant to say that much.

"I know what you mean," Violet said quickly. "I'm a total disaster when it comes to men. I'm always picking the wrong one. If I'm attracted to a guy, run far and fast. He's a loser. Probably an unemployed loser who will charm you out of every penny you have." Or worse. But she had no reason to admit that. At least not on her first day.

"My new plan is to not date," she finished with a shrug.

"Ever?"

"I wish, but I'll give in. This time I'm determined to get it right," Violet said. "I'm going to keep saying no until I'm sure. Except all the ones I say no to turn out to be great. My radar sucks. I guess next time I need to say yes when I want to say no. Reverse psychology and all that."

Jenna raised her perfectly plucked eyebrows. "You get asked out a lot?"

"Sure. Hourly. Don't you?"

"Not exactly."

Violet didn't believe that. Jenna was that irresistible combination of fire and class. "Maybe because you were married."

"I don't think so. Guys are rarely interested in me."

Violet nearly choked on her drink. "Then you're not paying attention. Trust me, men are interested."

"I'm sort of avoiding men right now," Jenna admitted. "Aaron cheated, so I'm being cautious."

Her ex had cheated? Violet had to consciously keep her mouth from dropping open. If a guy would cheat on someone like Jenna, what chance did the rest of them have?

Someone tapped on the front door, then pushed it open. "Hi. I hope I'm not interrupting."

Jenna stood gracefully and crossed to the other woman. "Perfect timing. We were just taking a break."

As Violet watched, the two women embraced.

They couldn't have been more different. Jenna was tall and thin, with fiery auburn hair. The other woman, older, was a petite, curvy blonde with big blue eyes and a ready smile. Violet had seen enough fake relationships to recognize real affection, maybe even love, when she saw it.

She'd already guessed their connection when Jenna turned and said, "Violet, this is my mom, Beth Stevens. Mom, this is Violet."

Violet scrambled to her feet and held out her hand. "Nice to meet you, Mrs. Stevens."

"Beth, please." The other woman shook her hand, then touched the half dozen or so silver bracelets on Violet's wrist. "I love these." She fingered the black leather woven through a thick chain. "Do you change the cord?"

"I could but I usually don't."

"I should wear something like that."

Violet did her best not to look surprised. Beth was elegantly dressed in tailored pants and a fitted long-sleeved shirt that had more than a passing resemblance to silk. Her jewelry was delicate and understated, except for a honking big diamond next to an eternity wedding band. Violet would guess the watch alone would cover her rent for close to a year.

So this was how the other half lived, she thought, curious rather than envious.

Beth studied Violet's face. "You've conquered the smoky eye," she said with a sigh. "I've tried and tried. I end up looking tired or as if I have makeup smudged over half my face." She wrinkled her pert nose. "I suppose I should let it go. I suspect the smoky eye look is like a miniskirt. Ridiculous after a certain age."

Before Violet could figure out what to say, Beth had linked arms with her. "So what are you two girls up to? Unpacking, obviously. Is it coming together?"

Jenna explained about the chart on the wall and how the store would be set up. Violet was caught up in the maternal hold of a woman she'd barely met. Normally she didn't like to be touched by strangers. An unexpected backlash, given her previous profession. But there was something warm and welcoming about Beth. As if she were the kind of woman who took in strays of all kinds.

"I love the kitchen," Beth said, leading Violet toward the rear of the store. "People are going to be so excited to learn new cooking techniques. With you right there, they can practice until they get it right."

"Jenna's going to be doing the cooking," Violet said, not surprised that Beth had assumed the customers would get to do it. That was the plan that made the most sense. It was easy for people to drift away from a cooking demonstration.

"Oh." Beth glanced at her daughter. "That will work, too, I'm sure."

Jenna shifted uncomfortably. For a second, Violet almost felt sorry for her. Retail was its own world and not an easy place for the inexperienced. Wouldn't Jenna have done better to open a restaurant? That was her area of expertise.

"Look at the beautiful ceramic bowls Jenna picked out," Violet said, leading Beth toward a row of shelves. "Don't you love how the colors pop?"

"They're perfect. Very cheerful." Beth smiled at her daughter. "You're going to do very well here. I can feel it."

"I hope so." Jenna drew her brows together, looking more determined than optimistic.

Beth squeezed Violet's arm, then released her. "I have a few errands to run, then I thought I'd get you girls some sandwiches." She picked up her purse and pulled out a pad of paper. "Order away."

After writing down what they would like, Beth hugged Jenna, then surprised Violet by giving her a quick squeeze, as well.

"I'm off." She grinned at Violet. "You've inspired me to buy black leather."

Jenna laughed. "Mom, that may not be a good thing."

"I think I'll let your father decide that. Back in a flash."

Beth left in a swirl of perfume with the door clicking shut behind her.

"We need a bell for the door," Violet said absently, thinking that Beth was unlike any mother she'd ever met or even heard of. "So we can hear customers come in if we're in the back."

"Good idea."

Jenna jotted a note down on the pad she'd placed on the counter by the cooktop.

When she'd finished, she looked at Violet. "She didn't mean anything by mentioning black leather."

"I know. It's fine." Violet knew she was different from Jenna. From all of them. It wasn't good or bad—it just was. She turned to her boss. "You must really take after your dad. You don't look anything like your mom."

Jenna smiled. "Not surprising. I'm adopted. Mom says I come from a tribe of redheaded Amazon women and she's jealous."

Adopted. Violet turned the idea over in her mind. There would be advantages of not knowing where you came from, she thought. "You two are really close."

"We always have been. My mom's my best friend." Jenna wrinkled her nose. "That sounds so fake, but it's true. She's always been there for me."

"Nice," Violet said. "What about your biological parents? What are they like?"

"I don't know. I've never met them."

"Did you ever think about finding them?"

Jenna shrugged. "I never saw the point. I have a family. I'm not looking for another one."

Because the one she had was so good, Violet thought, more bemused than jealous. It was like watching a zoo animal. They were cute and all, but nothing she could relate to.

She couldn't imagine what it would be like to be close to her mother. Hers had beaten her, same as look at her, and Violet had taken off when she'd been fifteen.

She'd lived on the streets for five long years before realizing that if she stayed there, she would end up dead before she was twenty-five. Change hadn't come easy, but she'd managed.

And now she was here, she thought, looking around at the store, seeing it as it would be, rather than as it was.

Maybe Jenna didn't know what she was doing, but she had Violet. Together they would make Grate Expectations a success. Jenna had class and money and something to prove, while Violet knew how to make it, no matter the odds. An unlikely match, she thought, but a good one.

Jenna added spices, one after the other. She quickly stirred the strips of flank steak, searing them with the spices, over the high heat. The late news played in the background and she was already on her second glass of wine.

Telling herself it didn't matter, that no one would know, she picked up the bowl containing the sauce she'd created on a whim and dumped it in the pan.

The liquid snapped and boiled, reducing to almost nothing immediately. She rotated the pan, then used a spatula to flip the strips over one last time before dumping the contents onto the warm flour tortilla.

After setting the hot pan on another burner, she turned off the heat and took a fortifying sip of wine.

There it was. A taco of sorts. She'd been mentally playing with the idea of combining Mexican and Indian cuisine. Many of the spices were rooted in the same plants.

Jenna grinned. Rooted in the same plants. That was funny. Then her smile faded as she turned her attention back to the food she'd made.

She was nervous about tasting it. Experimenting used to be so easy, so joyful. Now it terrified her. Worse, it made her feel sick inside, as if something that had once been a part of her was now lost. She ached to be who she'd been before and didn't want to admit that woman was probably gone forever.

After squaring her shoulders, she picked up the taco and took a bite. The unusual blending of spices didn't sit well on her tongue. She found herself unable to chew, let alone swallow. She spit the meat into the sink and flushed it down with water. After running the garbage disposal, she threw out the rest of the taco.

When the tears came, she ignored them.

"I'm worried," Beth said as she stacked rinsed dishes on the counter. "Jenna doesn't know anything about making a store work. She doesn't even like shopping, unless it's for knives. Then she could spend hours. But this is different. This is working with the public."

"She's a smart girl," Marshall said as he loaded the dishwasher. "Give her a chance. She'll figure it out."

"She doesn't have much time to make it work. All her money is tied up in that place. Her savings and her half of what she and Aaron got for that sad little house they owned. If the city hadn't wanted to buy it and tear it down for that road, she would have had even less. You should have seen the inventory in her store. Thousands of dollars' worth of kitchen equipment."

Her husband glanced at her. "Did you want her to start a business without something to sell?"

"Don't be logical. You know how I hate that." Beth sighed, wishing she could learn how to let go. But when it came to anyone she cared about, she couldn't help worrying. Obsessing, Marshall would say.

"She knows what she's doing," Marshall told her.

"I'm not so sure. She's a chef. She should be cooking. She understands that world. I wish I knew what really happened with Aaron."

"Do you think there's more than she's telling us? Isn't Aaron cheating on her enough?"

"It is," she admitted, although her mother's instinct told her there was more to the story than Jenna had admitted. Something was different with her daughter. Not just the expected sadness and hurt from the breakup of a marriage. It was bigger than that.

"Jenna will figure out her store. Didn't she hire someone?"

"Violet. She's wonderful. Pretty. Black hair and dark eyeliner. I'm sure she has tattoos." Beth thought of the other woman's stacked bracelets and her three silver hoops in each ear and wished she had the courage to be unconventional.

"Does Violet have retail experience?"

"Yes. Several years of it."

"Then she'll help Jenna."

The statement drew Beth back to the subject at hand. Her chest tightened a little. "What if it's not enough? I understand that Jenna needs to regroup. She has to think and come up with a plan for the rest of her life, but opening a store? I don't think that was smart."

She finished rinsing the last two pots. Marshall fitted them into the dishwasher. She handed over the soap. He filled the cup, then closed the dishwasher and started it.

The end-of-dinner ritual had been the same for years. When Jenna had still been in the house, the three of them had cleaned the kitchen together. It had been a time of conversation and laughter.

"If she fails at this, too, she'll be crushed," Beth whispered, aching for her only child.

"You need to let it go, Beth. You can't protect her from everything. Jenna's a smart girl."

"Worry's my thing."

He moved toward her and slid his arms around her waist. "I'll admit you've turned it into an art form. Now you need to practice letting go."

She rested her hands on his shoulders and stared into his dark eyes. Even after all these years, being close to him made her breath catch.

"I can't help it. I love her."

"If you love something, set it free," he began.

She laughed. "Don't you start with me."

"Why not? I plan to finish with you."

He bent his head and kissed her.

Jenna stood in the center of her store and listened to the sound of silence.

Upbeat background music—something perky and Italian— played through speakers, but there wasn't any conversation.

No talking at all. Probably because to have the spoken word required people. AKA customers. And there weren't any.

It was eleven-fifteen on her first morning. She'd been open for seventy-five minutes and not a single person had walked through her sparkling clean glass doors.

Less than two weeks ago she'd stood in her parking lot and had watched as her sign had been lowered into place. She'd filled every shelf, figured out how to work the cash register, had talked to an accountant about keeping track of the sales. A problem she didn't currently have.

Happy Birthday to me, she thought sadly as she adjusted her white chef's coat. And hey, now she was thirty-two. This wasn't exactly how she wanted to spend her birthday. Talk about a disaster.

She'd been so sure that people would come. That they would be enticed by the pretty store window displays and the promise of great kitchen supplies. Over the past week Violet had casually mentioned taking out an ad in the local paper or getting a flyer into some kind of mailer. But Jenna had blithely refused. Because she'd been so damn sure.

She had the sudden need to bake. To sink her fingers into warm dough, to smell yeast and create crusty rolls slathered with sweet butter. Or maybe a tart. Quiche with a flaky crust and filling of eggs, cheese and garlic and nuts.

Or a brisket. She was back in Texas now. Something falling-apart tender with tang and spice. Grilled potatoes that tasted like heaven. She had an idea for using…

She shook her head, dislodging the wishful thinking. She didn't do that anymore. She cooked, she didn't create. Hadn't she already proved that to herself?

Behind her she heard Violet carefully rearranging shelves in an effort to keep busy. Jenna had to give the other woman points—so far she hadn't even hinted she wanted to shout, "I told you so." This despite the fact that Violet had been pushing for some serious advertising.

Fear tasted metallic on her tongue. Every single penny she had was tied up in this store. She had a three-year lease and her landlord expected monthly payments, regardless of her failure as a businesswoman.

She spun toward Violet. "I don't know what to do," she blurted.

Violet straightened from behind the shelf she'd been dusting. "Start cooking," she said quickly. "Something snacky and delicious that I can put on a tray and carry around."

"What good will that do? There's no one to eat it."

Her assistant smiled at her. "If they won't come here, I'm going to take the food to them. While you're doing that, I'll print out coupons to hand out to everyone I see. Ten percent off. Part of our grand opening. That will get people in."

Jenna nodded and did her best not to calculate how much that ten percent would eat into her profits. Better to lose a part of something than keep all of nothing, she told herself as she moved to the back of the store and started pulling out ingredients for a very familiar and easy appetizer.

A half hour later, she had a spicy goat cheese filling sitting on small crackers. She already had mushroom tarts in the oven, but they would take about fifteen minutes to bake.

"The trick is the spices," she told Violet. "Fresh is best and they have to be chopped really fine."

"Save the explanation for the customers," Violet told her, grabbing one of the trays. "I put the coupons on every car windshield in a five block radius. Hopefully that will bring people in. Now we're going to seduce them with food." She paused. "Are you going to be okay in here by yourself?"

"Of course," Jenna lied. The thought of being alone with

customers terrified her. Something she should have thought through *before* opening a store.

"Just offer them food and be prepared to talk recipes," Violet said with a smile. "I'll be back as soon as I've handed all these out."

Jenna nodded and offered a confident smile while Violet walked out.

While Jenna had put on black pants and her familiar chef's coat, Violet had dressed in a straight skirt in dark purple and a multicolored long-sleeved blouse. Three or four necklaces filled the open collar. The familiar half dozen bracelets clinked by her wrist. Her black hair was spiky, her bangs stick straight, and the smoky-eye look Beth had so admired was firmly in place.

Of the two of them, Violet was the one who should have looked out of place, yet Jenna felt as if everyone looking at her would know she was a fraud.

Before she could beat herself up even more, the front door opened with a tinkle of the bell Violet had hung there. But instead of her assistant returning, two women walked in. Each carried a coupon in her hand.

"Ooh, look at that," the shorter one said to her friend. "I love the colors on that trivet. It would look great in your kitchen."

"It's nice," the friend said, then spotted Jenna. "Hi. We just tasted that cracker. It was fabulous. Do you have the recipe?"

"Ah, yes. It's an easy spread or it can be a tart filling. You can use what you have on hand to fudge the ingredients."

The short woman laughed. "What I have on hand is a bottle of white wine and a few Lean Cuisines."

The oven timer beeped. Jenna pulled out the mushroom

tarts. The women rushed over and took napkins, then juggled the hot appetizers until they could take a bite.

"Delish," the taller one said with a sigh. "I don't suppose you have this recipe, too?"

Jenna had the recipes in her head. "I could write it down, if you'd like."

The women exchanged glances and started to leave. Just then Violet burst through the door, her tray empty, and about a half dozen people behind her.

"I know," she was saying. "If you think those are great, wait until you try the mushrooms. You'll die. I'm serious. They're fabulous. We don't have the recipes printed up yet. New store glitch. But by the end of the week, we'll have the recipe cards ready. And Jenna, the brilliant chef and owner, is doing a whole class on appetizers. So come back and get the recipe cards, then sign up for the classes."

Jenna felt anything but brilliant. Regardless of what she'd been in the rest of her life, she'd always felt good in the kitchen. Now she didn't know what to do there.

She watched as potential customers swarmed around the tarts. Soon the tray was empty. She'd already put another batch in the oven. At least they liked the food. That was something.

While she answered questions about getting the crust right, Violet rang up several purchases. The idea about the recipe cards was a good one. Maybe they could offer different recipes every week. Although Violet had made an excellent point when she'd said that people needed something to buy on a regular basis. Maybe she could come up with recipes that used different gadgets or something.

"Jenna? Is that you?"

She turned toward the speaker and saw two women her own age had entered the shop. They were both tall, exquisitely dressed, with perfect hair and makeup. Kimberly was as dark as Caitlin was fair. They were beautiful and familiar.

Jenna smiled. "What are you two doing here?"

"Beth called our moms," Kimberly said with a smile, as she hurried toward Jenna and hugged her. "Why didn't you tell us you were back? You're opening a store! It's darling." She stepped back. "Look at you, all cheflike."

Caitlin gave her a hug, too, along with a double air-kiss. Her white-blond hair swung in around her face before falling back into place.

"I was so worried about you," Caitlin said, resting her long, pink-tipped nails on Jenna's arm. "We heard about Aaron," she added in a low, sympathetic voice. "So sad, but you're obviously just peachy. The store is to die for. Really. I love it."

"We should get together," Kimberly said. "Call Jolene and go out. The four of us. It'll be like it was in high school."

Affection surged through Jenna. "I'd like that," she admitted. Hanging out with friends would be good, she thought. A reminder that life could be normal.

"Me, too," Caitlin said. "Soon."

"How about dinner?" Jenna asked. "Sometime this week."

The two other women exchanged glances, then turned back to Jenna.

"God, no," Caitlin said with a laugh. "If you could see my schedule."

"Mine, too," Kimberly told her. "I thought once the twins were in school, my life would finally slow down. But not at all. And keeping a decent housekeeper is practically a full-time job. But maybe we could get together for coffee. You know, some morning."

Caitlin nodded. "I can do coffee. I'll call Jolene and see if she has an hour free."

An hour. Jenna forced a smile. "Sure. Let me know." She

pulled a business card out of her pocket and wrote her cell on the back. "Give me a call."

"Will do," Caitlin promised as they headed for the door. "We love your little store."

The afternoon went pretty much like the morning. A few customers drifted in, there were a handful of sales, mostly driven by the coupons Violet had printed. Jenna made more trays of appetizers, which brought in people, but when they found out she didn't have recipes, they drifted away.

By five, Jenna felt tired and discouraged. She looked around at the full shelves, the carefully planned stock she'd been so proud of, and realized operating a successful business was more complicated than she'd ever thought. She needed a plan and some knowledge about the market and a good dose of common sense. Something she'd apparently missed out on when she'd been busy learning how to debone a chicken.

At exactly six, Violet locked the front door and turned the sign to indicate they were closed.

"It was a pretty good day," she said cheerfully. "Nearly five hundred dollars in sales."

Jenna nodded. "Great."

Considering the cost of the goods they'd sold, her overhead and salaries, not to mention the ten percent off coupons, she was probably in the hole about two hundred dollars. And that was just on the first day. Imagine how much she could fail in a week.

Violet crossed to her. "It's okay," she said. "This will get better. People will start to talk about the store, and before you know it, we'll be bustling with activity."

"Bustling?" Jenna managed a smile. "There's a word I haven't heard in a while."

"It works in this situation. We'll be slow for a while, but things will get better. You'll see."

"I know you're right," Jenna lied.

Violet tilted her head. "Want to get a drink? I know a bartender who makes a mean margarita."

"Thanks, but my mom's expecting me for dinner."

"Okay, sure. Tell her hi from me."

Violet left and Jenna quickly followed. No matter where she looked, all she had seen was potential. Now she felt as if she'd been playing a game where everyone knew the rules but her. The worst part was, the only person she could blame was herself.

She crossed the parking lot to her car. On the drive over, she would have to figure out how to spin her day so her parents didn't worry. They were already concerned enough.

As she slipped into her car, she heard the sound of laughter and glanced up toward the store next door. Only Ewe was busy with customers. Dozens of people held baskets overflowing with brightly colored yarn. She could see through to the back where a large table was crowded with knitters. A tall, handsome man moved toward Robyn, put his hand on the small of her back, then kissed her.

Jenna turned away and started the engine. Deep inside, she felt a stab of something that could only be envy. But whether it was for all the happy people filling her neighbor's store, or for the fact that she missed having someone special in her life, Jenna couldn't say.

Three

Violet passed out the list of ingredients to the half dozen customers sitting in front of the kitchen area of the store. It was the third day after opening and the first day of Jenna's classes. Yesterday had been a little better, with more people dropping by. Sales had been unimpressive, but she knew that could grow with time. Assuming they had time.

If she wanted to complain that it seemed as if Jenna had opened the store without much of a plan, she was just as guilty of leaping without looking. After all, she'd come to work for her without much in the way of guarantees. Still, her gut said this was the right thing to do. And if her gut had made its first mistake, she would simply find another job and start over. It wasn't as if she hadn't done it countless times before.

Jenna adjusted the mirror over the portable cooking table. "Can you all see what I'm doing?" she asked.

There were a few murmurs of agreement.

"Good. I thought I'd start with a quick tip on how to chop onions. It's fast and easy and will keep your fingers out of the way of a sharp blade."

Knives, Violet thought, making a mental note. They could do classes on different kinds of knives. What they were used for, how to care for them. That would encourage people to buy knives and sharpeners and knife blocks.

Jenna continued her lesson, explaining how to cut the onion in half, through the root, then peel it.

"Slice this way," she explained, demonstrating, "at an angle. Then turn the onion and slice it."

The slices fell away at a speed that was practically a blur. Jenna ran her fingers through the growing pile of onion, easily separating the slices into neat diced pieces.

"I didn't know how to do that," one woman murmured to her friend. "That's clever. I wish she'd let us practice."

"Me, too," the woman next to her answered. "I don't want to watch someone cook—I want to do it myself."

Violet agreed. But Jenna seemed determined to be the only cook in her kitchen. She had great ideas about products and even flow in the store, but she wasn't intuitive when it came to customers. Violet could only hope that Jenna's funding was generous so they could keep going until all the kinks were worked out.

Violet didn't get it. Jenna was nice and obviously intelligent. But clueless. It was as if she woke up one morning and said to herself, "I'm going to open a kitchen store." The total lack of advertising was problem enough, aside from the awkward people skills.

Jenna dropped the diced onion into sizzling butter, then smashed a clove of garlic and quickly sliced it. Chicken came next.

She did a good job of explaining what she was doing, but

despite that, the small crowd wasn't engaged. Several people shifted in their seats. A couple checked their cell phones. A woman on the end finally rose and headed for the door.

Violet followed her. "Thanks for coming."

The woman nodded, glanced at Jenna, then back at her. "She's obviously a really good cook, bless her heart, but no one wants to be preached to. Not unless it's Sunday morning. I would have loved to get my hands dirty."

Violet smiled. "I'll share that with Jenna."

The woman pulled a business card out of her jacket pocket. "I work around the corner at the bank and I'd love to learn how to make a few things. If she starts offering classes that are helpful to me, you give me a call and I'll come back."

"I will. Thanks."

The woman left.

Violet stared after her, wondering how many others were going to bolt before the chicken was even half done.

The door opened, and Beth, Jenna's mother, stepped inside. She smiled at Violet.

"Hi," she said in a low voice, then sniffed. "I don't care what it is, it smells delicious."

"I'm sure it will be. Jenna's a gifted cook."

"I want to tell you she gets it from me, but I'm more of a casserole kind of girl. I still remember when she was about eight or nine and I was making a chicken and pasta combo. I poured everything into the dish. But before I could crush the crackers and sprinkle them on top, Jenna gave me a very disapproving look and asked if I could please use something more original than saltines this time."

Violet chuckled. "That would have intimidated me for sure."

Beth grinned. "I'm not sure I cooked again for a week. Fortunately my husband loves to barbecue, so we didn't starve." She patted her left hip. "Although I could afford to lose a few pounds. With Jenna back in town I'm going to have to start going to my Weight Watchers meetings twice a week if I don't want to blow up to something the size of a building."

As Beth spoke, she glanced at her daughter, love obvious in her eyes.

They were a close family, Violet thought. Something she couldn't relate to on a personal level. You can't miss what you haven't had, she reminded herself.

Beth moved to the rows of chairs and slipped into the back. As she sat, two other women got up and left. Violet watched them anxiously. This was worse than not having a class at all. At least then people felt free to wander around and possibly buy things. But with Jenna lecturing, they only wanted to slip out as quickly as possible.

And never come back, she added silently.

Thursday morning Jenna sat in Cianfrani's Coffee Shop, sipping her latte as her friends chatted. Kimberly had gotten in touch with her two days ago, suggesting they all get together for coffee. Jenna had jumped at the invitation.

It was probably wrong to want to escape her business the first week it was open, but that was how she felt. So far the week had been a disaster. Sales had actually dropped, which was hard to believe. Except for her mother, everyone had walked out of her cooking class before it was over. Violet assured her things would get better, but Jenna had a feeling her lone employee was not only lying but was probably already looking for another job.

Thoughts for later, she reminded herself, turning her attention on Caitlin, who was talking about the problems her kids were having in their exclusive private school.

"One counselor talks about downtime," she was saying. "That children need instructional play to develop an imagination. I told her that my boys had spent the previous weekend trying to wallpaper the dog and imagination was the last thing they needed to work on." She sipped her nonfat soy drink. "Bill thinks they should learn to sail. Can you imagine? They're six."

"I know what you mean," Jolene said with a throaty laugh. She had always been pretty in college and now she was beautiful, with platinum blond hair that tumbled in curly splendor halfway down her back. "If Taylor wins one more dance championship, we'll have to buy a separate house for her trophies and ribbons. Little Amber is already singing in church. We've talked to a few agents and *they're* talking children's Christmas CD."

Kimberly smiled. "Little Jonathan is still throwing shutouts in Little League. I barely see him and Eric. They're always playing. We talked about having another one. A girl, this time, but I don't know. My stomach is finally flat again."

"Tell me about it," Jolene said. "I barely get in an hour at the gym. Did I tell you I have a new trainer? He's gorgeous. He comes to the house and even gives a postworkout massage."

Caitlin raised her eyebrows. "Which kind?"

Jolene smiled smugly. "The good kind."

The three women laughed together. Jenna tried to join in, but it was as if they were speaking a different language. She didn't know their husbands or their kids. She wanted to ask if any of them worked but already knew the answer.

Kimberly smiled at her. "You're so fortunate, Jenna. You only have to worry about yourself."

"It's true," Jolene chimed in. "I'm sure the divorce was difficult, but you got half of everything, right? So you're set."

Half of nothing was still nothing, Jenna thought, even as she smiled and nodded. There had been a few thousand in savings. The only reason she'd had the money to open the store was because the City of Los Angeles had needed to expand a road. They'd bought up four houses, including the tiny place she and Aaron had owned. A neighbor had hired a slick lawyer who had gotten them all a tidy sum above market value.

Caitlin leaned toward her. "How was it?" she asked in a hushed tone. "The divorce. Was it awful?"

The table went silent. All three women stared at her intently, as if she'd done something extraordinary. Or terrifying.

"It wasn't fun," she admitted. "But we'd grown apart." Which was better than saying being with her husband had sucked the life out of her. She'd been left with little more than a few skills she didn't trust and a gut-wrenching fear that she was mediocre.

"Was there another woman?" Jolene asked. "Was she younger and prettier?"

"I, ah—"

"It wasn't another man, was it?" Kimberly asked. "I heard that happens a lot in California. That would be the worst."

"Not worse than a woman," Caitlin told her. "At least with a man you never had a chance. With a woman, you have the same parts."

"Being left for any reason means you're still alone," Jolene said, tucking a platinum blond curl behind one ear. "Do you think it's because you didn't have children? A child binds a man to you. At least that's what I tell myself."

"A child would make things worse," Caitlin said. "Then she'd forever be tied to her ex."

Kimberly sighed. "He left her and now she's alone. To hell with him." She toasted Jenna with her coffee.

Jenna felt like the ball in a tennis game, being slapped back and forth. She grabbed her coffee, sucked in a breath and prepared to lie her way to sanity.

"I left him," she said quickly, before her blush could catch up with her. "He was holding me back. I came home because I wanted to and now I have the store. I can't believe how great it's doing. Speaking of which, I really have to get back to work. Violet is fabulous, but it's my responsibility. You know how that is. Being the one who makes it happen. It was great to see you three. We'll stay in touch, all right?"

She stood, gave a little wave, then quickly walked to her car. Once she'd backed out of the parking space, she drove to the other end of the parking lot and pulled into an empty space. Then she rested her head against the steering wheel and told herself that if she kept breathing everything would be fine. As long as she kept breathing.

Even as she drew air in and pushed it out, she felt her chest tighten and her eyes start to burn. Lying to her friends wasn't the answer, she reminded herself. Although the truth was equally impossible. What was she supposed to say? That Aaron *had* left her for another woman, but that she almost didn't care about that because the rest of it was so much worse? That she'd come home because she had nowhere else to go, and opening the store had been a stupid mistake? That would have been a conversation stopper.

And while she was being honest, Caitlin, Jolene and Kimberly weren't friends. Not anymore. They were women she used to know and little more. They were in different places, and she was…lost.

Which meant she had to do something about her life. But what?

★ ★ ★

The question plagued Jenna through the rest of the afternoon. She let Violet go early—it wasn't as if they had any customers—then closed right at six. After turning the lock, she walked through her empty store, touching the cool metal on the gourmet coffeemakers, the smooth surface of the mixing bowls.

The scent of cinnamon still lingered in the air. She'd made cookies earlier, in an attempt to entice customers. It hadn't worked.

She stood in the center of her store and turned in a slow circle. She liked everything about the space—the crowded shelves, the wide aisles, the cooking area in back. She liked the view out of the window, being next to the yarn store, leasing in Old Town. She liked it, but she didn't love it.

She hadn't wanted to make plain cinnamon cookies. She'd wanted to blend in ginger and try something fun like rosewater. She'd thought about going to the market and buying fresh spring vegetables, then making a red wine risotto with the crunchy, delicious vegetables served with a perfect roasted chicken stuffed with garlic and spices.

She'd heard two women complaining about all the ingredients they had in their pantries, items bought for a single recipe but never used again. When they'd listed a few, a dozen possibilities had occurred to her, and she'd almost spoken. But she'd been afraid.

She remembered experimenting with a salmon dish at the restaurant where she and Aaron worked. He was the high profile chef, the man who charmed customers, spending more time in the front of the store rather than in the back. He'd dazzled, while she'd worked the magic behind the scenes.

That night, it had been raining. Something that didn't

happen often in Los Angeles. The sound of the rain on the roof had made her think about murky seawater and all things green. She'd created a green sauce, then, borrowing from one of her favorite mole recipes, had added rich dark chocolate. While she hadn't been completely thrilled with the resulting color, the flavor had been perfect.

She'd offered a sample to a few regular customers, just to get their feedback. Aaron had swept in and taken the dishes from them. Worse, he'd apologized for what she'd made, as if she were some first year student who had burned toast. She'd been humiliated.

Later, when she'd yelled at him, he'd acted as if she was the one at fault. He'd had several of the staff taste her dish. One of the women had actually gagged. Jenna had been crushed, wondering if there was something wrong with her taste buds. Were they different from everyone else's?

During the divorce, she'd found out Aaron had been sleeping with the server, so her reaction was probably scripted, but the damage had been done. Jenna had started to question herself, to wonder if her instincts were off. As soon as doubt appeared, she found herself sticking to what was safe. She told herself it was the smart thing to do, but in truth, she was slowly dying inside.

Her cell phone rang. She pulled it out of her pocket, glanced at the screen and nearly jumped. Aaron? What would he want?

Almost afraid thinking about him conjured the call, she pushed the talk button.

"Hello?"

"Jenna. I only have a second. Some woman called, looking for you. She sounded strange. You're not in trouble, are you? She wasn't a bill collector, was she?"

I'm fine, she thought grimly. *Nice to hear from you. How are things?*

But Aaron had never been interested in polite conversation, not unless it got him something.

"Did the woman leave her name?" she asked, knowing it wasn't a bill collector. She might be failing at her business, but she hadn't stopped paying her bills.

"No name. When I said you'd moved back to Texas, she thanked me and hung up." He shouted something to a server.

The background noise told her he was in the kitchen of his new restaurant. If she were vindictive, she would have been hoping he gave everyone food poisoning on opening night.

"You're calling to tell me someone you don't know was asking about me and you don't have any more information than that?"

"I thought you'd want to know."

With that, he hung up.

She stared at the phone for a few seconds, then shoved it into her pocket. After collecting her purse, she let herself out the back, then checked the lock. Although her car was only a few feet away, she decided to walk around the area and see if she could figure out her next move.

The conversation with Aaron was confusing, but she decided to ignore it. Anyone looking for her could find her as easily here as in L.A. As for her ex, well, he had the emotional attention span of a gnat. Later, when he wanted something, he would point out he'd done her a favor tonight and would expect to be repaid.

It was fairly light, although dusk was approaching. The evening was warm—still in the mid-seventies. As she passed a restaurant, she noticed the bar crowd spilling out onto the patio. Maybe it was just her, but there sure seemed to be a lot of couples.

Looking at the heads bent so close together, listening to the intimate laughter, made her think more about Aaron. Not that they'd ever been like that. It seemed to her she and her ex hadn't exactly wallowed in the "in love" stage. They'd met when he'd been hired at the restaurant where she'd worked in Phoenix. He was already successful, flown in from L.A. to save an ailing establishment. The owner had promised him free rein and had vowed to fire anyone who didn't cooperate, so the staff had been nervous about his arrival.

Jenna remembered her first impression had been of a charming showman who captured everyone's attention. His style was so different from her deliberate way, his volume in contrast with her quiet voice. She'd been aware of him, intrigued by him and flattered when he'd asked her out.

They'd mostly talked business—cooking and how she created her recipes. She hadn't thought he was especially attracted to her and wasn't sure how she felt about him, so it was a surprise to end up in his bed. From that day on, they'd sort of been together. A couple. For a long time, she, too, had been intrigued by the public persona. Eventually she'd started to realize Aaron was more flash than substance, but for her, a flaw in a partner wasn't a reason to end a marriage.

Jenna paused on the sidewalk for a second, looking at the various couples. She'd always wanted what her parents had. One true love. Sure, that sounded like something out of a fairy tale, but she knew it was real. She'd grown up watching true love at work.

Her parents had met on Beth's first day of college, taken one look at each other and fallen madly in love. Already aware she couldn't have children, Beth had resisted Marshall's advances. Jenna smiled and started walking again. Those had been her mother's exact words when she told the story. "Marshall's advances."

She could imagine her handsome father pursuing the girl of his dreams. He wasn't a man who ever lost, and he'd wanted Beth. They'd been engaged within a year, married the following summer, after Marshall had graduated, and started looking for a baby to adopt by early fall. Jenna had shown up in their lives in the spring.

It was perfect, she thought, happy to have been a part of their storybook lives. And what she'd always wanted. But somehow that kind of relationship had eluded her. While Aaron had obviously cared at first, she'd never felt she was the love of his life. Not that she was so sure he'd been hers, either. But she'd never thought she would end up divorced and without children. She wasn't sorry she'd come home, she just didn't understand how she'd gotten so offtrack.

The store was a disaster. There was no other way to describe it. She knew she didn't have the experience necessary to be successful, and while retail wasn't her dream, it was all she currently had. Being smart and hardworking were great, but obviously not enough.

She lingered outside the window of a clothing boutique, wondering how their sales were.

The cooking class had been a disaster as well, she thought, remembering the bored looks of her squirming audience. Violet had been right. People didn't want to attend a lecture. They wanted to get their hands dirty. Have fun, like in the yarn store. There they were always *doing*. No instructor sat up front, *showing* them how to knit. They learned by practicing the techniques themselves.

Violet's other point about having something to sell that related to the classes made sense, too. Assuming anyone made it through one of her lectures, he or she simply left when Jenna was finished. The customer wasn't compelled to buy anything. Which made for a crappy bottom line. Even if she gave the occasional class on how to use different equipment, it wasn't going to be enough to sustain the store. They needed a product customers could buy regularly. Something they liked that made their lives easier. Most people didn't see the need to own more than one food processor or mixer.

If she wanted to be successful, she needed to completely change her game plan and her vision for what the store should be. This wasn't about educating the cooking public, it was about creating a place that was warm and welcoming. A place people wanted to go.

And while she was making all these changes to her store, she might want to look at herself, she thought. At least move toward having fun with her work and maybe even her life. Or really, what was the point?

Four

Violet arrived at nine-thirty, per usual. The store opened at ten, which gave her a half hour to get things in order. If nothing else, she needed to make sure they had enough cash on hand to make change. Less of a problem in a store where no one bought much of anything, but she had high hopes that eventually they would start to move product.

She pulled in next to Jenna's Subaru, then walked to the back door and used her key to let herself in. To the left was the small restroom, to the right, the storage area. Boxes were stacked nearly to the ceiling. Jenna had ordered with the idea that she would be selling things in the first week of business. Once they'd realized the store wasn't going to be an instant success, it had been too late to cancel the deliveries.

A sale might work, Violet thought. Although it wouldn't help the bottom line. Still, they had to start moving inventory or they would physically run out of space to put everything.

She made her way through the towering stacks of boxes to the entrance of the store. Jenna sat by the kitchen area, a small folding table set up in front of her. There were several pads of paper, a few pens and a waiting coffee from Starbucks.

Jenna looked up and smiled. "Oh, good. You're here. I have news. We're closed."

Violet felt her mouth start to drop open. She consciously kept it closed and did her best not to let any emotion show.

"Okay," she said slowly.

"Not permanently," Jenna added with a smile. "At least I hope not. I'm a little punchy. I didn't sleep at all last night. Everything's a mess. It's my fault. I didn't plan this at all. The store, I mean. You talked about research and projections and I don't know what any of that is. I literally stood in the parking lot, saw the 'For Lease' sign and called because I didn't know what else to do."

Violet pulled out the second folding chair and sank down. "I'd wondered," she admitted. "You didn't seem really prepared."

"*Clueless* is the word you're looking for," Jenna said with a laugh. "You can say it. I won't mind."

"I prefer overly optimistic."

"Very PC," Jenna said. "So in my hours of not sleeping, I thought about what needs to happen to make this place successful. I have every penny I own tied up in this store. Failure isn't an option. I want to close for a couple of days while we come up with a plan and get it ready to implement. Then we'll have a big reopening." She leaned forward. "Violet, you're the only one at this table who knows anything about retail. What do you think we should do?"

Violet was surprised by the question. Based on what she knew about Jenna, she'd been expecting a chart with a couple of lists.

"What kind of changes are you open to?" she asked tentatively.

"Anything. Everything. If you want me to paint the floors green and sell caterpillars, I will."

Violet's mouth twitched. "That might be going a little too far."

"Maybe, but you get my point. I know how to cook. I think I do a decent job explaining how to make something. But that's it. You were right about having stuff to sell. Not just big-ticket items. We need people coming back week after week, buying things. So how do we do that? I want the classes to be more exciting. I want people enthused. Tell me how to make that happen."

Violet looked at her boss. Jenna seemed to be telling the truth. She was intense but focused. "The store has a lot of potential," she began. "A great location."

"That's what I thought. Well, in the fifteen seconds I considered before signing the lease."

"You got lucky," Violet told her.

"Let's hope it wasn't the last time." Jenna watched as Violet seemed to consider her words. She leaned toward her. "I need you to be honest with me. Just say it. I promise I won't be upset."

Violet drew a breath. "Okay. There are a lot of different things you can do to bring people in and keep them coming back. For starters, lose the white coat. Yes, you're a chef, but it's intimidating. You want people to believe they can do what you do. That it's easy and fun. Dress like your customers. Maybe a little better."

Jenna did her best not to wince. "I love my white coat, but I see your point. My only concern is all my nice clothes are going to get stained. Cooking can be messy."

Violet thought for a second. "What about aprons? You

could wear different ones depending on what we're cooking. They could be fun and we could sell them."

"Sure. If you think anyone will buy them."

"They will if they think they'll help make the meal taste better."

"It's just an apron."

"It's all about making people feel better about what they do."

Jenna made a note on her pad. "What's next?"

"Recipes. We have to have them to give out. And we should always have a food sample to offer customers along with the recipe so they can go home and make it that night." She hesitated. "I mentioned this before, but…"

"Tell me again," Jenna urged. "What?"

"We should offer the items necessary to make the recipe. Put it in bags or baskets or whatever. All the ingredients, except the fresh stuff. So if it requires a can of tomatoes and pasta, they buy that here. We can go slightly gourmet, charge more and have a better profit margin. Sure the markup on a can of tomatoes isn't much, but multiply that by a hundred and it starts to pay the rent."

Jenna had never considered selling food. Her first instinct was to say no, but look at where her instincts had gotten her so far.

"That would work," she said slowly, thinking about some of her favorite recipes. "Especially when there are hard-to-find ingredients. I could special order items. Although some of them do require refrigeration."

"If they have a limited shelf life, we can tell people they have to preorder. Then they can stop by, pick up the food and then go home and cook it." Violet straightened in her chair. "We could do classes on cooking for company. A few impressive-looking but easy-to-prepare meals. After the class, people could give us a few days' notice and come by to pick up all the ingredients, then go home and make the meal."

"That sounds like fun," Jenna said. In the past she'd always cooked what interested her, but maybe she could think about what other people would enjoy, as well. She might not think appetizers were that compelling, but then she wasn't hosting a cocktail party for twenty.

And speaking of cocktails... "What about a bartender?"

"I don't understand."

"What if we had a bartender come in and show how to mix different drinks?" She frowned. "That might require a liquor license. But maybe we could set up something with one of the local restaurants around here. All those fancy drinks can seem intimidating."

Now Violet was taking notes. "I like that. It would bring in a younger crowd. Not that I don't love the ladies who lunch."

"They do have money." Jenna thought about her friends. Okay, not friends, but still. They were a potential customer group. "Mothers," she said slowly. "What can we do with them?"

"Healthy, organic cooking," Violet said immediately. "Maybe classes on baby food or what to feed toddlers. Remember that cookbook on burying vegetables into regular food? Something like that."

"I like it," Jenna said. "We could also feature a different cookbook every week. Cook two or three recipes. That would encourage people to try different styles of cooking." Plus it would be safe for her. Someone else's recipe.

"And give us a chance to sell specialty cooking items," Violet added. "Woks, different pans. That kind of thing, not to mention the cookbooks themselves. Oh, and don't forget the singles."

"What do you mean? Cooking for one? Isn't that kind of sad?"

Violet laughed. "Yes, but those of us who live alone have to eat, too."

"I live alone," Jenna said. "I just whip up something."

"That's because you know how. Those of us who aren't blessed with your cooking background are forced to eat frozen dinners night after night. If we advertised that class in the right places, we could get a lot of people. Meeting someone in a cooking class is a whole lot more appealing than meeting someone in a bar."

"Sure," Jenna said. Singles. She never would have thought of that. But it made sense.

They continued brainstorming. Violet suggested a website.

"I know a guy who does decent work for not a lot of money," she said. "Want me to have him write up a proposal?"

"Yes. My online experience is limited to finding professional cookware on sale."

By eleven, they had a master plan in place. Violet left to talk to the web guy and set up the newspaper advertising. Jenna investigated cookbooks, and came up with a cooking class schedule. She also bit the bullet and bought a large refrigerator for the back room. If they were going to sell perishables, she would need a place to store them.

She drove to the small print shop her mother had recommended and ordered flyers, copies of recipes, raffle tickets, and discussed the cost of getting custom-screened aprons with the store's logo. At quarter to five, she returned to the store to find Violet laying printouts of an initial web design on the counter.

"He was bored," Violet said cheerfully. "I love it when

that happens. He threw this together in about an hour and I have to say I think it's great."

Jenna bent over the different pages. The design was clean, the colors bright. On the side and top were navigation buttons for recipes, cookware, gadgets and more.

They played with the design and made a few changes.

"What about this?" Violet asked. "Move this button here?" She'd barely finished speaking when her stomach growled.

Jenna stared at her. "Didn't you stop for lunch?"

"No. I was busy."

Jenna stacked the papers together. "We'll finish this tomorrow. You've already put in a full day. You need to eat. Go on. I'll see you in the morning."

Violet hesitated. "Want to get a margarita at Dos Salsas?"

The invitation was unexpected. Jenna instantly felt both awkward and shy. It had been years since she'd made a new friend, she thought. Most of the people she worked with in restaurants were guys, and the friends in her life had all been Aaron's. She certainly hadn't kept in touch with her friends from here—her uncomfortable coffee date had proven that.

She wanted to say it was their fault, but she hadn't called, either. The question was why. Another area that required self-exploration, she told herself. Why had meeting Aaron and getting involved with him changed her so much? It was like he was a star in the heavens and she was simply a circling planet.

"It wasn't supposed to be a hard question," Violet said quietly. "It's okay. I'll see you in the morning."

Nothing on the other woman's face gave away what she was thinking, but Jenna knew she'd hurt her.

"No, wait. I'd love to get a margarita."

"You don't have to."

"I want to. I got caught up in thinking about my ex. Don't ask me how. Sometimes my brain is a scary place."

"Mine, too." Violet smiled. "Let's go."

"I swear, if you can figure out what they put in their nachos, I'll give you my life savings." Violet grabbed another chip as she spoke.

Jenna eyed the plate in front of them, then smiled. "How much do you have in your savings?"

Violet laughed. "Not much, but there would be gratitude, too."

"Well, if there's gratitude, how can I say no?"

"Seriously?" Violet asked. "You could make these?"

"Sure. Re-creating a recipe isn't that hard."

"Maybe not for you. I've tried a couple of times and I can't do it."

"I'll show you how."

Violet looked both pleased and surprised. "That's really nice of you."

"Hardly. You're saving my business. I seriously owe you."

"I'm helping. There's a difference."

Not in this case, Jenna thought, but she wasn't going to push. She didn't want to make Violet uncomfortable.

She took a sip of her margarita and glanced around the bar. It was big and open, with dark wood beams and ceiling fans. There wasn't a huge crowd yet, but she saw plenty of people and conversation.

She felt good, she realized. She had a plan to get the store up and running.

"I like all the changes we've come up with," she said, grabbing another chip. "Now if only I hadn't screwed up in the first place."

"You're really hard on yourself," Violet said.

"No, I'm…" Jenna pressed her lips together. "Maybe I am. An old habit." She thought about how critical she was of herself. "I wish I could blame my parents, but I can't."

"I know your mom's great."

"My dad's just as supportive. I didn't grow up feeling like I was always wrong. I was pretty normal."

Violet glanced at her. "Tell me what normal is like."

"You say that like you don't know."

Violet hesitated. "Everyone's normal is different. What was yours?"

Jenna wanted to talk about Violet instead but had the feeling it wasn't good to push. "Usual high school experience. Some fun, plenty of angst. I went to college, joined a sorority, couldn't pick a major. Nothing really appealed to me." She wrinkled her nose. "I got tired of the liberal arts classes. By my second year, I was spending more time in the house kitchen than anywhere else. That summer I had a long talk with my parents about my future. I wasn't sure what to do." She smiled. "My dad is the one who suggested culinary school."

"Smart man."

"He is. I was stunned, but it felt right. I headed off to Dallas and discovered I loved to cook. The classes were great. I stayed an extra semester just so I could learn more. I had several job offers when I graduated. I took one in Phoenix— mostly to live somewhere different. I was working at a restaurant when I met Aaron."

"What's he like?"

"Charming," she admitted. "He's the guy who walks in the room and knows exactly what to say to everyone. He can convince you of anything. I loved being around him, but at the same time when I was with him I felt different. I can't explain it."

Violet picked up her margarita. "Less shiny?"

Jenna considered the description. "Yes. That's it. I felt less than I'd been before. Looking back I can see that he wasn't especially brilliant in the kitchen, but he convinced us all he was. For years, I told myself I couldn't keep up. I guess that's when I started putting myself down."

She hesitated. "I used to be so inventive in my cooking. Aaron would pick my ideas apart, make me feel they weren't any good, then a few weeks later, they would show up on the menu. When I asked about that, he said he'd made changes, improved them. But I wasn't ever sure he did. I used to take chances."

She pressed her lips together. "Sorry. Too much information."

"It's not. What you're saying makes a lot of sense."

"You mean it explains why I'm not willing to do anything without charts and a plan? Structure makes me feel safe. It wasn't always that way."

Violet eyed her over the glass. "Don't take this wrong, but I don't think you started it. I'll bet it was Aaron."

"You think?"

Jenna thought about their relationship. She wanted to say he'd always been there for her. That he was supportive. But she knew it wasn't true.

"He wanted me to be less than him," she said slowly.

"Maybe you scared him."

"Nothing scared Aaron."

"Everyone is afraid of something." Violet spoke with a confidence Jenna envied. "If a guy pretends he's not, he's faking it. Trust me. I have experience when it comes to lousy guys. Show me a nice guy who wants to take me out and treat me well and I yawn. Parade a few losers in front of me and I can't get there fast enough."

"That's not good," Jenna said.

"Tell me about it. I have a whole list of wonderful men I'm not the least bit interested in. When you're ready for rebound guy, just let me know. I can suggest a couple dozen."

Jenna laughed. "I'm not the rebound guy type."

"Sure you are. Everyone is. It's kind of required. You've ended one relationship and you need to think about starting the next. Rebound guy gives you confidence."

"What does he get out of it?"

"Sex with minimal effort. Guys love that."

Jenna shifted in her seat. "I've never been much of a guy magnet. I'm not sure rebound guy will be worth the effort it'll take to get him."

Violet raised her dark eyebrows. "Have you looked in the mirror lately? The effort we're talking about is little more than wearing a short skirt and smiling."

If only, Jenna thought wryly. "I'm not good with guys."

"I doubt that, but even if it's true, it doesn't matter. The rebound relationship is about having fun. You get out there and remind yourself that yes, you can have a good time with someone else. You go out a couple of times, have hot sex, wake up feeling refreshed and move on."

Jenna wondered what Violet would say if she confessed to the fact that she'd only been with one other guy before Aaron. The thought of sex with a stranger was terrifying.

"My parents met in college," she said. "They knew right away that they were meant for each other. I always thought it would be like that for me."

"I didn't know it was like that for anyone," Violet murmured.

"I was holding out for perfect. Instead I got Aaron."

"Maybe it's time to try fun instead."

"I've never thought of dating as fun," Jenna admitted. "I guess I was doing it wrong."

"You're doing it again," Violet said.

"Doing... Oh, right." The put-down thing.

What was with her? When had she become that kind of person—always seeing the worst in herself?

"Okay," she said, straightening. "Rebound guy. You swear it's fun?"

"It can be. Give it some thought and when you're ready, I'll hook you up with Mr. Blow Your Socks Off." Violet grinned. "Unless you have other things you want him to blow on."

Jenna felt herself blush. She sipped her margarita. "It's been a long time," she admitted in a whisper.

"Then we'll get going on that."

"Business first, sex second."

"Are you sure you don't want to reverse those?" Violet teased.

"I have rent to make."

"Fair enough. But when you want the sock thing, just let me know and I'll find you someone completely inappropriate."

Jenna laughed. "I'd like that. It doesn't sound like me at all and I'm starting to think that might be a good thing."

Violet pushed her cart through the grocery store. It wasn't where she usually shopped, but after running a couple of errands in Austin, she'd impulsively pulled into the parking lot of the upscale establishment. Maybe hanging out with Jenna was rubbing off on her.

With that in mind, she ignored the frozen food aisle and walked purposefully toward the produce. The area was huge and well-lit, with rows of fruits and vegetables neatly arranged. She saw more types of lettuce than she'd ever seen in one place. Tomatoes were yellow and nearly purple, as well as red.

She quickly collected salad fixings, grabbed a gourmet salad dressing from the refrigerated shelves, then headed for the fresh pasta section. Tonight she was going to cook herself a real dinner. A real easy dinner, but still, it was progress.

As she maneuvered her cart, she noticed how nicely everyone was dressed. Men in suits. Women in expensive-looking jackets, with tailored skirts and great shoes. She saw a flash of red sole and stared, wondering if someone really was wearing Christian Louboutin shoes in a grocery store.

Trying to see the side of the shoe to decide if she liked the style, she wasn't looking where she was going and came to a shuddering stop as her cart collided with someone else's.

She glanced up. "Sorry. I wasn't looking."

The cart's handler—a tall, suit-wearing guy—smiled at her. "I could tell. What was more interesting than—" he looked to his left and picked up a bottle "—imported olives?"

She smiled. "Shoes. A female cliché, if there ever was one."

"Shoes, huh? Your thing?"

"I'm more a looker than a buyer. Sorry about the cart attack."

She started to go around him, but he maneuvered himself in front of her and gave her a smile.

"Wait. I have a question about these olives," he said.

"What makes you think I know anything about them?"

"Women always have knowledge about anything mysterious."

"You think of olives as mysterious?"

"And you don't, which proves my point."

He had sandy brown hair and hazel-brown eyes. His expression was friendly and interested without being too aggressive. His suit looked expensive but not crazy. He was clean-shaven, broad-shouldered and normal-looking. Not at all her type.

She would have excused herself and walked away except she was tired of always getting it wrong. Every guy in her life had been a disaster, probably because when it came to men, her gut didn't know what it was talking about.

So maybe she should ignore her lack of interest and see what else the nice man had to say. It was unlikely this one would steal her credit card or buy a car in her name, then not make payments.

"Olives can be difficult," she said, moving her cart to the side so other people could get by. "Now, when the oil is difficult, you know you're in trouble."

He laughed. The sound was low and pleasant. Easy. As if he were the kind of guy who laughed a lot.

"I'm Cliff," he said, holding out his hand.

"Violet."

"Nice to meet you, Violet."

"Nice to meet you, too." She paused, not sure what to say next.

Cliff continued to smile at her, as if she were the brightest part of his day. "I work in finance, which sounds more impressive than it is. I've been in town about five months and the only people I know are the ones on my floor at work. I'm putting in eighty hours a week because I don't know what else to do with my time. Have dinner with me?"

Nice, she thought. The guy was nice. And, of course, she wasn't the least bit interested.

"Thanks, but no."

He gazed into her eyes. "I know meeting a guy in a grocery store isn't much better than meeting a guy in a bar. What do you really know about me, right? Giving me your number wouldn't be safe. So let me give you my card."

He withdrew a card from his suit jacket pocket. "My work number is there, along with my cell. How about next Tuesday?"

"I don't get to Austin much. I live in Georgetown," she said without thinking, not sure what to do about the invitation.

"That works for me. How about the Wildfire Restaurant? It's next to the Palace Theater. Tell you what. I'll be there at seven. I hope you'll join me."

He held out the card until she took it.

"I'm a good guy," he told her. "Ask anyone on my floor."

She stared at the card. The company name was one she recognized and the location was a high-rise in Austin. Apparently Cliff really did have a job, and it was a good one.

She looked up only to see he'd turned away and was already at the end of the aisle. He rounded the corner without looking back.

He probably *was* a good guy, she thought as she tucked the card into the back pocket of her jeans. No man had ever gone out of his way to make her feel safe before. Women like Jenna were probably well-treated all the time. They didn't know the world could be different. But Violet did. She knew how ugly it could be.

She was tired of losers who made her heart beat faster. Of jerks who hurt her, either physically or emotionally. Jenna made normal seem pretty damned wonderful. Maybe it was time for Violet to experience normal for herself.

Five

The last time Jenna had had this many butterflies in her stomach, she'd been getting married. Hopefully the re-opening of her store would prove to have a happier ending. She waited anxiously by the oven as cookies baked. As per their plan, food would be available the second the doors unlocked.

While she waited for the three-hundred-and-fifty degrees to work their magic, she glanced around the store. She and Violet had rearranged a few shelves and reworked most of the displays. Gone was the rigid order she had so loved, and in its place was a welcoming riot of color and equipment. Dish towels spilled out of mixer bowls, mugs nestled next to coffee-makers. A gourmet coffee display was nearby.

The website was up and working, ads were in all the local papers, coupon inserts in two, and somehow Violet had managed to get them interviewed for a local blog.

She checked the cookies, then eyed the class schedule on

the wall. The big dry-erase board was filled with offerings from organic food for babies and toddlers during the late-morning to a singles cooking class on Friday night. Her perfect kitchen would be invaded by people who had no idea what they were doing, and she was actually sort of okay with that.

Even more surprising, she was trying something new. The organic food for babies and toddlers was completely out of her comfort zone. She'd nearly vomited when she'd agreed to the class, but she was going to do it. She figured an eighteen-month-old wouldn't be as critical as Aaron.

Giving up control was a good thing, she reminded herself. At least it would be when she got used to it and stopped hyperventilating at the thought. Trying to keep control of everything had become a habit in recent years. Maybe it had been a way not to notice how out of control her marriage had become.

She returned to the oven and pulled open the door. The timer dinged just as she drew out the tray and set it on the waiting cooling rack.

Across the room, Violet groaned. "What are those? They smell amazing."

"A brownie-cookie with a melted chocolate center."

"I'm going to gain weight working here, aren't I?"

"If I'm doing my job right."

Violet grinned. "Tell me when they're cooled. I want to taste one and make sure they're okay. For marketing purposes."

Jenna laughed. "Thanks. We wouldn't want to risk serving our customers anything that wasn't good."

"Exactly."

Jenna slipped the second batch into the oven and shut the door. Precisely two minutes after the cookies had come out of the oven, Jenna used a spatula to transfer them from the cookie sheet to a second cooling rack. She glanced at the clock. They were less than five minutes to the grand re-opening.

What if nobody came? What if all the changes didn't make a difference? What if she failed?

The swirling thoughts made her want to pound her head against the wall. Instead she forced herself to breathe slowly. Everything was going to be fine, she reminded herself. Her new plan was in place and it was based on making customers happy, rather than being everything she wanted the store to be. Even as she hovered, twenty dozen sugar cookies waited to be decorated for today's class on decorating with spring flowers.

The table by the register held fifty brightly colored lunch-size paper bags Violet had bought at the dollar store. Inside some were the nonperishable ingredients for the sugar cookies. The others held the same for the brownie-cookies. Recipe cards were attached. Everything was premeasured in sealed plastic bags. All that was required were eggs and butter.

Next to the bags, stacks of mixing bowls, cookie sheets and cooling racks partially blocked printed schedules of the cooking classes for the next two weeks. Later in the week there would be a ribbon-cutting ceremony with members of the Georgetown Chamber of Commerce stopping by.

They'd done what they could do, she reminded herself. What happened now was up to the good people of Georgetown.

"It's time," Violet said as she walked toward the door. "Oh."

"What?"

"There are people waiting outside. I hadn't noticed."

People waiting, as in customers? Jenna walked toward the front. Sure enough, there were five or six women standing on the sidewalk. As soon as Violet unlocked the glass front doors, they walked in.

Several of them held flyers or coupons in their hands. They looked around eagerly. A couple inhaled, then groaned.

"What are you baking?" one older woman asked. "It smells wonderful."

Jenna smiled. "A brownie-cookie. I just pulled some out of the oven. Have a taste."

She handed out the samples.

"Do you have the recipe?" another woman asked. "I came in for the sugar cookie class, but these are delicious."

"We have recipe cards," Jenna said, pointing to the front of the store even as she wondered if she recognized the woman. She might have been a retired teacher from her elementary school.

"We also have the ingredients ready if you want to buy those and make them at home yourself," Jenna added. "You'll need eggs and butter, but we've taken care of everything else."

Violet walked over with a few of the bags in her hand.

"How clever," a customer said. "I want one of each."

"Me, too."

A third woman eyed Jenna. "That apron is adorable. Are you selling those?"

By six o'clock, Jenna's feet hurt and her back ached. She also felt a weird stretching sensation in her face, which came from having spent the whole day smiling. It was all pain she could happily live with, she thought as she watched Violet lock the front door. When she turned, they stared at each other, then both began to laugh.

"We did it!" Jenna said, bouncing on her already-throbbing feet. "I can't believe how many customers we had."

"I know." Violet pointed to the lonely bag sitting on the table. "I figured the ingredient bags would be popular, but I wasn't expecting them to go this fast. We're going to have to make more for next time. People are going to tell their friends and we'll have customers showing up, wanting to try what we've been cooking."

Jenna sank into a chair. "Did you see those women with the cookies? They were so happy decorating."

"Nearly everyone bought cookie sheets and cooling racks."

The day had been crazy busy. She would have to come in early in the morning to restock shelves and prep for the next cooking class. If this kept up, she would need to hire a part-time person to prepare the bags and stock the shelves. Talk about a happy thought.

"You did this," she said, turning to Violet. "You made it happen."

"I helped," the other woman corrected.

"If I'd been left on my own, I would have failed spectacularly."

Violet studied her for a second. "Then I have a favor to ask. Say yes, and we can be even."

Jenna smiled. "Unless you want a kidney, sure."

Violet shifted uneasily, as if nervous. She fingered the bracelets on her wrist. "I have a date on Tuesday."

"Is that all? Of course you can leave early."

"No, that's not it. I met this guy. Cliff. He's nice. A business type." She pulled a card out of her skirt pocket and held it out. "He has the kind of job where they give you business cards."

Jenna took the card and studied it. She couldn't see anything noteworthy about the information. Cliff worked for a big financial firm. He was a senior manager, which probably meant he was one step away from being a vice president.

"I don't know what to wear," Violet admitted. "We're going out to dinner."

Jenna frowned. "You always look great. Fun and pulled together."

"I have a unique style," Violet said. "It's wrong for Cliff."

"Not if he asked you out. What do you want to dress like?"

"Not what. Who. I want to dress like you."

Jenna sat up straight. "Trust me. Stick-up-the-ass isn't a style to attract a guy."

"You dress great," Violet told her. "Sophisticated. Elegant."

"Boring."

"Classy."

Jenna had never applied that word to herself. She wore tailored clothes because they tended to suit her body and weren't trendy. Shopping wasn't her thing. Those big mirrors in dressing rooms intimidated her. Looking at her butt in a three-way mirror wasn't her idea of a good time.

"You're serious?" she asked.

"Yes. I want to look right for my date with Cliff."

"I'm really the last person you should be asking, but sure. I'll help."

Violet sighed. "Thank you."

"Don't thank me yet. I haven't the faintest idea how to help you. Want to come to my house and look at my closet? It'll give us a place to start."

"That sounds perfect."

Jenna's townhouse was relatively new, with comfortable furniture and hardwood floors. She had a few scattered rugs, artwork on the walls and extra shelving in the kitchen for her impressive collection of cookware.

The built-in, under-the-counter wine cellar and stainless steel appliances were about as far from Violet's somewhat rundown apartment as it was possible to get while staying in the same city.

Violet sat at the stool by the bar counter and wondered what it would be like to live like this for real. To have no need for extra locks, while enjoying garage parking for her car. The differences were both inspiring and depressing.

She accepted the glass of white wine Jenna offered, then waited while her boss shuffled through the contents of the refrigerator. In a matter of minutes she had loaded a plate with various cheeses, some cut fruit, and a dip she'd whipped up using sun-dried tomatoes and some mystery ingredients, and water crackers.

Violet eyed the offering. "Your life really is perfect," she said without thinking.

Jenna nearly choked on her wine. "Excuse me? I'm getting a divorce, my husband cheated on me, I've just turned thirty-two, I have no kids, I own nothing and if not for you, my business would have failed."

Violet nodded slowly. "When you put it like that."

They both laughed.

Jenna held out her glass. "Today was a good day. Thank you."

"It was good and tomorrow will be better."

They clinked glasses.

"If you're right," Jenna said, "then I'm going to break out my comfortable shoes. My feet are killing me."

"Retail is all about standing."

"Robyn's on to something with her knitting," Jenna grumbled. "She gets to do it sitting down."

"It's worse," Violet said cheerfully. "Have you seen her fiancé? He's gorgeous."

"Some people have all the luck." She picked up the tray of food. "Come on. We can eat while you ponder my wardrobe. Please don't get your hopes up, though. You'll be wildly disappointed."

The two bedrooms were upstairs. The smaller one, just off the stairs, was mostly empty. Jenna led the way down the short hall to the master.

They entered through double doors. The space was large. Even with the bed, dresser and two nightstands, she had room to hold an aerobics class. French doors led out onto a balcony. Violet didn't care if the view was only of a parking lot. No one she knew had a balcony off their bedroom. She had a feeling the master bath would be about the size of her entire bedroom, then nearly fainted when she saw the walk-in closet.

"Nice," she murmured.

"More than I need," Jenna said, as she put the tray on the dresser and set her wine next to it. "I'm not big on clothes. Plus, working in a restaurant means wearing a uniform of sorts. Black pants, white jacket. I'd put on a T-shirt underneath. Not exactly high fashion."

Jenna joined Violet at the entrance to the closet and turned on the light. Shirts and pants hung on double racks. Dresses hung at one end. Boxes of shoes sat on shelves, and what looked like eight or ten white kitchen coats stayed dust-free in dry cleaner bags.

"My former life," Jenna said, touching the plastic.

Violet couldn't decide if she sounded wistful or just plain sad. "Do you miss it?"

"Sometimes. Working in a restaurant kitchen is crazy. Orders come in together, there are too many people in too small a space. There's lots of yelling and swearing. But making people happy is great. I loved being part of the celebrations. Someone's anniversary or birthday. It's like they chose me to make the event memorable."

Jenna shrugged, ducking her head. "Not me personally. I'm not that self-absorbed. But they came to where I worked and trusted me with something special. I liked that."

"It sounds wonderful."

"It took a while to get there. I spent years slicing and dicing to prove myself. The hours are long. It's impossible to have much of a social life. Unless you're married to a chef, which has its own problems. It's not like the store, where I have a lot of direct contact with customers. When you're back in the kitchen at a restaurant, you don't get much interaction."

Violet had never thought of what happened behind the scenes when she went out to eat. She'd never considered that the person cooking the food cared about her experience one way or the other.

"You put a lot of yourself into what you do," she said.

"Which is both good and bad." She shrugged. "So tell me about your date. Where are you going?"

"Wildfire. It's in Old Town."

Jenna studied her. "We're nearly the same height, but you have more curves. Not that I'm bitter."

"You don't have to worry about your weight," Violet pointed out.

"Yes, and you get to have breasts." Jenna sighed. "My mom is always worrying about her weight. She gains and loses the same fifteen pounds nearly every year. What she can't see is she's beautiful no matter what. When I was a teenager, I would see my dad watching her and I knew what he was thinking. It totally freaked me out. Parents should not have sex. But now, I think it's great. Well, in theory. I still don't want the details."

She moved into the closet. "Your date is on Tuesday, right?"

"Uh-huh."

"So he'll probably be coming from work. Which means a suit. I think you should wear a dress. That's my mother's training coming out, by the way." She raised her voice to a slightly higher pitch. "A man likes to see a woman in a dress."

Violet knew she had plenty of experience when it came to the likes and dislikes of the average male but didn't think it was helpful when it came to things like dating this particular kind of guy. This wasn't her world. Who was she trying to kid?

Jenna pulled out three or four dresses. "Why don't you try these."

The top one was a short-sleeved cotton dress in dove gray. The bodice had tight horizontal ruffles with some banding at the waist. The skirt had wider ruffles.

Not really her style, Violet thought, eyeing the dress doubtfully. She wasn't exactly a ruffle person.

"I have a belt that could go with this," Jenna said. "It actually looks really great on."

"Okay. I'll try it." After all, her goal was to look like someone else.

Jenna handed over the dresses. "Can't wait to see the fashion show."

She stepped out of the closet and returned to the bedroom. Violet pulled off her black pants, the tank top and lace overshirt she wore, then stepped out of her boots. She drew the ruffled dress over her head and buttoned the front.

"There's a full-length mirror on the back of the bathroom door," Jenna said, pointing, then leading the way.

Violet trailed after her. Once in the huge bathroom, complete with separate shower and massive soaking tub, she closed the door and stared at herself.

The color wasn't bad, she thought, turning back and forth. The fit was great, but the style just wasn't working.

"I look like I'm twelve," she said.

"It's not quite right," Jenna agreed. "There's a black dress that should be better. Let me get it."

She left the bathroom, then returned seconds later. The dress she held looked more fitted. A simple scoop neck, tank straps and a skirt that fell to mid thigh. Some tucking detail on the front gave the shape definition.

"Simple, elegant, silk," Jenna said holding it out.

Violet's gaze dropped to the tag still attached. "I can't wear that. It's new."

"What does that have to do with anything?"

"It's your dress. You should wear it first."

"If we wait for that, a millennium will have passed." Jenna pushed the dress toward her. "You have to at least try it on."

Violet took it reluctantly. She didn't have any silk in her wardrobe. It was costly to buy and usually had to be dry-cleaned. Not an expense she needed. But the fabric was whisper soft and the style appealed to her.

After hanging the black dress on the towel rack by the light switch, she unbuttoned the front of the dress she had on and shrugged out of it without even thinking. When she reached for the black dress, she felt more than heard Jenna's surprise. A second too late, Violet remembered that stripping down to a thong and bra in front of her boss probably wasn't the smartest thing to do.

Jenna stood slightly behind her, so she had a full view of

the delicate scrollwork on the small of her back and the roses between her shoulder blades. Chinese characters trailed along her left thigh, a Celtic design extended up both arms and a dolphin arced just above her right ankle.

"They're beautiful," Jenna said, sounding very close to meaning it.

Violet drew the black dress off the hanger. "It was a geographical necessity," she said, undoing the zipper. "I lived on the streets for a while. I got my first tattoo on a dare and the next couple to fit in."

The others had followed because they'd seemed like what she should do at the time. Now she regretted them, but it wasn't as if they could be scrubbed off.

"Why were you on the streets?" Jenna asked. "Or is that question too personal?"

"I was independent." Violet slipped into the dress. "This is great."

Jenna moved behind her and pulled up the zipper. "It's perfect. You have to wear it. I think it needs a little jacket. I have a couple you can choose from. My mom is very big on accessories."

Violet was grateful for the change in subject. "She trained you?"

"Actually, she does my shopping." Jenna shrugged. "I know it's weird, but she loves to shop and she's good at it. She'll show up with bags of clothes for me to try on. I keep the ones I like and she returns the rest."

"Nice system."

"It is. I'm spoiled. If things get serious with this guy and you want to change your look, you should talk to her. I'm sure she'd love to help. She can suggest stores or even take you shopping."

The thought was nice, Violet thought. Impossible, but

nice. In her world, the mother of her boss didn't bother with an employee. Of course in her world, her boss didn't usually lend her brand-new dresses.

"Let's go see what jackets I have. I'm thinking short and tailored, but not too severe. We want him to be impressed, not afraid you're into discipline."

Violet trailed after her, wondering what life would have been like if her own mother had cared about her. As it was, Violet had run away at fifteen and never gone back. When she'd been younger, she'd dreamed about finding a family to take her in. A place to belong. She'd always wanted that.

Without meaning to, she thought of Cliff. He wasn't anything like the guys she usually dated. He was normal—at least on the surface. She would bet he'd never gone hungry a day in his life.

They had nothing in common. She would be foolish to allow herself to hope. But maybe, just maybe, a little anticipation couldn't hurt.

She wasn't too proud to buy love, Jenna thought humorously as she delivered paper plates filled with lemon bars to the businesses around her store. Or at the very least, good neighbors and potential customers.

She saved Only Ewe for last and was pleased to see Robyn behind the register.

"How's it going?" the other woman asked when she saw Jenna. "You've been getting a crowd over there."

"Finally." Jenna handed over the plate. "A little sugar rush to keep you going."

"Thanks. These look delicious." Robyn lifted the plastic wrap and sniffed. "You're killing me, you know that, right? Those brownie-cookies were beyond wonderful. I bought the bag of ingredients and made them over the weekend. It was really easy. What a great idea."

"Violet came up with it. We're going to keep offering pre-measured ingredients with recipe cards. And not just desserts, for actual meals."

"It's perfect," Robyn told her. "I'm tired when I'm done working and I don't want to think up what to cook and then have to stop at the store. This is nearly as easy as fast food, but healthier and fresh. Not to mention, it will impress my boyfriend, T.J."

The front door opened and several older women entered. Robyn waved.

"A few of my regulars," she said in a low voice.

"You have a great store," Jenna told her, looking at all the bins filled with yarn. "It makes me want to learn how to knit."

"We have beginner classes starting all the time. My grandmother teaches them. She's incredibly patient."

"I'd like to try." She thought about the classes she had lined up at her own store. "Maybe when things calm down a little."

"Don't hope for that," Robyn said with a smile. "Not in retail."

"Good point. How about when my schedule starts to make sense?"

"Better."

Jenna excused herself and returned to her store. Violet had already set up for the class, and several women and men chatted by the chairs. She saw her mother and waved.

Beth broke away from the group and hurried toward her.

"They're very excited about the class," she said in a low voice. "Advertising in Sun City was brilliant. Especially for a class like this. People who live there have plenty of money and are the type to be interested in cooking."

"As long as it brings in customers," Jenna said.

"It will. You're going to be so successful. I can feel it."

Beth hugged her, then gave her a push toward the kitchen area. Jenna grabbed an apron and pulled it over her head, then washed her hands.

"Are we ready?" she asked, smiling at the rapidly growing crowd. There had to be more than twenty people in the store for the class. They only had seating for thirty. Something she'd never thought of as a problem. The space would get a little crowded when everyone got up to cook, but she told herself that would make it more fun.

"Low salt doesn't have to mean low taste," she began, re-peating the name of the workshop. "Salt does many things to food, but what we're most interested in is how it brings out the flavors. Most people believe that no salt means no flavor. What we're going to discover today are ways to make a meal even more delicious using herbs, rubs, spices and sauces. Are you ready to get started?"

Everyone nodded.

"Come on up," she said.

The cooking class quickly spiraled into a disaster, with not enough burners, pots and utensils. But no one seemed to mind. The soup team experimented with the spices she'd put out for them, while the men who'd taken over the grill pan admitted that her custom rub really did make the chicken taste great. Jenna moved from group to group, offering sug-gestions and answering questions.

She watched anxiously as the chili group tasted their food. She'd played with that recipe, adjusting a few things, and now wondered if she'd made a mistake. Although her changes had been minor—a teaspoon each of coffee granules and mocha powder—she couldn't help doubting herself.

She hated her indecision, she thought grimly. But the two men and three women were all grinning as they tasted, and then went back for bigger spoonfuls.

"This is delicious," one woman said, glancing toward Jenna. "What did she put in the spices?"

Jenna sighed with relief. Facing the self-defeating voices in her head was the first step in getting herself back. Maybe that spark was still there. At least the chili was good.

"You're going to have those prepacked ingredients, aren't you?" one gray-haired woman asked her.

"Yes. They're up front. You can also buy the rubs individually or as part of a basket."

The class had so many different dishes that the ingredients hadn't fit in a paper bag. Violet had found a craft supply store with a sale on baskets and had bought them out.

"Oh, I like the baskets," a second woman said. "But when I come back for more ingredients, can I just reuse the same basket?"

"Of course," Jenna said, making a decision on the spot.

"Good. I want what they're having." She pointed to the chili group. "My sons love chili."

When the class was finished, Jenna helped Violet ring up all the purchases. Beth joined them, doing the bagging. They sold every basket, nearly all the spices and rubs, ten cookbooks and over five hundred dollars' worth of pots and pans.

After the last customer left, Jenna leaned against the counter. "I love Sun City."

Violet and Beth laughed.

"That was a fun class," Beth said. "I'm going to make that chili and not tell your father it's low-salt. You know how he is—anything new makes him nervous." She paused and winked. "At least when it's new in the kitchen."

"Mom," Jenna said, rolling her eyes. "Don't frighten Violet."

"I'm not frightened, I'm jealous," Violet teased. She leaned toward Beth and lowered her voice. "Although Jenna *is* your daughter and that would fall under the category of too much information."

"You're right. I'll keep it to myself. I wouldn't want to seem like I'm bragging." Beth hugged Violet, then Jenna. "You girls are a great team. Call me if you need anything."

"We will," Jenna assured her.

When she'd left, Violet sighed. "I really like her. She's great."

"I know. I was lucky when they picked me."

"Speaking of luck...or getting lucky..."

Jenna laughed. "Are we going to talk about your date next Tuesday?"

"I thought we'd talk about a certain doctor I know. I'd forgotten all about him, but I spotted him last night at Three-Legged Willie's and I thought of you."

Jenna took a step back and held up both hands. "No, thanks."

"I haven't offered anything yet."

"But you're going to."

"He would be the perfect rebound guy," Violet told her. "He's cute, he's funny, sophisticated. The best part is he's a total player. He never wants to get involved. Rumor has it he's great in bed. The exact qualities you want in a rebound guy."

Jenna shifted uncomfortably. "I don't think so."

"Why not?"

"He has too much experience. I don't want to be compared

to other women and found wanting. Can't I start with someone who's grateful I would even consider sleeping with him?"

Violet laughed. "See, this is why you'd be great together."

Jenna thought about pointing out she hadn't been kidding, but why sound even more pathetic with the truth?

"Can I give him your number?"

Jenna hesitated, then drew in a breath and nodded. "I can't wait," she lied.

Six

"Have you tried the cookies?" Beth asked, holding out the tray. "They're beyond delicious. If you're having anything close to a bad day, they'll make you feel better. I think they cure just about anything emotional." She flashed a smile. "My daughter made them. And no, she doesn't get her cooking skills from me. I wish she did."

Jenna smiled to herself as she rang up a large purchase. Beth was working a few hours so Violet could leave early and get ready for her hot date with the finance guy. Her mother was the best PR person around. So far she'd sold two of the most expensive mixers in the store, an entire set of pots and three Keurig coffeemakers.

The two women Beth was speaking to each sampled a cookie. Their tiny, polite bites were followed by moans that made Jenna feel all quivery inside. She loved it when people appreciated her food.

The smell of chocolate drifted through the store, the result of her morning baking combined with the sweet scent of the berries she'd pureed earlier. Fruit and chocolate was always a winning combination.

She had the sudden urge to work with crepes. Chocolate with an unexpected bite. Or maybe rolled chocolate, like a cannoli, filled with a fruit and cream mixture.

"Is there a recipe?" the taller woman asked, bringing Jenna back to the moment.

"Yes." Beth leaned forward and lowered her voice. "Even better—there are bags by the register with all the dry in-gredients already measured. You only have to add eggs and butter at home. Isn't that the best? You could make these tonight. I know I'm going to. My husband loves them."

The two women turned and looked at Jenna. She finished with her customer, then held up the bags.

"Were you talking about these?" she asked innocently. "The cookies? We're having trouble keeping the ingredients in stock."

"I'll take three," the shorter woman said firmly. "I have my grandchildren coming by next week."

Jenna rang up their purchases, then glanced at the clock. It was nearly six. When the women left, she walked to the door and turned the sign, then locked it.

"And we're done."

Beth carried the tray to the kitchen and set it on the counter. "Aren't you exhausted? I don't know how you do this all day."

"It's not that much harder than working in a restaurant."

"It feels hard. You were busy and you didn't even have a class today. You're going to have to hire some part-time help."

"I know." The thought pleased her. After that first disas-trous week she'd been afraid she couldn't sell enough to pay the light bill, let alone the rent. Now she was actually scrambling to get everyone taken care of. Her store was making it.

"Having all these customers is what the self-help gurus would call a quality problem."

Beth laughed. "The only kind to have." Her gaze turned speculative. "Tell me about Violet's date."

"There's not much to tell. It's a first date. He works in finance. She's a little nervous because he's not her usual type. Apparently Violet prefers bad boys to nice guys."

"A lot of women fall into that trap. But she's getting out there, trying something new." Beth put the leftover cookies into baggies. "You could go on a date."

Jenna wasn't even surprised. "I'm impressed. I've been home nearly three months and this is the first time you've mentioned me dating."

"I wanted to give you time."

"Which has run out."

Her mother's mouth twitched. "Yes, it has. There are several very nice young men working in your father's bank. Or if you don't want to date someone who reports to him, which I understand, there are customers. Single men with good prospects."

Jenna crossed to Beth and took her face in her hands. "I love you. Stay out of my love life."

"Someone has to do something. You're spending all your time working."

"My business is all of forty seconds old. Let me get it going before I get distracted."

"You need to get out there, have a life. You don't have to get serious, but you need to start dating. Aaron was a charmer, that's for sure but, as my grandmother would say, when you met him, you led your ducks to a dry pond. Find a better pond."

Jenna dropped her hands and thought of Violet's doctor friend. The one who didn't get involved and was supposed to be a god in bed. Probably not a news item to share with her mother.

"I'm considering it," she admitted. "Violet says I need a rebound guy."

"That's true," Beth said thoughtfully, dropping the bag of cookies into her purse.

"You know what a rebound guy is?"

"I have cable. I know things."

Jenna laughed. "I'm sure you know more than me." The laughter faded. "I know I need to get out there. I still want to meet someone great and fall in love. Have a family. My biological clock is ticking, but I also don't want to make another mistake. I always thought I'd have what you and dad have."

"Every relationship is different."

"Aaron was a bad choice. I see that now. I don't regret the divorce, I don't want to be with him, but all that time is lost and I can't get it back."

"You're thirty-two. You have lots of time."

"It doesn't feel that way. The girls I was friends with in high school are all married with kids."

"You went a different way. You wanted a career."

Which was true but also surprising, considering Beth had always stayed at home. Jenna had loved her mother and hadn't been looking for a way to rebel. Maybe she was just different.

"You'll find your own happy ending," Beth told her. "No one path is right for everyone. We all make compromises."

"You didn't compromise. You wanted to be a wife and a mother and you are."

"I wanted more children," Beth said. "I wanted a big family."

Jenna had forgotten that. Beth had been in a bad horseback riding accident when she'd been young. The resulting injuries and surgery had left her damaged enough that it was unlikely that she could ever have children. She'd explained her situation to Marshall on their third date and had bravely told him she would understand if he didn't want to see her again. A man like him wanted sons of his own.

Jenna had heard the story a dozen times. He'd dropped Beth off at her sorority house and had been back first thing in the morning. He'd taken her in his arms, brushed away her tears and told her he loved her. That they would adopt. They'd started the process the day after they'd returned from their honeymoon.

Less than six months after their marriage, they'd been given Jenna.

"You should have adopted more," she said gently, touching her mother's arm.

"In hindsight, maybe. But I'd heard so many stories about women who adopted, then got pregnant."

Which had happened, Jenna thought sadly. Beth's body had figured out a way to get pregnant but carrying to term had been impossible. She'd miscarried half a dozen times over several years.

Beth and Marshall had then turned to adoption again, only to have two pregnant teens change their minds at the last minute. From what Jenna had figured out, they'd stopped trying to adopt after that.

"We were grateful to get you," Beth said. "We stopped with perfection."

"I'm not perfect, Mom. You know that."

"I disagree. You were never like other teenagers. You didn't talk back, or turn surly."

"What about the year I refused to clean my room?"

"Easy stuff when compared to drugs or sleeping around."

Jenna widened her eyes. "Mom, I slept with the entire football team. Didn't you know?"

Beth grinned. "Uh-huh. I don't think so."

Her mother was right, Jenna thought. She'd loved her parents, had enjoyed her life. Only once had she acted out in teenage rebellion. It had been because she'd been grounded for a weekend after breaking curfew. Sure her "real" parents would understand her better, she'd decided to find them.

Two days later, filled with guilt and remorse, she'd returned to the agency and withdrawn her name from the registry.

Her mother hugged her. "You're all I've ever wanted, sweetie. You know that, right?"

"Yes. I love you, Mom."

"I love you, too. Now think about getting a social life."

Jenna shook her head. "You can't ever stop trying to make things better, can you?"

"No. It's in my DNA. You're going to have to suffer through my quest for you to be happy."

"I will be," Jenna said.

But when her mother had left, she stood alone in the store and wondered what was the next step toward happiness. She was making a success of something that could have been a disaster. She was trying new things, making real connections with people. So why did she still feel a gnawing emptiness inside?

Violet hesitated outside of Wildfire. The restaurant looked welcoming. There were just enough people to make her feel as if the food was good but not so many as to be intimidating. It was five after seven on Tuesday—which made her fashionably late for her date.

She'd changed her mind about coming at least seventeen times in the past two hours. Even as she'd dressed, done her makeup and driven to Old Town, she'd kept thinking it was a mistake. She wasn't even sure she liked Cliff. He wasn't anything like the guys she usually dated, which was a point in his favor. The actual paying job that included an office and business cards was new. He'd been nice. Not too pushy.

She smoothed the front of the black dress she'd borrowed from Jenna. Over it she wore a three-quarter sleeve red-and-black cropped jacket. The nubby fabric contrasted with the smooth silk. She'd added a single pair of silver dangle earrings, had backed off on the bracelets and put on ridiculously high-heeled pumps.

Indecision poured through her. Stay or go?

She glanced into the restaurant again and saw Cliff. He stood inside the door, watching her. He looked…hopeful, she thought. His mouth seemed to be fighting a smile, but she knew he was wondering if she would come in or walk away.

Once again he was dressed in a tailored suit. His white shirt collar was open and she saw part of his tie peeking out of his jacket pocket. His sandy brown hair had been recently brushed.

He had a nice face, she decided. Regular features. He was average-looking—the kind of guy who fit in anywhere. One who most likely paid his bills on time, liked sports and probably considered having an extra beer during the game the extent of being bad.

Did men like that really exist? She knew they did in other places, like in Jenna's world. But for her? Not so much.

Maybe it was time to change that.

She held her clutch purse more tightly and walked toward him. His smile took over his face, brightening his eyes. He hurried to meet her.

"Hi," he said. "You came."

"I did."

"You look amazing. I remembered you being beautiful, but then I tried to talk myself out of it. I figured it was probably the glow from the olives. But it was you."

Her cheeks warmed. It took Violet a second to realize she was actually blushing. She didn't think she'd blushed since she'd been eleven.

"Thank you."

"Shall we?" he asked, motioning to the restaurant. "I was an optimist and asked them to hold a table for us."

She nodded and started inside.

He moved next to her, putting his hand on the small of her back. She felt the heat of his fingers. Usually when a man touched her there it was simply on the way to grabbing her ass, but Cliff's hand didn't move.

They were shown to a corner table. The restaurant was appealing, with white walls and a dark ceiling. Ceiling fans circled lazily above them.

"Have you been here before?" he asked when they were seated. "A few people at work recommended the food. It's supposed to be excellent. A lot of different choices." His face tightened. "Let me know if I'm talking too much."

Violet didn't know what to say to that. How could someone like her make a guy like Cliff nervous?

Their server appeared. He was a tall man in his mid-twenties. His gaze settled on Violet for several seconds. The attention made her nervous. Had he guessed? Was he going to tell Cliff she didn't belong in a place like this?

"Good evening," he said instead. "Welcome to Wildfire. We have three specials tonight." He listed them, then took drink orders.

Cliff ordered a Scotch on the rocks. Violet wanted something a little safer and asked for a glass of the house white.

She turned to find Cliff staring at her.

"What?" she asked, touching her hair.

"I can't believe you're here. Did you see the waiter staring at you? He thinks you're gorgeous. Why aren't you married to some rich guy who owns half of Texas?"

"We dated for a while, but he got on my nerves."

Cliff grinned. "That's a break for me. So Violet of the olive aisle, tell me about yourself."

"I work here in Old Town. In a store called Grate Expectations." She spelled *grate*. "It's new. The owner is a fabulous chef without a lot of retail experience. It's fun and we're a good team. What about you? Your card says finance. What area of finance are you in?"

"I work with companies who want to raise money in the stock market."

He briefly explained about offerings, preferred and common stock, then stopped when the waiter appeared with their drinks.

"Have you decided?" the server asked.

"No," Cliff told him. "I can't take my eyes off her."

"Understandable," their waiter said. "I'll give you a few more minutes."

Violet was flattered by the attention but a little confused by it, too. She knew she was pretty, if slightly off the center of conventional beauty, but Cliff seemed to think she was fascinating. Is this how normal guys acted? Maybe she wasn't used to compliments because when a guy was paying for sex, he rarely bothered.

"Tell me about yourself," she said before sipping her wine. "You said you were new to town."

"Before here I lived in Chicago and before that, Boston."

"Miss the snow?"

"Not even for a second. What about you?"

"I've been in the Austin area for a few years now. What do you like to do for fun?"

He shrugged. "Pretty typical stuff."

"Watch sports?"

"Football and baseball."

"Good choices," she told him.

"Thanks. I like to travel. I plan a big trip every couple of years. Next spring I want to go to Thailand. I hear it's beautiful. And I like wine." He nodded at her glass. "Have you been to Santa Barbara?"

"No."

"It's beautiful. I was there a couple of years ago. I drove from Chicago, saw a lot of the country, filled my trunk with wine and drove home."

"Sounds like a good time."

"It was."

He told her about other trips he'd taken. They spared a couple of minutes to look at the menu and had their orders ready when their server returned, then resumed their conversation.

Violet found that she liked the sound of Cliff's voice. He was well-spoken without being stuffy. He laughed easily, never looked at other women, and while he was obviously interested, he wasn't touching her all the time.

She found herself relaxing more than she would have expected, leaning in when he spoke. Partway through her meal, she realized she felt a flutter, low in her belly. Attraction, she thought happily. That was a good sign.

"Have you been married before?" Cliff asked, passing her the bread.

She took a slice, then set it on her plate. "No."

"Get close?"

"Not really."

"I'm surprised," he admitted. "A beautiful woman like you? You must have to beat guys off with a stick."

She laughed. "Not as much as you'd think. I've worked in retail for years, mostly in cookware. Not a lot of guys hang out there and I don't go to bars very often."

Picking up a strange man and taking him home wasn't her idea of a good time. She'd done that enough before—to make money. It had been a horrible life, and she'd vowed she was never going back to it.

"What about you?" she asked.

He sighed. "Divorced."

"What happened? Or is that too personal?"

"I don't mind talking about it. We were too young. We met in college, fell in love and thought it was forever. We got married after college, moved to Boston and started our careers. We had a plan—kids in a couple of years. Instead of growing closer together over time, we grew apart. Suddenly we'd been married four years and didn't seem to be getting any closer to starting a family. We fought about that, then we fought about everything else. One day we both realized it was over."

"That sounds sad," she told him.

"It was, but I recovered. Moved to Chicago. I thought I'd meet someone there, but it's tough. I'm not a guy who likes going to bars. I don't want to date anyone at work. It can be messy."

"I can imagine," she murmured.

He hunched his shoulders a little and leaned toward her. "I

tried a dating service. Talk about a disaster. I couldn't believe the women they were fixing me up with. We had nothing in common. One of the women had twelve cats. I'm not kidding. I don't mind a couple of pets but twelve of anything isn't normal."

Violet laughed. "I agree. Plus, how would you get the hair off your suits?"

"Tell me about it."

Conversation drifted to favorite movies. They both liked comedies and action movies. Neither of them enjoyed foreign films. He admitted he was a closet Harry Potter fan and she whispered that she was probably the only person in the area who didn't like burnt orange—the University of Texas color. When their server asked if she wanted more coffee, she glanced at her watch and was shocked to find it was after ten.

"It's getting late," she said. "I didn't realize."

Cliff nodded. "You probably have to get home." He hesitated. "I was wondering…"

All her warm feelings tumbled. Three hours of great conversation, seducing her into thinking he was nice and normal and that she really liked him was going to end in him asking her to his place. For a drink. Because that was always how it started.

She grabbed her purse and jerked it open. She'd put a hundred dollars in twenties right on top. Just in case she had to pay and run. No way she was going to let him buy her dinner and think that she owed him.

He cleared his throat. "Now that you've spent some time with me, I was wondering if I could see you again. And if…" More throat clearing. "If you'd, ah, trust me with your phone number."

She stared at him. "Excuse me?"

"Your number," he said again. "So I can, ah, call you and see you again."

She blinked. That was it? He wanted her phone number? Not sex?

Relief tasted sweet.

"Cliff, I would very much like to see you again. And yes, you can have my number."

His whole expression changed. His smile lit up his face and he looked as if she'd just handed him the keys to a Ferrari.

"Great." He pulled out his cell, prepared to input the info. "Okay, shoot." She gave him her number.

He paid the bill and they walked outside. After escorting her to her car, he lightly touched her arm.

"How about Saturday night?"

"I'd like that."

"Good. Me, too." He leaned in and lightly kissed her cheek. "I'll call you with the details."

No one had ever kissed her cheek before. At least not that she could remember. She hadn't allowed kissing with clients, and the guys she'd been involved with had been more interested in getting their tongue down her throat than in anything remotely sweet and tender.

He stepped back. "Would you mind texting me when you get home? So that I know you got home safe?"

"Sure."

"Great. Thanks, Violet. I had a perfect time with you."

And then he was gone. No touching, no hinting, no feeling her up. Just a nice guy on a first date. It was like something out of the movies.

Jenna practically danced in impatience when Violet walked into the rear entrance Wednesday morning.

"Tell me everything," she said by way of greeting. "You said hello and he said hello and then what?"

Violet laughed. She was wearing her usual dark makeup and dozen or so bracelets, but still she looked different.

"You're happy! I can see it in your eyes." Jenna examined her. "Are you blushing?"

"Maybe. I don't know. It's crazy. I barely know this guy."

"But?"

"But I like him. He's nice. Funny and charming and normal. I've never wanted to be with a normal guy before. They don't interest me. But I gave Cliff a chance and it turns out I like him."

"See!" Jenna grinned. "This is so cool."

"It kind of is." Violet put her purse on a shelf, then moved through the stockroom into the store. "He deals with the stock market. Helping companies raise money. He travels, he likes wine, he's into football and baseball. He's divorced."

"Why?"

"College sweethearts who grew apart. He says he wants kids and a family, that he's looking for something serious." Violet hugged herself. "I can't believe he actually said that, but he did."

"Did it sound needy?"

"No. It was nice. He was sincere." She closed her eyes, then opened them. "He wants to see me again."

"Of course he does. If he hadn't, he would be an idiot." Jenna ignored the twinge of jealousy she felt. "I'm glad it went well."

"It was the dress. Pure magic. I'm getting it dry-cleaned, then I'll return it."

"There's no rush. Unlike some people, I don't have a personal life." She glanced at her watch. "I'd better open up."

She impulsively hugged Violet. "I'm really happy for you and only slightly bitter."

"There's still the sexy doctor."

"That will be its own brand of fun," she admitted, then hurried to the front door.

Ever since the grand reopening, there had usually been customers waiting to get in. Today a couple in their late forties or early fifties stood patiently.

She opened the door. "Good morning," she said cheerfully.

"Good morning," the woman said, stepping inside.

She was about the same height as Jenna, with dark red hair that fell to the middle of her back. She was thin and dressed in a flowing floral print dress that nearly went to her ankles. More striking than pretty. The man with her was a little taller and ruggedly handsome.

Probably her husband, Jenna thought. The attractive couple didn't look old enough to have retired, and yet they were in the store on a weekday morning. People had interesting lives.

"Feel free to look around," she said with a smile. "Violet and I are both available if you have any questions." She glanced at the clock on the wall. "There's a class on risotto starting at eleven, if you have time."

"I love risotto," the woman said, tilting her head. "You're Jenna, right?"

"Yes." Jenna didn't remember meeting her, but there had been so many customers lately. "Have you been in before?"

"No, but we've heard about the store. It's very nice. It feels friendly and welcome. No dark spirits here."

"Good to know," Jenna said, taking a step back. She glanced at Violet who was obviously trying not to laugh. "Okay, then. I'll be right here if you need anything."

The man and woman exchanged a glance. The woman moved closer. "Have you owned other stores?"

"Ah, no. This is my first. I used to be a chef."

"Yes, I..." The woman cleared her throat. "Here locally?"

"In different cities. Mostly the southwest. Also Los Angeles."

"But you've only been back in Texas a few months, right?"

Jenna stared at her. "How did you know that?" she asked slowly.

"Serenity has always enjoyed cooking," the man said, not answering the question. "She can make anything."

The woman sighed. "That's not true." She wrinkled her nose. "Not meat. We're vegetarians. Partly because of the animals and partly the environment. If we stopped growing corn as animal feed we could cure hunger in a single generation."

"I didn't know that," Jenna murmured, wondering how to politely excuse herself from the couple. While she was always pleased to have new customers, these two made her nervous. How had the woman known Jenna had been in Georgetown only a few months?

"We're from California," Serenity added. Her eyes were dark green, her cheeks pale. "The Napa area. Have you been there?"

"For a couple of weekend getaways. It's very beautiful." She took another step back, feeling uneasy. "I'll let you look around."

"Oh, Tom," Serenity said softly. "I can't believe this is happening."

Happening? What did that mean? Whatever it was, it couldn't be good.

Jenna glanced at Violet, who was already heading for the

phone. Jenna wondered if they were going to rob her or if it would be worse. Worry settled like a rock in her stomach.

"Should we tell her now?" Serenity asked.

The man—Tom—nodded.

"Jenna, we're Tom and Serenity Johnson." He grinned, looking suddenly boyish. "Tom, short for Atomic."

Great, Jenna thought fighting hysterics. They were going to be robbed by hippies. How humiliating.

"I thought you'd feel it," Serenity said, staring intently at Jenna, as if searching for something. "The connection. I'd hoped you would. At first I was waiting for you, but now…" She sighed. "I want you to know, but only because it's time. I hope you know that. I couldn't wait anymore. Am I making sense?"

"Not in the least."

Serenity smiled and held out her hand, as if expecting Jenna to take it. "We're…" She swallowed, looked at Tom, then turned her attention back to Jenna. "We're your birth parents."

Seven

Violet had only gotten to the nine in 9-1-1. Slowly she put the phone down and stared at the three people standing in the middle of the store.

Serenity and Tom gazed at Jenna with expressions that were almost beatific. Love, hope and happiness shone in their eyes. Jenna, on the other hand, looked as if she was going to bolt the second she found the ability to move.

Jenna's birth parents? Violet remembered Jenna telling her she'd been adopted, but she'd had no interest in getting in touch with her biological parents. It was obvious from her wide eyes and scary-white face that Serenity and Tom were completely unexpected.

Not knowing what else to do, Violet crossed to Jenna and lightly touched her back, wanting her to know she wasn't alone.

"Are you okay?" she whispered.

"No," Jenna breathed.

Serenity's smile never wavered. "I'm sure this is a surprise. It is for me, too. I've been waiting to meet you, but I knew it was important for you to come to us. That you would have questions. I was as surprised as you when the universe instead told me to come to you. I'm so delighted we can finally be together."

Violet felt Jenna stiffen. Personally, she wanted to ask what the message from the universe was but didn't think Jenna would appreciate that.

"I don't understand," Jenna whispered, her voice breathless and soft.

"Your mother is Beth Stevens, your father is Marshall Stevens. We knew that much from the adoption." Serenity leaned into Tom. "They were so in love. We liked that about them. We could feel it and see it in their eyes."

"You met my parents?" Jenna asked.

"It was a condition of the adoption. We had to know you were going to be well taken care of." Her smile faded. "Giving up a child isn't an easy thing, but we were young… Still, all these years, we've wondered. I've sent you vibrations. Have you felt them?"

"I'm going to throw up," Jenna whispered.

"Keep breathing," Violet told her.

"Let her get used to us," Tom murmured to his wife. "Let her ask her questions in her own time. You don't want to scare her off."

"You're right, my love." Serenity's smile returned. "I'm just so happy, Jenna. You're lovely."

"She looks like you," Tom said quietly.

Violet looked between them and realized he told the truth. Serenity and Jenna were about the same height. Their faces were similar, and they had the same eyes.

"I don't know what to say," Jenna said, taking a step back. "How did you find me?"

Violet felt Jenna's confusion and pain. She wanted to dismiss the Johnsons but couldn't. It was all too plausible.

"We've always known your parents' names," Serenity said easily. "Once we knew we were meant to come and see you, finding you wasn't difficult. We called your restaurant in California where a helpful man named Aaron told us you were here. We drove, of course. I'm not one who flies easily, except in my dreams. The country is so beautiful."

Serenity tilted her head. "I have so many things I want to tell you. About your past and your family."

Jenna seemed frozen in place. Violet glanced at the couple.

"This is a bit of a shock," she said. "Jenna wasn't expecting your arrival."

"She's right," Tom told his wife. "Our girl needs time."

Jenna shuddered.

"We're staying in town for a while," Serenity said. "Close by. We very much want to get to know you, Jenna, and have you get to know us. That's why we're here."

Jenna cleared her throat. "Excuse me. I have an appointment."

She turned and fled through the stockroom. Seconds later, Violet heard the back door slam shut.

"Oh," Serenity breathed. "She's gone."

Hardly a surprise, Violet thought. Who walked into someone's business and announced they were family with no warning? Talk about an insensitive introduction. While she could appreciate the theory of families getting back together, some kind of delicacy seemed appropriate.

"She'll be back," Violet said. "I'm sure she needs a little

time to adjust to everything you've told her. Why don't I take your number and she can call you later?"

"All right," Tom said. "We got a cell phone for the trip. I'll write down the address where we're staying, as well."

Violet pulled one of their business cards from her pocket and handed it to him. He wrote on the back.

"I'll give this to her as soon as I see her," Violet promised. Although she had a feeling Jenna might not take it willingly.

"I suppose that's the best we can do," Serenity said, sounding wistful. "I had hoped…"

"It'll happen," Tom said, taking her hand in his. "Trust the universe."

"I will."

Serenity smiled at Violet. "Do you know any good vegan restaurants in the area?"

If it was Wednesday morning, it must be yoga, Jenna thought frantically as she drove through Old Town. She headed for the studio and prayed her mother was keeping to her schedule. If not, she would have to hunt her down.

Aware that she was not at her best, she focused on her driving and kept her breathing steady. Every time Serenity and Tom Johnson popped into her brain, she pushed the image away. Not now, she told herself. She would have her breakdown as soon as she was parked.

She found a spot just around the corner from the yoga studio and quickly walked inside. In a small foyer, the girl behind the low desk looked up.

"Class has already started," she said. "I'm sorry but we don't allow late arrivals."

"I'm here to get my mother," Jenna told her. "There's a family emergency."

"Oh. I'm sorry. Let me get her for you. What's her name?"

"Beth Stevens."

The woman walked to the closed door and quietly pushed it open. Jenna paced the small space until the woman returned with her mother in tow.

"Jenna! What are you doing here? Not that I mind the interruption. I swear, I was seconds from snapping a bone. There are some things my body simply won't do."

Without thinking, Jenna moved toward her. "Mo-om," she said, her voice cracking.

Her mother took her in her arms and held her tight.

Everything was familiar, she thought gratefully. The feel, the scent, the secure embrace that never let go too soon.

Beth guided them to the wooden bench across from the desk. The young woman who had gone to find Beth excused herself and disappeared into the main room of the studio. Beth touched Jenna's face.

"Tell me what's wrong. Are you hurt?"

"No. I'm fine." She couldn't figure out where to start. "We're talking no warning. One second they were just *there*, saying…" She touched her chest. "I can't breathe."

"You can." Her mother kept an arm around her and studied her. "Tell me what happened, Jenna. This is starting to scare me."

"My birth parents are here."

Beth's mouth dropped open. "What?"

"Tom and Serenity Johnson. They waltzed into my store this morning. Right when it opened. They acted as if they knew me. I thought they were going to rob us or something. Then they announced they were my birth parents."

Jenna didn't want to think about any of it. Her stomach flipped over, making her swallow against rising nausea.

"They're hippies and weird and vegetarians. Serenity said

she'd been waiting for a sign from the universe to come find me and it arrived."

"Via FedEx?" Beth asked.

Jenna glared at her. "This isn't funny."

"Oh, honey, it kind of is."

"These are my *birth parents!* What are they doing here? I don't want to know them. I don't want this."

Beth smoothed Jenna's hair. "They're family."

"They're biology. You're my family."

"You came from them. That's something."

"Why are you taking their side? You haven't met them. Oh, wait. You have, back when you adopted me. You never told me about them. Why?"

Beth touched her cheek. "Calm down. You're making too much of this."

"Because it's a big deal. Why aren't you upset? Why aren't you threatened? Tell me I can't ever see them again, please."

Her mother smiled at her. "They gave me the greatest gift of my life. I am grateful every day for you, Jenna."

Oh, sure. Rational thought. Like that was going to help.

"I think it's nice that they're here," Beth told her. "They can answer questions I never could. About where you come from and your DNA."

"I don't care about my DNA," Jenna muttered, annoyed that Beth wasn't shrieking and insisting she keep her distance from the Johnsons.

"You will when you have children of your own."

"Like that's ever going to happen."

Her mother kissed her cheek. "I know this must be a shock. How did you leave things with them?"

"I told them I had an appointment and I ran."

Beth raised her eyebrows.

Jenna stood. "Don't you dare get on me, Mom. This was horrible. I had to get out of there. I'll be polite later."

Nothing made sense. Not the unexpected arrival of her biological parents or her mother's calm acceptance. She knew for sure her mother had watched soap operas in the past. Beth understood how these things were supposed to go. Where was the insecurity, the melodrama, the terror of losing her only child?

"You're too calm," she told her mother. "It's not natural."

"I'm curious about these people. I want to meet them again."

"You didn't think to warn me what they were like?"

"Back then they were teenagers, Jenna. We were delighted to be given a chance at adopting. They weren't very different from any other young couple. You need to talk to them." Beth stood. "Give me a few minutes to get changed, then we'll go see them."

Jenna tucked her hands behind her back. "No. I don't want to." She didn't need another set of parents. The ones she had were perfectly fine. "Besides, I have a risotto class in fifteen minutes."

"Then I'll pick you up after that."

"That doesn't work for me."

"Jenna, they've come a long way to see you."

"They could have called first, or sent a letter. You don't just drop in on a kid you gave up at birth."

"Maybe not, but this is the situation we have. It will be fine. You'll see."

"And if it isn't?"

"Then you can say you told me so."

"I'm not sure that's enough of a reward."

★ ★ ★

Beth drove her Mercedes through the midday traffic. Jenna sat next to her, arms crossed, her expression stubborn.

She had to admit, she was surprised by her daughter's reaction. For herself, she was very curious about seeing Jenna's birth parents after all this time.

Just over thirty-two years ago, she and Marshall had gone to San Francisco to meet with the pregnant teenager who had picked them to adopt her baby. Serenity had been young and scared and very pregnant. Her parents hadn't been with her—instead a young man had been at her side. Tom, Beth remembered. Funny how they'd stayed together all these years.

Serenity had asked most of the questions, had cried more than once and explained that her parents were making her give up her baby. They told her it was for the best. Serenity said she hadn't believed them until she'd met Beth and Marshall. And then she'd known they were the ones.

The four of them had signed the necessary paperwork. Two weeks later, Beth and Marshall had flown back to pick up their baby daughter. They'd never seen either of the teens again.

To think that after all this time, they were going to meet again was amazing.

"Give me the address," she said as she turned onto a quiet residential street.

Jenna did, sounding more like a sullen teen than a successful businesswoman.

"I'm glad Violet thought to get their address."

Jenna rolled her eyes. "Yes, it was very thoughtful of her."

"Why are you being so difficult about this?"

"I don't need them," Jenna told her. "I don't like how they

just showed up. If they've had the contact information for all this time, why now? Why is this moment better than ten years ago or ten years from now? What do they want? I'm also worried about you. I don't want you to get hurt in all this."

"It's sweet of you to worry," Beth told her, "but I'm fine. Jenna, you're my daughter. No one can take that away."

They pulled in front of a pretty two-story house with an apartment over the garage.

"Violet said they're renting an apartment while they're in town," Jenna said grudgingly.

Beth parked the car and led the way upstairs. She had a few nerves, she admitted to herself, but more curiosity. At the top of the stairs was a small landing and a red front door. Beth knocked.

It was opened quickly by a tall, slender redhead who looked enough like Jenna to make Beth blink.

"I knew you'd come," the woman said happily, then embraced Beth. "I knew it would be exactly like this."

"Serenity," Beth said and hugged her back. "It's been a long time."

"I know. Too long."

The other woman stepped back to let them in. Beth glanced at the small but tastefully furnished apartment. Jenna barely slipped inside the door.

Beth returned her attention to their hostess.

Serenity was as tall as she remembered but more beautiful. She'd aged well and stayed slim. There had only been the one meeting, and they hadn't exchanged pictures. Over time, she'd forgotten what Jenna's birth mother had looked like.

Now she saw the similarity in the shape of their faces, the eyes. By contrast, Beth was short and round—not exactly a comfortable way to think of herself.

"Tom's out getting us some lunch," Serenity said. "I was resting. Travel exhausts me." She turned to Jenna. "It's nice to see you again."

"You, too," Jenna said, sounding more grudging than pleased. "I have to admit, I don't know what to say to you. I wasn't prepared to meet you."

Serenity sat on the square footrest, leaving the two wing chairs for Jenna and Beth.

"Perhaps we should have called," Serenity murmured, looking concerned as she studied Jenna. "Tom mentioned it. I never wanted to hurt you or frighten you, but the idea to finally come and find you was so strong."

"From the universe," Jenna told her mother, then pressed her lips together.

"I've been waiting," Serenity admitted to Beth. "For her to come to us. I started to think she never would, but then the universe let me know I needed to go to her."

Beth wasn't usually critical of people, but this time she had to agree with her daughter. Serenity definitely fell in the crazy category. Although this kind of crazy was often harmless.

"How long are you in town?" she asked.

"We're not sure. A few weeks." Serenity smiled at Jenna. "We wanted to give you the chance to get to know us, to ask any questions."

"That would be nice," Beth said, before Jenna could respond. "Jenna's busy with her store, but I'm sure there will be time for you to discover each other. Where do you live?"

"Napa Valley. We have a family winery. It's beautiful there."

While Serenity answered Beth's questions, she looked only at Jenna. The hunger in her eyes made Beth a little uncomfortable. But she was determined to do the right thing.

"Any other children?"

Serenity finally turned to her. "Two boys. Despite our parents' refusal to believe Tom and I were in love, we stayed together all this time. We married out of high school. I got pregnant almost right away. I did love being pregnant."

She would have loved it, too, Beth thought grimly. If she'd been able to carry a baby to term.

"What do your boys do?"

"Wolf, our youngest, runs the winery. Dragon—" The smile returned. "Dragon is a lawyer. We can barely believe it ourselves, but he swears he loves it. I'm not sure how he can exist in a city, away from the land and the sun. He's not one with the earth, but he never has been."

"Children will go their own way," Beth said, refusing to look at her daughter. The last thing she needed was to see Jenna right now. Odds were they would both break out into hysterical laughter. *One with the earth?*

Then her humor faded. Serenity had been blessed with two more children. Beth would have liked that.

"Would you like some tea?" Serenity asked. "Dandelion root. I dried it myself."

"No, thank you," Beth murmured. "Two boys. That's so nice."

"But you're my only daughter." Serenity turned back to Jenna. "You would have loved growing up with us."

"I'm happy with the life that I had," Jenna said. She cleared her throat. "Although you do paint a vivid picture."

Serenity swayed slightly on the sofa. "We would have called you Butterfly. If we'd kept you. Tom wrote a song about you. You'll have to ask him to play it when he gets back."

★ ★ ★

Jenna did her best not to choke or run for the door. Butterfly?

"The boys got to be animals and I'm a bug?" she asked before she could stop herself. Only to slam into the realization that the "boys" in question were not only adults, but her brothers. As in *brothers*. She'd been an only child her whole life and now she had brothers.

"Technically Dragon is short for Dragonfly, but he's asked us not to call him that."

Jenna looked at her mother, only to see Beth mouthing the words "Be nice."

"Dragonfly?" Jenna asked, then wished she hadn't.

Serenity laughed. "He wasn't happy about it, but I kept seeing dragonflies when I was pregnant."

Jenna thought about saying that it was good that Serenity hadn't been near a farm with really big pigs, but kept her mouth shut.

Everything about this felt completely surreal. How could people she'd never known show up and expect to have a connection with her?

"Do your boys look like you or Tom?" Beth asked.

"Mostly Tom."

"Jenna looks like you."

Jenna had to consciously keep from scowling.

"I think she's much prettier," Serenity said.

"You won't have to worry about your weight as you get older," Beth said to Jenna. She turned back to Serenity. "That's nice. I'm a lifetime member of Weight Watchers. Show me a food and I can tell you the points value. I just love their program."

Jenna wanted to tell her mother to stop talking about her weight. She was beautiful, and Jenna wanted to be just like her. Shorter and curvy and lush. And while she was at it, she wanted to walk away from this apartment and never talk to Serenity again.

She was angry with her birth parents for bursting into her life and really pissed at Beth for not being upset. Which probably didn't make sense, but at this point, she didn't care.

"Have you tried avoiding meat?" Serenity asked. "It's very healthy, and many people I know have lost weight with a vegetarian lifestyle."

Jenna wanted to stand up and scream. Was Serenity implying her mother was fat?

Instead of getting upset, Beth laughed. "We're in Texas. Eating meat is practically a religion. Speaking of eating, I think we should all get together. You and Tom, Marshall and me and, of course, Jenna."

"Jenna who brought us together," Serenity said. "That would be very nice."

Beth dug a piece of paper out of her purse and wrote on it. When she handed it to Serenity, she said, "Here's my home number and our address. How about brunch on Sunday?" She drew her eyebrows together. "Do you eat eggs?"

"We can," Serenity said in a tone that implied she would rather not. "I'll bring a dish, as well."

"That would be good." Beth smiled. "I'll have to warn you, I'm not half the cook my daughter is."

Without wanting to, Jenna looked at Serenity and knew in that second the other woman was thinking, "No, *my* daughter." But she didn't say the words, which meant Jenna didn't have to scream. Probably best for all of them.

The need to attach herself to Beth, to proclaim their relationship, unnerved her. She and her mother didn't have anything to prove. Yet somehow Serenity's arrival had changed everything.

"How about eleven?" Beth asked.

"That would be lovely."

Jenna stood. "I need to get back to work. It was, um, nice to see you again."

Serenity rose, looking oddly elegant in her hippy dress. Her long hair should have made her look old, but it didn't. Somehow it suited her face.

"I guess I'll see you Sunday," Jenna added, then fought unexpected guilt for not wanting to spend more time with them while they were here.

Screw that, she told herself. She hadn't asked for this visit, and they sure hadn't given her any warning. Sunday was plenty of time.

She'd barely spent a moment thinking about her birth parents. Now they were here. Just as strange, her mother was only about fifteen years older than she was.

"Lovely to meet you," Beth said as they walked to the door. "Call if you need anything."

"I'm sure the universe will provide," Jenna muttered, when they were back outside.

She thought Beth would snap at her, but instead her mother laughed. "Serenity has a distinctive charm."

"How can you say that?" It was practically a betrayal.

"Because she's unique and there aren't enough unique people in the world."

Jenna shook her head. "There's something seriously wrong with you, Mom. You know that, right?"

Beth linked arms with her. "I've known it for years."

Eight

There was nothing like the unexpected arrival of birth parents to put something as inconsequential as a blind date out of one's mind, Jenna thought as she studied herself in her bathroom mirror.

She'd spent most of Thursday and today trying to forget Serenity and Tom had ever shown up in her life, which proved impossible. Even work hadn't been enough of a distraction. But considering she was about to go on a date with a strange man who had a reputation for being a god in bed, getting her birth parents out of her mind should be relatively easy.

She studied the ruffled dress that Violet had rejected and decided it suited her just fine. She wasn't trying to be sexy or sophisticated. She simply wanted to get through the evening without embarrassing herself.

After slipping on high-heeled sandals, she grabbed her small purse, a pashmina wrap and headed for the door.

Fifteen minutes later she'd arrived in Old Town, parked her car and was standing in front of the restaurant where she was to meet Dr. Mark of the gifted penis. She eyed the bar and wondered how dangerous it was to get completely drunk. After all, the restaurant would call a cab to get her home and she could phone Violet and get a ride to work with her. Not that getting plastered would do much for her first impression in the dating department.

She walked into the Mexican restaurant and found a tall, good-looking blond guy chatting with the hostess. Judging from the way they were looking at each other, they were obviously enjoying getting to know each other.

Player, Jenna thought in disgust, and felt a flash of pity for the guy's date. Then her mind hiccupped as she recalled Violet's description of Dr. Mark and realized he very well might be *her* date.

She cleared her throat, and they both looked up. The hostess looked annoyed while the guy gave Jenna a not-very-subtle once-over. He moved toward her and smiled, showing dimples that only enhanced his looks.

"Please tell me you're Jenna," he said in a low sexy voice. "If not, will you pretend to be?"

She wasn't sure if she should be flattered or insulted.

"I'm Jenna," she said, figuring the truth was always a good fallback position.

"I'm Mark." He took her hand, then brought it to his mouth where he lightly kissed her fingers. "I owe Violet big time." He led her to the hostess.

"Table for two, somewhere private."

The girl he'd been flirting with flashed him the hate stare, but he didn't notice. Jenna got the message, though.

Note to self, she thought. Violet wasn't kidding about this

guy being a player. Absolutely no emotional engagement was allowed.

As they were shown to a quiet table in back, Jenna tried to figure out if she could really have sex with a stranger. Mark was handsome enough and obviously practiced, but her body had never been one to perform on command. The theory of rebound sex was interesting, but she wasn't sure it was for her.

When they were seated, Mark moved his chair closer to hers. "Hello, Violet's friend. I understand you're new in town."

"I've been back a couple of months."

"Back from where?"

"Los Angeles."

He studied her appraisingly. "I can see you on the beach."

"I'm not really a beach kind of person. But I did go a few times."

"I love the beach."

She stared into his blue eyes. "You love the girls in bikinis."

His smile was unrepentant. "God gave us beautiful women for a reason."

"So you could admire them?"

"Something like that."

The waiter appeared. Jenna risked ordering a margarita. Mark got a beer on tap.

She waited until they were alone before angling toward him. "Tell me about yourself."

"I'm a doctor." He paused, as if waiting for appropriate oohs and ahs.

"Violet mentioned that. What kind?"

"Orthopedic surgeon. Show me a broken bone and I'll heal it."

"Just like Jesus."

"Almost." He flashed her a grin, then shifted his chair a little closer and took one of her hands in both of his. "I'm very good with bodies."

He was close enough that she could inhale the scent of his skin. The smell was pleasant enough, but he was invading her personal space, which she didn't like.

"Do you handle any of the local sports teams?" she asked as a way to distract him.

"Mostly the Longhorns. I've fixed up several of their players. They have a team doctor but I'm called in for the difficult cases. Teams in other cities fly me in for consults."

He got into his story, telling her about private jets, operating rooms in different cities and what it was like to watch a game on Sunday morning, knowing if someone got injured, he could get the call.

Their drinks arrived. She used the moment to inch her chair back and slide her glass away from him so he wouldn't hold her hand as much.

From his work, Mark segued to his personal travel. Jenna found herself thinking about Serenity and Tom and wondering what they were doing, alone in a strange city. While she didn't want to spend time with them, she also felt a little guilty for ignoring them. Telling herself they would be at brunch on Sunday wasn't enough.

This was all Beth's fault, she told herself. If her mother hadn't raised her to have good manners, she could cheerfully ignore her birth parents.

"Jenna?"

She looked at Mark.

"That was funny," he said. "You're supposed to laugh."

"Oh, I'm sorry." She squeezed her eyes shut, then opened

them. "I'm distracted. You're great and this is fun, but I've had the weirdest week."

"I know how that goes." His smile was back, and interest danced through his deep, blue eyes.

"This is different from work issues though. Wednesday morning two strangers walked into my store. They seemed nice enough—maybe a little hippy. They announced they were my birth parents. I always knew I'd been adopted, but I never had any contact with them before. And there they were, in my store."

He stared into her eyes and nodded. "That's rough."

"Tell me about it. I totally freaked. I'm not looking for more parents. I love the ones I have. I just want the new ones to go home. Worse, they're hippies. Serenity and Atomic, if you can believe it. They would have called me Butterfly. Who does that to an innocent kid?"

He sipped his beer and nodded.

"But they're my blood relations, and they have two sons, who are my *brothers*. So there's this whole other part of my life I don't know about. It's confusing and kind of scary. I don't know what to do. My mom—my real mom—is having them over for brunch on Sunday. So I'll see them then. Part of me thinks that's plenty of getting-to-know-you-time while another part of me feels guilty about not hanging out with my biological parents more. Still, it's not like I asked them to show up."

She sucked in a breath, then let it out slowly. "And I've just done the emotional dump thing, haven't I? Sorry."

"It's fine."

He captured her hand before she could pull it away and lightly kissed her knuckles. The contact was the most erotic thing to happen to her in close to six months, so she waited for the tingle or a whisper of heat. All that surfaced was the realization she was going to have to wash her hands before she was comfortable diving into the chips and salsa.

"What's the plan?" Mark asked, running the tip of his tongue across the pads of her fingers.

"Plan?" Weren't they having dinner? This was a restaurant, right? Those sheets of paper in the corner of the table really looked like menus.

"Did you want to eat, or should we go somewhere private?"

Now she felt stupid. "Private?"

He leaned in close and pressed his mouth to her ear. "You're beautiful, Jenna. Soft and feminine." His hand dropped to her knee, slipped under her dress and started a purposeful journey up her thigh.

She jumped and scooted the chair back about a foot. "What are you talking about?"

Mark looked more puzzled than annoyed. "Violet said you were looking for a rebound guy and I'm good with that."

Jenna's mouth dropped open. She closed it only to have it fall open again.

"I thought this was a date," she said at last. "I don't think I can have sex with a stranger."

"That's because you've never tried." He winked at her. "If you're worried it won't be good for you, there isn't a woman alive I can't please. I'm up for anything." He grinned. "If you'll excuse the pun."

She collected her purse and stood. "Mark, you're really, um, unexpected. I appreciate the offer, but I can't right now."

"Want to go make out in my car? I bet I could change your mind."

"Flattering, but no. I guess I'm not ready for a rebound guy."

He stood. "I understand." He reached into his jacket pocket and pulled out a business card. After writing on it, he handed it to her. "I've given you my cell phone number. When you change your mind, give me a call."

He moved toward her, put one hand on her shoulder and bent to kiss her. While her instinct was to turn her head, she stayed where she was as his mouth brushed against hers.

The contact was soft and exploring. And she felt nothing. Yup—a hasty retreat was exactly right.

He straightened enough to whisper, "I make house calls."

"Good to know." She turned to leave, then looked back at him. "You going after the hostess?"

He chuckled. "Sure. Did you get a look at her ass?"

"No."

"It's impressive," he said with a wink.

"Okay, then." Jenna couldn't find it in her heart to be angry. Violet had promised a player who was good in bed and that's who Mark was. There was an ick factor she couldn't overcome, but he was probably exactly what some other woman was looking for.

Once she got to her car, she grabbed her cell.

"Hello?"

"Hi, Mom. Are you and Dad up for some company?"

"Of course. Have you eaten?"

"No. Are there leftovers?"

"Yes, although I doubt they're up to your standards."

"They'll be perfect. See you in a bit."

She hung up, then started her car and drove the familiar route to her parents' house. Beth was waiting and opened the front door before Jenna could ring the bell.

Her mother took in the dress, the fluffy hair and extra makeup. "You look pretty. Were you on a date?"

"If that's what you want to call it."

Beth grinned. "Really? That's wonderful. Tell me every-thing." Her smile faded. "Wait. If you're done already, it didn't go well, did it?"

"Not exactly."

"Come on, honey. We'll go in the kitchen and you can talk about it. I warned your father there might be girl talk, so he found a baseball game to watch."

Jenna loved everything about being in the house. It was warm and welcoming, happy and familiar. Her mother settled on a bar stool in the kitchen while Jenna pulled containers of leftovers from the stainless steel refrigerator.

As she turned on the oven and reviewed the leftover po-tential, she explained Violet's theory of rebound guy.

"Makes sense," her mother said. "You don't want to get serious too quickly."

"I guess." Jenna checked the vegetable drawer for herbs and pulled out some fresh basil. "But Dr. Mark was a pro."

She detailed her date as she got out a premade single serv-ing pizza crust from the pantry, then smoothed on the left-overs. After topping it with grated mozzarella, she added fresh basil, then put the whole thing in the oven.

Maybe she should do a pizza class, she thought absently. How pizza could be made with just about anything. It was a fun way to use up leftovers, and the mothers might appreci-ate it as a way to get their kids to eat all kinds of things.

Beth was laughing by the end of her story. "He actually said he could please any woman? There's a claim. You should have taken him up on it."

"I'm not sure sex with a stranger is a stress I need right now."

"It might make you feel better. Clear out the pipes, so to speak."

"Mom!" Jenna was shocked. "I'm your daughter."

"You're an adult. It could be fun. Dr. Mark sounds in-triguing."

"Then you go out with him."

"I'm married."

"I'm not sure that would bother him at all."

Jenna moved toward her mother, who hugged her tight.

"You doing all right?" Beth asked.

Jenna knew they weren't talking about her date anymore. "I'm dealing. They haven't been in the store again, which is good. I'll see them Sunday."

"Yes, you will. It will be fine, you'll see. We'll all get along." Beth touched Jenna's cheek. "Want to spend the night?"

Jenna thought about her familiar room upstairs. The bed she'd had since she was a teenager. Not that she'd used it much, once she'd left for college. The attached bathroom was probably still stocked with her old perfumes and acne treatments.

"You should clean it out and make it a guest room."

"We have a guest room."

"Then take up a hobby. Scrapbooking or knitting. Only Ewe has classes."

"I like that it's your room. It makes me happy."

Jenna held on to her mother and kissed the top of her head. "I would love to stay the night."

Violet was waiting when Jenna arrived at work the next morning.

"Now it's my turn to want details," her friend said. "Tell me everything."

Jenna laughed. "Mark was exactly as you promised. Hand-some and more than willing to take care of my personal plumbing."

Violet's dark eyebrows drew together. "Why don't I like the sound of that? It didn't go well, did it?"

"Not exactly. Mark was thinking that sex was a sure thing, while I wasn't sure I was ready to date."

"Oh, God. That's not good. What happened?"

Jenna gave her the basic details as she put her purse on the shelf and led the way into the store.

"I'm sorry. I should have been more clear with him."

Jenna shook her head. "I don't think that would have helped. He's a man on a mission. When last I saw him, he was off to seduce the restaurant hostess. What I'm curious about is the potential pool of women. The way he goes through them, isn't he in danger of running out?"

"True, but he travels a lot." Violet winced. "I'm sorry it was so horrible."

"Actually, it wasn't. I liked going out and seeing if I could date. I think maybe I could, but I'm not up for a professional rebound guy. Maybe if my biological parents hadn't popped into my life with no warning, but they pretty much burned up all my extra energy. I just wish they'd go away."

"They weren't that bad," Violet said.

"You want them?"

An expression of longing briefly passed over Violet's face.

The look surprised Jenna. "You're looking for a family?"

"I never knew my dad and I haven't seen my mom since I was fifteen. She's probably dead and I don't know if I care enough to find out."

Jenna was stunned. "I'm sorry," she said quickly. "I was very insensitive."

"You didn't know," Violet told her. "It's fine. I haven't had a real family, so it's not like I know what I'm missing. It would be weird if my dad just showed up. I wouldn't know it was him." She frowned. "I don't think I'd believe him." The frown faded. "I have trust issues."

"We all have something," Jenna said.

"You have too many parents. It's cool that Beth isn't freaking out. She could be and that would make this all really awkward." Violet motioned to a stack of boxes by the cash register. "Those Bundt pans finally came in. We can schedule the cake class."

Jenna wasn't sure if the change in subject was deliberate or not, but she went with it. The last thing she wanted to do was hurt Violet's feelings. As much as she and the other woman had started to become friends, Jenna realized she barely knew anything about Violet's previous life.

"Now I have to find a killer recipe," she said. "Is chocolate too much of a cliché?"

Violet laughed. "Your primary customer base is women. I don't think chocolate is ever a cliché."

They went over the rest of the class schedule for the coming week.

"Are we sure about working with kids?" Jenna asked more to herself than to Violet. "It's going to get messy."

"But their moms are looking for new ways to cook healthy."

"I know." She wrinkled her nose. "I'm thinking I should embrace the messiness. What about turkey meatballs? They're packed with protein and very lean, which the moms should appreciate. We can make them relatively plain for the kids and then do a nice spicy sauce for the parents."

"That would work. It's a finger food. Children love finger foods."

"Right. Oh, and for our classic Italian cooking class, I want to feature a Rachael Ray recipe for baked ziti. Everyone loves her and I've tried the recipe. It's great."

She spoke easily, careful not to let on how much it bothered her to use someone else's recipe. It was worse than
cheating—it was admitting she was a failure. Before, she
would have simply come up with a recipe herself. Before,
when she'd trusted herself.

A few days ago, she'd played with a cake-cheesecake combination. The idea had been so clear in her head. She knew
how it was supposed to taste. But halfway through the
baking, she'd pulled the cake out of the oven and dumped it
in the trash without even tasting it. Because thinking it was
horrible was better than being sure.

"I'm sure the Rachael Ray books would sell in the store,"
Violet told her, drawing her back to the present.

"Me, too."

The front door opened. They both turned to greet the
new customer. Jenna held in a groan when she saw Serenity.

Today the other woman was dressed in a long, flowing
tunic in lavender, and stone-colored loose pants that came
to just below her calves. A delicate chain circled her ankle,
while sandals showcased a pedicure of purple nail polish.

"Good morning," Serenity said, sounding happy. "I woke
up just before dawn and knew I wanted to see my daughter
again."

Jenna did her best not to bristle at the "my daughter" comment. She would take the words in the spirit in which they
were meant, she told herself. Or at least give it a good try.

"Nice to see you again," she said. "Did you meet Violet
last time you were here? She's the brains behind the organi-
zation. I'm the cook."

"We spoke," Violet said, moving toward Serenity and offering her hand. "But I don't believe there were introduc-
tions. Nice to meet you."

"You, too."

Serenity took Violet's hand and held on to it. She put her other palm close to Violet's cheek without touching it.

"Your aura is troubled," Serenity said. "You're unsure. But your future will be happy." She frowned. "There's a bump in the road ahead, but once you're through that, you'll be fine."

Jenna stared, unable to think what to say. All this and no tarot cards, she thought, trying to find the humor in the situation. It was that or scream, and it seemed a little early for a full-throated yell.

Serenity dropped her hands and beamed at Violet. "I hope you don't mind. I get a sense about people. Tom reminds me not everyone wants to know what's going to happen to them. He thinks I should edit more."

Yay, Tom, Jenna thought.

"A happy future is good," Violet said. "Thanks for sharing."

"Just watch out for the bump."

"I will."

Jenna wondered how Violet could be so calm and rational. Maybe she was more experienced with those slightly off the road of normal.

"We were planning menus for our cooking classes," Jenna said into the silence. "We try to have a class every day. During the class we feature cookware or cookbooks. For some, we have the ingredients prepared ahead of time, along with a recipe card. Customers can buy them and re-create the dish that night, if they want."

"That's very innovative." Serenity picked up the printed list of classes. "I see you're doing organic but not vegan."

"Not many in the community have embraced the vegan lifestyle. It's tough." There had been a lot of vegan eaters in L.A., but Jenna and Aaron hadn't catered to that crowd.

Vegetarian they could do, but vegans didn't eat animal products of any kind. In her opinion, the world was a sad place without butter. Not to mention cheese. A little sprinkling of the right cheese could save almost any dish.

"Have you tried any vegan recipes?" Serenity asked.

"No. I don't have much experience in that area."

"You should. Even if you don't plan on becoming a vegan, you can try a completely different way of thinking about food. You might find it's fun."

Fun. Jenna couldn't remember the last time cooking had been fun. Although the idea of trying vegan intrigued her. As she'd never done it before, there would be no expectations.

"Why don't I whip up a few things and bring them by for you to try?" Serenity offered.

"All right." Jenna did her best to sound more enthused than doubtful.

She realized she'd failed when Serenity laughed. "I promise the food won't be horrible. You inherited your cooking ability from me, Jenna. I've been creating recipes since I was very young. My mother and her mother were also great cooks. In fact your grandmother, who was French, by the way, owned a bakery. Her pie crust alone generated three marriage proposals before she was sixteen."

Her smile turned impish. "When I occasionally go off the vegan wagon, so to speak, I confess it's with a fresh baguette and some cheese. Organic, of course."

"You're French," Violet said. "That's good to know."

It was, but somehow Jenna still resented having the information. Even more uncomfortable, she wanted to ask questions. To know more about her ancestry, even though that seemed like a betrayal of Beth and Marshall.

Serenity flipped her hair over her shoulder. It was a casual gesture, but one that Jenna recognized—mostly because she did it herself.

"I'm not trying to get in the way," the older woman told her. "I want to get to know you, just a little. And you to get to know us. That's why we're here. Because we miss you."

It had been thirty-two years, Jenna thought grimly. It sure took them a long time to miss someone.

She recognized the twisted reasoning of being annoyed they'd shown up at all and resenting how long it had taken them to come find her in the first place. Probably a defense mechanism, she thought. A way to protect her emotions.

"Getting to know each other is probably a good idea," she said, her voice neutral.

Beth would be so proud. But in truth, Jenna had no plans to connect with her birth parents or even like them very much. They were intruders. She already had a mother and father she loved, and for some reason she couldn't escape feeling that Serenity and Tom were a threat to them.

Violet found herself anticipating her second date with Cliff more than she would have thought. They'd been texting throughout the week. Despite having gotten her number, he hadn't called. She had a feeling he was trying to play it cool, which was intriguing. It implied that he cared enough to have a strategy. Very different for a girl who had pretty much always been a sure thing.

They met in front of the Silver and Stone Restaurant. When she arrived, Cliff was already waiting near the elevator.

For this date Violet had gone with fitted black pants and a white silk blouse—one of her ten classic wardrobe pieces. She finished her outfit with black sandals and silver earrings. Casual chic, she told herself as she walked up to Cliff.

He'd traded in a suit for jeans and a long-sleeved shirt. He looked good, she thought. Normal. He smiled when he saw her, delight brightening his hazel-brown eyes.

"You came," he said as he approached, then took her hands in his and lightly kissed her cheek.

"Does that surprise you?"

"Yeah," he admitted. "It kind of does. Are you hungry? I've eaten here before and the steaks are great. So's the service and they have a nice wine list."

He was talking a lot again. The obvious nervousness was charming, she thought happily, and made her like him more.

They walked up to the hostess where Cliff said he had a reservation. Calling ahead was a small thing, Violet told herself, but still thoughtful.

They were shown to a table by the window and handed menus. Cliff ignored his and stared at her.

"You look beautiful."

"Thank you."

"You're welcome. Would you mind if I ordered a bottle of red wine to have with dinner? This place has a great wine list and they carry several of my favorites."

"That would be nice. I enjoy red wine."

She had a feeling anything he ordered would be nicer than the stuff she bought at the grocery store.

"Wine is one of my things," he told her. "I've owned a couple of condos, but never a house. When I finally buy one, I want room for one of those freestanding wine cellars. One with temperature and humidity controls."

"Something to keep in your man cave?" she teased.

He grinned. "I don't think I need a man cave."

"But there are all those sports to watch."

He glanced at the table then back at her. "I'm hoping I'll

find someone who likes to watch them with me. When I get married again, I want my wife to hang out with me. I'm not looking for space for myself."

"That sounds nice."

"I know there are guys who want to be with their friends, and that would be okay, from time to time." He grinned. "But I prefer the company of women."

"We smell better."

"Yes, you do."

The server appeared. She was a pretty woman about Violet's age, with huge breasts and big Texas blond hair.

She introduced herself and talked about the specials. Violet was surprised when Cliff barely glanced at her. Instead, he smiled at Violet as the other woman spoke.

"What can I get you to drink?" she asked when she'd finished her list of specials.

Cliff ordered his bottle of wine. The server's eyes widened.

"Yes, sir. I'll bring that to the table right away."

She picked up the wineglasses already there and quickly replaced them with much larger, more expensive-looking glasses.

Violet raised her eyebrows. "So this isn't the fourteen-ninety-nine special."

"You'll love it."

Now she was curious and made a note to check out the label, then go online later to find out what a bottle of Cliff's favorite wine cost.

"Are you planning on being in the Austin area long enough to buy a house?" Violet asked when they were alone.

"I'm hoping to be. My boss has made it clear he wants me here for at least ten years. I've looked around at several of the neighborhoods and they're family friendly. I want a nice house, though. With lots of room."

"Do you want a family?" She couldn't remember the last time a guy talked so easily about his future. Most of them were reluctant to make plans more than two days in advance.

"Two kids, maybe three. A boy and a girl, for sure. A dog." He ducked his head. "I know what you're thinking. Pretty boring, suburban dreams. I can't help it. I'm a guy who likes the 'burbs. It's where I grew up."

"I'm not thinking that at all," Violet admitted, a little surprised to feel herself longing for what Cliff mentioned.

A husband and kids. She'd never seen herself with either—probably because girls like her didn't get happy endings. But she'd been changing her life for a while now. Making better choices. That had been the hardest thing—walking away from her old way of life and taking responsibility for acting differently. She'd done it day by day, choosing what was right for her future rather than what was expedient. Maybe Cliff was her reward for the hard work.

"I hope you get exactly what you want," she added, smiling at him.

"I will. I always do."

The server appeared with the wine and made a show out of uncorking it.

Cliff tasted the small amount she poured. Violet braced herself for a whole swirling, twirling, sucking dance, but he only sniffed it once, took a sip, then nodded.

"Very nice." He looked at Violet. "I hope you'll like it."

"I'm sure I will."

The server poured wine into both their glasses, then left.

Cliff waited while Violet tasted the wine. She didn't know enough to say anything other than, "It's nice," which was true.

"You like it?" He sounded anxious.

"Very much."

"Good." He leaned toward her. "I've done all the talking so far, Violet. Tell me more about yourself. Where did you grow up?"

"A small town in Louisiana," she admitted.

"You don't have much of an accent."

"I can when I want," she said in a drawl, then shifted back to her regular speech. "I watched a lot of movies when I was young and I wanted to sound like them." Rather than her mother, she added silently. "I had a typical childhood." She smiled as she lied.

Why get into the truth? It wasn't early dating material. It might never be something she told anyone. Why share that her mother had been the local town whore? That when Violet was two weeks shy of her fourteenth birthday, a man in town had given her mother a few hundred dollars for the privilege of raping her daughter.

Oh, it wasn't called rape. Her mother had promised her a special night. Violet had seen enough of her mother's business trade to know what was going to happen. Running away had earned her a whipping that had put off the deflowering a good month, but eventually the old man had taken her to a small house in a neighboring town and done his thing.

She'd cried and screamed until he hit her so hard, she was nearly unconscious. When she got home, her mother gave her fifty dollars and told her to go buy herself something pretty.

Instead, she'd saved the money, stolen from her mother when the woman was drunk and had run away the summer she turned fifteen.

She edited as she spoke. "I moved to New Orleans when I was still a teenager."

"Great city. Did you like living there?"

She faked a smile. "Sure. There's always something going on. Lots of tourists."

Her time in the city was mostly a blur. She'd discovered getting high made her life bearable, and she'd been young enough and pretty enough to find men who were willing to finance her habit. She'd mostly serviced the tourist trade, but had a few local regulars.

One of them, Sam, had taken her in when a particularly nasty customer had beaten the crap out of her. He'd warned her that if she didn't get out, she would be dead in five years. Violet wasn't sure why, but she'd believed him. She'd decided to make a change.

"From there I went to Pensacola. I got a job in an appliance store, answering the phones."

It hadn't been much, but she'd gotten off drugs with help from a free program through a local church and had supplemented her pitiful income with a few customers a week. She'd learned to save, to plan and had gotten her GED.

"After a few years there, I came to the Austin area. My apartment is in Georgetown and I really like it. There's a sense of community."

She'd wanted to go somewhere that no one knew her. She hadn't sold herself in six years and had no plans to go back to the business. She saved nearly a third of her salary, investing it safely. No matter what happened, she wanted to be able to take care of herself. Life had taught her to never trust a man.

"Have you always been in retail?" Cliff asked.

Violet nearly choked on the wine she'd sipped. "Pretty

much," she said. "I love the store where I work now. Jenna's a great boss. Our customers are fun."

She shifted the conversation back to him.

By the end of the meal Violet had a greater appreciation of a really great cabernet sauvignon and of Cliff. He was funny, charming, smart and apparently crazy about her. They talked more about his job. He admitted to being terrified of his assistant, a stern woman who had been with the company nearly thirty years. He liked his boss, enjoyed bike riding, hadn't dated much in high school and had never cheated on a woman. The most interesting part was she sort of believed him. Even about the not cheating.

Now, with the bill argued over—she'd offered to pay—they walked outside in the cool, clear night. Cliff reached for her hand as they moved toward her car in the parking lot next to the restaurant.

"I had a great time," he said.

"Me, too." The best part was she was telling the truth.

"Want to do this again?"

"Yes."

They reached her car. Before she could pull her keys out of her purse, he stepped in front of her and cupped her face in his hands.

The kiss was inevitable, she thought, bracing herself for contact. She knew the drill, how to get through it without letting her indifference show. Because touching and being touched wasn't the same for her as it was for other girls. It wasn't that she didn't like the contact, it was that she could barely feel it. Doing what she'd done had messed with her body. She'd gotten so used to disconnecting from what was happening that it was nearly impossible to experience desire.

He leaned forward and pressed his mouth to hers. The touch was tender, soft and gentle. He offered rather than took, and she found herself relaxing. It was nice, she thought. In time, if she was patient, there might be something more.

"I'll call you," he whispered, before stepping back. "Good night."

"Night."

He was a good guy, she told herself as she drove away. Other women might take that for granted, but not her. She knew the other side too well, and had promised herself she would never go back.

Nine

Jenna arrived at her parents' house Sunday morning at ten-thirty, just in time to see a catering truck pulling out of the circular driveway. She stared at the van, horrified.

She'd been so careful to keep her problem a secret, guessing that if she told her mother how unhappy she was that Beth would blame herself. But the catering truck seemed proof that her mother had guessed her secret and either felt sorry for her or didn't want to trust her with an important meal.

She collected the cinnamon rolls she'd made—the only thing her mother would let her bring—and went inside.

"What was that?" she asked as she entered the kitchen.

Beth looked up from the quiche she was sliding into the top oven. "What was what?"

"You called a caterer?"

"I had to. I wanted to make a good impression on Serenity and Tom."

Jenna swallowed, feeling she'd just been hit in the stomach. "Mom, I'm a chef. I would have done the cooking." Brunch food was easy. She could follow a recipe with the best of them.

"I know, but you're so busy with the store. I didn't want to bother you. This way, you can just enjoy yourself." Her mother touched her cheek. "I hate to burden you when you have so much going on."

Jenna stared into her eyes and told herself to accept Beth's words at face value.

"Okay." She set the cinnamon rolls on the counter. "These need a three-fifty oven for forty minutes."

Her father strolled into the kitchen. She walked toward him as he held out his arms.

"How's my girl?" he asked, hugging her as he kissed the top of her head.

"Good."

"Did your mother tell you she wanted the meal to be vegetarian?"

"I never said that," Beth said primly, setting out champagne glasses. "I said we were having vegetarian dishes. Serenity said they would eat eggs and cheese. I'm being supportive. Besides, there are going to be breakfast meats, too."

"Only because I insisted." Marshall winked at his daughter. "God put us at the top of the food chain for a reason."

"Brace yourself," Jenna said. "Serenity is bringing a dish."

"I'm sure it will be delicious," Beth said. "You are both to behave."

"Breakfast lentils," Jenna teased. "Yummy."

Marshall groaned. "Tell me again why they're coming?"

"Because I invited them. They're family."

Her dad squeezed her. "Your family, not mine," he whispered. "They're not related to me."

Jenna laughed.

Beth pointed to the doorway. "You're making trouble, Marshall. Get out until you hear the doorbell. Then you may greet our company and open the champagne."

"We're drinking at breakfast?"

"We're having mimosas. Now git."

Marshall strolled out the way he'd come.

"That man," Beth grumbled. "He torments me because he can."

Watching her parents together made Jenna feel a little better. At least some parts of her world were where they should be.

"All right," she said, crossing to the refrigerator. "What did you pay those people to bring you?"

"Two kinds of quiche," Beth said, motioning to the oven. "One with only eggs, cheese and vegetables and one that is the quiche equivalent of an all-meat pizza. For your father."

"And?"

"A fresh fruit plate, scones, a tray of breakfast meats I only need to warm for ten minutes and petit fours."

"Petit fours?"

"Those are for me. For later."

Jenna laughed. "Mom, you make me crazy."

"Then I must be doing something right. Come on. Let's put in your cinnamon rolls."

Serenity and Tom arrived right on time. Jenna was determined to be pleasant and welcoming, offering to be the one to go and greet them.

"Good morning," she said as cheerfully as she could, while

trying not to let her eyes bug out when she caught sight of Serenity's outfit.

Her birth mother wore a long, flowing dress of rainbows. Not rainbow colored, which would be marginally better, but fabric covered in brightly colored rainbows. They swirled, they flowed, they circled into a kaleidoscope of color that nearly made her dizzy. Dangling earrings that looked like stained glass competed for attention. By contrast, Tom was practically normal in jeans and a tie-dyed shirt.

"My little girl," Serenity said as she entered the house. She passed her casserole dish to Tom, then approached Jenna and lightly kissed her on each cheek. "You look beautiful."

"Thanks. Um, so do you."

Tom gave her a smile and also leaned in for a kiss—single cheek this time. Jenna took the casserole dish from him and stepped back.

"Serenity, you remember my mother, Beth Stevens. Mom, this is Tom." Jenna saw her father making his way toward them. "And this is my dad, Marshall. Dad, Serenity and Tom."

The men shook hands.

"Come into the kitchen," Beth said. "For years I tried to get people to hang out in the living room, and it never happened. So I've given up. Now we simply migrate to the kitchen and keep it casual."

Part of the reason Beth had remodeled the space, Jenna thought, proud of her parents' home. There was a big work area, bar seating at the high counter, a sofa by the window and a fireplace tucked into the corner.

"Refrigerator or oven?" Jenna asked Serenity, raising the casserole slightly.

"If we're eating in the next half hour, it can stay out. I

made a breakfast rice pudding with vanilla rice milk and dried fruit."

Which didn't sound too awful, Jenna admitted. "Rice milk, not soy or almond milk?"

"Too much soy can mimic estrogen. Almond milk is delicious, but too sweet for the recipe. I use rice milk often. Most people who have grain issues are fine with rice."

"God's food," Tom added, coming up behind Serenity and putting his arm around her waist.

Serenity laughed. "That's what we used to tell our boys."

Jenna didn't know what to say to that. Fortunately, Beth had already handed Marshall the bottle of champagne.

"I thought we'd start with mimosas," she said. "Toast to our new relationship. I'm so delighted you've come to get to know Jenna." She pulled out a pitcher of orange juice. "I squeezed it myself, from organic oranges."

Serenity looked pleased. "That was very thoughtful of you."

"Wait until she gets a load of the plate of breakfast meats," Marshall murmured in Jenna's ear.

Jenna did her best not to grin.

While the champagne was opened and mixed with the orange juice, Beth got Serenity and Tom seated at the counter. She disappeared for a second, only to return with an armful of photo albums.

Jenna groaned. "Mom, no."

"They'll want to see them."

"We will," Serenity said, taking the glass Jenna offered.

Beth set the largest of the albums between Serenity and Tom. "Jenna, stand here and explain what everything is."

"You've labeled every picture. It's very clear."

Beth shot her a warning look behind their backs.

"Fine," Jenna mouthed and took up the position.

The first page showed Jenna as a newborn, in Beth's arms.

"Oh." The soft sound seemed to barely escape Serenity's lips. "They wouldn't let me see you," she whispered. "They said it would be easier to give you up. I wasn't going to change my mind, but I would have liked to hold you."

The words hit Jenna in the gut. For the first time since her arrival, Serenity seemed like a real person and not a caricature. While still in high school, she'd gotten pregnant and had given up her child. That had to have been tough. Not anything Jenna would have wanted to go through.

Serenity turned the page. There were dozens of photos of Jenna through the first few months of her life. The first steps, the first taste of real food, several bath pictures. Tom touched the school picture from when Jenna was seven. She was surprised to see tears in his eyes.

"She looks like your mother there," he said, then cleared his throat. "The shape of her face."

"I know." Serenity glanced at Beth. "I was telling Jenna that her grandmother was an excellent cook. She was French, as was my grandfather."

"When did you see Jenna?" Beth asked, her voice more curious than concerned.

"I stopped by the store yesterday."

"She wants me to teach vegan classes," Jenna added.

"That would be different," her mother said. "It's all about finding the right recipe, I would imagine."

"Are your parents still alive?" Marshall asked, pouring more champagne into his glass.

"My folks live in Hawaii," Tom said. "We visit them when we can. Mostly they come to see us. Serenity's not much of a flier."

"It's unnatural," his wife said. "I've done it a few times, but it feels so dangerous." She sighed and smiled at a picture of Jenna at twelve. "Your grandparents grow organic coffee. We have some at the apartment, if you'd like to try it."

"That would be nice. Thank you."

"My parents were killed several years ago," Serenity said. "A boating accident. They were lost in a typhoon. I was devastated, but they died doing what they loved."

"Sailing?" Beth asked.

"Sailing around the world. They did it every couple of years. They had a beat-up sailboat they'd owned forever. There were places they'd stop every time. It was a good life."

Jenna excused herself to put the quiches into the lower oven to warm. As she straightened, her head spun, but not from a blood rush. It was too much information, too many people and facts. Grandparents. She hadn't thought of that. The grandparents she knew were Beth and Marshall's parents. Beth's had moved to an upscale retirement development in Boca, while Marshall's folks were still in the same house they'd lived in for forty years in Houston. The only change in their lifestyle was now the help lived in to give them a bit more assistance.

The grandparents she knew flew to Europe and took cruises on giant ships. They didn't sail around the world over and over again or grow coffee in Hawaii.

She didn't know these people. She had no emotional connection to them, but she couldn't escape a biological one. She was who she was, at least physically, because of Serenity and Tom. She had brothers and apparently a couple of grandparents. She might have aunts, uncles, cousins...

Over the next few minutes, she busied herself checking on the dining room table, then setting out the food that didn't have to be warmed or cooled. She noticed her mother had put Tom and Serenity on the same side of the table, which meant she was sitting across from them in her usual spot.

No escaping it now, she told herself and refilled her champagne glass.

Serenity followed her into the kitchen. "How are you doing?" the other woman asked.

"Fine," Jenna said automatically.

"I'm only asking because I'm sensing you're struggling with something."

Jenna stared at her, wondering if Serenity's direct line to the universe really gave her unexpected insight. "Everything is great," she said, lying. "There's no struggle."

"Of course there isn't," Beth said as she walked into the kitchen. "Jenna is very happy with her store and what she's accomplished in such a short period of time. Aren't you, honey?"

Jenna nodded but couldn't shake the feeling Serenity wasn't convinced.

It didn't take long for the quiches to finish, the cinnamon rolls to brown and the breakfast meats to heat. She and Beth carried in everything while Marshall seated their guests.

"The quiche in the white dish is only eggs and cheese and vegetables," Beth said as she set it down next to Tom. "The other has bacon and ham in it. I'm sorry to say, we're meat eaters in this house."

"I understand," Serenity told her. "But I hope you'll try the rice pudding."

"Of course," Jenna said. "I'm looking forward to it."

Serenity smiled, then showed them a couple of pictures. "My boys. Dragon is the one on the left."

Jenna stared at pictures of two men she'd never met yet were related to her. They were both dark-haired and good-looking. Dragon looked as if he were holding in a smile, and she found herself thinking she would like him. Wolf was more serious but still appeared friendly.

"They're very handsome," Beth said with a sigh.

"I hope you can meet them one day," Serenity murmured, taking back the pictures.

"Sure." Jenna smiled brightly. "Let's eat."

When they were all seated, they paused for a moment to say grace. It was a Sunday morning tradition. When Marshall had closed with "Amen," heads went up and food started to circulate.

Jenna put both bacon and sausage on her plate before passing it to her father. She sampled from both quiches and then, because she was curious, she took a scoop of the rice pudding. With Serenity watching, she took a bite.

The rice was well-cooked, the texture creamy. It was sweet, and the dried fruit was just moist enough to balance the consistency.

"This is good," Jenna said, hoping she didn't sound as surprised as she felt. "Could I get the recipe? I think it's something I could make with my mothers and kids class. A few of the children are lactose intolerant."

"Of course. Commercial dairy is filled with hormones," Serenity said. "I hope you tell your customers to buy organic."

"Pass the butter," Marshall said.

Jenna knew better than to look at her dad. If she did, she would start laughing. Instead, she glanced at her mother, who was giving her husband a "You're going to get it later" glare.

Tom put down his fork. "I have some wine for you back at the apartment," he said. "We brought a few bottles with us."

"You have a winery?" Marshall asked, looking interested for the first time.

"I told you that," Beth said.

"I must have forgotten."

"We own about a thousand acres in Sonoma and Alexander Valley," Tom said. "We grow mostly reds. Merlot and Cab, Malbec and some Petit Verdot. We're a small winery, but we're growing. Everything is organic."

"What is the winery called?" Beth asked.

Serenity smiled at Jenna. "Butterfly Wines."

Jenna set down her fork.

"After our little girl," the other woman added.

"I inherited some money right out of high school," Tom said. "Enough to buy an old winery and their land. It was all overrun and poorly maintained, but we were young and determined."

Serenity laughed. "We didn't know anything about making wine, but it seemed the right thing to do."

"A suggestion from the universe?" Jenna muttered under her breath.

"I took classes at UC Davis," Tom said. "Worked for a few wineries. After a few years, we started to get some decent grapes. When it came time to bottle it, we had to design a label, which meant coming up with a name."

"We wanted you to be a part of things," Serenity said. "We always felt your spirit was with us. That it was just a matter of time until you wanted to connect with us."

Jenna did her best to look pleased with the information, but inside she was angry and confused. They had named a winery after her but had never bothered to come find her. It's not that she was sorry they hadn't been a part of her life, it was more that she was having trouble believing their sincerity. And what was with the pressure of expecting her to go find them?

"There's a Butterfly Creek in the area," Tom continued.

"Which gets confusing, but we like what they do so it's all good."

"It sounds wonderful," Beth said. "What a great place to live."

"It is," Serenity said. "You should come visit."

Jenna scooped up some quiche and refused to glance up to see if Serenity was looking at her as she spoke.

"I have to go back for a couple of weeks," Tom said. "Wolf's wife is pregnant and he's distracted. I'm going to help."

Jenna did look up then. "Are you both leaving?"

"I want to stay," Serenity said.

Tom took her hand in his. "I can't convince her otherwise, although we try never to be apart. Every moment together is precious. Especially no—"

"We've been together since the first day of high school," Serenity interrupted, leaning her head on her husband's shoulder. "We took one look at each other and just knew."

The story was similar to Beth and Marshall's, Jenna thought. Apparently, she came from a long line of people who met early and fell immediately in love. So where had she gone wrong with her love life?

"Would you like to stay here while Tom goes back to Napa?" Beth asked.

Jenna nearly choked on her quiche. She managed to swallow it, then grabbed her mimosa. She glanced at her dad and saw he'd paused with his fork halfway to his mouth. Obviously they hadn't discussed this in private.

"That's lovely of you to offer," Serenity said. "But I'm enjoying our apartment. I'll be fine there."

"All right, but if you change your mind, let me know."

Jenna stared at her mother, wondering why she felt compelled to bond with Serenity and Tom. Once again she had the sense that Beth should feel at least a little threatened by everything that was going on. But then her mother had always been one to do the unexpected.

"Everything went so well," Beth said as Marshall loaded the dishwasher. "The food was excellent. I saw you took seconds on the quiche."

"Don't tell anyone. Real men and all that."

She smiled. "The rice pudding was good."

"You're not going to get any ideas, are you? Start serving tofu?"

"Probably not. I like a good steak too much. But it was fun to try. I'm glad we did this. Jenna needs to spend time with her birth parents. This is good for her."

Marshall straightened. "Why are you doing this?"

"Doing what?"

"Getting involved. Inviting those people over to the house?"

"Those people?" She laughed. "They're a part of our family."

"No, they're a part of Jenna's. Have you really thought this through, Beth?"

She put the orange juice in the refrigerator, then turned to him. "What are you talking about? This couple is the reason we have Jenna."

"True and I'm grateful for that. But we adopted her thirty-two years ago. Why are they showing up now?"

"That's what Jenna wanted to know. Does it matter?"

"Yes, it matters a lot. They're nice enough, but what do we know about these people?"

She put her hands on her hips. "What does that mean?"

"We shouldn't get too involved."

"But we need to be there for Jenna. This is important. Do you want me to ignore them?"

"No." He sounded as frustrated as she felt. "I think what you're doing is admirable, but it's also dangerous. We're not all going to be one big happy family. Life doesn't work that way. I don't like how they've just shown up with no warning. What do they want?"

"Why do they have to want anything?"

"Because everybody has a motive."

"That's cynical," she told him, glaring.

"It's realistic." He sucked in a breath. "I don't want to fight with you. I also don't want you or Jenna to be hurt. I'm saying be careful. You don't want to lose your daughter."

"That's not going to happen," Beth said firmly. "Jenna and I have a special relationship. I'm her mother."

"So's Serenity."

"That's different."

"No, it's reality. You're pushing them together. Make sure you can live with the consequences."

"Why do you always have to see the worst in people?" she demanded. "This is a good thing."

"I hope so, Beth."

He pushed the start button on the dishwasher, then walked out of the kitchen. She stared after him, still angry and suddenly hungry.

Men were stupid, she told herself. They didn't understand how important relationships were to women. It wasn't possible that she could lose Jenna. They meant the world to each other.

One of Jenna's earliest cooking memories was how excited she'd been about Tuesday nights. That was the night she got to cook dinner for her parents. The weekend before, she would pore over her *Cook's Illustrated* magazine, deciding what she wanted to tackle.

The magazine had been one of her favorites for years. What she loved was how they explained all the different variations of a recipe they'd tried and why each one worked or didn't work. *Cook's Illustrated* had given her the idea of experimenting with a recipe.

Once she'd chosen her menu, she'd give her mother a shopping list. Beth would faithfully buy everything, even when it meant going to specialty stores to find the right spice or an imported oil. When Jenna got home from school, she'd go to work.

Some dinners had turned out exactly as she'd planned, and some had been disasters. But even when the roast burned or the sauce was curdled, she had been delighted with her effort. She'd known she could fix what had gone wrong and would do better next time. Growing up in her mother's kitchen, she'd found her calling.

Now she stood in the small kitchen in her rented townhouse and carefully stirred the rice pudding. She'd written down Serenity's recipe and had risked making a few changes of her own. When the sauce had thickened to the correct consistency, she scooped the mixture into a bowl and let it cool.

For the first time in a long time, she was excited about tasting something she'd cooked. Deep down inside, she knew it was going to be okay. Maybe not brilliant, but good.

After fifteen minutes, she couldn't stand it anymore and took a taste. The texture was perfect, creamy without being too soggy, sweet without being sugary, with a hint of hazelnut. That was her addition. The twist. And it had worked.

★ ★ ★

"Are you sure this was a good idea?" Jenna asked nervously, as she put out cans of Italian tomatoes onto the various workstations. "I'm afraid it makes me look desperate."

"It's going to be great," Violet assured her. "First Fridays are special in Georgetown. All the downtown businesses get involved, staying open later. Come on, it's just one class. Relax."

"It's a class for singles on a Friday night. What if no one shows?"

"Then you don't have to be worried about anything."

"I guess."

"And you're not desperate."

"Maybe. I'm afraid everyone will assume I'm teaching this class so I can meet eligible guys."

"Want me to make you a button that says you're not?"

Jenna glared at her assistant. "Don't make me hurt you."

"Oh, please. I'm the tough one here." Just then her cell phone chirped. Violet grinned as she reached into her apron pocket. "It's Cliff."

"Oh, yeah. You're really tough. Practically a marine."

"I'm ignoring you," Violet said as she looked at the screen, then laughed. "He wants to know if he should feel threatened by all the good-looking single guys trying to pick me up."

Jenna glanced around the empty store. "I would say that's a no."

The class for singles had seemed like such a good idea at the time, but now she wasn't so sure. She didn't know which would be worse—if no one came or if there were a lot of people. She was still mentally recovering from her date with Dr. Mark. Not to mention the stress of getting her business up and running and hey, new parents. Not much room or time left for a social life.

Violet slipped her phone back into her pocket. "I reminded him I'm still at work and can't text with him."

"You're seeing him tonight?" Jenna asked, already suspecting the answer.

"Uh-huh."

"You've been going out with him a lot."

"This is the third date this week."

"That's nice." Jenna could be genuinely happy for Violet. Cliff sounded great.

"It is and so is he." Violet leaned against the counter and sighed. "We're taking it slow, physically. I like that. It makes me feel that he's in it for more than sex."

"Why wouldn't he be?"

"A lot of guys just want to get laid."

"You mean like Dr. Mark?"

Violet winced. "I really am sorry about that."

"I know. It's okay. If I change my mind, I know who to call."

The front door opened and Serenity breezed in. She'd taken to dropping by the store every few days, so Jenna wasn't surprised.

"Hi," she called. "Does Tom know you're here for my singles class?"

Serenity laughed. "He trusts me. Our souls have connected in a way that can never be undone. Hello, Violet. How's that young man of yours?"

"Good. I'm seeing him tonight."

As they chatted, Jenna studied Serenity. As always, she wore colorful, loose-fitting clothing. This evening's outfit was cream-color pants with several red ribbons sewn down the side. Her top fell to midthigh, with bell sleeves, the fabric a paisley explosion of red.

Serenity was someone who could talk about souls connecting in a very New Age kind of way, only to ask about Violet's boyfriend in the old-fashioned terms of "your young man."

"What's on the menu for tonight?" Serenity asked.

"Pasta," Jenna told her. "Something easy to make for a date. You'll be pleased to know it's vegetarian."

"I'll get you converted before you know it."

Jenna smiled rather than respond. She thought about mentioning the rice pudding recipe she'd experimented with but decided not to.

"By the way," Serenity said, tilting her head. "I want to talk to you about a young man I met today. His name is Ellington and he works at the healing center I've been going to."

Jenna wasn't aware of any healing center in the area, but then she'd never gone looking for one.

"Thanks, but I'm not really…"

Serenity touched her arm. "He's in his mid-thirties, tall, very good-looking. Divorced. He's been going through a lot and now feels ready to start dating again." The corners of her mouth turned up. "He eats meat."

"There's a plus," Violet murmured.

"I think you two would do well together. Your auras have a lot in common."

Jenna wanted to pound her head against the wall. Couldn't Ellington hook up with a nice massage therapist and call it a day?

"I'm not looking to date," Jenna began.

"You'll never move on if you don't release the past."

"I think the past is pretty much gone. I'm over Aaron. I've started a business. It's all good."

Serenity gazed into her eyes. "Your heart and soul are crying out for a connection. I can hear it and it makes me ache inside."

Jenna stared into Serenity's intense gaze. "All right," she said with a sigh. "I'll meet Ellington."

"We could double-date," Violet offered. "Meet for dinner somewhere."

Jenna wanted to hug her. "That would be great." Having another couple around could keep the evening from being a total disaster. "I've been wanting to meet this Cliff guy and make sure he's good enough for you."

"Excellent," Serenity said. "I'll give Ellington your number."

"Just the number for the store," Jenna said quickly. "In case things don't work out."

"Of course. Whatever my daughter wants."

Ten

Beth studied the cookbooks on display, stacked on a shelf, with a couple open to specific recipes. Handwritten notes mentioned the dates and times the recipes would be prepared in the store.

"Sorry," Jenna said, rushing up to her. "We're swamped."

"Swamped is good."

"I know. We went from dead to crazy in a few short weeks. Violet's already hired one college student part-time and I think we might need another one."

"How are the cookbook classes doing?" Beth asked.

"Great."

They walked toward the kitchen end of the store. Jenna poured them each a cup of coffee, while Violet took care of the customer by the cash register.

Jenna handed Beth a small bowl of soup. "Tell me what you think," she said.

Beth picked up the spoon and took a taste. The soup had

an obvious tomato base, but it was so much more. Rich and spicy with a hint of something smoky.

"I love it," she said between spoonfuls. "It's so unusual."

"It's Brazilian."

Beth stared at her. "When did you start cooking Brazilian food?"

"I've been experimenting with different things lately."

"Well, it's delicious. Is it hard? Could I make it?"

"Sure." Jenna wrinkled her nose. "You really like it? You're not just saying that?"

If Beth didn't know better, she would swear her daughter was waiting to be scolded. "You know you always have brilliant ideas for new recipes. This one is great. You should use it in one of your classes. Speaking of which, how did it go? Any likely prospects?"

"There were three guys and twelve women. I didn't have a chance." Jenna shrugged. "But the class itself was good. I did an easy pasta dish. I'm going to work up complete menus and also some ideas for dishes that can be prepared in advance and then frozen."

"Sounds like a great idea. Not everyone has your ability to whip up a delicious dinner with soda crackers and pepper."

"Even I would have trouble with that." She glanced over Beth's shoulder.

Beth turned. "What?"

"Oh, just wondering when Serenity is going to pop in. She's here nearly every day."

"She's in a strange city and her husband is gone. She's lonely."

"I know and I appreciate her interest, but does she have to come here all the time?" Jenna looked at her mother. "While I'm complaining, why do you always take her side?"

"I understand her. Don't forget, I'm the one who got you, Jenna. She's the one who gave you up."

"That was her choice. I'm not angry she did. I had a great childhood. It's just that sometimes she talks about how she's been waiting for me to come to her. That she and Tom thought I would be interested in finding out about my biological past. Then I feel guilty for never having seriously wondered about them."

Beth glanced around at the colorful store. Music played from hidden speakers. The sound was appealing and faintly Italian. The scent of basil and chicken lingered from the last class. Sunlight poured in through large windows.

"This is a welcoming place to be," she said gently. "Try to be patient."

"She's calling me her 'daughter.' At first it was just the one time, but now it's in every other sentence." Jenna paused, as if waiting for Beth to pounce.

Beth took another sip of her coffee. "You *are* her daughter."

Jenna groaned. "You are so annoying. Be possessive, like everyone else. She's also fixing me up on a date. She met Ellington at a healing center. Apparently our auras match or something."

A date did seem as if it was going too far, but Beth only shrugged. "Maybe you'll like him."

"Doubtful, but I'll go." Jenna lowered her voice. "It's not that I really mind any of that, but everything feels forced to me. If we're going to have a relationship, it will take time. She's pushing things."

"Maybe she wants to make up for lost time. You should give her a chance, honey. The two of you have a lot in common."

"DNA doesn't make a relationship."

"It's a start. You look a lot like her, you have similar characteristics. They say intelligence passes through the mother."

Jenna set down her coffee and crossed her arms over her chest. "She doesn't know me. If there's any love it's for who she thinks I am or who she wants me to be. She wasn't there when I was little. She's not the one who read to me or taught me to ride a bike or took care of me when I was sick."

Beth nearly got lost in a wave of memories. "We were so lucky to get you."

Jenna hugged her. "I'm the lucky one. I love you. I don't want her getting in the way of that."

Beth straightened. "Is that what you think? That you have to pick? You don't. I'll always be here for you. Maybe it would help if you thought of Serenity as someone to be friends with."

Jenna looked startled, then laughed. "Typical. You come up with a solution while I'm still defining the problem. You're right. That is the best way to deal with her. Stop thinking of her as someone who wants to be my mother and think of her as a friend." She wrinkled her nose. "A slightly pushy friend who won't eat cheese."

The front door opened. Jenna looked past Beth. "Speak of the devil."

Beth turned and saw Serenity had entered the store. She was so tall and beautiful, Beth thought. For once she was in jeans that showed off her long thin legs.

She touched her blond hair and wondered if the short cut was too matronly. Serenity's long hair was young and appealing.

"Good morning, daughter of mine," Serenity called as she crossed to Jenna and embraced her. Jenna glanced at Beth over the other woman's shoulders and rolled her eyes.

Beth held in a giggle.

Serenity turned to her. "You're here! That's wonderful. How is everything?"

"Good. Are you enjoying your stay?"

"I am. A few days ago, I explored Austin. A wonderful city. And the parks here in Georgetown. Yesterday I took the trail from the lake all the way into town and then walked to the university."

"Walking?" Beth asked. "That had to be over five miles."

"Yes. Don't you sometimes feel you have to be outside, communing with nature?" She drew in a breath. "I was refreshed by it."

Beth had the feeling she would only be crippled. A five-mile walk for fun? The whole point of her yoga class was it was exercise without sweat. Plenty of groaning and pain but not so much on the sweat.

"When I got back to the apartment, I did a mini-cleanse."

Beth looked at Jenna who shrugged. Beth wasn't sure what went into a mini-cleanse, but she was comfortable not knowing the details.

"I'm a new person," Serenity said, then sighed happily. "Which probably explains what happened when I was meditating this morning."

"Being one with the universe is kind of a full-time job, isn't it?" Jenna asked.

Beth pressed her lips together to keep from smiling.

Serenity nodded seriously. "It requires dedication." She linked arms with Jenna. "I was meditating about you."

Panic chased across her daughter's face. Beth didn't know if she should rescue Jenna or let things play out.

Before she could decide, Serenity said, "I was wondering if this store is really right for you. While I love the space and can feel the happiness here, I'm not certain it's where you want or need to be."

Beth stiffened. Talk about meddling. Jenna loved the store. She'd gotten off to a shaky start, but she'd recovered and was doing very well. It was so much better than working her butt off in restaurants where she had crazy hours and never got to have a social life.

Jenna pulled her arm free and faced Serenity. "I just opened the store."

"I know. It was a decision you made in a time of need. You put out a request to the fates and it was answered. But was it the right thing for you?" Serenity smoothed Jenna's hair. "You have so many gifts. Most people only have one or two, so their choices are easy. But you have paths going in multiple directions."

"I like the store," Jenna said, sounding less sure of herself.

"Of course you do," Beth said quickly. "It's going well, and you're having so much fun. You said how you enjoy being able to cook at your own pace. Plus you're helping other people with your classes."

"I do," Jenna said. "I like working with the public, which is a nice surprise. I love seeing people cook something they would have sworn they couldn't make and then going home and re-creating the experience for their families."

"I didn't mean to suggest the store was completely wrong," Serenity said gently. "I'm simply wondering if it's your calling."

"That's for Jenna to decide," Beth told the other woman. "It's her life."

"True, but we must guide our children."

Jenna is my child, not yours.

Beth thought the words but didn't speak them. Irritation burned inside of her, but she did her best to keep her expression calm.

It was a style difference, she told herself. Nothing more. Serenity was only here for a short time. Eventually she would have to go back to her regular life and all this would be behind them.

"There were elements of being a chef I really loved," Jenna said. "But it wasn't for me."

"The journey is exploration," Serenity assured her.

"Interesting."

Beth realized Jenna was taking Serenity's words and supposition seriously and was actually considering that the store might not be for her. She wanted to grab her daughter and tell her to ignore the other woman's weirdness. She'd barely gotten her daughter back, and now she was going to lose her again?

She fought back the panic. Nothing was going to happen in the next few weeks. Everything would calm down.

She managed to slow her breathing and relax enough to smile. But when she looked at Serenity, she found she didn't like her nearly as much as she had before.

Jenna worked frantically in her kitchen. Tonight was her blind date with Ellington of the healing center. Despite knowing it was good for her to get out on a date, she was sorry she'd agreed to be set up. Bad enough to go out with someone she didn't know, but worse when the results would be reported back to Serenity. No doubt her birth mother would want to dissect the evening in terms of moon placement and chakras.

Adding to the impossibleness of the situation was the fact that she'd decided to cook.

Oh, sure, it would have all been fine if she'd decided to

crack open a cookbook and pick a recipe. But she hadn't. Instead, she was creating something from scratch.

Her first thought had been to make Indian food. Serenity had made her think of it, mentioning Ellington liked it. Jenna had never made more than a few Indian dishes, simple things that wouldn't impress anyone. But she'd been determined to try something new—breaking out of her cooking rut seemed to be helping.

She'd started with basic Indian spices only to realize Indian flavorings had a lot in common with Mexican food. They both used cumin. Mexican food used cilantro and Indian food favored coriander, but they both came from the same plant. Could they be blended?

Three hours later she poured sauce on her chicken curry enchiladas and wondered what the hell she'd been thinking. The food could be a complete disaster.

Or it could be wonderful.

Not sure which, she popped the dish in the oven, offered up a prayer and shook tortilla chips into a bowl. Seconds later, her doorbell rang. She drew in a breath for courage and went to answer it.

The man waiting for her was tall and good-looking, with blond hair and blue eyes. When he saw her, he smiled and Jenna felt a little whisper of anticipation. Maybe she'd been too quick to judge Serenity and her taste in men.

"Jenna? I'm Ellington."

"Nice to meet you," she said. They shook hands and she felt a very distinct spark. Nice, she thought. This could be nice.

"We're having dinner with friends of yours?" he asked as he followed her inside.

"Violet works for me. I've never met her boyfriend, Cliff, but I hear he's pretty great."

"I like meeting new people."

He smiled again, but instead of a spark, she thought she recognized something. No, not something. Someone. She studied him more closely.

"Have we met?"

"I don't think so." He shrugged. "You might have seen me on TV. I do a lot of interviews, discussing homeopathic healing techniques. I've appeared on most of the local talk shows and have a regular segment on the morning news."

"You're a local celebrity."

The smile returned. "It's no big deal."

Uh-huh. Big fish in a small pond. That described Aaron perfectly. She studied Ellington more carefully and saw all the signs. Good looks, nice clothes, an ease with strangers. Her biological mother had set her up with the healing center equivalent of her ex-husband. She sighed. It was going to be a very long evening.

"Thanks for doing this," Violet murmured to Cliff as they walked toward Jenna's townhouse.

He smiled at her, then lightly kissed her. "Anything for you. You know that."

He was so perfect, she thought happily. The past few weeks with Cliff had been a revelation. She hadn't known a guy could be so sweet and funny and nice.

She'd been concerned about telling him she'd offered to double-date with Jenna, but Cliff had been all for it, more than willing to help her friend.

This was their sixth date. They'd gone to a concert, had spent a Sunday afternoon bike riding, been to the movies and he'd cooked dinner for her at his place. At the end of each date, the kissing had gone on a little longer, with more intensity. She knew what he wanted, and after tonight, she was determined he would get it.

She still had trouble losing herself in their kisses, but he was such a good guy and she really liked him. If they waited for her to be panting with desire, it could be well into the next century.

"Poor guy," Cliff said with a chuckle. "Going around with a name like Ellington."

"I know," she said, gazing up at him. "It's like wearing a 'kick me' sign."

"You'd never do that to a kid, would you?" he asked.

"I'm the one who grew up named after a flower. I'm very big on regular names."

"Good." He kissed her again.

This time she felt a tiny tingle deep in her belly and hung on to it with both hands.

"What is a naturopath?" Cliff asked.

"I think it's about alternative medicine," Violet said. "I've never gone to one. They use herbs and organic cures. Supplements, that kind of thing. Ellington also does acupuncture and massage."

Serenity had raved about him, claiming his acupuncture was amazing.

"Is he a real doctor?"

"I don't think he went to medical school, but I know there's some study involved."

They knocked on the door and Jenna let them inside. Violet was curious about Ellington. "Not bad," she whispered to Cliff, taking in the good looks. Ellington obviously believed in working out.

"Welcome," Jenna said with a smile. "I've made margaritas. They're good but I'm a little nervous about dinner."

"It will be terrific," Violet said, sniffing the delicious scent drifting in from the kitchen.

Violet introduced Jenna, who, in turn, introduced Ellington. As they all sat down in the living room, Violet smiled at Cliff, only to find him studying Ellington.

"Violet tells me you're a doctor," he said, taking the margarita Jenna offered.

"Naturopath," Ellington said easily. "It's a form of alternative medicine. I'm interested in a holistic approach when treating my patients."

"What does that mean?" Cliff asked, sounding slightly challenging. "You couldn't get into medical school?" He added a chuckle at the end of his question.

Violet stiffened.

"I did go to medical school." Ellington paused. "Harvard. The more I learned about traditional medicine, the more it didn't work for me. When I graduated, I went to China and studied there for a few years."

Violet blinked. Ellington must be older than she'd first thought. She would have pegged him as early thirties, but now as she looked closer, she saw he had a few lines, a touch of gray in his hair. Maybe early forties then. Eligible, intelligent and the man knew how to give a massage. Go, Jenna.

"China," Cliff said. "Not on my list of places to visit. I prefer Europe."

Ellington nodded. "What do you do, Cliff?"

"I work in finance. I help companies raise money through issuing stock. It's technical."

"I'm sure it is."

Violet wondered if it was just her, or if a not-so-subtle tension filled the room. It was as if the two men were in competition. No, that wasn't right. It was as if Cliff had something to prove.

"You drink?" Cliff asked, motioning to Ellington's glass. "Is that allowed?"

"My practice doesn't define my personal life," Ellington said, still looking comfortable.

"We're having an unusual dinner tonight," Jenna said, picking up a tortilla chip. "Indian-Mexican food."

"Sounds great," Violet said, confident anything her friend cooked would be amazing.

Cliff barely acknowledged Jenna's comment. "You've probably been to India," he said.

Ellington shrugged. "Yes. Several times."

"What do you think about it?"

"I found a lot of beauty and peace there."

"I thought it was crowded and dirty."

"There are challenges in the country. Poverty. But it is one of the most spiritual places I've ever been. There's a sense of unity there that I haven't experienced in my other travels."

"I'd rather have a five-star restaurant and an ATM."

"They're good, too," Ellington said.

Violet was confused. It was almost as if Cliff was drunk. But he'd barely sipped his margarita. She glanced at Jenna, but her friend looked completely calm, as if nothing unusual was happening.

As she clutched her glass, she couldn't help hoping she was the only one who was uncomfortable.

Jenna stood in her kitchen and wondered what she was supposed to say. On the one hand, dinner had been everything she'd hoped for, and she was practically floating with happiness. On the other hand, the company had been less than perfect.

This was her first time meeting Cliff. The way Violet had talked about him, she had expected a charming, funny guy.

But the man with her friend had been more than difficult. He'd been rude and challenging, acting as if Ellington was little more than a medical con man.

The most unexpected part of the evening hadn't been her food. Later she would revel in her cooking experiment being delicious. Taking a chance had felt good. Right.

But Ellington had overshadowed even that. Talk about a pleasant surprise. Not just good-looking, but nice and smart and tolerant of Cliff. Aaron would have thrown a fit and stormed out. Ellington had seemed more amused than insulted.

She leaned against the counter and looked at him.

"I'm genuinely speechless, which doesn't happen often."

Ellington smiled. "Impossible. I haven't kissed you yet. That's when you're supposed to become speechless."

She laughed. "I meant about tonight. I've never met Cliff before. He wasn't what I expected."

Ellington shrugged. "A lot of people are threatened or confused by what I do. They make assumptions. Cliff was trying to impress Violet."

"You're not mad?"

"Why would I be? I had a great time with you. I wish we'd had more time to talk privately."

"Me, too." Although that was her fault. She hadn't thought she would have such chemistry with Ellington, so she'd gone out of her way to keep the evening casual and anything but private. Once she'd found out he was a local celebrity, she'd wanted to run for the hills.

It said something to her about her ability to judge first impressions.

"How about trying this again Friday night?" he asked. "Just the two of us."

She shook her head, feeling more than a little regret. "I can't. I'm working."

"I thought you owned a kitchen store."

"I do. We have a class on Friday. For singles." She paused. "You're welcome to come, if you'd like."

As soon as the words came out, she wanted to call them back. What was she doing inviting a good-looking single guy whom she was interested in to an evening with a bunch of single women? Talk about stupid.

But she couldn't retract the invitation, so she had to stand there, hoping he would say no.

Instead, he smiled. "I'd like to see you work. What time?"

"Six."

"I'll be there." He leaned toward her and kissed her cheek. "I'm seeing Serenity tomorrow," he said as he straightened. "I'm going to thank her for introducing us."

Jenna stared into his dark blue eyes. "Me, too."

Despite the disaster of an evening, Violet found herself back at Cliff's condo. She'd been there before, once, when he'd cooked her dinner. Then she'd admired the open space, the view, the masculine décor. Now she roamed his living room, feeling restless and confused.

The guy she knew, the guy she'd gone out with and liked and laughed with, had been noticeably absent tonight. Instead, her date had been condescending and had gone out of his way to make everyone else uncomfortable. She hadn't recognized him at all and he'd embarrassed her.

"Want something?" he asked as he poured himself another Scotch.

"No, thanks." She'd lost count of the drinks he'd already had and wondered if that was the problem. Was Cliff a lousy drunk?

After taking a swallow, he moved toward her. "I know you want to help out your friend, but let's not do that again," he said, putting his arms on her waist and lightly kissing her neck. "I don't want to share you with anyone. It's not the same when other people are around."

He moved his lips against her skin. She felt the physical contact but had no reaction. No tingle, no anticipation.

"You didn't like Ellington," she murmured.

"I know his type. Sanctimonious. Jenna can do better. She's great. But that guy. I've seen him on cable. He thinks he's hot stuff."

Violet got it. Cliff had been threatened by Ellington. He'd reacted out of fear. "He's different, but I don't think he's that awful."

"Did you like him?"

So much in those four words. She saw the worry in Cliff's eyes. As she watched, he swallowed and put down the drink. His body shifted, as if he were bracing himself for a hard blow.

"He's famous. At least around here," Cliff added.

Violet sighed and her irritation drained away. "I don't care about stuff like that," she said, moving toward him. "I'm more into who the guy is than what he does."

She put her hands on Cliff's shoulders and kissed him. "There's only one guy I like and he's in this room."

She felt his muscles relax, even as he leaned in and kissed her.

"You sure?" he asked, his mouth against hers.

"Very."

Cliff kissed her. "I don't want to talk anymore. Do you?"

"Not if you have something else you'd like to do."

He chuckled, then kissed her deeply. She leaned into him,

wanting to respond, even as she felt her body begin the process of shutting down. She felt nothing, reacted automatically, did what was expected.

When he thrust his tongue in her mouth, she responded in kind, tasting only the Scotch. As he touched her breasts, her mind joined her body until nothing but the mechanics were left.

Tears burned in her eyes. She didn't want to be like this, she thought, frustrated and hurt and afraid she would never be normal again. She wanted to feel what he was doing. She wanted to want him. But there was no connection between his touch and her brain. She could see what he was doing, but she couldn't feel it.

He pulled off her shirt and bra, then stared at her breasts. "You're so sexy."

He touched her everywhere, carefully removing her skirt, then lowering her panties. She moved as if he excited her because she was too ashamed to tell him the truth. She made the noises, gasped at his touch. She did what was expected— helping him out of his clothes, saying all the things customers had paid to hear. She lied.

He was already hard and shaking. Instead of bothering to move into the bedroom, she shifted against the back of the sofa and parted her legs for him. He pushed into her and groaned.

It didn't take long. She sensed when he was close, arched her head back and panted several times before moaning and pretending to shudder. Another trick she'd learned. Otherwise some guys wanted to make it last longer.

"Oh, yeah," he growled as he pumped harder and faster. "I knew you'd like it." Then he closed his eyes and came.

When he was done, he withdrew with far more care than she deserved. He touched her cheeks, her breasts, then kissed her.

"I knew it would be like this," he said, staring into her eyes. "I knew it would be perfect."

More tears threatened. She felt like a whore, only the currency wasn't money. It was respect and honesty. She could never tell Cliff the truth, and by withholding, she would never be as close to him as she wanted.

"You okay?" he asked.

She nodded and reached for her clothes.

He stared at her. "Was I too rough? Didn't you like it?"

She forced a smile. "I loved it." She kissed him. "Couldn't you feel me?"

He gave her a long, slow grin. "Oh, yeah. You're amazing." He pulled her into a hug. "I'm so lucky to have you in my life."

His words got through to her in ways his touch hadn't. Slowly she relaxed. She let him lead her into the bedroom where they snuggled.

Curled up against him, her head on his shoulder, she told herself it would get better. That with time, she would find her way to all that Cliff offered her. She wasn't going to give up. She'd come too far for that.

The next morning Jenna opened the store by herself. There were no classes until later in the day, and Violet wasn't due in until noon. She took a second before opening the front door to savor the sense of accomplishment. The business was succeeding, and last night she'd cooked completely out of her comfort zone and it had worked.

Her mother had always told her that being brave meant knowing you were afraid but doing whatever it was anyway.

She'd done that and allowed herself a moment of pride. Just as exciting was the desire to try something new again. To continue experimenting.

But despite that thrill, she felt torn about other parts of the previous evening. Cliff had been a disappointment, but she'd liked Ellington a whole lot more than she'd expected, even if he did remind her a little of Aaron. Now she was sorry she'd assumed the worst and had set up a double date. She wouldn't have done it with someone Beth had introduced her to, but she hadn't been willing to trust Serenity. Maybe it was time to actually give her birth mother a break.

A few minutes later, the woman in question breezed into the store. "I know this is the worst possible thing I could ask," Serenity said with a laugh, "but I have to know about last night. I actually couldn't sleep because I was wondering and hoping." She paused and drew in a breath. "Did you like him?"

Jenna grinned. "Ellington was a very unexpected hottie."

Serenity raised her hands and turned in a circle. "I knew it! When I met him, I could see the two of you together."

"Don't start planning the wedding. It was one date."

Serenity lowered her hands to her sides. "Are you seeing him again?"

"Friday. He's coming to the singles cooking class." Where she hoped he wouldn't be seduced away by any of the other women.

"He gives a wonderful massage."

Jenna winced. "Don't take this wrong, but that falls into the category of too much information."

"I'm draped," Serenity assured her. "It's not like he's seen me naked."

It was all Jenna could do not to cover her ears and start humming. "Good to know. What do you see him for?"

"Oh, this and that. I need a little alignment now and then. I've been fighting an infection for a while now."

"You don't want to use antibiotics?"

"They wouldn't help with what I have. Anyway, I'm glad you had a good time."

"Ellington was great, but I was kind of surprised by Violet's date."

"Cliff? From what she's said, he's wonderful."

"I know. That's what was so confusing. I get being cynical about alternative healing and all that, but a date isn't the place to have the discussion. Especially when you're just meeting the person. He made me uncomfortable. There's something about him I don't trust."

"What's the something? Can you define it?"

Before she could stop herself, she blurted, "A darkness."

Oh, great, she thought. Serenity's weirdness was contagious. What was next? Talking to trees? Only, Serenity had been right about Ellington, so maybe she was a little less crazy than Jenna had assumed.

"That's very insightful," the other woman said. "You're seeing past his facade to who he really is. You get that from me. I've always been able to read people."

Jenna ignored that. "I'm not going to say anything to Violet and I would appreciate it if you wouldn't, either. She really likes Cliff and maybe he was just having an off night."

"You know that's not true."

Jenna hated to admit it, but Serenity was right. "I can feel it in my gut. But it's my problem, not hers."

"I agree. Until she comes to you for help, she has to follow her own path. She'll appreciate your silence and see your support. Violet is smart and intuitive. She already knows the truth, but she's not willing to face it. The time will come, though, and then you can be there for her."

Jenna wanted to gag but instead found herself agreeing with Serenity. She had to admit, her birth mother showing up was turning out to be a more positive experience than she first thought. Maybe, with a little time, they could be friends.

Eleven

Jenna double-checked the supplies. "I want to make sure I have everything," she said, feeling more nervous than the last time and knowing her butterflies had little to do with teaching and everything to do with a certain student who had promised to attend.

"You'll be fine," Beth said. "Look how many reservations you have. There will be a big crowd. I'm looking forward to seeing the man Serenity set you up with. I think it's fascinating you two hit it off."

"I know. I didn't know what to expect and I was terrified." She lowered her voice. "Serenity isn't exactly in the mainstream."

"But she found a nice man."

"Yes. At least I think so. It was a double date so we didn't get much time to talk."

Beth looked across the store to where Serenity chatted

with a couple of customers. "She's fitting in very well. Some people have that gift."

Jenna glanced at her mother to see if Beth meant anything else by the comment, but her expression was open and unguarded.

Violet came up to them. "The Italian bacon is all cut up," she said. "I've divided it into the little bowls, so every station has the right amount."

"Thanks," Jenna said. "I appreciate you doing that."

Tonight's class was a recipe for spaghetti carbonara, an easy pasta dish that anyone could prepare.

Beth excused herself and walked toward Serenity.

"Everything else is set up, right?" Jenna asked. "I'm sorry to keep checking. I don't know what's wrong with me tonight. I feel like I'm driving everyone crazy."

"The nerves aren't helping, are they?"

"No. Why did I invite him to this class? I'm not sure I even like him."

Violet raised her eyebrows. "Seriously? You're going to try to sell that to me?"

"Maybe not." She sighed. "One second I tell myself that it was just one date and so what? The next I want to ask you if you think some woman is going to steal Ellington away from me."

"No, and if someone does, then you're better off without him."

Jenna sucked in a breath. "Thanks for being rational. It's important that one of us is. I don't usually have trouble with it, but there's something about that guy."

"He's gorgeous."

Jenna grinned. "I know. Wasn't that surprising? I nearly fainted when I opened the door. No wonder he's a local celebrity—he's probably very telegenic." Ellington being well-known still made her uneasy. After all, Aaron had been charming at the beginning of their relationship, too.

Violet's cell phone chirped. She pulled it out of her apron pocket and glanced at the screen, then put her phone away.

"Cliff," she said. "He's heading home from work and wanted me to know he was missing me."

Jenna wondered if that had really been the message. "Things are still good between you?"

"Yes, they're great. He's sweet and caring."

Jenna could think of many descriptions for Cliff, and neither of those came to mind. "I'm glad you're happy," she said instead, then glanced at the clock. "It's nearly time."

Over the next fifteen minutes, people arrived for the class. She handed out appetizers she'd made. Of the three samples, two were recipes she'd made before, but one was tiny cups of the soup she'd been playing with. She watched anxiously as people tasted the soup and relaxed when nearly everyone asked for more.

The need to create was coming back to her. Like an itch she couldn't reach, it dogged her, appearing when she least expected it.

Jenna was on the lookout for Ellington and still managed to miss him when he showed up. One second she was handing out recipe cards, the next, someone tall and male was beside her.

"You look busy," he said. "I just wanted to say hi before everything started."

She turned to him and quickly got lost in his blue eyes. Yikes. He was better-looking than she remembered. His smile flashed, effectively blanking out her brain and leaving her unable to speak.

"Jenna?"

"Yes?"

"You okay?"

"I'm fine. The class… We're expecting a lot of people. I'm glad you could make it. Here." She thrust out a recipe card. "What we're making tonight. Of course Serenity isn't happy. Nothing vegan about our meal. So don't expect her to taste anything. She said you give a great massage."

Jenna clamped her lips together and wished for a mini tornado to whisk her into another reality. She hadn't just said the massage thing, had she? Maybe she'd just thought it.

Ellington chuckled. "I'm glad she approves. Is it all right if I stay after class so we can talk? Or do you have somewhere to be?"

"I don't have anywhere to be," she squeaked.

"Good."

She managed to pull herself together enough to start the class. She let the students divide themselves up into groups, then assigned them stations and explained how to make the pasta. She'd brought in bottles of chardonnay to be sampled during the cooking process. Soon the store was filled with the smell of simmering garlic, onion and Italian bacon and the steam from boiling pasta pots.

Serenity said she was tired and left about halfway through the class. Beth went with her, while Violet manned the cash register. Jenna moved from station to station, demonstrating how to whisk the eggs, showing how much salt and pepper to add.

She was aware that Ellington was in a group comprised of him and three women. The females in question were about her age, all pretty and obviously interested in him. They jostled each other in an attempt to be the one standing closest to him and kept up a running conversation.

Violet was right, she told herself. If he was the kind of guy who was easily distracted by other women, then she didn't want him in her life anyway. But saying the mature thing and believing it were two different things.

As the cooking continued, the sound in the store rose. Jenna noticed Ellington's group seemed to be having the most fun. The women had progressed to practically hanging on him.

She ignored the knot in her stomach and demonstrated how to pour the eggs into the pasta and stir until the eggs were cooked. She poured in the bacon, garlic, onion mixture from the frying pan and tumbled the entrée onto a serving dish.

The various groups then repeated her steps, some with more success than others. She went around and helped, then she and Violet passed out small plates and forks so everyone could sample what they'd made.

"You okay?" Violet asked in a low voice.

"Bitterly jealous."

"Don't be. He's enduring, not enjoying."

Jenna frowned. "How can you tell?"

"Let's just say I have a lot of experience with reading men's body language. See how the blonde is leaning into him?"

Jenna didn't want to look, but she turned her head anyway. Sure enough, the tall, curvy blonde was all over Ellington. Like white on rice, as her grandmother would say.

"Uh-huh."

"Look at how he's standing. He's leaning away from her, not toward her, and he has his arms folded. See how the left one is blocking her from getting too close?"

Jenna hadn't noticed that, but now she saw that Violet was right.

"He's smiling but he keeps looking at you," her friend added.

Sure enough, Ellington glanced in her direction, then winked.

Jenna felt the jolt all the way down to her toes. "Have I mentioned how much I adore you?" she asked Violet.

"Just doing my job."

Jenna laughed. "You're the best, seriously. I was living in the bad place."

"No need to go there with Ellington. He's interested."

Violet proved to be right. It took nearly an hour for the last of the customers to leave. The women who'd cooked with Ellington seemed determined to leave with him until he said something Jenna didn't catch. All three of them turned to glare at him, then collected their purses and left.

Everyone else bought something from the store. The kits for the spaghetti carbonara all sold quickly. By seven-thirty, Violet was walking toward the back.

"I'm heading out," she said. "Cliff's waiting. See you to-morrow."

"Night," Jenna called after her.

Most of the lights were off, the front door was locked, leaving only her, a lot of pasta and a good-looking guy. Now what?

She turned to find that Ellington had poured them both a glass of wine and served up some pasta.

"From what you made," he said, handing her both and motioning to the empty chairs. "I wouldn't trust any of the others."

"I'm sure they were fine."

He collected his food and joined her. They sat on folding chairs, facing each other over the small table that had held the pasta kits.

"You're a patient teacher," he said. "You give a lot of en-couragement."

"I want people to enjoy cooking."

"You make it look easy."

"It actually is easy. Once you master a few basic techniques and procedures, it's just a matter of practice and finding out what you like to eat."

"I don't think so," he told her, his eyes bright with interest. "I'm a lousy cook."

"You did fine tonight." She picked up her wine. "Your group seemed to have a lot of fun."

"They were interesting."

She sipped and did her best to look casual. "And interested in you."

He shook his head. "I tried to be subtle, then I told them I was with you. When that didn't work, I said I was gay."

Jenna nearly choked. "Seriously?"

He grinned. "Works every time."

"What if you find a woman who wants to convert you?"

"So far I haven't." He studied her for a second. "You've been here all day, haven't you?"

"In the store? Sure, but I'm here pretty much every day."

"You're tired." He held up a hand. "I'm not saying you look tired—you look great." He put down his plate and stood, then walked around her chair.

"Sit up," he instructed. "Close your eyes and concentrate on your breathing."

Feeling just a little wary, Jenna did as he said. Seconds later she felt his large, warm hands settle on her shoulders. His strong fingers immediately found her tense muscles and began to massage them.

Relaxation blended with pleasure, making her want to purr. It was all she could do not to roll her head back and forth and beg for more.

At his urging, she leaned forward so he could move a little

lower down her back, then he shifted to her upper arms. The gentle yet deep rubbing was amazing, she thought. If he could do this with a simple back rub, what would Ellington be like in bed?

Images followed the question, and she felt heat on her cheeks. Oh, great. Her own imagination was making her blush. At least he couldn't see her face.

The massage continued for a few more minutes, then he stopped. "I hate to end this now," he said. "But I need to get going. I promised my son I would be home in time to put him to bed."

Jenna rose and faced him. "You have a son?"

"Isaiah. He's seven."

Serenity had left that piece of information out of the conversation, Jenna thought, trying to decide if it mattered.

"Are you free tomorrow night?" Ellington asked. "Would you like to go to dinner?"

"I'd love that."

"I see the store's open until six. Want me to pick you up here?" he asked.

"That would be great."

He stepped toward her and put his hands on her waist. "Tonight was fun, but I think it's time we risked an evening with just the two of us."

Her heart began to flutter like a trapped bird. She felt breathless. "Me, too," she managed.

He lowered his head and kissed her. The contact was light and quick and just enough to make her knees go a little weak.

"I'll see you tomorrow," he said as he straightened.

"Uh-huh."

She let him out the front, then did her best to act dignified until he had driven away. Then she did a little dance all the way through the store.

Beth stopped by Jenna's store on her way to the market. She wanted to hear about the singles class the previous evening. Ellington had arrived as promised, and she was curious if Jenna had liked him as much the second time around.

He'd certainly been good-looking enough, Beth thought as she walked toward the store. But what, really, did they have in common? She had asked Marshall if he knew any suitable single men in the local business community. Although he'd refused to get involved, she knew she could convince him that this was important.

She pulled open the glass doors and stepped in to find a class in session. But instead of her daughter helping people through a cooking project, Serenity was explaining the recipe.

Beth came to a stop so quickly, the door bumped her in the butt. She moved inside, then searched for Jenna and found her stocking shelves.

"She's teaching a class?" Beth asked as she approached. "You didn't tell me."

Beth felt oddly breathless and confused, as if she'd suddenly found her kitchen chairs nailed to the ceiling.

"She mentioned it a week or so ago," Jenna said. "I wanted to tell her no, but you kept saying I should give her a chance, so I put out a sign-up sheet and we had ten people interested within three days." Her daughter smiled. "She has a welcoming style. Very inclusive and warm."

Beth eyed the large crowd. "What's the class?"

"Introduction to vegan cooking. They're even baking,

which I don't understand. How can you bake without eggs for binding?"

"But this is your store," Beth protested.

"I know, but I don't think the customers care who's cooking." She frowned. "Are you upset?"

"What? No. Of course not. Just surprised. You never mentioned it. I wondered if you were keeping it a secret."

Jenna stared at her. "Why would I do that? I forgot to tell you. It's not a big deal."

"Oh, I know. I'm fine." Beth smiled as widely as she could. "You go ahead and finish your work. I just wanted to stop by. I'll see you later."

Jenna nodded slowly. "If you're sure."

"I am."

They hugged, then Beth turned to leave. She still felt a little shaken inside. It was because she'd been so surprised, she told herself. Having Serenity a part of Jenna's life was a good thing. She'd thought so from the start.

Before she could reach the door, Violet stopped her.

"Morning," she said.

"Hello, Violet. It looks like you have your hands full."

"I know. It's a nice way to start the morning. Were you leaving?"

"I have errands to run."

"I'll walk you out."

Beth led the way. When they were out on the sidewalk, Violet stopped.

"I have a favor to ask, but I want to make sure you don't feel obligated." Violet bit her lower lip and ducked her head, then looked back at Beth. "Agreed?"

"Of course." Beth was more intrigued than concerned.

"I was wondering if you would mind going shopping with me sometime. You're always dressed so stylishly and I've seen the clothes you've bought for Jenna. They're wonderful. I don't have a huge budget, but I want to make some changes in my wardrobe."

Beth smoothed the front of her jacket and smiled. "Violet, that's very sweet of you, but I'm old enough to be your mother. Why would you want to dress like me?"

Violet shook her wrist with the half dozen bracelets. "I like my look, but I want to upgrade it. I'm dating this really great guy. He's a professional, in finance. Suits and ties, that kind of thing. I want to fit in better."

"You shouldn't change yourself for a man."

Violet laughed. "Excellent advice that no woman takes. At least not at the beginning of a relationship."

"True." Beth wondered if the man in question had asked Violet to do this or if it was her idea.

"You know what you're doing," Violet said. "I don't have a clue. I've been coloring my own hair since I was seventeen. I rarely go to a salon and I usually cut my hair myself."

Beth eyed her spiky style. "You do great work."

"Thanks, but I want to be classy. Myself but better."

Beth tried to remember the last time she and Jenna had gone shopping. It had been a while. Once she'd met Aaron, Jenna had hardly ever come home. There had been very regular phone calls and Beth had flown out to see her a couple of times a year, but it wasn't the same. She'd missed doing things with her daughter.

"I'm happy to help you pull together a few outfits. When's your next day off?"

"Tuesday."

"Why don't we go then?" Beth pulled a piece of paper out of her bag and wrote down her cell number. "Give me a call and we'll set up a time."

"Thank you so much," Violet said earnestly. "I really appreciate it."

"I'm happy to help," Beth told her. "We'll have fun."

Ellington arrived right on time. Customer traffic had slowed enough that Jenna had been able to change and retouch her makeup. As Violet had returned the sleeveless black dress and sworn it had great date karma, Jenna had decided to wear it. Hopefully she would have as much fun with Ellington as Violet had claimed to have had with Cliff.

She unlocked the store's glass door and let him in, then found herself unexpectedly overwhelmed by his long, lean body in jeans and a long-sleeved white shirt. Had his eyes always been that blue, she wondered as she got lost in the pleasure of looking at him.

"You look great," he said, leaning in to kiss her cheek. "How was your day?"

"Busy, but fun. I'm getting a lot of foot traffic, which is great. People are telling their friends about the store. Business is excellent."

"I'm glad. Starting new in retail is tough."

"Especially for someone coming from a completely different industry. If it wasn't for Violet, I would have failed. She's saved my butt and my bank account. Thanks to her good ideas, we've hired two part-time people."

She pressed her lips together. "Sorry. I didn't mean to go on like that."

"Don't apologize. It's nice to hear someone excited about what they do. Are you hungry? We're having dinner around the corner. Fish City Grill. Have you been there?"

"Not in years, but I remember liking it."

"I doubt they'll have anything as good as your enchiladas," he warned.

She laughed. "I'm okay with that. Last night I tried to make a kale pesto. Can you spell *yuck?* I don't know where I messed up, but it was awful."

"Do you try different things with food a lot?"

Good question, she thought. "Not for a while, but it's coming back. Slowly." She smiled. "I'm starting to remember that it's okay when things don't turn out right the first time. I can always try again and get it right."

"Good philosophy." He motioned to the door. "Shall we?"

She collected her purse and followed him outside.

They walked to the restaurant. Ellington gave his name, and they were shown to a corner table by the window. Once they were seated, he leaned toward her.

"Thanks for coming out with me tonight," he said. "I haven't been on a real date in a long time."

"Why not?" Someone who looked like him and who was also nice and successful should have women taking numbers.

He hesitated.

"You're not going to tell me you were waiting for the universe to tell you it was time, are you?" she asked before she could stop herself.

He laughed. "No. I don't communicate much with the universe. That would be your mother."

Birth mother, Jenna corrected silently. "How much did she tell you?"

He looked startled. "About what?"

"The adoption. Our relationship."

"Oh." His expression relaxed. "That she gave you up for adoption when she was a teenager and recently she's reentered your life."

Jenna had a feeling he knew a whole lot more than he was saying, but she wasn't sure she wanted to find out what.

Their server appeared. They both ordered wine.

When the woman had left, Jenna said, "Why haven't you been dating? It can't be for lack of opportunity."

He laughed. "Thanks for the compliment. I suppose it's a combination of things. I won't date a client."

"Hearts are breaking all over Georgetown."

"I've had a few women leave my practice because of that," he admitted. "No one I was truly interested in."

"Ah, so you are interested in *some* of your clients."

"Not at all."

"That's what you implied."

His teeth flashed white as he grinned. "You're trying to get me in trouble."

"It's kind of fun. You're so perfect."

"Far from it."

"Oh, please. Harvard medical school, but it was too traditional, so you went to China to study there. You're athletic, spiritual, have a kid, give a great massage, are holistic, but eat meat. Does it get any better than that?"

"Many women see my son as a liability."

"Many women would see him as a bonus."

The server appeared with their drinks. Ellington asked her to give them a few minutes before ordering.

Jenna took a sip of her drink and studied her date. She enjoyed teasing him, mostly because she sensed he would take it in the spirit she meant it.

"I'm far from perfect," he said when they were alone. As he spoke, he leaned toward her. "For one, I'm divorced."

"So am I."

"My marriage fell apart because I was caught up in my

work. I would rather have been with a patient than my wife. Or traveling."

"Was that about you or what was going on at home?"

"Both. It's hard to stay with someone who travels all the time. Even after Isaiah was born, I spent several months in India every year. I believed that what I was doing was more important than anything else." He shook his head. "I wish I could say I was the good guy."

"What changed?"

"She left and took my son with her. At first I kept doing what I'd always been doing, then one day I realized Isaiah was my responsibility. That I had deliberately brought him into this world and that he needed me. But the parenting plan was set. When I wanted to change things, she wouldn't agree. I supposed it was her way of punishing me for emotionally abandoning her. I can't really blame her." He shrugged. "Unfortunately Isaiah suffered, as well."

Jenna stared at him. "Something must be different now. He spent the night last night."

"He didn't spend the night, he lives with me. About a year ago, she was killed in a car accident. I became a full-time single dad. It's been a tough year for him. He was six. First he lost his dad, then he lost his mom. We had a lot of adjustments to make."

Jenna couldn't imagine an adult going through something like that well, let alone a little boy. "How's he doing now?"

"Thriving." Pride filled Ellington's voice. "I bought a house in his school district so he could stay close to his friends. My mom moved in and my mother-in-law lives around the corner. Between them, they handle the day care and everything about my life and his. I stopped traveling and opened a permanent practice at the healing center."

"You were able to reconnect with him?" she asked.

"It took a while, but yes. We're doing all kinds of things together. We have a deal that I'm home to tuck him in bed." He grinned. "I had to get special dispensation for our last date and for tonight."

"Please tell him I appreciate his generosity."

"I can see I'm going to have to continue to negotiate the bed tucking issue with him," he said, gazing into her eyes. "For the past year, it hasn't been much of a problem, but that might be changing."

Jenna willed herself not to blush. "I'd like that."

"You're ignoring the fact that I live with my mother."

"I'm not scared about it, if that's what you're asking."

"Good."

The server returned and they quickly ordered. After she left, he said, "Enough about my life. Tell me about yourself."

She gave him a few highlights, explaining about being a chef, her marriage and subsequent divorce and her move back to Georgetown.

"You don't want to tell me about your ex?" he asked.

"There's not much to tell."

Ellington didn't say anything. He simply watched her.

"All right," she said slowly. "He reminds me of you a little."

"Ouch."

She smiled. "You don't look alike. But you're both... charming."

"Is that a bad thing?"

"It turned out to be with him. I've always been creative with my cooking. At first he encouraged that, but in the last couple of years he seemed more interested in making me feel like I wasn't good enough." She shook her head. "The worst part wasn't what he did, it was that I believed him."

He reached across the table and touched her hand. "We often tend to believe the people we love. Even when they're wrong."

"I hadn't thought of it that way, but you're right. So now I have to figure out where I left my confidence and start trying things again. I've been taking a few very small risks. Our dinner was one. It's strange, in the past couple of weeks, I've felt my experimental side returning."

He raised his eyebrows. "Maybe that's because Serenity is around."

"Why would you say that?"

"She's very creative, you're a lot like her. Maybe having her show up jolted you out of a rut."

"I was just getting my store up and running when Serenity and Tom arrived," she mused.

"Interesting timing. Trust the Force."

As soon as he said the words, his expression froze. Jenna blinked at him.

"The Force?"

Oh, God. First Serenity with the universe and now Ellington with the Force? She found herself glancing toward the exit.

He cleared his throat. "Sorry. I'm a huge *Star Wars* fan. I had the lunch box and everything when I was a kid. Isaiah has seen the first movie with me and we've been playing with our light sabers, so it's on my mind." He looked completely humiliated. "When I said 'huge fan' I meant I like the movies. I don't have costumes or think there really is an Empire."

She relaxed, finding the confession more charming than scary. And seeing the somewhat perfect Ellington squirm didn't hurt, either.

"Light sabers?"

"Toys. They're toys."

"Do they make the noises?"

He sighed, as if surrendering to the inevitable. "Sure. Otherwise, where's the fun?" He stared at her. "Do you think I'm an idiot?"

"I think you're a lot less like my ex-husband than I realized."

"That's good, right?"

"Very good."

They smiled at each other.

He cleared his throat. "Now what were we talking about before I stuck my foot in my mouth?" He paused. "Serenity and Tom."

Jenna would rather have talked *Star Wars,* but okay.

"You know they're good people, right?" he asked.

"I do," she admitted. "At first I resented her. I have a family, I wasn't looking for more parents. But my mom—" She paused. "I know Serenity is your client or patient or whatever, so don't take this wrong, but the woman who raised me will always be my mom."

"Fair enough."

"My mom thinks I should get to know Serenity and Tom. That my connection to them is important."

"She sounds very wise."

"I think so, which means I'm listening. Maybe Serenity isn't as strange as I first thought. I can see she's a lovely person, but she's nothing like me."

"You have a lot in common with her."

"That's the second time you said that." Jenna wrinkled her nose. "I cook with butter, eat meat and the universe has never once sent me a message. Or the Force."

He laughed. "I was thinking you shared other characteristics. You look alike."

"True." At least she knew she would age well.

"You're both caring, nurturing people."

"I don't nurture," Jenna protested.

"The act of cooking, of feeding people, is nurturing by its nature. Food is life."

"I think you're taking my work a little too seriously."

"Or you're not taking it seriously enough." He mitigated the intensity of the words with a smile. "Appreciate the gift you bring."

"Now you do sound like Serenity."

"Occupational hazard." He took her hand in his. "Have I totally scared you away?"

"No," she said honestly. "You've intrigued me. You're full of contradictions. And, according to Serenity, you give a great massage."

He chuckled. "You've already had a sample of that."

"I have and I'm surprised you have time to do anything else in your day. I would think your massage clients would keep you busy."

"I don't usually offer massage to my clients," he said, releasing her hand.

"Really?"

"Serenity's a special case." He hesitated for a second. "What with her being from out of town and a temporary client."

Before she could ask anything more, the server returned with the bread basket.

"Is it hard for you to eat out?" he asked, leaning toward her and speaking quietly. "Are you thinking about how you'd do it better?"

"I try not to," she admitted. "Eating out is fun and I don't want to lose that by being critical."

"Sort of like me taking an over-the-counter pain reliever for a headache."

She turned to him, pretending shock. "You don't."

"Sometimes."

"What would your patients say?"

He laughed. "They'd be appalled. Can I convince you to keep my secret?"

She found herself getting lost in his blue eyes again.

"Maybe," she said, trying to sound casual. "For a price."

"A woman who negotiates. I like that."

Which was good, because she was quickly beginning to realize that there were many things that she liked about him.

Twelve

Jenna floated home from her date. Oh, sure, a car was involved, but that was a technical detail. In her heart, she was floating.

They'd laughed and talked and laughed some more all through dinner. She couldn't remember anything she'd eaten because she'd been so wrapped up in Ellington. Then he'd walked her to her car and kissed her with an intensity that had left her breathless.

As she parked in her garage, she told herself not to get too excited. That one great date did not a relationship make. But it had been so long since she'd had such a good time with a guy, including the last few years in her marriage. Sad but true.

Instead of going directly into her townhouse from the garage, she went out the open double door to collect her mail. On her way back, a man stepped out of the shadows.

She stopped in midstep, not sure what to do. Run?

Scream? With her garage door standing open, he could get directly into her house, possibly dragging her with him to do who knew what. Except this was Georgetown, not exactly a hotbed of murderers and rapists.

Indecision kept her in place, and in that second when she couldn't decide, she realized the man was on his cell phone. More than that, he was holding up his hand in the universal "wait and be quiet" signal.

"...the Baxter files. Email me the results. And double-check the billing. They screwed up the hours last month. Thanks, Cathy. Have a good day."

Jenna relaxed. She doubted many criminals left messages while on a stakeout or told anyone to have a good day.

"Sorry about that," the man said, stepping closer to her and into the light from her garage. "Work stuff. My assistant gets frantic when I'm gone, and that's never good."

She recognized him immediately from the pictures Serenity had brought to the brunch.

"I know you," she said.

He flashed her a smile then, one that looked exactly like Tom's.

"So you're feeling it then," he said. "The connection? Our familial oneness?"

She laughed. "Actually I recognize you from a picture your mother showed me. Hello, Dragon."

"Hey, sis. I'm glad it was a picture because, honestly, the oneness thing is so last year."

She laughed. "It's nice to meet you. What are you doing here?"

"I came to meet you. Sorry it's so late, but my flight was delayed. I would have waited until morning but my curiosity got the better of me."

Jenna studied her clean-cut brother. He seemed so normal. "Want to come in? I can make you something to eat."

"That would be great, if you're sure? Mom said you were a chef. Very convenient. I'll bet you never go hungry."

"And you do?" She led the way through the garage and into the house.

"Not now, but when I was a kid, it was a nightmare. All that vegan food." He shuddered. "I started working in the vineyards when I was seven just to earn money. I told my parents it was for comic books but it was really so I could buy my lunch at school. No kid wants lentil loaf in his lunch box."

She set down her purse in the living room and made her way into the kitchen. "What happened to the connection that flows between us?"

He grinned and took a seat on one of the bar stools next to the island. "Total crap," he admitted cheerfully. "I'm a constant disappointment to my parents. Now, Wolf is perfect. Totally into everything organic. I'm the bad, nonorganic seed in the family."

Jenna checked her refrigerator. "I could make you chicken piccata over angel-hair pasta with asparagus. How does that sound?"

"If you weren't my sister, I'd kiss you. I'm sorry I didn't bring wine."

She motioned to the small under-counter cellar. "Help yourself."

He did as she suggested, pouring them each a glass. Because she had been so busy talking with Ellington that she hadn't even finished her wine at dinner, she accepted and took a sip. Then she got to work, making the meal.

"Mom said you were on a date," Dragon said as he took

his seat again. "As your brother, I don't want any details. I'm not looking for more responsibility in my life."

"What responsibility would you have?"

"Beating him up if he hurt you."

The matter-of-fact tone was kind of comforting. She finished buttering bread from a baguette she'd bought, then squeezed on crushed garlic, topped it with fresh Parmesan cheese and popped the slices into the broiler.

"I already know everything about you," he continued. "Mom's been making regular calls. You probably want to know about me."

Jenna finished pounding the chicken and dredged it in flour. "Every detail," she told him, holding in her amusement.

"Well, I'm a lawyer. Corporate. When I first said I wanted to go to law school, my parents expected me to study something like immigration law and then spend my career working for earnest praise."

"Not your style?"

"Hardly. I'm corporate all the way. Gotta pay for the steaks and fancy car some way. It's worked out great for me. I'm in San Francisco. Do you know what it's like to be successful and straight in that town? It's good to be me."

She supposed Dragon could easily fall into the arrogant jerk category, but he was so at ease with himself that she couldn't help liking him.

"Trust me," he added. "I'm due. Growing up with a name like Dragonfly wasn't easy. I got beat up on a regular basis."

She turned the lightly browning chicken and added the pasta to the water. The diced asparagus would be parboiled and served on the side. While he was talking, she pulled out the browned garlic bread.

"Something to keep you from fainting while the rest of this cooks," she said.

He took a bite, then moaned. "Amazing," he mumbled over his food. "I saw you make this in, what, a minute? I can't believe how good it is."

"You're an easy audience," she said.

"That's what all the girls tell me."

Jenna laughed. "I'm sure there are dozens."

"Of course. Although lately..." His voice trailed off.

She squeezed lemon juice into the pan. "No way. Don't tell me you're thinking of settling down."

"Maybe. I'm nearly thirty. Wolf is married and Jasmine is pregnant."

"Jasmine?"

Dragon grinned. "They're perfect for each other. Jasmine never met a bean sprout she didn't like. Her nose wrinkles when I walk in the house, like she can smell the animal products on me. But she's sweet and pretty. Wolf runs the winery." He grabbed for his glass. "You know about that, right?"

"Butterfly Wines?" she asked drily.

"It's not like they named it after me."

"I wish they had. And Butterfly?"

"Hey, you're complaining to the wrong guy. Do you know what it was like the first day of school?"

"Sorry, no, but I can imagine."

She dropped the asparagus into the boiling water in the small pot, then dumped the pasta into a colander. While it drained, she stirred the sauce, spooning it over the chicken.

"We're ready," she said and grabbed a plate from the cupboard.

After scooping pasta onto the plate, she collected the chicken breast and poured the sauce over it. By then the asparagus was done. She dashed a little extra virgin olive oil onto the pasta, topped it with grated cheese and passed it to him.

"Enjoy," she said. "Oh. Flatware."

She handed him a knife, fork and napkin, then took the seat next to him.

"It'll get cold," she said, when he didn't move to take a bite.

"I know, but I'm savoring the moment. This looks great, smells better. If I could meet a girl who cooks like this, I would so marry her."

"You're easy."

"Tell me about it." He cut into the chicken. "The boyfriend. What does he do?"

She hesitated.

Dragon chewed and swallowed, then looked at her. "What? It's not a difficult question."

"He's a naturopath."

Dragon groaned. "Let me guess. Mom introduced you."

"Yes, but he's really nice and smart. He went to Harvard medical school."

"I'm a Yale man, myself."

"Really? Ivy League?"

"I could have gone to Stanford, but it was too close to home for my taste. And I do mean taste. My mother could smell a burger on my breath from a mile away."

He devoured his dinner while asking her questions about her life. When he was done, he leaned back in his chair and sighed.

"That was the best. Thanks."

"You're welcome. If you'd like, I could teach you how to cook a few simple things."

He picked up his wine. "Do I look like a guy who cooks?"

"No, but that could change."

Dragon grinned. "No, thanks. Now when I find the one, I'll take you up on that offer. Not for me, of course. For her."

"Pig."

The smile never wavered. "That's me."

"I met one of my brothers," Jenna told Violet Monday morning as they opened the store.

"I was going to ask about your date, but this might be better. Which one?"

"Dragon. He's completely adorable, in a confident, cocky, lawyer kind of way."

"You liked him," Violet said. "I can tell by the look on your face."

"I did. He looks a lot like Tom. He's actually really handsome. It's weird, but I already feel like I know him." She wasn't completely sure about extra parents, but siblings she could deal with. "He's nothing like his family. Expensive suit, loves meat. I'm going to guess his car is a gas-guzzler. He jokes about growing up eating tofu surprise."

Now that she thought about it, Serenity hadn't mentioned any of what she would consider Dragon's "negative" characteristics. She'd said her son was a lawyer and not much else.

Serenity was accepting, Jenna thought. And not judgmental. Her birth mother had that in common with Beth.

"He sounds great," Violet said.

"He is."

The front door opened and Robyn from Only Ewe stepped in.

"Morning," she called. "I wanted to let you know our beginning knitting class is starting next week, in case you're interested."

"I am," Violet said.

"Let me think about it," Jenna said. "I really want to learn, but I have some things I need to work out for the store."

"No problem. We always have them starting. Your mom, ah, Serenity, is in one of my classes. She's pretty good."

"I didn't know that she could knit."

"She's great. She helps the other knitters. Actually, she's assisting in a couple of my classes."

"I shouldn't be surprised," Jenna said. "She does love to get involved." A couple of weeks ago the information would have annoyed her, but now she accepted it as a part of who Serenity was.

"I need to get back," Robyn said, moving toward the door. "But I wanted to let you know. Oh, and thanks for those marshmallow cookies. They were fabulous. Thank goodness I had a class come in after you brought them over or I would have eaten them all myself."

She waved and left.

Jenna turned to find Violet studying her.

"What?" Jenna asked.

"Is everything all right with the store?" Violet sounded concerned.

"Of course. I just want to make a few more changes."

Violet tensed.

Jenna touched her arm. "I was going to ask you to stay a few minutes later today so we could talk about it, but I don't want you to suffer. Everything is fine. In fact it's wonderful. You're doing a terrific job. I love the girls you hired to work part-time."

"Okay. Good." Violet's expression relaxed.

"It's me. I'm not loving taking care of all the details. Or-dering, managing the supplies. I really want to spend more time with the classes. I was wondering if you would be will-ing to manage the store. I could either give you a raise or cut you in for a percentage of the profits."

Violet's voice caught while she was answering. "I'd love handling things for you."

"I was really hoping you'd say that. Let's talk more after work."

"Absolutely."

A half dozen or so customers arrived together, interrupting their discussion. Each had a question about a different class. At one point Jenna looked up to see her mother discussing Bundt pans with one woman and Serenity demonstrating a Swiss-made cheese grater to another. She wasn't exactly sure when they'd arrived, but she was grateful for the help. Finally about eleven-thirty, there was a brief lull.

"You're doing well," Beth said. "It's a Monday morning and you're still crowded."

"I know. It's so good, it's almost scary." She led her mother toward the kitchen. "I'm making Violet the manager of the store. We're going to talk details tonight after work. I want more time to focus on the classes."

"What a great idea. Violet is organized and experienced."

"I'm organized," Jenna said with a laugh.

"True, but running a store is new for you. I'm glad you're having fun."

"I am. I thought I'd made a huge mistake when I rented the store, but I didn't." She was about to mention her date with Ellington when the door opened and Dragon strolled in. "Check it out," she said, pointing.

Beth turned in time to see Dragon and Serenity embrace.

"Who is that?" Beth asked, sounding slightly shocked.

"One of my brothers. He's a corporate lawyer. I'm not sure it's possible for him to be more different than his parents."

"Really?" Beth eyed him. "Come on. You can introduce us."

Violet wrapped a set of pots in the generic gift wrap they had in back. As she cut and folded and taped, she found it tough to keep from breaking into a happy little dance. As it was, she settled on grinning like an idiot.

Her promotion probably wouldn't mean all that much to a lot of people, but to her it was confirmation that she'd made the right choice to take the job. Her gut was in working order—something always good to know.

She was delighted that Jenna was pleased with her work and excited by the opportunity the store represented. She had lots of ideas about ways to advertise the store and different promotions to bring in customers. Over the next few days she would come up with a plan and share it with Jenna.

So far, Tiffany and Kayla, their college help, had both worked out. If all went well, they would also need to hire a full-time person.

She carried the wrapped package back to the customer, then turned and bumped into a tall, dark-haired man.

"Sorry," she said automatically, stepping back.

"No problem."

He was attractive, she thought absently. Well-dressed in an "I have money" kind of way without being flashy. She liked his eyes and the kindness lurking in his expression. That or she'd been hanging out with Serenity for too long.

"I love a good bad girl," the man said.

Even though his words should have annoyed her, they didn't. Odd, she thought. "Sorry. I'm neither bad nor available."

"Would you be willing to make an exception?"

"No."

"My loss."

His easy grin made her want to smile in return.

Serenity and Beth joined them.

"I see you've met my oldest son," Serenity said. "Dragon, this is Beth, Jenna's other mother."

Violet noticed that Beth tensed slightly at the description, but she was gracious as she shook Dragon's hand.

"I didn't know you were coming to visit," she said.

"I decided at the last minute. I wanted to meet my sister."

"Where are you from?" Violet asked.

"San Francisco. I'm a lawyer."

Serenity winced. "A corporate lawyer," she added, sounding as if her son also kidnapped children in his free time.

Dragon looked unrepentant as he leaned toward Violet and murmured, "Worse, I eat M-E-A-T. Don't say the word too loud. She either cries or faints."

"My husband runs a few banks here in Texas," Beth said. "The corporate world can be challenging."

"Exactly." Dragon winked at her. "That's why I like it." He turned back to Violet. "Have you worked for Jenna long?"

"Since the store opened, so a couple of months."

"Don't," Serenity said, resting her hand on her son's back. "It's not yet time."

"Time for what?" Violet asked, confused.

Dragon sighed. "She's telling me not to pursue you. That it isn't our time."

"You know this how?" Beth asked.

"I can sense it." Serenity's voice was as calm as always. "Violet, when the time comes, you can trust Dragon. Despite his appearance of wickedness, he's kind. When he was little,

I watched him play with the smaller children. He was so gentle."

Dragon groaned. "Mom, come on. I have a reputation here. Don't start with the small children and rescuing bunnies talk. Women don't find it sexy."

Violet was more startled by Serenity's statement that she could trust Dragon. Why would she have to?

She glanced at Beth and saw Jenna's mother rolling her eyes. Violet held in a grin. The two mothers were so different. Serenity tall and thin, with long dark red hair and no makeup. Her flowing dress fell nearly to her ankles, the colors bright enough to stand out anywhere. Beth was blond with makeup emphasizing her pretty features. She wore tailored pants and a cropped jacket that suited her petite frame.

On the surface Serenity was exotic and had her own appeal, while Beth fell into the category of normal. Still, if Violet had to pick, she found Beth safer.

"How does the universe speak to you?" Beth asked. "Email? A voice in your head?"

Serenity was unruffled by the question. She slipped her arm through Dragon's and leaned against him. "It's more as if an unasked question has been answered."

"That's convenient."

Violet might not have a hotline to the universe, but she could sense rising tension. Apparently Dragon felt it, too. Before she could draw Beth away, he wrapped his arm around his mother's waist.

"Are you up for a walk?" he asked. "I want to see that park you told me about."

"I would love that."

She smiled at Beth, then turned and left.

Beth watched them go. "I really do like her but sometimes she can be a little too much."

"She does jump in the middle of things," Violet said.

"How did her vegan class go?"

"You saw the crowd, so that was good. The question is, will they come a second time?"

"We can only hope," Beth said brightly.

"She's in everything," Beth told Marshall that night over cocktails. "Since she arrived, I have yet to show up in Jenna's store without finding her there, or having her walk in five minutes later. I can't get a second alone with my own daughter. Plus, the whole thing about the universe. She receives private messages, then shares them with everyone else. Aren't we the lucky ones?"

She sipped her vodka tonic. "Serenity is trying to take over Jenna's life. I don't know how to stop her. Did I tell you one of her sons is in town?"

"You mentioned it."

"It's Dragon. He's actually fairly nice and a corporate lawyer, so he knows what life is like in the real world, as opposed to the planet where Serenity lives. But still. She has two children of her own. She needs to leave my daughter alone."

Marshall looked at her. He didn't say anything, he just looked.

"I know," she snapped. "You warned me not to get involved. Well, you were right but that doesn't change the situation. Does you being right mean I can't talk about it?"

"Of course not."

"I don't want to dislike her, but she's making it difficult." She took another drink. "I'm the one who encouraged Jenna to welcome them into her life. Can you believe it? I did this to myself."

The rational side of her brain knew she had nothing to

worry about. That her daughter would always love her. But she felt both frantic and scared. It was one thing to be annoyed with Serenity, but the fear was much, much worse. Jenna was all she had. Two months ago she would have been confident that her relationship with her daughter was untouchable. Now, she wasn't as sure. Telling herself to snap out of it wasn't helping.

"What if she doesn't love me anymore?" she whispered.

Marshall set down his drink and crossed to her. After putting her glass on the living room table, he pulled her to her feet and held her in his strong arms.

"Nothing is going to change," he said. "Have a little faith."

"Faith isn't the problem. You can't know everything is going to be all right."

"I can. There's nothing they can do to take her away, Beth. You were right to encourage her to get to know her birth parents. This is all new. She's adjusting. In time things will settle down. You'll see."

"What if you're wrong?"

"I'm not."

She didn't say anything else. But the truth was, he couldn't know. Which left Beth wondering, for the first time in thirty-two years, if she was going to lose her daughter.

Thirteen

"You sure this is all right?" Ellington asked as he unpacked the lunch bags and set the contents on a picnic table. "It's the middle of your work day."

"Yours, too," Jenna reminded him, sliding onto the wooden seat of the picnic table. "Let me put this in perspective. I have a store full of customers, my mother and birth mother are having issues, my new brother is hitting on my manager and I have a class to teach in a couple of hours. If you were me and a handsome man called and invited you to lunch, wouldn't you jump at the chance?"

Ellington passed her a panini. "I'm not into guys."

She laughed. "You know what I mean. I'm happy to see you and delighted to get away for a little while."

"Then I'll tell Mrs. Ruley we're thrilled that she canceled."

"Please do."

It was a perfect late-spring day, she thought, raising her

face to the sun. Blue skies, warm temperatures, a light breeze. The picnic table sat in the shade of a two-hundred-year-old live oak next to the San Gabriel River. When Ellington had first called with the unexpected invitation, she'd told herself she didn't have the time. But then she'd realized a break was exactly what she needed.

"What's your class?" he asked.

She sipped her soda. "It's actually a really fun one. A couple of weeks ago a customer complained that she had ingredients in her pantry that she didn't know what to do with. A spice she'd bought for one recipe, or some exotic sauce that had been on sale. Different flavored oils. Things that weren't a part of her usual cooking style."

"My mom has a bunch of those in her kitchen."

"Everyone does. Eventually the product goes bad, which makes that first recipe really, really expensive. I asked my customers to bring in a list of anything strange in their pantries. I took the top ten most common items and have built a couple of recipes around them."

Ellington shook his head. "That's brilliant."

"Actually Serenity is the one who encouraged me to hold a class." She held up a hand. "Don't say it. I'll admit she has good ideas."

"I'm glad you think so."

"I do. And I'm really looking forward to the class. It's fun, for them, but mostly for me. I used to…" She paused, not sure how much to share. "I told you before, I used to be really inventive in the kitchen. After the last year or so with Aaron, I've been scared to try new things." She smiled. "But even when I fought the urge to experiment, I couldn't seem to stop myself."

"I'm glad you couldn't and I'm sorry your ex treated you that way."

"Part of the fault is mine. I kept giving in to him. I think I knew in my gut if I wasn't everything he wanted, he wouldn't stay." She thought for a second, remembering how much she'd worried in her marriage. About doing the right thing, about being what Aaron wanted.

"Now I find myself wondering why he wasn't as worried about making me happy. I've realized it's because the relationship wasn't that important to him. He had other things he would have rather been doing, so he did them. Including other women."

Ellington looked uncomfortable.

"Too much information?" she asked quickly. "We can change the subject."

"You're hitting too close to home," he admitted. "I didn't cheat, but I wasn't present in my marriage."

"The difference is you realized your mistake." Jenna knew that Aaron would never care about anyone as much as he cared about himself. Even if he begged her to return to him—which he wouldn't—she wasn't interested. Next time, she wanted someone as committed as she was. More important, she wanted someone who saw the best in her and encouraged her to succeed.

"I like helping people discover that making something delicious is a whole lot easier than they first thought. I like them surprising themselves with what they can do."

"A natural teacher," Ellington told her.

"I'm not sure about that but I am having fun." She'd been terrified at first, creating on the fly, but then she'd told herself to let go. To believe in herself. Ironically, the first time she'd been brave enough to play with a recipe had been after the brunch with Serenity and Tom. She'd re-created the rice pudding dish, making it her own.

"We're going to have an ongoing class in the store where

people can write down what they're trying to get rid of and I'll come up with a recipe. We'll print out the recipes I've already created and have those out for people to take."

"You're good at this," he said, sounding impressed. "Do you miss being a chef?"

"Sometimes, but less and less as time goes on. I know people who thrive in the controlled chaos, but I'm not one of them. Aaron loved the constant pressure. He charmed the customers and the staff."

"Did you know it was over when you stopped being charmed?"

Her first instinct was to say it had been over when he'd told her he was sleeping with other women and wanted a divorce. But that wasn't right.

"I'm not sure when I left emotionally," she admitted. "I'd been shut down for a while. Afraid, not trusting myself."

She studied him, taking in the good looks, the easy smile, the warm, friendly nature. He was practically perfect—no, better than perfect. He was a man who had learned from his mistakes.

"What were you like, predivorce?" she asked.

"What do you mean?"

"Before the introspection—before you learned from your mistakes." She had a feeling he'd never been all that terrible.

He finished chewing, then swallowed. "It's not a story designed to make you like me more."

"I'm willing to risk it."

"I'm not sure I am." He put down his sandwich. "Let's just say I came into my own pretty early and I used it to my advantage."

"The hot guy in high school?"

"I could get dates the football captain couldn't. I wanted

to be a doctor, some for the money, mostly because I knew it would make my life very easy when it came to women."

She thought of Dr. Mark and knew that was very possible.

"College was more of the same." He looked at her. "School was easy for me, so I had plenty of free time to play. You'd think that having been given so much, I would be gracious, but I wasn't. I took what I wanted and when I was done, I walked away without looking back. I left a trail of broken hearts everywhere I went."

Jenna tried not to look surprised or disappointed, even though she felt both.

"The summer before my junior year of college, my grandmother took me to India. It had been her lifelong dream. My parents didn't want her to go alone and they sure didn't want to go, so I volunteered. I figured it would be an adventure, plus there was a whole new continent of women to conquer." His mouth twisted. "Back at college, I'd already worked my way through most of the coeds."

He pushed his sandwich aside. "What I didn't know was that my grandmother had plans for me. She was determined to teach me some compassion. We didn't stay in a luxury beach resort. Instead I spent my days working in a clinic for the poorest of the poor. They were starving, without any kind of sanitation. Bugs everywhere, the noise was incredible. When I wanted to leave early, my grandmother told me this was the other side of medicine. The side that mattered. And that I'd better be careful because leprosy, which still existed there, was sexually transmitted."

"Is it?"

"You get it from fluids, mostly from the nose and mouth. It's not that contagious, but at the time I was young and had no way to check what she said, so I was careful." He shrugged. "That trip changed me. A kid I'd made friends with had an accident and his leg was crushed. I was there while it was cut off, using a saw and minimal anesthesia. The food and water made me sick, the crowds were everywhere. It was the longest month of my life. In some ways it was also the best. When we flew home, I was different. I couldn't care about the things I had before. I finally wanted to be a doctor to actually help people."

He grinned. "Only to walk away from it all and go to China to study alternative medicine."

"You still heal people."

"Yes, but not in a traditional way. I've learned there are many answers to the same question. Traveling allowed me to learn more and treat them better. Too bad I didn't apply the lessons to my personal life."

"Didn't your wife travel with you?"

"She didn't want to go where I went. Had I been attending a seminar in Paris, I think she would have been very happy. From my perspective, she was making me choose between her and the work I loved. From her point of view, I was a husband who was never home and when I did manage to stop by for a few days, I made it a point to make sure she knew my work was far more important than her."

Jenna winced. "That's not fun."

"Your husband did the same?"

"Sometimes. He wanted me to know that everyone was more intriguing than me and that he was only home because he had to be." Aaron had rarely said it in words, but he'd made the meaning clear.

"When she left," Ellington said, "I continued on as if nothing had changed. It took her dying to make me realize I'd lost her and my son. It's not easy to convince a six-year-old whom you practically abandoned and whose mother died that you're not going to disappear." He sipped his soda. "It's been a hard lesson for me. Now I'm focusing on what's around me. My family, then my work. I'm trying to find some balance, so I've been cautious about dating. I don't want to screw up again."

"Everyone makes mistakes."

"True, but mine have been very hard on everyone *but* me. I don't want to be that guy anymore." He leaned toward her. "Which is why I want to wait before introducing you to Isaiah."

"Of course." She hadn't thought they were anywhere close to that point.

He grinned. "You could meet my mother, if you want."

"I have enough mothers in my life right now, but thanks for asking."

He had a depth she hadn't expected. An honesty. Aaron would never see the truth about himself, never begin to understand the point of self-examination. But Ellington saw his flaws and was trying to change. She appreciated that.

They returned to their lunches, talking about local events and Isaiah's quest to convince the adults in his life that he really, really needed a puppy.

"There's a bake sale in a couple of weeks," Ellington told her. "My mother says she draws the line at baking, so Isaiah and I are going to make cupcakes together."

"Should be a good time. I'm no pastry chef, but things like dessert can be fun. Anything with sugar."

He laughed. "I'll let you know how it goes."

When they'd finished their lunch, they stood and tossed their trash, then started for their cars.

Halfway down the path, Ellington grabbed her hand and drew her to a stop.

"Have I scared you away?" he asked.

She stared into his dark blue eyes and allowed herself to get lost there. "You've given me a lot to think about," she admitted.

"Is that a polite yes?"

"You're not just a pretty face and you have a complicated past. What I took away is that you learned from your mistakes."

"I'm still learning. Balance is tough for me. I love my work and my son, but they're not my world. Something is still missing." He turned away. "Now I sound like a thirteen-year-old girl."

She reached up and touched the side of his face, turning him back to look at her. "No. You sound like someone I want to get to know better."

"Are you being polite?"

"I'm mostly impatient. This is where you're supposed to kiss me."

His mouth turned up at the corners. "You sure?"

"Very."

"Right now?"

"This second."

He wrapped his arms around her and drew her against him. She went willingly, wanting to feel his body against hers. He was tall and muscled, different from Aaron's leanness. She had to stretch a little for her mouth to meet Ellington's, and she liked that, too.

His mouth was firm yet gentle, exploring rather than taking. He moved against her, creating heat and friction. He wrapped his arms around her waist, his fingers pressing into her skin. They touched from shoulder to knee, and even that wasn't enough. She found herself wanting more, needing to deepen the kiss. Heat exploded inside of her, surprising her with its intensity. But this was the middle of the day, in a public park. She drew back.

"If I were still that guy," Ellington said ruefully.

"The backseat of your car?" she asked, then wanted to clamp her hand over her mouth. What if he hadn't been as affected as she had been? What if he'd thought the kiss was only okay? The heat moved from the feminine places in her body to burn her cheeks.

"I was thinking of that thick grove of bushes," he admitted, "but the car works, too."

Relief tasted sweet. She smiled. "If we weren't so responsible."

"Exactly." He kissed her lightly. "I'll call you later."

"I'd like that."

They parted, each returning to their cars. Jenna drove back to the store, singing along with the radio and feeling happy and quivery at the same time. It was going to be a very good day.

"There's a trick to shopping," Beth said as she pulled into the parking lot of a consignment store Violet had never noticed before. "One or two really nice pieces can fool people into thinking you have a very expensive wardrobe. I had a friend who had a couture Armani jacket. She would toss it over chairs, label side up. We all saw it and assumed everything else was designer, too, when in truth she bought most of her casual clothes at Target."

"I like that," Violet said. "Discount is more my budget."

"You're trendy," Beth said, parking the car. "Why would you want to spend a lot on something that's only going to be in style for a few months? But for classic pieces you'll keep for years, buy the best you can afford. Consignment is often the way to go."

"Good advice," Violet said, following her into the store.

It was open and bright, with high ceilings and lots of windows. Racks of clothes stretched out in all directions.

"Impressive," Violet said, when what she meant was "intimidating." Where was she supposed to start?

Beth pointed. "The designer section is over there. You're skinny enough that everything will fit you. Ignore the bitterness in my voice, by the way. Although I did lose two pounds last week."

"Good for you," Violet said. "You're not dieting are you?"

Beth patted her hip. "I can't find anyone to do it for me, unfortunately."

Violet looked at the other woman's curves. "You're beautiful. Why would you want to change anything?"

Beth smiled, then hugged her. "Thank you. These days I'm feeling short and stout, much like the little teapot."

Violet was going to ask why, then realized the reason had Serenity written all over it.

She wanted to tell Beth not to compare herself to the other woman—that they were totally different, but it was unlikely Beth would listen. No matter how many times Violet managed to fit into a situation, she was still braced to be found out. For someone to stand up, point their finger and call her a whore. She supposed everyone had demons.

Beth searched through jackets, pulling out two or three, studying them, then putting half of them back. When she'd loaded Violet down with half a dozen, she led her to the triple mirror by the dressing rooms and plopped into a chair.

"Let the fashion show begin."

At Beth's instruction, Violet had worn a plain white tank over black jeans. Of her own accord, she'd left her signature bracelets at home and had only worn one pair of earrings.

Her makeup was unusually soft, her hair more tousled than spiked.

She took the first jacket and tried it on. The black fabric was a soft wool, tailored, and yet it hung loosely.

"I like it," Beth said as she stood, dumping the remaining jackets onto the chair. "Very simple. The shoulders are right." She moved behind Violet and smoothed the fabric. "It's all about fit."

Next to the mirror were a couple of pincushions filled with pins. Beth picked up a few and went to work. Violet couldn't see what she was doing in back. She felt a few tugs, and suddenly the jacket fit her perfectly, emphasizing her waist while still looking classy.

"What did you do?"

"Pinned it in a little, just to give you an idea of how it's supposed to look. Life is a lot better with a good seamstress, let me tell you. I can give you the name of the person I use. She's not cheap, but she's the best. I'm faking it, but at least you can get an idea of how it will be."

She moved around to Violet's front and studied her. "Maybe shorten the sleeves by a hair, too," she murmured before handing Violet a hanger and holding up the next jacket.

They went through each of the jackets the same way, with Beth studying them, then adjusting with pins when necessary. She found a couple of adorable cocktail dresses, one of which was only twelve dollars, and several pairs of Stuart Weitzman shoes in her size.

Two hours later, Violet had two dresses, a skirt, four tops, a jacket, three scarves, four pairs of shoes and a Prada handbag. The prices ranged from twelve dollars to two hundred. The latter should have made her whimper, but she pulled out her credit card happily. She had the savings to spend more on clothes but had never seen the point. Until Cliff.

"You've been great," she told Beth as their purchases were rung up. "I can't thank you enough."

"I've had a wonderful time," Beth assured her. "I don't get to shop like this much anymore. Now, we're going directly to my seamstress so you can get fitted."

"I don't want to keep you. You can just give me the address."

"I want to come. It's fun for me. You're so pretty. It should annoy me, but it doesn't."

Violet laughed, then felt an unexpected pang. The longing and loss were for what had never existed in her life.

"Jenna is fortunate to have you."

Beth smiled.

Violet signed the credit card receipt. Together they carried the bags out to the car.

"I wanted a lot of children," Beth said as they drove out of the parking lot. "I knew at an early age I couldn't have them. Marshall and I started the paperwork to adopt even before we were married. We were delighted that Serenity chose us. Jenna's been a blessing."

Violet knew her mother had never described her in those terms.

"Do you want to have children?" Beth asked as she came to a stop at a red light.

"Maybe. Someday."

"Jenna mentioned you're seeing someone. Is he special?"

"I think so. It's still pretty new." And as much as she liked Cliff, she couldn't seem to let go with him and totally be herself. Probably because of the secrets she kept. He didn't strike her as the kind of guy who would accept her past.

"If he's not the one, you'll find him."

"Like you found Marshall?"

Beth smiled. "Exactly."

"If I don't find the right guy, I have my career," Violet said.

"Jenna mentioned she'd made you manager of the store."

"Uh-huh. I'm pretty excited."

"You've done excellent work. You're a natural with the customers."

"I like being with people."

"You're very patient with Serenity."

Violet knew this was potentially dangerous ground. "She's unique."

Although Jenna had problems with Serenity, Violet found that she liked the other woman. Sure, she was unusual, but there was a kindness about her. She truly cared about people, in a way that asked for nothing back. Violet had seen the longing in Serenity's eyes when she looked at Jenna. She regretted having lost her daughter.

Violet wanted to feel bad for her, but at the same time she understood that Jenna had been an incredible blessing for Beth. Like many of life's complications, the situation was confusing.

"Tom's back in town," Beth said. "He and Serenity are coming over to dinner tomorrow. There's a challenge. We're barbecuing burgers. Both kinds. Jenna's bringing a few sides, as is Serenity."

"Brace yourself for soy," Violet teased.

"Don't I know it. Marshall's threatened to get takeout on the way home, so he can eat before dinner. I've promised him that our burgers are going to be the old-fashioned kind, but I think he's afraid I'll try to slip him some tofu."

Violet laughed. "It's not as bad as he thinks."

"I don't think he wants to test the theory."

They turned into a strip mall. Beth pointed to the small store at the end. "It doesn't look like much, but she can work miracles."

When they'd parked, Violet turned to the other woman. "Thank you so much for helping me today."

"You're welcome." Beth patted her arm. "I don't know much about your past, Violet, but I sense it wasn't especially happy. If you ever want to talk, I'm here. If you just need a friend, I hope you'll think of me. For anything."

Violet had learned early not to let her emotions show and to never let them be in charge. But now, she found herself leaning close and hugging Beth.

"Thank you," she whispered, fighting unexpected tears. "You have no idea how much that means to me."

Beth held on tight. "One day you can tell me."

"Isn't she beautiful?" Tom asked, pointing to a picture of a very young and very pregnant Serenity.

Jenna stared at the photo, seeing a lot of herself in it. An odd reality she was slowly getting used to.

She sat between her birth parents on the sofa in Beth and Marshall's family room. Somehow they'd all gotten through dinner. The combination of traditional and vegan food had been consumed, and there had been enough wine to smooth over any rough edges.

Jenna turned to the next page, which showed young Tom and young Serenity together. They looked happy and in love.

"My parents insisted I give you up," Serenity said with a sigh. "They didn't believe that Tom and I would stay together. Having me pregnant was hard enough on my family—keeping a baby and being a single teenage mother was more than they could handle. But I wonder..."

"Coffee anyone?" Beth asked briskly, rising to her feet. "I think I'd like some."

"I'll take some as well," Tom told her.

"No, thanks," Serenity said.

Marshall nodded.

Jenna felt her mother's tension. While she felt badly that Beth didn't like how things were going, she wanted to remind her that this had been her idea. Beth had been the one to insist they all get to know each other.

The last picture in the album showed a very scared Serenity in a wheelchair as she was taken into the hospital to give birth. Jenna felt sympathy for the young girl whose life had been so changed by her pregnancy. Although she suspected most women found the process altered everything. Still, Serenity had been a teenager and not a grown woman who'd been ready to get pregnant.

"Here's a few pictures of the winery," Tom said, taking that album from Jenna and replacing it with a slimmer one. "They're recent pictures."

She studied the vineyard at sunset, the light streaming across the grapevines.

"It's beautiful."

Beth returned to the family room and glanced at the picture. "It is."

Serenity took Jenna's hand. "I have to go back. I need to see Wolf and Jasmine. She's seven months pregnant and I want to commune with her unborn baby."

Jenna barely blinked at the thought. "I'm sure they've both missed you."

"They have, and I've missed them, but this was important." Serenity squeezed her fingers. "Jenna, please come back with me."

"What?"

Jenna pulled her hand free, then closed the album and rose. She stepped out from behind the coffee table and faced her birth parents.

"Just for a little while," Tom added, making it clear they'd discussed this already. "For a few days. We want you to see everything. The winery, our home. Meet Wolf and his wife."

Visit them? She'd barely gotten used to the fact that they existed.

"Dragon will be there, too," Tom added.

Jenna had to admit seeing her brother again was an enticement. He'd only stayed in town overnight and then had flown back to San Francisco. But the rest of it was less appealing.

"You have Violet to take care of the store," Serenity said. "She can handle things."

Jenna looked at Beth, who was carefully ignoring the conversation.

"Mom?"

Reluctantly, Beth looked up. Her smile was forced. "Why not go?" she said, her tone neutral. "It would be fun. It's only for a few days."

Because it was weird. Because the thought of it made her uncomfortable. She found herself back at the same set of questions she'd had when Serenity and Tom had first shown up. Why now? What made this time special?

She felt everyone watching her. Tom and Serenity were so hopeful, her parents, carefully noncommittal.

"I'll bet that coffee is ready," she said and ducked into the kitchen.

She hurried into the other room, knowing her escape was temporary. When she heard footsteps behind her, she turned, expecting to see Beth. Instead Tom stood there.

"I know it's hard," he said, his dark eyes watching her. "But we'd really like you to come. Everything is beautiful right now. Growing. New life. Your mother..." He cleared his throat. "Serenity cried every night for the first six months. I would see her swollen eyes every morning when we went to school. Beth and Marshall are wonderful, but they've had you your entire life. Please, Jenna, just give us this."

His plea, so obviously from the heart, was difficult to ignore. Maybe she didn't understand Serenity, but everything her birth mother had done had been kind and loving. The least Jenna could do was respond the same way.

She drew in a breath. "Sure," she said at last. "I'll go with you."

Fourteen

Violet nearly danced with impatience. She was so excited about her new dress. Cliff was taking her to the theater that night and she'd wanted to look perfect. For once she'd blown out her hair instead of leaving it casual. The soft curls complemented her more subtle makeup and subdued jewelry.

But the dress itself was the star. It was a vintage-inspired blue cocktail dress that fell to the middle of her calf. The fitted bodice was decorated with black jet beads, while the skirt was full with layers of tulle.

She'd found a beaded black evening bag at a thrift store and was wearing a pair of the Stuart Weitzman pumps she'd bought with Beth. For the first time in her life, Violet felt like a princess.

When Cliff knocked on the door, she had to bite her lip to keep from laughing with delight. She hurried to the door and threw it open.

"Hi!"

Instead of responding, he stared at her. "What are you wearing?"

She grabbed his hand and drew him into her apartment, then she spun in a circle. "Isn't it amazing? I love this dress more than I've ever loved any piece of clothing in my life. I'm so excited we're going somewhere I can wear it."

But instead of looking happy, Cliff scowled.

"What?" she asked.

"Where did you get it?"

"The dress? At a consignment store." Her pleasure faded a little. "Don't you like it?"

"I know your style. You don't dress like this."

She stared at him, trying to read his emotions. But for once she couldn't tell what he was thinking.

"I went shopping with Beth," she said, trying to keep the hurt from showing in her voice. She'd done this for him, and somehow it had gone terribly wrong. "Jenna's mother. She helped me buy a bunch of clothes. I wanted to dress better. I wanted you to be proud of me."

Cliff's shoulders rolled forward and his face relaxed. "You didn't have to do that, Violet. I'm always proud of you. You're always beautiful." He smiled. "Especially tonight."

She stared at him. "Why were you upset at first?"

He shrugged. "I wasn't upset exactly," he began, then shook his head. "Who am I kidding? I was jealous as hell. You looked so amazing and I know I don't deserve you. I thought you were going to tell me you didn't want to see me again. That it was over."

"Why would I get dressed up to do that?"

"To show me what I was losing."

Raw shame darkened his eyes, a wounded expression that told her somewhere in his past, something like that had happened. Someone had been that cruel.

"Cliff," she whispered. "I would never do that. I bought this dress for you. I want to be everything you could want."

He lightly touched her face. "You don't know how much that means to me. I'm sorry I was a jerk."

"It's okay. I understand." They'd both been hurt, she thought, going to him. They had that in common. The truth was Cliff wasn't the most exciting guy on the planet, but she was just fine with that. He was safe, and that would always be the most important thing to her.

When a voice whispered that she couldn't truly give herself to someone who didn't know the truth about her past, she ignored it. If the price of being with Cliff was a sin of omission, then she was willing to accept the consequences.

Serenity sliced the coffee cake and set the pieces onto paper plates they used in the store. Jenna tasted it, fully expecting it to surprise her, and it did. The cake was moist and the cinnamon filling just spicy enough to counteract the sweet. Even the frosting was the right consistency.

"This is great," Jenna said. "Are you going to have them prepare this during your next class?"

"I haven't decided."

Despite her initial concerns, the vegan cooking classes were going very well. They were always full, and the baskets of ingredients sold out every time.

Serenity looked at her. "This is exactly what I wanted," she admitted. "The two of us working together. I imagined it in some form or another. Sometimes I would think about what it would have been like if you'd grown up as my daughter, living at the winery, always a part of things."

While Jenna could understand Serenity's need to have closure, she wasn't comfortable talking about a life that had never been hers. No matter how she grew to enjoy spending time with Serenity, Beth would always be her mother, and she didn't want that to change.

"It would have been different," was all she could manage for a response. At least the store was quiet right now and they weren't having this intimate conversation in front of twenty strangers.

"I had a lot of guilt," her birth mother continued. "About giving you up for adoption. I used to wonder if I'd given in too easily. If I should have fought my parents harder. The past can be tricky. If I had kept you, and Tom and I had married sooner, things would have been different. I'm not sure how, but history builds on itself. Who knows where we would have gone? I wouldn't have had Wolf and Dragon. There would have been other children, though. An alternate universe."

Jenna could almost understand her slightly strange logic. "You don't have to feel guilty. I had a wonderful childhood. You did the right thing."

"Perhaps. I suppose we'll never know." She managed a shaky smile. "I'd always wanted a dozen children but never felt I deserved them."

"Why wouldn't you?"

"Because I'd walked away from you. I suppose it was my way of punishing myself."

"I'm sorry you did that," Jenna told her. "You're a great mother."

"Guilt comes at us in different forms."

Jenna knew that was true. She'd wrestled with her own feelings of guilt about her marriage, wondering what she'd done that was so wrong. She'd felt guilty about resenting how he ignored her, about accusing him of cheating, although the latter had turned out to be true. It seemed to her that a large part of guilt was a complete waste of time.

Serenity rinsed the knife in the sink. "I wanted to come find you so many times over the years. I kept telling myself that you had to be the one to come to us. I was willing to wait for as long as it took. Only, things changed."

And speaking of guilt, Jenna thought, there it was. Slapping her on the back of the head.

She wanted to protest that it wasn't her fault that she hadn't been interested in finding her birth parents. She'd had a life and a family. She hadn't been looking for more.

"I'm not trying to make you feel bad," Serenity said quickly.

"I know." The kicker was, Jenna really did believe her. "We'll make new memories when I come to Napa."

"It will be wonderful," Serenity promised. "I can't wait for you to see our house. There's a wall of glass looking out onto the vineyards. It's beautiful and there's a healing energy there. Wolf's house is nearby. You're going to love his wife. Jasmine is sweet and precious. She weaves her own cloth."

Of course she does, Jenna thought, barely able to keep from rolling her eyes. "That's time-consuming."

"It is. She buys raw cotton from some farmers we know. Instead of a garbage disposal, Jasmine and Wolf have a pig. You'll see their place and the vineyards and we'll meet the neighbors. There are so many places I want to take you."

"I'll only be there for a few days," Jenna reminded her, wondering if anything about the trip was going to make her feel trapped. "And I'll be back. I don't have to see it all at once."

"I want to make memories," Serenity told her. "As many as we can."

Jenna wasn't sure if that was good or bad. Or just a little bit scary.

"I've worked out a schedule with Violet," she said. "The store will be covered."

"Are you worried?"

"Not really. I completely trust Violet and we have the part-time help. My mom will come in every day." Jenna chuckled. "I know her. She'll hover, filling in wherever she's needed."

Serenity's expression tightened slightly. It was only a faint pulling around the eyes and mouth, but Jenna caught it.

"She's very good to you," Serenity said.

The words were right but without emotion.

Jenna went over what she'd said, trying to find the place that had upset Serenity. Was it that she called Beth Mom? Beth *was* her mother in every sense of the word. Now that Serenity had come back into Jenna's life, did she expect that to change?

Jenna excused herself to help a customer. A few minutes later, Serenity said she was going back to the apartment to pack.

Jenna handled the customer, then reached for the ringing phone. "Grate Expectations."

"Jenna Stevens please."

"I'm Jenna."

"Oh, wonderful. My name is Tara Peters. I'm a book editor in New York. I specialize in cookbooks."

Jenna was confused by the call. "Do you want us to carry more of your books?" she asked, not sure it was an editor's job to promote sales.

Tara laughed. "That would be nice but it's not why I'm calling. I just got back from an intriguing trip to Los Angeles. I met someone I think you know. Aaron Candellano."

"I think we've met," Jenna said drily.

"Don't worry. I have an ex-husband, too. On my good days I only want his legs broken. Aaron's been working with my assistant. He pitched a cookbook to us and we were interested. We have a relationship with the Food Network and were considering him for the show. However, it seems he's not the creative genius we first thought. On my trip I found out very quickly Aaron is all flash. From what several people told me, you were the creative energy in the relationship."

Jenna sank down onto the stool behind the cash register. She heard a faint buzzing sound and told herself this was a really stupid time to faint.

"Someone said that?"

"More than one person. In fact, the only employees I could find who liked Aaron were the ones sleeping with him. If I flew to Texas next month, could we talk?"

"About what?"

Tara laughed again. Jenna was starting to like the sound. "About a potential book deal and perhaps a show. I understand you have a store in Georgetown. From what I saw of it on your website, I think it would be a great backdrop for filming."

"I, ah…" She sucked in air. A cookbook deal? A show? Her? "We could talk," she managed to say. "Sure."

"Great. I'll be in touch in a couple of weeks. Oh, and Jenna? It's none of my business, but I think you're better off without him."

With that, the New York editor hung up.

Jenna slowly replaced the receiver. It was Violet's day off. Tiffany, a pretty, bright, blonde business major at Southwestern University, efficiently handled the few late-morning customers, leaving Jenna free to blink and breathe and wonder if she'd imagined the whole thing.

When Beth showed up a little before noon, she was grateful to have her to talk to.

"How are things?" her mother asked, then frowned. "What happened? Did Serenity do something?"

"No. It's good, I think. Weird, but good. I got a call."

Jenna told her about the short but unbelievable conversation she'd had with Tara Peters.

"She wants to come here and talk to me. She thinks Aaron is all flash." Jenna couldn't explain how validated she felt without admitting to her mother how broken she'd been when she'd returned from L.A.

"I love smart women," Beth told her. "Good for you. This is great. You're going to write a cookbook and people everywhere are going to know how amazing you are. You are so talented."

Beth hugged her.

Jenna held on, appreciating the familiar sense of love that washed over her.

Beth straightened. "You know Serenity is going to take credit for this," she said with a sigh.

"How can she?"

"You get your creativity from her."

"I guess. There's plenty of cooking on her side of the family tree."

"Something to talk about when you go visit."

Jenna touched her arm. "Mom, are you okay with me going to California?"

"Of course. It's important for you to get to know them. Aren't you excited about the trip?"

"In a cautious way. Serenity wants to cram everything into a five-day visit. I'm more in the 'let's take it slow' camp."

"She wants to make up for lost time."

"That's what she said." Jenna paused, wondering how much it was safe to share.

Her mother smiled. "It's all right. I know the two of you

talk. I know you're developing a relationship. I think that's a good thing. If you'll remember, it was my idea."

Jenna decided to take her at her word. "We're getting along. She's not as strange as I first thought, so that's good. And you're right—we do have things in common. Biology can't be denied. The cooking seems to come from her side of the family. I want to meet Wolf and his wife and see the winery. But I don't know what to say when she talks about feeling guilty about giving me up for adoption. I'm happy she did."

"Is that what she said?"

"Yes. I think she regrets it. She was talking about how she should have fought her parents more and kept me for herself."

Beth pressed her lips together. "She has other children. Isn't that enough?"

"Apparently not. She mentioned that she wanted to have even more kids but couldn't get past the guilt."

"Oh, please," Beth snapped. "She was irresponsible as a teenager and got pregnant. It's been happening since the beginning of time. She gave up her child for adoption and got on with her life. Doesn't this all strike you as dramatic? Just another bid for attention?"

Jenna stared at her mother. "What do you mean?"

"Serenity is quite the drama queen. Everything is about her. Haven't you noticed that every conversation is about her feelings or her holistic ways or her connection with the universe?" Beth used her fingers to make air quotes around the last word.

"She never talks about anything that isn't directly related to her," her mother continued. "She doesn't ask about anyone else. She's myopic and narcissistic."

Jenna was stunned. "You really don't like her. I thought you did. I thought you two were getting along."

"She's fine, in her own way," Beth said grudgingly. "As long as you don't mind only talking about her. And that's not even what bothers me. What pisses me off is her assumption that you would have been better off with her."

"She didn't say that."

"It's implied in her guilt. As if she'd left you at the side of the road. What is there to be guilty about? You were loved and nurtured every second of your life. Is she saying she could have done it better? That we were lousy parents?"

"I don't think it was about you at all," Jenna said slowly, feeling odd about having to defend Serenity.

"Of course not—because that would mean thinking about someone other than herself." Beth shook her head. "She's good, I'll give her that. She's managed to weasel her way into every corner of your life. She even picked your boyfriend."

"It wasn't like that."

"Really?"

"You wanted me to get to know her." Jenna couldn't figure out what they were fighting about.

"I know and I still stand by that." She sighed. "She's just so damned annoying. Now you're going off to see the winery they named after you. If you were so precious to them, why didn't they get in touch with you before? Why didn't they contact us when you were younger?"

Jenna had wondered the same thing herself but not with Beth's energy. This probably wasn't the time to admit she'd started to like Serenity and appreciate having her around. Watching the vegan classes had opened her eyes to cooking possibilities. She couldn't deny that Serenity had inspired her in some important ways.

"Do you not want me to go to California?"

Her mother took a deep breath. "Of course you have to go. It's important that you see whatever it is they want you to see." She looked at her. "I'm fine. Most of the time I can deal with her but every now and then she rubs me the wrong way. Like I said, it's the drama thing." Beth paused and looked down. "You've been the center of my world so long, it's difficult to share."

"Finally," Jenna said, putting her hands on her hips. "All this time I've been telling you the whole thing is strange and you've been pushing me toward them. It took you long enough to feel threatened."

Beth laughed. "Well, I am. I know it's irrational, but I can't help it."

"Mom." Jenna hugged her. "I love you so much. I'm not going anywhere."

"You're going back to California. You might adore it and want to stay there again."

"Different circumstances, I swear." She paused. "As for Ellington, Serenity didn't pick him. She introduced us."

"A subtle difference. You weren't interested in meeting anyone I mentioned."

Jenna winced when she realized her mother was right. "I will. When I get back you can set me up to your heart's content."

"I thought you liked the naturopath."

"I do."

"So why would you want to go out with anyone else?" She shifted her handbag over her shoulder. "It doesn't matter. I want you to be happy. That's the most important thing." She glanced at her watch. "I need to run. I'm getting all my errands out of the way so I can stop by the store every day and get in Violet's way."

"You won't be in her way."

Beth ignored that. "You're leaving day after tomorrow?"

"Yes."

"Give us a call when you arrive."

"I will." She hugged her mother again. "It's only for five days."

"I know. I'm happy you're going. Really. You'll have a wonderful time."

The words were right, as was the tone, but pain darkened her mother's eyes and something that might have been fear.

Jenna watched her leave, then rubbed her forehead. Nothing about this was turning out how she'd planned. The last thing she'd wanted to do was hurt Beth. Ironically, she was only going because her mother had suggested she give Serenity a chance.

Relationships were complicated, she reminded herself as she turned to answer a customer's question. Complicated and unpredictable.

Tiffany left at five, so Jenna was alone as she shut down for the day. After locking the front door, she closed out the cash register, then started stocking shelves. She wanted to leave the store in good shape when Violet arrived the following morning. She was just about to turn off the lights and head out the back when she heard a knock on the front door.

Why people couldn't read a Closed sign was beyond her, but it happened more often than not, she thought as she crossed to the front of the store. But instead of a customer, she saw a familiar dark-haired man. He was only a couple of inches taller than her and slim. When he saw her, he flashed a smile that used to have the power to bring her to her knees.

Yesterday she would have been terrified to see him again, worried about what he would say and how he could hurt her.

It was amazing what a short phone call could do to change a woman's perspective.

She opened the door and smiled. "Hello, Aaron."

"Sweet Cheeks," he said, sweeping into her store and lightly kissing her. "You look great. And this store. Amazing. How are you? I've been thinking about you, so I decided to stop by and see how you're doing."

"L.A. is about twelve hundred miles away."

He gave her his best smile, the sexy, slightly lazy one that had always made her want to push him down on the kitchen table. Now she saw the smile for what it was—an act.

"I miss you, Jenna. More than I thought I would. I miss us."

"Really? You haven't called. Oh, wait. I take it back. You did call to tell me that someone you'd never met was trying to find me. You gave out my personal information. That was nice."

"It wasn't bad, was it?" he asked, sounding horrified. "God, did someone try to hurt you?"

"No. It was fine. So why are you here?"

He drew in a deep breath and took both her hands in his. "Let's go have dinner. Or we can stop by a store and pick up some ingredients. We'll cook together. I miss that, Jenna. Us cooking, side by side. You were always so brilliant."

"Um, I don't think so."

He blinked in surprise. She could almost hear him thinking, "But hey. It's *me*."

"Don't you want to spend time with me?" he asked, sounding more petulant than sexy.

"Not really."

"But we have things to talk about. Jenna, you can't be happy here. A store? Really? Your heart and soul belong in a kitchen. We did so much together. I hated it when you left."

She pulled her hands free of his. "Hated it? You told me you'd never been faithful and that I was holding you back."

"I was drunk."

"It was ten in the morning, Aaron."

She knew she could let him keep talking, get her pound of flesh, so to speak. Or she could be mature and tell him he was too late. It was the mature thing to do.

Besides, being mature was going to feel really good.

"You don't have to pretend," she told him. "Tara Peters already called me."

He stiffened, then relaxed into a smile. "Did she? Good. Then you know about her idea for us to work together. I think it's great."

"No, that's not really what she said. She's interested in working with me, but she didn't seem that impressed by you."

The friendly facade slipped. "What the hell did you tell her?"

"Nothing. She was doing all the talking. Oh, wait. I said yes."

He glared at her. "I never thought you would play the bitter ex."

She felt happy and free and filled with possibilities. "That would make me a bitter woman with a book contract, Aaron. You probably want to leave now."

He started to speak, but she didn't stay to listen. Instead, she walked to the front door and held it open. "Have a safe trip home."

He stalked past her, then turned. "You're nothing without me. This store is ridiculous. It can't possibly support a book deal."

She stared at him, wondering what she'd ever seen in him and why she'd ever thought his opinion mattered.

"You know the best part?" she told him. "I don't even care if the book thing works out or not. I'm happy here, Aaron. I've made it work and you can't take that away from me."

He was still sputtering when she closed and locked the door.

As she turned out the lights and walked into the back to collect her purse, she had to ask herself why she'd thought he was so special. She'd finally figured out she'd been wrong about him.

Fifteen

"I'm sorry," Ellington said, sounding frazzled. "Isaiah picked up this stomach bug somewhere and now my mom has it. He's finally feeling better, but she's worse and I can't get away."

"I understand," Jenna said, keeping the disappointment from her voice. She and Ellington had been planning an evening together before she left for California.

"Do you?" he asked. "I'm sorry I won't be able to see you."

She smiled. "I'm sorry, too. Anything I can do?"

"No, but thanks for offering. The pediatrician said he would be okay to go to school tomorrow. Now I just have to keep my mom hydrated."

"You take your son to a pediatrician?"

Ellington chuckled. The sound was both weary and amused. "Sure. There are a whole lot of laws about doctors treating their own family members. Plus kids aren't my specialty."

"But you've given him tree bark or whatever it is you'd prescribe."

"Are you mocking me?"

"I've heard tree bark is very helpful."

"It is, but you're mocking me."

"Maybe a little."

"Nice. I like a little mocking now and then." He paused and she heard muffled conversation. "Sorry, I gotta run. Call me while you're gone?"

"Promise."

"Good. Talk to you soon."

She hung up and glanced at the clock, then wondered what she was supposed to do with the rest of her evening. She'd already packed and had been planning to spend the time with a certain handsome doctor.

She felt badly that he'd been having to deal with a sick kid and now a sick mother. If it was anything but tummy trouble, she would have taken over food. But with a stomach issue, it was best to leave the special dishes for another time. There were—

She sat up straight as she remembered Ellington saying something about a bake sale. Wasn't that this week?

Five minutes later she'd logged on to his son's elementary school and saw that the bake sale was tomorrow.

It was close to nine-thirty when she stopped in front of her garage. She pulled out her cell phone and dialed Ellington.

"Hello?"

"It's me," she said. "Hope I'm not disturbing you."

"Both patients are sleeping. Isaiah's energy is back, which is both good and bad, and my mom's improving."

"I'm glad. Did you remember that tomorrow is the bake sale?"

There was a second of silence, followed by a lot of swearing.

She held in a laugh. "I'll take that as a no. It's okay. Go look on your front porch. I'll wait."

"What are you talking about?"

"Go look."

She heard him open the front door.

"You didn't," he said. "Jenna, I don't know what to say."

"Be careful when you pick it up. Then look inside."

"I need to put the phone down."

"I'll wait."

A moment later he was back. "I can't believe you made these."

She smiled, picturing the cupcakes she'd baked, then decorated to look like a bright gold C3PO from *Star Wars*. "My homage to your obsession. I hope Isaiah likes them."

"He's going to love them. That was very thoughtful." He cleared his throat. "Thank you."

"You're welcome."

"I'm going to miss you."

She leaned back in her seat. "Then my work here is done." She heard him laugh.

"I'm going to miss you, too," she admitted.

"Then we have that in common."

"I'll call you while I'm gone," she promised.

"I look forward to that and seeing you when you get home."

"Night, Ellington."

"Good night."

Dragon was waiting at the San Francisco airport, looking as tall and handsome as she remembered. Several women eyed him as he took Jenna's suitcase.

"Do you get that everywhere?" she asked as they hugged. "The female attention."

"Everyone suffers," he said with a grin. "I bear my pain as best I can."

She laughed. "Thanks for picking me up."

"You're welcome. I'm part of the entertainment for the weekend, so you're not getting rid of me. Mom and Dad got in late last night. Rather than make them take the drive again, I said I'd bring you."

They walked to his car—a silver BMW 550i—and she watched as he put her suitcase in the trunk.

"I'll warn you my parents have the entire visit planned down to the second. There's going to be plenty of eating and drinking. While I don't object to the drinking part, I was thinking we could stop and get a burger on our way out of town."

He looked so hopeful as he spoke that she had to laugh.

"That sounds great," she told him.

"It won't be up to your excellent standards. I'm still dreaming about that dinner you fixed for me."

"Next time you're in town, I'll make you something else."

"Promise?" he asked, holding open the passenger door for her.

She made an X over her left breast. "I swear."

They stopped at a diner with big windows and comfy booths. They both asked for burgers with the works, an order of fries and an order of onion rings to share. Dragon pulled two small disposable toothbrushes out of his shirt pocket and waved them.

"For after," he said. "Mom can smell meat on my breath from a mile away. When I was a kid, I tried chewing grass to disguise what I'd been eating, but it never worked."

She stared at him. "You're what? Thirty? A successful attorney who has his own life. Can't you simply tell her this is your choice and to lay off you?"

He scrunched his face and shook his head. "I don't think so. When was the last time you really stood up to your mother? How did that work for you?"

"Good point."

Dragon sighed. "I'm saying it all wrong. Mom is great. I joke about her, but seriously, she couldn't have been more supportive. Maybe I didn't always love the food, but there was lots of freedom at our house. There were just enough rules to keep us safe, but otherwise, we got to do what we wanted. I knew whatever happened, whatever I chose, she would be there for me."

"I've heard Serenity talk about you and Wolf. It's obvious how much she loves you both."

"We love her and Dad just as much."

The waitress brought their sodas.

"I'm looking forward to seeing the family home," Jenna said. "From what I've heard, it's beautiful."

"You'll like it. It's big and bright, with lots of windows. Nearly all the materials are recycled, which gives the place a lot of character." He grinned. "Wolf is just like Mom and Dad. Totally organic, vegan."

"I heard Jasmine weaves her own cloth."

"Oh, yeah. She's currently weaving diapers from organic, unbleached cotton. She's sweet enough, but not my style." His gaze sharpened slightly. "How's Violet?"

"Still seeing Cliff."

"Bummer. Let me know if they break up."

While she kind of liked the idea of Violet dating her brother, it wasn't what she would call a practical relationship. "You live a thousand miles from her."

"For the right motivation, I could move."

She raised her eyebrows. "That's a long way to go to get laid."

He fell back in the booth, his hands spread across his chest. "You wound me. I'm a good guy."

"You're a hound dog. You sleep with women because you can."

"I'm looking to change. I'm older now." He grinned. "Not as old as you, of course."

"Of course."

"I liked her."

"If you tell me the universe said she was the one, I'm not sharing my onion rings with you."

"The universe and I don't talk much. I just liked Violet. I want to get to know her better. I could get a temporary assignment in Austin and see where things went."

Which all sounded nice, but as much as she liked Dragon, she couldn't help wondering if he was all flash and no substance.

"Have you ever been in a serious relationship?" she asked.

He sighed. "Once. College. She was brilliant. My age, but in a master's program. I was crazy about her. But I was eighteen, newly freed from parental restrictions. My big plan was to finish my freshman year with decent grades. She was graduating and heading off to Europe to work for NATO. I couldn't be what she needed. She married a Swedish prince or something."

She stared at him. "Is any part of your story true?"

"The broken heart part is. Since then I haven't met anyone who intrigues me. Until Violet. Mom says that there is more than one right someone for each of us and not to give up hope."

"I hope she's right about that," Jenna murmured. "Although she and Tom have been together since high school."

"Not everyone gets that lucky." He grinned. "She's fixed me up a few times and the relationships have gone surprisingly well."

Something Jenna could relate to. Ellington had been Serenity's idea. Still...

"If you're serious about Violet, you're putting a lot on a thirty-second conversation."

"I'm a romantic."

She laughed. "While I wouldn't change a thing about my past, I have to say, it would have been fun to grow up with you as a brother."

He winked.

After they'd finished their lunch and brushed their teeth, they got back on the road. Dragon kept Jenna entertained with stories about growing up. Tales of recycling experiments gone wrong and the cow Serenity had bought to provide milk, only to have it get loose in her spring garden and eat everything back to the dirt.

"The winery itself has some old vines, which gave my folks a place to start," he said as he followed the signs pointing to Napa. "They didn't have the usual downtime waiting for the vines to mature. Mom made different kinds of crafts to supplement the money coming in. We lived pretty simply."

"No TV?"

"We had TV. They thought it was good for us to experience the world, and television brought the world to us."

"The original house on the property is now the tasting room," he continued. "Dad, Wolf and I built our house ourselves, with a little help from local contractors. Like I said, nearly everything is recycled, repurposed or reused. She did want new appliances, though."

"I've seen a couple of great stoves from decades ago," Jenna said, remembering a white monster with three different ovens in a friend's house in Los Angeles. "They're beautiful, but not always practical."

"The kitchen is Mom's pride and joy, so you'll get points for noticing." He glanced at her. "Not that you need the points."

Jenna turned to him. "When did you know about me?"

He shrugged. "Always. I can't remember when I didn't. They would talk about you now and then. Our big sister. When I was little, I would ask when I would get to meet you."

"What did they say?"

"When the time was right you would come to us."

The information only confused her more. "Why would they talk about me, make me real to you, and do nothing about it? What if I'd never wanted to find them? I mean, you."

He kept his eyes on the road. "If you're looking for logic, you've come to the wrong place. Mom lives by her own rules. I never knew what she was waiting for and now…"

"Now, what?" Jenna asked.

"Now's when she decided it was time for her to find you." He flashed her a smile. "The universe doesn't check in with me."

"Me, either," Jenna said, staring out the side window.

It wasn't that she *wanted* her birth parents to have shown up sooner, exactly. But an explanation would be nice.

"Families are complicated," she murmured.

"Yes, they are."

They drove around vineyards and small towns. The sky was blue, the grape leaves a vivid green in neat rows that stretched out for miles. As Dragon signaled a right turn, she saw the sign pointing toward Butterfly Wines.

She found herself wishing she'd brought someone with her for a little moral support. Ellington, she thought wistfully. He would be fun to travel with.

Her hamburger sat heavily in her stomach, making her wonder if eating it had been the smart thing to do. Not that she had anything to be nervous about. She already knew Serenity, Tom and Dragon. She only had Wolf and his wife left to meet.

"Wolf doesn't resent me, does he?" she asked, trying not to sound anxious.

Dragon patted the back of her hand. "No. Don't sweat it. We're family. Everybody here wants you here." He flashed another smile. "Trust me."

They drove past the beautiful old farmhouse that was now the tasting room, continuing down a road with a sign declaring it "Private."

They dipped down into a valley. The vineyards stretched out on either side, as far as the eye could see. After a couple more curves, she could see a two-story house sitting on a slight rise.

"You didn't say it was a log cabin," she breathed, taking in the huge house, the wraparound porch and the flowers blooming from pots and planters.

"It's sixty-five-hundred square feet. Hardly a cabin."

She turned to him. "You said you built it with your dad. You can't have built a house this big."

"I said we had help."

She laughed. "What exactly did you do?"

"I hung a door."

She was still laughing when he pulled up in front of the house and parked. Before she could do much more than climb out of the car, Serenity had burst through the front door and hurried toward her.

"You're here," her birth mother said, rushing toward her, arms held open wide. "You're finally here."

As Serenity embraced her, holding on as if she would never let go, Jenna realized the "finally here" comment wasn't about the fact that Serenity and Tom had flown in the night before. It was the relief of a mother who had been waiting thirty-two years for her child to come home.

Jenna didn't know what to do with that information. She hugged Serenity back, hoping the contact was enough and that words weren't required.

Tom joined them, smiling broadly. When they both stepped back, Jenna saw a tall, thin redheaded man standing next to a petite blonde with a very big belly.

Serenity wrapped her arm around Jenna's waist and propelled her toward the stairs.

"This is Wolf and his wife Jasmine."

Jenna climbed the stairs. "Nice to meet you," she said, facing another stranger who was her brother.

Wolf stared at her. He looked much more like Serenity than Tom, but he had his father's quiet strength. His gaze appraised her with such solemnity that she started to feel guilty. Not just about the burger but on general principal. She had a momentary flash of sympathy for his yet-to-be-born child.

She braced herself for some accusation only to watch as Wolf's eyes filled with tears. He lunged at her, wrapping both his arms around her.

"I've missed you so much," he breathed.

Jenna stood stiffly, her arms trapped at her sides. She appreciated the sentiment, but how could he miss someone he'd never met?

"I knew it would be like this," Serenity said, then joined the embrace.

"Group hug," Dragon called.

Jenna found herself in the middle of a family moment. She could feel the love flowing around her and did her best to let it inside of her. But all she felt was a little weird and uncomfortable.

When everyone had stepped back, Wolf wrapped his arm around his wife.

"This is Jasmine."

"Nice to meet you," Jenna said, half holding out her hand, half pulling it back at the same time.

"Oh, Jenna."

The very pregnant woman lunged at her, gripping her in a surprisingly strong embrace.

"I'm so happy we're finally really sisters," Jasmine whispered.

"Ah, me, too."

"All right, break it up," Dragon said. "It's too much like girl-on-girl porn. Seeing as you're both relatives, that's just gross."

Jenna stepped back. "You're all making me feel so welcome. Thank you."

"It's what we've always wanted," Serenity told her, then linked arms with her. "Please. Come inside."

Jenna let herself be led into the house.

The foyer was open to the second floor, with a catwalk stretching between each side of the house. She could see all the way through to the back of the living room where floor to ceiling windows seemed to draw the outdoors in.

The furniture was more rustic than contemporary—big pieces framed in wood with brightly colored fabrics. To the left was a dining room with beautiful arched windows accented with stained glass.

"Dragon, you take Jenna's bag up to her room," Serenity said. "We're going to go into the kitchen and have a little girl time."

Jenna would rather have gone with her bag and freshened up, but she followed Serenity to the other end of the house.

They passed the formal dining room with a table big enough to seat twenty, then went into a huge kitchen. There was an eight-burner stove, triple ovens, two warming drawers, more cabinet space than in a showroom and a big butcher block table that easily seated ten.

"The cabinets are from an old hotel," Serenity said, touching the one closest to her. "We had them refinished. The countertop is a mixture of materials."

Jenna turned around and saw granite on the island, a few sections of wood, some stainless and what looked like poured concrete. What should have been a mess looked comfortable and perfectly at home in the huge space.

Windows looked out onto a massive garden. She could see a couple of goats in the distance, along with something that looked like a llama or an alpaca.

Serenity followed her gaze. "We use the goats for their milk and the alpaca fibers for knitting. In the barn, I make cheese." She smiled. "To sell. We don't really eat it. Well, maybe every now and then."

"I'm shocked."

Serenity laughed. "Everyone gets to be bad occasionally. Come on."

They went out the back door to where a couple of golf carts were plugged into charging stations. Jenna slipped into the passenger side of the one Serenity pointed to. Serenity unplugged it, then got behind the wheel.

"I thought we'd take a quick tour of the place before we start dinner," Serenity said as they took off down a dirt path toward the vineyards.

"Tom and I bought this place when we were still in our twenties. We had a clear vision for what we wanted. Land was still relatively cheap, so we added on when we could." She smiled as they bounced along. "However, making wine is an art form we've never truly mastered. We bottle about eight or nine hundred cases a year, but most of the grapes are bought by several of the big wineries in the area. It makes what we do more profitable."

She drove around the merlot grapes, then turned left to head past the old house that had been converted to the tasting room.

"We'll go there tomorrow," Serenity said. "They do a very nice lunch at the tasting room. And some of the new releases are impressive. Wolf seems to have more ability when it comes to making wine than either Tom or I do." She sighed. "I wish Dragon had been interested in being a part of this."

Jenna thought about all her brother had told her. "I think his course was set a while ago."

"You're probably right. He was his own person, even before he was born. I could tell."

Jenna pressed her lips together to keep from asking how. She'd grown used to Serenity's unusual ways and could even appreciate some of them. Instead she focused on the clear blue sky, the warm breeze and the beauty of the landscape around them.

"We're working on new labels for the winery," Serenity told her as they parked in the shade and stared out at the rolling hills covered in grapevines. "We're going to be looking at designs while you're here. I'd love your input."

"It's not for me to say," Jenna protested automatically.

"You're family."

She smiled rather than answer that. Technically, she was family. A biological member—full sibling to Wolf and Dragon. But DNA aside, she didn't exactly feel that she belonged.

"Are you all right?" her birth mother asked.

"Just a little tired from the travel."

"I'll take you back so you can rest before dinner."

Jenna's room was as beautiful as the rest of the house. Big, with high ceilings and east-facing windows with more views of vineyards. The only strange touch was the butterfly motif. There were butterflies on the bedspread and several carved butterflies on the dresser.

After showering in the attached private bath, she changed her clothes and made a brief call to Violet, who assured her all was well at the store. She'd barely hung up when someone knocked on her door.

She opened it to find Dragon lounging against the door frame.

"Are you my unofficial guide?" she asked, her voice teasing.

He grinned. "I'm the closest this family has to normal, so yes. I'm here to introduce you to all the idiosyncrasies you can imagine and some you can't. Tonight, we're having Mexican. Fajitas."

"I love fajitas."

"This is different."

"How?"

He raised his eyebrows.

She ran through the list of traditional ingredients. "Oh."

He guided her to the stairs. "Exactly. Tonight, the role of meat will be played by portabella mushrooms. The cheese is sadly absent. However, there are fresh ingredients, guacamole that will make you find religion, and my very sweet, one hundred percent natural sister-in-law makes a killer margarita. I suggest we get drunk and count the hours until we can eat chicken again."

She laughed. "Deal."

"Good. Because I've already planned our route back to the airport, and there's this great little place that makes Southern fried chicken and biscuits you're not going to believe."

They walked into the kitchen to find everyone was already there.

"Feeling better?" Serenity asked.

"Yes, I am. Thanks."

"Good. We saved you some peppers to chop." Serenity turned to Jasmine and Wolf. "Your sister is a master with a knife."

"A good reason not to piss her off," Dragon said, grabbing at a tortilla and getting his hand slapped by his mother.

Jenna washed her hands and went to the cutting board where several red, green and yellow peppers were waiting, along with serrano chilies. Tom stood over a big pot of beans, while Serenity doctored rice.

As Dragon had promised, Jasmine took control of a professional-size blender and began making margaritas while Wolf made guacamole and Dragon set the table.

Fifties music played from hidden speakers. The sun sank lower in the sky, sending streamers of light through the windows.

As everyone worked, they talked about their day, the winery, what was happening locally. Wolf brought them up-to-date on what had been going on in the vineyards. Jenna didn't understand all the technical terms about growing and thinning and production, but she was able to follow the main concepts.

Jasmine passed out large glasses rimmed with salt and filled with slushy light green mix. She picked up a glass of lime juice over sparkling water and held it up with everyone else.

"To Jenna," Tom said, smiling at her. "Daughter and sister. Missing from our lives until now. Welcome home."

Echoes of "welcome home" filled the kitchen.

Jenna smiled and accepted the toast, then took a drink. Work resumed on the dinner. She showed Jasmine how to safely cut chilies without getting the juice on her hands and tasted Tom's famous beans. Wolf caught her in an impromptu hug, and Serenity and Dragon danced to "Rock Around the Clock."

As the sun slowly set, someone turned on the lights. Jenna leaned against the counter and watched, not exactly sure where she fit in, but knowing being here now was starting to feel more right.

Sixteen

"I love the responsibility," Violet said. "Running the store. It's great."

"You're doing good work," Cliff told her, the words right, but his expression more tense than happy.

They were sitting at her small dining room table, having dinner together in her apartment. Since Jenna left, Violet hadn't had as much free time, but as always, Cliff had been understanding. Or so she'd thought. He'd been acting strange tonight.

"I wasn't even looking to change jobs, but when I saw Jenna's ad, something inside of me said I needed to go there and talk to her. Do you ever get that? A feeling in your gut?"

Cliff stared at her without answering.

She raised her eyebrows. "Are you still with me?"

He shrugged. "I was thinking about something else. So is all of Jenna's family with her in Napa?"

"Her whole birth family."

"Even Dragon?"

Violet couldn't remember if she'd mentioned Jenna's brother. "Yes. He's there. Why?"

"He sent you a text message."

Her first instinct was to get pissed that Cliff had looked at her phone. Then she reminded herself that they were in a relationship and that she'd been the one to leave her phone out on the counter. Mostly so she could grab it in case Jenna called to ask about the store.

"He wanted to know how you were doing," Cliff continued, something flashing in his eyes. "So you're seeing him?"

"I'm not. I've met him and he's nice enough, but he lives in San Francisco."

The second she said it, she knew it was wrong. "Not that I would be interested in him if he was here."

Cliff stared at her for a long time, then returned his attention to his dinner.

Silence filled the room.

She felt guilty, even though she hadn't done anything wrong, and a little annoyed.

She stood and walked around to his chair. After taking his hand in hers, she pulled him to his feet.

"I'm not seeing Dragon," she said. "He's my boss's brother."

"He texted you."

He was jealous and insecure. If the situation were reversed, she would probably feel the same way.

"He can text all he wants," she told him. "I'm unavailable."

Cliff studied her for several seconds, then he lowered his mouth to hers.

She wrapped her arms around his neck and gave herself over to his kisses.

They were making progress, she thought as she parted her lips. Every time they were together, she felt a little bit more. It was as if her body was awakening, inch by inch. Last time they'd made love, she'd actually become aroused and had been eager for him to be inside of her.

Sometimes she thought about telling Cliff the truth. That sex was more difficult for her because of her past. That she held back and it took a lot for her to trust enough to let go. She wanted to be honest—to have all the barriers between them gone—but she wasn't ready. Probably because she knew her past would be a game-changer. Once he knew the truth, he would be gone.

She'd tried to tell herself that a man who wouldn't accept all of her wasn't worth having. But then she thought about how nice he was, how he was so different from anyone she'd ever gone out with, and she put it off for a while longer. But soon, she thought.

He kissed his way down her neck. She wore a T-shirt over jeans. Her feet were bare. When he drew the T-shirt over her head and lightly touched her breasts, she felt an actual shiver.

Nice, she thought hazily. This was nice.

He kissed her neck again, moved down to her collarbone, then lower to the top of her breast. When he reached the curve, she snuggled close in anticipation of his soft, wet kiss. Instead she felt the sharp pain of his teeth.

"What?" she yelped and jumped back.

"You okay, baby?"

Cliff looked so normal, so much like he always did, that at first she couldn't figure out what was wrong. She glanced down and saw he'd bitten her hard enough to break the skin. She saw the clear indentation of his teeth and blood seeping up through the broken skin.

"What was that?" she demanded.

"Don't you like it?"

His voice and demeanor were so at odds with his behavior, that she couldn't understand what was happening.

"You want me to do it again?" he asked, still speaking softly, warmly.

She reached for her T-shirt and started to pull it on.

He ripped it out of her hands. She never saw him raise his fist. The next thing she knew, light and pain exploded in her cheek.

Instinctively she turned away, but she wasn't fast enough. She could see the front door, her purse with her cell phone. If she could get to either.

But she didn't have a chance. He hit her face again.

"Whore," he whispered into her ear. "You think I didn't know? That I wouldn't find out? I had a friend check up on you. He called me today and said that someone with your name was arrested in New Orleans for solicitation. I told myself it wasn't you, but then I saw that text message and I knew what you were. What you'd always be."

Violet cried out. "Stop!" she screamed. "Stop it now!"

She'd been beaten up twice before in her life—both times while she was still on the streets. Back then she'd been high and that had helped to dull the pain. Now she felt the sting of the smack, the blood and loosened teeth of his punch.

Cliff raised his arm again. She ducked, determined not to be hit. But somehow she slipped and then she was falling. The side of her head hit the coffee table.

Agony exploded. She felt the hot wetness of blood. She couldn't seem to catch her breath, she thought as she went down on her knees.

Survive, she told herself, wishing the high-pitched scream-ing would stop. Stay alive.

Someone pounded on her front door. "What's going on in there?"

She recognized the voice of her elderly male neighbor. Mr. McAllister was maybe a hundred-and-thirty pounds and used a cane.

I'm fine.

Violet meant to say the words, but they wouldn't come out. It was only then she realized that she was the one screaming and she didn't know how to stop.

Blood filled her mouth from the cut on her head, and she vomited.

Her front door opened. She heard Mr. McAllister demand, "Who are you? What were you doing to Violet?" then the sound of hurried footsteps on the stairs.

She allowed herself to fall to the carpet. As she hit, the room went blurry. She struggled to stay conscious.

Someone moved past her. She heard a voice saying something about a beating and giving an address. Mr. McAllister, she thought, slipping away. She would have to thank him later.

The police officer's gaze was both sympathetic and unsurprised. Violet knew she saw this kind of thing all the time. You didn't have to be poor or unemployed to be abused.

Violet did her best to stay very, very still. Her head throbbed with a pain she'd never felt before. The nurse had promised to return and hook up the IV as soon as they confirmed her head injury wasn't serious. There was also the issue of her swollen jaw, black eyes and assorted other bruises from the fall.

Things would be better soon, she told herself. As soon as the pain medication hit her system, everything would be better.

"We're going to find him," the officer said. "He'll be charged."

Violet nodded slightly.

"Charged is good," she said, knowing it wouldn't matter at all. He would post bond and be back out on the streets. Probably looking for her. A restraining order was only a technical aid. It wouldn't physically keep him from coming after her.

There had to be others, she thought sadly. He'd snapped too easily, too quickly. She would bet a lot that he'd done this before. Other women out there who had lived through the same. She hoped the police found out if he had.

As usual, her gut had been no help. But when compared to what he'd done to her, the losers she usually gravitated toward were actually looking pretty good. The obvious solution was to avoid men altogether, she told herself. To just accept that she was alone and go with it. She just hoped she wasn't going to have to leave Georgetown to get away from him.

She closed her eyes and told herself that in a few days she would feel better. That her body would heal. She was less sure about the rest of her, though. That would take longer.

The nurse returned. "We'll be keeping you tonight for observation, but as of now, all indications are that you're going to be just fine. You've got a big bump though." He hooked up the IV and offered something to eat.

"I'm not hungry," Violet told the male nurse, who looked concerned. "I'm fine."

"Does it bother you that I'm a man?" he asked. "Do you want me to switch you to one of the other nurses?"

Unexpected tears filled her eyes. She wasn't prepared for kindness. The last time this had happened, she'd been maybe nineteen and strung out on drugs. She'd been more concerned about getting discharged so she could get high again than thinking about staff or worrying about healing.

Violet looked at the guy. He was maybe five-eight and a hundred-and-fifty pounds. His eyes were soft brown and there were flecks of gray in his blond hair. His wedding ring looked a little battered, as if he'd been wearing it for years.

"I'm not worried. I could take you."

He grinned. "Probably. Try to rest. The pain medication should already be working."

She frowned, then realized the sharpness had faded, leaving behind only dull throbbing.

"It is," she told him. "Thanks."

"I'm going to bring you a sandwich later. If you argue with me about eating it, I'll arm wrestle you."

She caught her breath and winced. Her ribs weren't broken, but they were bruised from where she'd apparently smacked them on the table, as well. "Okay, okay. Just don't make me laugh."

The nurse—his name tag said Henry—touched her hand. "You're safe here, Violet. Try to get some sleep."

"I will."

She waited until he'd walked out, then closed her eyes, only to open them immediately. The fear she didn't want to acknowledge was still there.

She was safe, she reminded herself. Cliff would be in jail for at least the night. When she was discharged, she would figure out where she could go that was safe. A hotel, she thought.

"Violet?"

She looked up and saw Beth standing in the doorway. Jenna's mother looked pale and was obviously trying to stay calm. Violet felt herself flush as shame rushed through her.

Women like Beth didn't deal with situations like this in their normal lives.

"I'm sorry," Violet whispered, dropping her gaze to her hands. "They insisted on contact information and I wasn't thinking. They promised they wouldn't call."

"Don't," Beth whispered, rushing to her side, tears filling her blue eyes. "Oh, Violet, honey. What did he do to you?" The tears slipped down her cheeks.

Violet shook her head. "Don't cry. I'm fine." She winced. "My head hurts is all and I got that from falling."

Beth took her hand and squeezed her fingers. "You're not fine. He hurt you. I talked to Henry. Cliff hit you. That's not supposed to happen. You liked him so much. We went shopping so you could make him happy."

"Not a mistake I'll make again," Violet said. "Really, I'm fine."

"Stop saying that!" Beth sounded furious. "You're not and that bastard is the reason." She brushed the moisture from her cheeks with her free hand. "How bad is it?"

"A lot of bruising."

Beth winced. "Oh, Violet." Her lips quivered, as if she were on the verge of crying again, then she got control. "All right. You're staying here tonight. They'll be letting you out in the morning. I'll be here to pick you up."

"You don't have to." She didn't want to put anyone out.

"I want to. I'm bringing you home. You're staying with us until you're healed. Do you hear me?"

The generous offer bewildered her. "I'll be okay on my own."

"Violet, you need taking care of."

Simple words, spoken as if they were nothing more than a polite response to "How are you?"

"You barely know me."

Beth bent over and kissed Violet's forehead. "I know plenty. You're coming home with us and staying in the guest room."

Violet was about to protest when she remembered. "The store. Jenna. I've let her down."

Beth actually rolled her eyes. "Right. Because you knew Cliff was going to beat you up and you deliberately waited until Jenna was gone just to mess with her. What a great plan."

Despite the pain it would cause, Violet giggled. "Okay. Good point."

"Thank you. Don't worry about the store. Jenna's due back on Tuesday and I can take care of things until then. I'll call Tiffany and Kayla and have them come in extra hours. There weren't any cooking classes scheduled, so that part is easy."

Beth kissed her forehead again. "I need to let you get some rest. Henry was very clear about that. Marshall is going to pop in for a second to say good-night, then we'll be back in the morning to take you home."

"Thank you," Violet whispered. "For everything."

"You're welcome. Try to sleep, honey."

She left, and Marshall stepped into the room. He was big and broad, yet Violet wasn't afraid of him. Not even when he looked so fierce and angry.

"I don't know what to say," the older man admitted as he stood by her bed. "I've never had to deal with anything like this."

"I'll heal," she promised. "It's okay."

"It's many things, but okay isn't one of them." Marshall drew in a breath. "Can I hug you? Would that hurt too much?"

It would probably jostle the hell out of her, but at that second, she didn't much care. "It would be fine."

He bent over and gathered her gently into his arms. She held in the wince as pain seared through her rib cage. He smelled of the night and leather and Scotch, kind of like she'd always imagined a father would smell. His touch was caring and safe. So very safe.

For a second she wondered what her life would have been like if she'd had a father to take care of her. If she'd mattered to someone...anyone.

"We'll be back in the morning," he whispered.

"Thank you."

"We take care of our own, Violet," he told her as he straightened. "For better or worse, you're a part of our family now. There may come a time when you regret that, but you're stuck with us. You hear me?"

She nodded.

"Go to sleep."

The instruction was firm, and Marshall Stevens expected to be obeyed. For once, Violet did as she was told and closed her eyes.

Despite the late hour, Jenna couldn't sleep. She pulled on jeans and a T-shirt and went downstairs. Although she expected to find the great room empty, she saw Tom standing by the window. He looked up when she entered.

"Oh, sorry," she said, coming to a stop. "I didn't mean to intrude."

"You didn't."

He walked toward the large sofa and motioned for her to join him.

"Can't sleep?" he asked.

"Every now and then." Generally one night a month, when she was ovulating. Her doctor had said it was hormonal. Not anything she wanted to share with Tom.

"What about you?"

He shrugged. "I have a lot on my mind." He smiled at her. "Your mom really appreciates you visiting. Having you here means the world to her."

Jenna ignored the "mom" part of the statement. "She's pretty amazing."

"That she is. I knew from the first second I saw her that I was going to love her for the rest of my life." He turned away then and swallowed. "Sorry. Sometimes it feels like I can't hold all the love inside."

"It's nice," Jenna said, wondering if anyone would ever feel that way about her.

"It's inescapable. When we were first together, we were young. Everyone said it wouldn't last."

"They were wrong," Jenna said lightly. "Did you tell them 'I told you so'?"

He chuckled. "I wanted to. Serenity wouldn't let me. She's so giving. So caring."

"She knows how to fill a room." Jenna hesitated. "I've sort of felt you and I haven't gotten to know each other as well."

Tom looked at her. "I've held back. Your relationship with her is the important one. She's an extraordinary woman, Jenna. Knowing her is a blessing."

Which was the oddest response, Jenna thought. Why did everyone keep pushing Serenity to the front of the line? It was as if she was the only one who mattered.

"Dragon told me a little about what it was like to grow up here," she said. "She sounds like she was a great mom."

"Yes, she was. The perfect wife."

He stared out the window. Jenna started to feel as if she were intruding. She excused herself and went back to her room. Only a few more days, she reminded herself. Then she would go home and be back where she belonged.

★ ★ ★

A dozen or so wine labels lay on the kitchen table. The designs were variations on a theme—a wolf, a dragon and a butterfly in some form or another. Next to the different designs were blank labels in different colors. Gold, green, red, blue.

"I like the gold color," Jenna said. "The gradation from pale to dark at the bottom."

"I agree." Serenity sat next to her, holding a mug of tea. "But choosing the design is more complicated."

Jenna did her best to avoid looking at them. The old labels showed a sketch of the original farmhouse, which she really liked. The new drawings, incorporating the animal manifestations of the names, were just too weird.

"Maybe just a new color would be enough," Jenna said. "Rather than changing everything. You want your customers to be able to find you on the shelf."

Serenity tilted her head, her long red hair falling over her left shoulder. "Maybe. I'll talk to Tom about it." She glanced toward the timer. "Would you check the muffins for me? I'm a little tired this morning."

"Sure."

Jenna got up and walked to the top oven. Inside, the blueberry muffins were turning a light, golden brown.

"I don't have your eye for baking," she admitted, "but my guess is another couple of minutes."

Yet another family meal. This time brunch—without eggs, of course. Yesterday she'd seen Wolf and Jasmine's house—a smaller version of the bigger log home that Serenity and Tom lived in. Jasmine had also shown her the baby's room and had tried to teach Jenna how to weave cloth.

From what she could tell, the Johnson family was very close. Dragon had gone off the previous afternoon to visit a couple of his local friends, but otherwise he'd been around. Wolf and Jasmine had spent more time here than at their own place, and Tom was never far out of sight.

It was family intimacy at a new level. Jenna believed it was genuine, but something lurked in the background. Something she couldn't put her finger on.

"I should show you pictures of the boys when they were little," Serenity said when Jenna had returned to sit across from her.

"I'd like that," Jenna said, "but I think it would be more fun when they're in the room to watch."

"Tormenting your brothers?"

Jenna laughed. "Yes. I do like that part of having siblings."

Serenity sighed. "I wish you'd been here when you were little. We missed you so much. I talked about you all the time, trying to make you real to Dragon and Wolf." She paused, her green eyes flashing with humor. "We celebrated your birthday every year."

Which fell under the category of creepy, Jenna thought. "But you never came to find me," she said. "Why? You knew how to find my parents."

Serenity flinched slightly as Jenna said the *P* word. Jenna felt both guilty and defiant. Beth and Marshall *were* her parents. If Serenity had wanted that to be different, she shouldn't have given her up for adoption. It was as if she wanted it both ways—to have the world as it was and to have changed the past.

"Why now?" she asked for maybe the twentieth time.

"There are things we can know right away," Serenity said calmly, "and knowledge that comes with time."

"What does that mean?"

"I always thought it was up to you to come to us. Then that changed. So we came to you."

She spoke so calmly, with such certainty.

Jenna wanted to argue, but knew she couldn't win. This conversation reminded her of being with Jasmine the previous day. She'd asked if Jasmine knew the sex of the baby.

"We're having a boy. Serenity told me."

Jasmine had spoken with the same quiet confidence.

"Did you get that confirmed by an ultrasound?" Jenna had asked.

"Oh, no. Serenity knows those kinds of things."

Jenna refused to believe her birth mother had mystical powers, but did that matter? Life was different here. Maybe she should stop fighting it and simply accept the truth. Accept that they were her family, too.

"I was never sure that Beth and Marshall were the right parents for you," Serenity said unexpectedly. "My parents picked them because I wouldn't make up my mind. I think I was trying to find the courage to keep you myself. Tom and I talked about running away together, but we were so young. And not very brave. But yes, I think that would have been better for you and for us."

The complete dismissal of her parents drove Jenna to her feet. Anger coursed through her. How dare Serenity assume Beth and Marshall had been anything but loving, supportive parents who had given her every advantage and made her feel special and adored?

The timer dinged.

Literally saved by the bell, she thought as she crossed to the oven and pulled out the muffins. She stared blindly at the tray, then shook her head.

Getting annoyed served no purpose. She would only say

things that would make the rest of her visit uncomfortable, and what was the point of that?

She could almost hear Beth's voice in her head telling her that Serenity believed what she had to in order to accept what she'd done. That giving up a child was never easy, regardless of the circumstances or outcome. Serenity's decision had been harder than most because she had married the father of her child and knew that things would have worked out.

Jenna knew Beth would urge her to be compassionate and remind her that she had less than forty-eight hours left until she could get on a plane and head back to her regular life.

She carried the tray of muffins over to Serenity. "What do you think?"

Her birth mother lightly touched one muffin. "Perfect."

Jenna set the pan on the cooling rack, then slipped the second one into the oven. She leaned against the counter and wished her mother was with her now. Beth would enjoy the house and the winery. Her eyes would probably bug out when she saw Jasmine's stack of handwoven diapers, but she wouldn't say anything.

Longing filled Jenna's chest, making her want to speak to her mom and tell her she missed her. Now that she thought about it, the last few weeks had been so busy that she couldn't remember the last time she'd told her she loved her.

The house phone rang. A few seconds later Tom walked into the kitchen.

"Jenna, it's Beth." He handed her the cordless phone.

Maybe the universe really did listen, Jenna thought humorously.

"Hi, Mom."

"Oh, Jenna, I'm sorry to interrupt." Beth's voice trembled.

"What's wrong?"

"It's Violet. I didn't know if I should call or not. She said to wait, but I wasn't sure."

Jenna tightened her grip on the phone. "Tell me! What happened to Violet?"

"Cliff went crazy or something. He beat her up."

If Jenna had eaten anything that morning, she would have thrown it up. Fear gripped her. "How bad?"

"She's all right. A couple of broken teeth. She smacked her head on the table, but she's going to be okay."

"He punched her?"

"He's in jail, at least for twenty-four hours. The hospital released her this morning and we've taken her home to look after her."

"Thank you," she breathed. "She can't be by herself and I know she doesn't have any family." Now that she thought of it, Violet never mentioned any friends. Just people she used to work with.

"I've already called Tiffany and Kayla," her mother continued. "They're coming in tomorrow and Tuesday and I'll work there, as well. So you don't have to worry."

Jenna wasn't concerned about the store. It was her friend who mattered.

"I'm coming back," she said. "As soon as I can get a flight."

She heard a noise behind her, but she didn't turn to look. Right now Violet was who she had to focus on.

"Don't cut your visit short," her mother began.

"Mom, Violet's boyfriend beat her up badly enough to send her to the hospital. I'm coming home."

Jenna got out of San Francisco that afternoon and arrived in Austin after dark. After collecting her car, she drove directly to her parents' house and raced inside. She met her mother at the bottom of the stairs.

"Oh, Mom," she said, hugging Beth close. "I missed you."

"You were only gone a few days."

"I know, but I still missed you."

She did her best not to think about what Serenity had said about Beth and Marshall not being a good choice as parents. The other woman couldn't be more wrong.

"How's Violet?" she asked as she straightened. "Feeling okay?"

"I think so." Beth led the way upstairs. "She's pretty banged up." Beth paused at the landing and faced Jenna. "She has a black eye and is feeling horrible about all of this. Not just the bruising." Her mother's voice quivered. "It's just terrible what that man did to her."

They went down the hall to the guest room. Jenna paused by the open door.

Violet lay back on several pillows, her bare arms outside the covers. The TV was on with the sound muted, and the nightstand lamps offered soft light in the early-evening gloom.

Jenna knocked, then stepped into the room. Violet turned toward her, exposing the dark purple bruise on her cheek and the black eye.

Jenna had to consciously keep from gasping.

"How are you feeling?" she asked, hoping she sounded normal, instead of shocked.

"Okay," Violet said. "Your parents are taking good care of me."

Jenna crossed to the chair by the bed and took a seat. "I'm so sorry."

"Don't be. It's my own fault. I picked Cliff."

"How could you have known what he was like?"

Something flashed in Violet's eyes. "I should have guessed." She shrugged, then winced. "It's over now."

"You're staying here until things are settled," Jenna said firmly, knowing it was what her parents would want.

"You don't mind?" Violet asked.

"Not at all."

"I'm sorry about screwing up."

Jenna shook her head. "Violet, you didn't screw up. Just rest and heal. We'll take care of everything else."

"I don't know how to thank you," Violet whispered.

"You don't have to."

Seventeen

Jenna opened the store the next morning. Tiffany was in until her noon college class, then Kayla would arrive for the afternoon shift. While the work would all get done, she felt weird being in the store without Violet.

It wasn't that Violet had been there every second, but this was different. She felt as if a part of her daily structure was missing. She depended on Violet in ways she hadn't realized.

About eleven-thirty, Ellington strolled in. He was as handsome as she remembered, and seeing him lifted her mood. She crossed to him.

"Hi, you," she said.

"Hi, yourself." He pulled her into his arms and gave her a quick kiss. "I missed you." He touched her face with his fingers. "And I wanted to thank you in person for those great cupcakes. They were the star of the bake sale."

"I'm glad."

"It was incredibly thoughtful."

"I just happened to remember. It was no big deal."

"It was a very big deal."

She stood in his embrace and felt all warm and safe. There were possibilities, she thought happily. Ellington was special. Who knew where this could go?

The bell dinged on the front door as a customer arrived. Jenna stepped back a little, thinking PDAs weren't exactly professional. Very nice but not the image she wanted for the store. Ellington winked.

"Rain check."

"Absolutely." She watched Tiffany approach the customer, then turned back to him. "How did you know I was back? I'm a couple of days early."

"Your mom called and told me."

Jenna shook her head. "Why would my mom…" Okay, now she got it. Her good mood faded, and she was left feeling oddly unsettled. As much as she'd enjoyed her trip to Napa, as much as Serenity had become a friend, she was tired of being pushed into an emotional place that wasn't comfortable.

"Serenity isn't my mother. Beth Stevens is my mother. She's the one who raised me and took care of me. Serenity gave me up for adoption when I was born. For thirty-two years she's been waiting for me to magically show up and when that didn't happen, she received some mystic message to tell her it was time to get in touch with me. I'm happy she did. I resisted at first, but now I can see she's a wonderful person and I'm glad to have her in my life. But that doesn't make her my mother."

Ellington stared at her for several seconds. "Feel better?" he asked.

"About what?" Annoyance sharpened her words.

"Getting that out. Obviously something happened while you were in California."

"Everything was fine. My trip was great," she said shortly.

"I'm glad to hear that."

He didn't seem upset by her irritation, and that pissed her off more. "You don't know what you're talking about. I don't care what Serenity told you. Just don't even talk to her."

His voice gentled. "She's my patient, Jenna. I will talk to her whenever either of us feels it's necessary."

"Fine. Do that. But I'm just saying, you don't know about my private life."

"Why are you angry?"

"I'm not," she snapped, then sighed. "I'm sorry. There's a lot going on."

"She mentioned Violet was hurt."

"She wasn't hurt. She didn't fall or get in a car accident. Her boyfriend, the man she trusted, hit her. He beat her up. Even though he was arrested, he's going to be out soon. And then what? How does she stay safe? How does she know it's okay?"

"I don't have an answer."

"Right. Sure. Because men only like to create the problems. If they're not hitting women, they're cheating on them, then saying it's the woman's fault."

"Is that what Aaron did to you?"

"What? We're not talking about Aaron."

"I think we are."

He was right, and she couldn't say why. Everything was great with Ellington. Why was she acting this crazy? He hadn't done anything wrong.

She glanced around to make sure no customers were listening, then stepped into the back room. Ellington followed.

"Jenna, you're dealing with a lot right now. I can see that. I understand it."

"Aren't you generous?" she snapped when she knew she should be grateful.

"Why are you fighting with me?"

The one question she didn't have an answer to. "I don't know."

"Is it about your mo— Is it about Serenity?"

"I'm not sure. Maybe. I'm confused. I want her in my life, but every time I get comfortable with where we are, she pushes me past where I want to go. I'm worried about my mom." She caught herself. "The person you would call Beth. I don't want her hurt. Violet got hurt by someone she should have been able to trust."

"That's a big list. Why don't you take it one item at a time?"

Which sounded reasonable but she just *knew* he was going to bring up Serenity first.

"Despite her faults, Serenity genuinely cares about you."

"I knew it!" she said between gritted teeth. "It's always about her."

"Maybe it should be. You're not seeing things clearly," he continued. "Your blind loyalty to Beth…"

"Blind loyalty? Are you serious? Beth—Mom—raised me from the time I was an infant. She has always been there for me. I've known Serenity a few months. Don't you dare compare those relationships."

"I'm sorry," he said stiffly. "I shouldn't have said that. But my point is valid. You're missing the big picture."

You're so sensitive. You don't know what's best. Variations on a theme, she thought, fuming with rage. Just like Aaron. What was it about men that they thought they knew everything?

Maybe it wasn't all men. Maybe it was just the ones who had been given too much a little too easily.

"Not to take away from what you have with Beth, but Serenity is your mother," he said.

"Biologically."

He stared at her as if silently pointing out that was the relationship that was most significant.

"We're going to have to agree to disagree," she said stiffly, doing her best not to hit him on the head with a nearby sauté pan.

"I didn't come here to argue with you."

"Why did you come?"

"Because I was glad you were home." He studied her for a long minute. "My mistake."

He walked out before she could say anything else. She stared after him, angry at him for being difficult and angry with herself for being stupid. None of this was Ellington's fault. He had known Serenity first, so of course he would be loyal to her.

Fine, she thought. Let him leave. This wasn't a good time for her, anyway. Better to not get involved. At least then she could avoid getting hurt.

Jenna spent the next couple of days trying not to think about Ellington. She told herself she didn't need a man in her life, and most of the time she believed it. Robyn from Only Ewe dropped by on Wednesday.

"Violet missed class," the other woman said as she walked in. "I wanted to make sure everything was okay."

Jenna hesitated. "She's doing better." She wasn't sure if Violet wanted her to share what had happened but figured Robyn would see the truth when Violet returned.

"Her boyfriend beat her up," Jenna said quietly, so the

other customers wouldn't hear. "She was in the hospital over-night and is staying with my parents for a few days while she starts to heal."

Robyn's eyes widened. "Oh, no. That's so horrible. Can I help? Or go see her?"

"I'm sure she would enjoy company, but I don't know if she wants everyone knowing what happened." She wrote down her parents' address and gave her Violet's cell number.

"I'm glad you told me," Robyn said. "I'll know to play dumb if any guy comes asking about her. I'll leave it to her to tell me what happened. How are her hands?"

"Fine."

"I'll take her some yarn and a simple pattern," Robyn said. "It might help pass the time."

"I'm sure she would appreciate that."

Robyn excused herself and went back to her store.

Jenna helped a few customers, answered questions about the next low-salt class and worked on a couple of recipes. When it was time to close, she locked the door, then walked through the aisles, straightening stock and making notes of what needed to be ordered.

A few weeks before, Serenity had questioned whether or not Jenna had made the right decision when she'd opened the store. She'd suggested Jenna's "destiny" lay elsewhere.

At the time, Jenna had listened, wondering the same her-self, but now she knew. She'd come back from Los Angeles with little more than some money, furniture and a broken heart. From that she'd created a place she could be proud of. She'd started over, made friends and was finding a home in the community. She'd risked being creative again and had rediscovered her soul.

The local Chamber of Commerce had talked to her about coming to meetings. Rotary wanted her to join. She was thinking of being one of the sponsors of a 5K run for charity. She was happy. It had taken a while, but she was happy.

Unless she thought of Ellington, which she wasn't about to do.

But she couldn't escape all his words, and she wondered about Serenity and Beth. Was she being unfair to one because of the other?

Her cell phone rang. She glanced at the number and sighed. "Hello?"

"You were thinking about me, weren't you?" Serenity asked with a laugh. "I sensed it."

"I was," Jenna admitted. "How are you?"

"Good. Jasmine saw her doctor today and everything is going well. He's still very disappointed he won't be delivering her baby, but she wants a midwife and to give birth at home."

Jenna winced. "I'm glad she's following her heart."

"So am I. How's Violet?"

"Recovering. She's getting stronger. The bruises are hideous though. He really hurt her."

"Payment will come to him. I believe in karma."

"I'm not surprised."

Serenity laughed again, then drew in a breath. "I miss you, Jenna. I wish you were still here."

Jenna knew what she was expected to say. As for the truth, she couldn't be sure. She liked her life here but had to admit, Serenity added something unexpected, in a good way. Maybe a lot of something.

"I miss you, too," she said softly.

"Thank you for saying that. Tom and I will be back soon. It will be a few days. We're driving. See you then."

"I can't wait. Bye."

Jenna closed her phone, then turned and saw Beth standing in the doorway leading to the back of the store.

"I let myself in," her mother said, her voice low and a little stiff. "I take it you were talking to Serenity?"

Jenna swore silently, then nodded, confident Beth had heard her say she missed the other woman.

A thousand excuses flew into her head, but she hadn't done anything wrong, so what exactly was she supposed to apologize for?

More complications, she thought wearily.

"I stopped by to invite you to dinner," Beth continued. "Violet is coming downstairs for the first time."

"Thanks," Jenna told her. "Let me finish locking up and I'll be there."

"My life sucks," Jenna said later that night, sitting on the chair next to Violet's bed.

Dinner had gone better than she'd thought, with Beth acting relatively normally. She'd avoided looking at Jenna too much, or maybe Jenna had just been expecting trouble. Or wallowing in guilt.

Violet shifted against the pillows that allowed her to sit upright. "I have a body full of bruises and a broken heart. Want to trade?"

"Well, no."

"Okay, then. What's going on?"

Jenna sighed. "I'm sorry. I'm talking about my problems when that's the last thing you want to hear."

"Not true. I want to hear about your problems. We're friends."

Something Jenna appreciated. "Thank you for that."

"You're welcome." Violet studied her. "Now start at the beginning. What happened?"

"I had a horrible fight with Ellington a couple of days ago. Part of me says he's just like Aaron and part of me says it's really my fault but I'm trying to blame him. Then I hurt my mother." Jenna drew in a breath. "Did she, ah, say anything about that to you?"

"No. And I couldn't tell anything was wrong. Are you sure you aren't imagining all this?"

"I don't think so." Jenna explained about Ellington dropping in to welcome her home and how he'd called Serenity "your mother."

"I went off on him," Jenna admitted. "Everything kind of exploded in my head. I'm dealing with a lot—getting to know another family, figuring out how I feel about them. He knows Serenity, so he's totally on her side."

"Do there have to be sides?" Violet asked.

Jenna got up and closed the bedroom door, then returned to her chair. "When I was in California, Serenity said she thought giving me to my parents had been a mistake. She implied I would have done much better with them or someone else."

Violet's gaze was steady. "That bothered you."

"In multiple ways. I love my parents. Why can't she respect that? She's the one who gave me up. Because of that I had a great life. I'm not saying it wouldn't have been as good with her and Tom, but that's not what happened. Now she's back and I feel like she's trying to force a level of intimacy that we simply don't have. That kind of a relationship can only grow with time."

"Is that what you fought with Ellington about?"

"Sort of." Their argument had been confusing, and she couldn't remember exactly what each of them had said. "Earlier today Serenity called. She and Tom are coming back. They're driving. Anyway, she said she missed me, and I said I

missed her, as well. When I turned around, Mom was standing there."

"Beth understands."

"I'm not so sure," Jenna said. "I believe she's fine with all
this, in spirit, but not so much in reality. This has been hard
on her."

"It's been hard on you, too."

"Maybe. I don't want her to think she's losing me."

"Beth knows better than that," Violet reminded her. "She
has faith in your relationship. No matter what, she'll always
be your mother." She paused. "Are you afraid that you can't
have them both? That you'll have to choose?"

Jenna shifted in her chair. "I hadn't thought of that. I'm
not choosing."

"So you can love them both?"

Love Serenity? She supposed it was a possibility. That if
their relationship progressed, her feelings would grow stronger. She wasn't sure if that was okay or not.

"I want everyone to back off," Jenna said, rather than answer the question. "To give me more time. It doesn't all have
to happen today."

"You could tell them that."

"When they show up, yet again?" She shook her head. "I
guess I have to."

Talk about complications. She'd come home to lick her
wounds. Instead she'd found a whole new life. Parts of it
were great, but parts of it weren't anything she expected.

"How pissed do you think Ellington is?" she asked.

"You could ask him," Violet suggested.

"What if he won't talk to me?"

"He's not that kind of guy."

Violet couldn't know that for sure. Jenna's instinct was to
hide from the problem, but she knew that wouldn't accom-

plish anything. But the idea of facing Ellington, of apologizing, made her want to whimper. Which was probably why
she had to do it.

It took Jenna two days to get up the courage to call Ellington. She carefully left a message at his work, when she
was pretty sure he would be with a patient. Perhaps not the
most mature act, but these days she was already on the edge.
She told herself if he called her back, then she would invite
him over so they could talk. If he didn't, then he was an idiot
and better to find that out sooner rather than later.

He phoned back in less than twenty minutes.

"It's Ellington," he said, when she picked up her cell.

That was it—an announcement of his name and nothing
more. No hint as to his mood or what she could expect from
him.

"Um, hi. I was wondering if you could come over some
night. I'd like to talk to you." She drew in a breath and
clutched her cell tighter. "Explain."

"What about tonight?"

"Your mom can watch Isaiah?"

"Yes."

"Okay. Um, great. Seven?"

"I'll be there. Oh, and Jenna? Don't cook anything."

"All right. Why not?"

"You hide behind your cooking and I don't want you
doing that tonight."

He hung up before she could react.

Probably for the best, she thought as she snapped her phone
closed and inwardly ranted.

"I don't hide behind my cooking," she told the stacks of
boxes in the back room of her store. "I don't hide behind

anything. Who does he think he is, saying something like that and then hanging up? Jerk."

Tiffany appeared in the doorway. "Are you all right?"

"Sure. I was just finishing a call." Jenna smiled and dropped her cell phone into her apron pocket. Hopefully Tiffany hadn't heard what she'd been saying.

Note to self, she thought as she returned to the front of the store. No ranting to boxes unless she was sure she was alone.

Violet dressed carefully after her shower and walked back to the room she was using at Beth and Marshall's house. She felt stronger today. The bruises were still scary-looking, but the pain was less. She was healing. Although she'd known it would happen, she was pleased to see proof.

She'd barely finished making her bed when her cell rang. She picked it up without looking at the screen, sure it would be Jenna with a question about the store.

"Hello?"

"Violet."

The sound of Cliff's voice sucked the life out of her. She felt dizzy and afraid and had to sit on the bed to keep from sinking to the floor.

"I'm sorry," he told her, his voice thick with emotion. "If you knew how sorry. I never m–meant—" His voice cracked. "Baby, I'm sorry. Can you ever forgive me? It won't happen again, I swear. When I found out about that guy and then your past—I just snapped. It's not even my fault, completely. You were wrong, too, but that doesn't matter. I want to see you."

He was still talking when she hung up.

The phone slipped from her hands. It took her a second to

realize it was because she was shaking. Coldness seeped into every cell and she was afraid she was going to throw up.

"I was thinking we'd rent *Funny Girl* for this afternoon," Beth said as she walked into Violet's room. "I love that movie, but I can't get Marshall to watch it with me. Are you—" Beth froze. "Violet, what happened?"

She looked up, sure that the fear was written on her face. "Cliff called. He wants to see me again."

Ellington arrived right on time, which was good because his instruction not to cook made her antsy.

She had gotten home at six-twenty, had changed her clothes by six-thirty and then had little to do but pace. Normally she would have been in the kitchen, whipping up a snack. Even as she tried to sort through her thoughts and figure out what she wanted to say, she found herself yearning to be slicing something or mixing or blending.

She pulled the door open as soon as the doorbell rang.

"I don't hide behind my cooking," she said by way of greeting. "It relaxes me and, like you said, giving someone food is a way of nurturing."

He stepped into her townhouse, looking tall and handsome, but she refused to be swayed by a gorgeous pair of blue eyes.

"Usually," he agreed. "But sometimes, you use cooking to put distance between yourself and others. There are the physical barriers—a counter, a bowl, even a knife—and the emotional ones. Your attention is always divided between what you're cooking and the person you're with. If you're cooking, you always have an escape."

She blinked at him. Talk about insightful, not to mention annoying.

"I assume drinks are acceptable," she grumbled, deciding

she would simply ignore his point. "I opened a bottle of wine. Would you like some?"

He surprised her by reaching out and putting his hands on her waist. When he drew her close, she found herself stepping into his embrace, then closing her eyes in anticipation of his kiss.

His warm mouth gently teased hers. She wrapped her arms around his neck and parted her lips. His tongue brushed against hers, sending sparks dancing down her spine.

As quickly as the kiss had begun, it was over. He stepped back.

"I would like a glass of wine. Thank you."

She eyed him. "Are you playing with me?"

"I was showing you I wasn't mad."

"You couldn't just say that?"

"Would that have been better than the kiss?"

She considered the question. "Probably not."

"Good."

She poured them each a glass of Syrah. They settled on opposite ends of the sofa, angled toward each other.

"I don't suppose you would go first," she said.

"You're the one who called the meeting."

"That's true." She sighed. "I guess the problem is my husband was always telling me what was wrong with me. He told me how I should feel and at the end of the marriage, he tried to undermine my creativity. And I let him."

Ellington watched her without speaking.

"Aaron was so different from me," she continued. "Outgoing, charming. Everyone wanted to be around him. He could make any event into a party. I liked that about him and he seemed to like me. We dated and then moved in together. I wanted more. I wanted what my parents have."

She looked at him. "Both sets of parents. A long, happy

marriage. I wanted to find 'the one' early on, fall in love and live happily ever after. Once I fell in love with Aaron, I needed him to make my dreams come true."

"But he's not that guy," Ellington said quietly.

"Not even close. I pressed for marriage, he resisted. Finally he agreed, but I don't think he really wanted to." She ducked her head, afraid to admit what she'd always been ashamed of. "He wouldn't buy me an engagement ring. He said he was marrying me and that should be enough. When my mom asked about it, I lied, telling her a diamond ring would get in the way of my cooking. That a simple gold band was easier in my line of work."

She risked glancing at Ellington, half expecting to see him scrambling for the door. Instead he only looked concerned.

"That hurt you," he said.

"Looking back, I know it was a big red flag. He was telling me flat out that I didn't matter as much to him as he mattered to me. Now I can see we were doomed from the start."

"Every marriage has challenges."

"Most of the time both parties are at least pretending to be interested. I was looking for the storybook ending and I completely chose the wrong man."

"It may sound like a cliché, but marriage isn't always about how it started, it's about what happens on the journey."

"I've sort of figured that out," she admitted. "Besides, I've already blown through following in my parents' footsteps."

He studied her. "Perfection is an impossible standard. If that's your goal, you're setting yourself up to fail."

"I don't want perfect," she said automatically, then stopped. "Well, maybe a little perfection wouldn't hurt."

He put down his wine and leaned toward her. "Jenna, please take this in the spirit in which I mean it. You have a lot of rules about how things should be. Whether it's the fact that Serenity and Tom waited until now to get in touch with you to how you run your business. Sometimes rules are good things, but sometimes they blind us to possibilities."

His words made sense.

"I was the opposite of you," he admitted. "I didn't want any rules. I felt my marriage was there to serve me. That despite pledging myself to another person and later having a child, that I could still do anything I wanted. Even if that meant disappearing to another country for three months at a time. I didn't care enough about the other people in my life to change for them. And so I lost them both."

He picked up his wine again. "I'm not sorry about the divorce, except for how it affected Isaiah. He deserved better from me. I'm still learning, and occasionally I resist the rules, but I know that a few are there for the better good."

"Just not all of them?" she asked.

"Exactly."

He was right. She did have a lot of rules. Maybe that was why Serenity's claim to hear messages from the universe annoyed her so much. In her world, no mystic messages need apply.

"Serenity wants to embrace everything at once," he said. "She wants to pretend the last thirty-two years never happened and the two of you are close and loving, with a lifetime of memories between you. You want to take things slowly, to be cautious and careful. You're protective, of yourself and those around you. You're worried about Beth and Marshall as much as yourself. I think that's reasonable."

"You're saying we have a style difference."

He nodded. "I can't claim to know what it means to give up a child, but I do know what it's like to almost lose one because of the choices I made. I know the guilt I feel. I was able to become a part of my son's life and because of that, I've changed. Serenity can't undo what's been done. She can only move forward, perhaps with a little too much enthusiasm. There are things about her…"

"Like what?"

He was quiet for a long time, then he smiled. "I think you should give her a chance."

"I can do that," Jenna said. "I already have. She has a way of sneaking up on a person."

He looked at her. "I see a lot of her in you."

A month ago, that statement would have bothered her. Now Jenna could see the value of being like Serenity. "Let me be clear. The universe and I aren't on speaking terms."

"Fair enough."

She looked at him. "I'm sorry I snapped at you before."

"You're under a lot of pressure."

"You reminded me of Aaron."

She expected him to get mad or accuse her of something. Instead, he nodded slowly. "I can see that. I'm sorry I push the same buttons with you. I don't want to. I don't need to belittle you to feel better about myself. I only want you to be happy."

She believed him, which felt good.

"I don't want to take any side but yours," he told her.

"Thank you."

When he put down his wineglass and slid toward her, she found herself uncertain, almost shy.

He took her glass from her and set it next to his, then cupped her face in his hands.

"Jenna," he breathed, before claiming her in a passionate kiss that sent heat surging all through her body.

As she kissed him back, she was aware of him dropping his hands to her shoulders, then rubbing them up and down her back. Anticipation quickened inside of her. Hunger burned. When his tongue touched her bottom lip, she parted for him.

He kissed her deeply. She met him stroke for stroke. He moved his hands to her waist, then up to her breasts. When he cupped her curves in his palms, she nearly groaned out loud.

His thumbs teased her already tight nipples. When he thrust his tongue back into her mouth, she closed her lips around it and sucked. The hands on her breasts trembled slightly.

He drew back so they could look at each other. His eyes were dark, his gaze intense.

"Am I moving too fast?" he asked, his voice just the slightest bit hoarse.

"That depends. What time do you have to be home tonight?"

His mouth curved into a very male, very predatory smile. "I don't."

"Then I don't think you're moving too fast at all."

Eighteen

Violet woke up early Tuesday morning with a sense of doom but also determined to get back to work. Her jaw still hurt, but not as much as it had. As long as she avoided gasping or laughing too much, she would be fine. As for Cliff—she couldn't hide from him forever. She wanted to get back to her life, and if she had to face him to do that, so be it.

The bruises were getting better. They were less painful, although the color palette wasn't any more subtle than it had been. She would hope for a makeup miracle to conceal the biggest one on her cheek.

She was also going to have to return to her own apartment. She couldn't continue to stay in Beth and Marshall's guest room. Although the thought of being alone at her place made her stomach hurt, she would simply have to suck it up and face her fears. She'd survived this kind of thing before, and she would again.

After showering and dressing, she went downstairs to pour

some coffee. Marshall was already there, leaning against the kitchen counter, talking on his cell phone. She smiled and waved, then quietly got a mug from the cupboard. Before she could pour her coffee and duck out to give him some privacy for his call, he hung up.

"You're up early," he said. "Sleeping okay?"

"I'm doing great. The room and bed are so comfortable." She walked to the refrigerator and collected the hazelnut coffee creamer. "I'm going back to work today."

"You up to that?"

"Physically, I'm much better. I know Jenna won't let me overwork myself, so I'll be fine. If nothing else, I need to get back into the world." She touched her bare cheek. "Assuming I don't frighten little children with my bruise."

Marshall nodded. "I'm sure routine will help. By the way…" He held up his cell phone. "I've been talking to a friend of mine in the police department."

She glanced at the clock. It was barely after six. "Your friend gets up early."

"He works nights. He's been doing some digging and has confirmed what we all suspected. You're not the first woman Cliff has hurt."

She wasn't surprised to hear that. "I don't suppose that's going to keep him in jail, is it?"

"Sorry, no." Marshall hesitated. "But I had a little talk with Cliff yesterday. I explained that it would be in his best interest to leave town. He's going to move back to Chicago. His company happened to have an opening there, so he should be gone in the next week or so."

She stared at him, not sure what to say. Gratitude and relief rushed through her. Cliff would be leaving. She would be safe.

She supposed she should ask what Marshall had said, or

what strings he'd pulled. For all she knew, he had threatened Cliff. But she couldn't bring herself to care.

Tears filled her eyes. "Thank you," she whispered.

"You're welcome." He crossed to her, wrapped his arm around her and kissed her forehead.

She leaned into him, wondering if this was what it felt like to have a father. "No one's ever taken care of me before," she admitted.

"Then you're going to have to get used to it, because we're not going anywhere. And neither are you. Don't take this information as a hint you should move out. Beth and I like having you around."

"I need to get back to my own life."

"Maybe, but not today. Oh, and I'll be following up with Cliff to make sure he really does move."

She nodded because there was too much emotion for her to speak.

Marshall set down his coffee and excused himself to finish getting ready for work. Violet sank down at the kitchen table, holding her mug in both hands.

Free, she thought. She was free, or she would be when Cliff was really gone.

Beth shuffled into the kitchen. Her blond hair was rumpled, her body covered in a pink fuzzy robe. Her hostess made it to the coffee, poured a mug and then drank deeply. When she'd swallowed, she looked up and wrinkled her nose.

"You're not even wearing makeup and you're beautiful. Do you know how depressing that is for me?"

Violet laughed, then pressed her hand to her side. "Ignoring the honking big bruise on my face."

"That will fade. My wrinkles won't."

"Your wrinkles are only in your imagination."

Beth smiled. "I love it when you flatter me." She crossed to the table and sat across from Violet. "Marshall told me the good news. You must be relieved."

"I am. I've been so scared he would come after me again."

"Marshall would be happy to fix you up with a nice little gun and some training on how to use it."

"I'm not exactly a weapons kind of girl."

Beth didn't look convinced. "If you'd had a gun when Cliff had first hit you?"

"He'd be dead now." Violet knew that was more than a possibility. Probably why she shouldn't be trusted with a gun.

"I'm going back to work today," she said, changing the subject. "And moving back to my own apartment."

Beth sighed. "I was afraid you were going to say that. We would love you to stay longer. At least until we know he's gone."

"I'd love it, too, but I'm concerned that if I don't get back to my life, the fear will win. I need to stay strong." For a lot of reasons Beth would never understand. "Besides, Cliff isn't going to hurt me after talking to Marshall." Something she felt in her gut. Not that she wouldn't sleep better when he was several states away.

"You're very brave," Beth told her.

"There's nothing to admire." On the contrary. She had plenty to be ashamed about.

"You're wrong, Violet. As you get older, you'll see that."

"Maybe."

"There's nothing I can do to convince you to stay?" Beth asked.

"Sorry. No."

"All my girls leave me. All right. I'll survive. It's the cycle of life and all that."

Violet stared at her, unable to get past the first part of what Beth had said. *All my girls leave me.* As if she were part of the family.

"And when you start dating again, you'll have to bring your young man around."

"I don't see a lot of dating in my future," Violet told her.

"I know it seems that way now, but you'll heal and then you'll get interested in someone."

Unlikely, Violet thought. She was tired of getting burned. "If the impossible happens, I'll be sure to do a background check."

"That's my girl."

Violet was at her apartment by nine that morning. She wanted to take back the few things Beth had collected for her, and to change into something suitable for work. As she stepped inside, she braced herself for the memories.

They were there, lunging out at her without a hint of subtlety. She could see everything that had happened, but this time as if from an aerial camera. Different perspective, she thought, willing herself not to flinch at the memory of Cliff's fist slamming into her face.

She ignored the instant replay and crossed to the kitchen. All traces of the meal were gone, the dishes were washed and put away. She couldn't see a hint of blood on the floor. No doubt Beth's doing, she thought, grateful to the other woman for everything. Beth had taken Violet's key, saying she wanted to get her some of her own clothing. Obviously, she'd done a lot more.

After changing into black pants and a long-sleeved blouse, she checked her makeup in the mirror. If the light was right and no one was looking, the bruise was fairly invisible. That was a plus.

Someone knocked on her front door.

Violet froze, then willed herself to relax. She couldn't jump at every sound. But just to be sure, she called out, asking who was there, before opening the door.

"Your neighbor," a familiar voice answered.

She crossed the small living room and opened the door to find her elderly friend waiting in the hall.

"Mr. McAllister," she said, smiling at him.

"Beth Stevens called to say you were coming back," the old man said as he hobbled over her threshold. "I thought I'd welcome you personally and see how you're feeling."

"Better," she admitted. "I don't know how to thank you. You saved my life."

The old man shrugged. "You looked after Buster when I had to go into the hospital last fall. It was a real load off my mind, knowing he was taken care of. Besides, I still believe a man has a responsibility to protect the women in his life. I only wish I were twenty years younger, so I could have beaten the shit out of your young man." He paused, then blushed a little. "Pardon my French."

She smiled. "He's not my young man anymore, Mr. McAllister. I swear. You don't have to worry. I'm not taking him back."

Mr. McAllister hugged her. "You're a good girl, Violet. You'll pick better next time."

Why did everyone assume she would ever want to be with another man?

"I want to thank you," she said. "May I make you dinner?"

"I'd like that." His eyes brightened with humor. "As long

as you understand we're just friends. I've started seeing Mrs. Brighten on the third floor."

She laughed, then pressed her hand to her jaw. "I promise I won't hit on you."

He grinned. "You can hit on me a little."

"A little then." She raised herself onto her toes and kissed his cheek. "Thank you again."

"You're welcome, Violet. You take care."

Violet arrived at work a little before nine-thirty. Jenna's car was already there. Violet hadn't warned her boss she would be in today, mostly because she wasn't sure she was up to a full day's work. It might take a while for her to get her stamina back. She'd also avoided calling because she was a little nervous about seeing Jenna.

She let herself in the back and set her purse on the shelf, next to Jenna's, then walked into the store. Jenna was attaching labels to brown bags filled with ingredients.

"Want any help?" she asked.

Jenna looked up, gasped, dropped the labels and came running.

"You're here," she said, hugging her. "How are you? Should you be back? Is it too soon?"

Violet held out her hands in the shape of a T. "I'll take those questions in groups of twenty."

Jenna laughed. "I'm so happy to see you. You look good."

Violet touched her bruised cheek. "Not yet, but I'm healing. I want to get back to work. I'm not sure if I can put in a full day, but I'd like to try."

"You're welcome to stay as long as you want. I've missed you desperately. Not only for your sparkling conversation, but I've had to place orders, and you know that's not my favorite thing. I might have accidentally ordered an extra two hundred spatulas. We'll find out Thursday."

Violet groaned. "I hope you're kidding."

"I am. Sort of."

"I'm glad you missed me."

"I was desperate."

Violet tried to smile and found herself with burning eyes again. "I'm sorry I was stupid," she whispered.

"You weren't."

"I was. I was taken in by a fancy suit and a guy who knew how to order wine. Amateur stuff. I should know better."

"Everyone makes mistakes," Jenna told her.

"My mistake landed me in the hospital. Did your dad tell you what he found out about Cliff?"

When Jenna shook her head, Violet filled her in on Cliff's background and how he would soon be moving.

"That's great," Jenna breathed.

"It's going to make sleeping at night easier."

"He would never find you at my parents' house."

"True, but I can't live there forever. In fact I moved out this morning. I'm back at my apartment."

Jenna looked concerned. "So soon. Are you sure?"

"I need to get back to my life. Which includes doing work around here. Why don't you tell me what's been going on?"

Jenna brought her up-to-date on the various classes, the new customers and how inventory had or hadn't been managed. She made a mental note to personally thank Tiffany and Kayla for picking up the slack.

"How are things otherwise?" she asked Jenna. "Last I heard, you and Ellington were fighting. Is that any better?"

Jenna's face flushed, and unlike Mr. McAllister, she hadn't said a bad word. Jenna's expression was a combination of guilty, smug and pleased.

Violet stared at her. "You slept with him."

"Maybe."

"You did. When did this happen? How was it? How do you feel?"

"Two days ago, fabulous and embarrassingly happy. I invited him over so I could explain why I'd had the freak-out. We talked and then one thing led to the other." She sighed. "It was great. He stayed the night. He had to leave early to get home before Isaiah woke up, then he called me about fifteen times." She pointed to a big bouquet of flowers. "Those were delivered yesterday and we're having dinner tomorrow."

"You're floating."

"I'm trying to keep my feet on the ground, but it's hard." She lowered her voice. "He's really nice."

"I'm glad." Violet meant it. One of them should have a successful love life.

Jenna was surprised when her father walked into her store later that week. It was early afternoon and there were only a few customers.

"You're an unexpected treat," she said, crossing to him.

"I thought I'd come by and see how things were working out." He glanced around the space. "Very nice. You're busy?"

"Most of the time. We're doing several cooking classes a week. They're turning out to be popular. We've also been selling a lot of food. Supplies for the recipes we make in the class."

She doubted hearing those details was why he'd stopped by. "If you're here thinking you can pick up something for Mom's birthday next month, I can't help. She's pretty much bought everything she already wants."

He smiled. "One of the things I love about your mother. She goes after what she wants." The smile faded. "I'm not here to talk about her birthday."

She waited, knowing her father would get to the point when he was ready.

He glanced around, as if making sure they couldn't be overheard, then said, "I'm worried about her."

"Mom?"

He nodded. "She hasn't been herself for a while now. Having Violet stay with us helped, but now with her gone…"

"She's seemed fine to me," Jenna said, even as she remembered Beth overhearing her say she missed Serenity. Her stomach tightened.

"She hasn't said much to me," he admitted. "I'm guessing here, but I know her pretty well. These last weeks have been hard on her."

Jenna put her hands on her hips. "This is so unfair. She's the one who encouraged me to get to know my birth parents. If you remember, she invited them over for brunch, where we all played happy family. Now she's mad that Serenity and I are getting along?"

"She's not mad. She's hurt and confused. I tried to warn her, but she wouldn't listen."

"What did you warn her about?"

"Getting involved. Beth never thought she would feel… threatened."

Jenna dropped her hands to her sides. "There's nothing threatening her. Regardless of my relationship with Serenity, she's my mom. She raised me. I love her."

"You're using logic. Your mother gets it in her head. It's her heart that's bruised."

The tension in her stomach increased. "I don't want her upset."

He shrugged.

Part of her wanted to stomp her foot and point out that if Beth had had her way, she would have given birth to several children and Jenna would have been expected to share her parents with them. But she knew that was a weak argument at best.

"She hasn't said anything."

"She wouldn't," Marshall reminded her. "Part of the problem is she really does want you to have a good relationship with Serenity. That's important to her. But I think she's feeling left out. When was the last time you did something together? Just the two of you?"

"It's been a while, but that goes both ways. She could have suggested something."

Her father's steady gaze made her want to squirm. "How much time does she spend in this store, Jenna? Helping you? Every time that happens, she's coming to you."

She hung her head, feeling about twelve. "You're right. I'm sorry."

"Don't apologize to me."

She looked at him. "I've been so caught up in my life."

"You've had a lot going on."

"Still."

She moved toward him. He held her close.

"I'll go see her," she promised.

"You won't say I was here?"

She smiled. "And get us both into trouble? I don't think so."

"That's my girl."

Beth stared into the refrigerator, trying to figure out what to serve for dinner. Normally she planned a menu for the week and then did her grocery shopping based on that, but lately she hadn't been in the mood.

Hormones, she told herself as she shut the refrigerator door, then crossed to the cupboard and pulled out a mug. After making tea, she took it outside and sat on the patio, sipping slowly.

She needed to change her life, she told herself. Take up a hobby. Maybe she could take a knitting class from Robyn at Only Ewe. Except she wasn't sure she wanted to be that close to Jenna's store. Or, more accurately, to Serenity, when she was in town.

All right—so if knitting was out, then what? Not gardening. She'd never been a big fan of grubbing in the dirt. She already belonged to a book club. Maybe something with crafts. Or she could learn how to make wedding cakes. That could be fun.

"There you are."

She turned and saw Jenna stepping onto the patio, then glanced at her watch. It was barely after three.

"Shouldn't you be at the store?" she asked, pleased to see her daughter, but cautious until she knew the reason Jenna had stopped by.

"Things are handled. You haven't been in for a while, so I thought I'd come see you."

"And?"

"And what?" Jenna sat in the chair next to her.

"And why else are you here?"

"No reason."

As quickly as that, Beth felt her world restore itself. Her mood lightened, her worry faded.

There were those who would tell her to get a life. They were probably right, she thought as she stared at her daughter. But her family—however small—had always been the most important part of her being.

"I'm thinking about learning to make wedding cakes. You know, for fun."

"Dad would love the samples."

True. Marshall enjoyed his sweets. And her, she thought, thinking of how he'd awakened her that morning. Sometimes it was like they were still teenagers.

"Oh, don't," Jenna said, squirming in her seat. "You're thinking about Dad. You have that look. I don't want to hear it."

Beth laughed. "I promise I won't share."

Jenna stared at her for a long time and moved next to her. After tugging Beth to her feet, she hugged her tightly.

"You're the mom of my heart."

"What brought that on?"

Jenna sighed. "I was thinking how much you and Dad mean to me. How happy I am to have you as my parents. You know that, right?"

Beth nodded. "You're the daughter of my heart." It wasn't the same as having given birth to her, but that was okay.

She thought about saying how she could practically see the connection between Jenna and Serenity. Almost as if their biological relationship was highlighted in Day-Glo paint. But that wasn't important, she told herself, holding the daughter she had loved for thirty-two years. The point was trusting the relationship she had.

The sound of the doorbell caused her to step back.

"It's probably UPS," she said, heading to the front of the house. "Your father can't get on the internet without ordering something. For a man who claims to hate shopping, he's quite the buyer online."

When she opened the door, instead of a young man in a

brown uniform, she saw Serenity and Tom standing on her wide porch.

"Surprise," Serenity said with a smile. "We stopped by the store and Violet mentioned Jenna was here. We thought we'd come over."

Beth waited for the surge of resentment, but it was gone. There was only the realization that these people were now part of her daughter's family, too. That they were all connected one way or the other.

She smiled with genuine affection and held the door open wide.

"Come on in," she said warmly. "Jenna will be happy to see you."

Nineteen

Jenna shook her head. "You're hoarding all the burners," she complained to Serenity, who'd taken a seat on the kitchen counter. "How many pots do you need to make tofu surprise?"

Serenity laughed. "You'll see what I'm talking about. My half of the meal will be finished long before your half."

"That's because you're making less," Beth teased.

After Serenity and Tom had arrived, Jenna had called the store to make sure Violet could handle things for the rest of the day and to invite her over for an impromptu family dinner. Marshall had been instructed to come home early, and while he and Tom watched baseball, the women had gone grocery shopping.

Now steaks were grilling on the barbecue. Beth had made her famous potato salad, with a nod to the vegans by using their mayonnaise, faux bacon and leaving out the egg.

The kitchen was crowded with the four women all working. Violet had taken over the blender and was mixing up margaritas. Beth and Serenity were each on their second and, from what Jenna could tell, not feeling any pain.

This was good, Jenna thought. Strange, but good. Both sides of her family coming together to...

Somewhere in the distance "You Are My Sunshine" began to play.

"My phone," Serenity said. "Jenna, do you know where my bag is?"

Jenna found Serenity's purse and pulled out her cell. "It's Dragon," she said, looking at the screen. She flipped open the phone. "Hey, you."

"Sis. Where is everyone?"

"At my mom's house. Why?"

"I'm standing in front of your closed store, feeling left out."

Jenna nearly squealed. "You're here? I didn't know you were coming. That's great."

"Ah, a fan. I need more of them in my life."

She gave him the address and directions. "Hurry. We're cooking dinner."

He hesitated. "What are we serving?"

"A little from both worlds. I'll throw on another steak."

"You're my favorite sister. I'll be right there."

She hung up. "Dragon's coming. He should be here in a few minutes."

"Wonderful," Serenity said from her perch on the counter. "Jenna, be a love and stir that back pot."

Beth shook her head. "I'll do it. Serenity, honey, don't take this wrong, but you sure can't hold your liquor."

"I know. It's always been a failing. I should drink more to get better at it."

"That's one way to handle the situation," Jenna said, then realized Violet was gone.

She ducked out of the kitchen and found Violet frantically applying makeup to her cheek.

"I don't want him to know," she said when she saw Jenna. "Don't say anything."

"I won't," Jenna promised, knowing it wouldn't matter. There was no way to completely cover what had happened. Plus he'd been at his parents' house when she'd gotten the call.

"He'll think I'm an idiot," Violet said, studying herself, then pressing powder onto the liquid foundation.

"He'll think some guy is a total jerk and want to go beat him up."

Violet shook her head. "You don't understand."

Which was true, Jenna thought. When had Dragon's opinion begun to matter?

The doorbell rang.

She went to go answer it and found her brother on the porch. He'd obviously flown in right from work. He'd removed his suit jacket and tie, but still had on suit pants and a white shirt.

"You really are a lawyer," Jenna said, feigning surprise. "I thought you were lying."

Dragon chuckled, then pulled her into a bear hug. "I heard there was a party."

"There is now."

She led him inside. He glanced around at the large house and whistled.

"Here I thought she'd given you to the first couple willing to take you off her hands. Didn't you get lucky?"

"Yes," she said, leading him into the kitchen. "But with the people more so than the place."

"Very PC," he whispered, before hugging his mom and greeting Beth.

Dragon quickly joined the men on the patio where the game played and meat cooked. Violet returned to the kitchen, slightly more subdued than when she'd left. Jenna noticed her friend kept looking toward the patio, as if bracing herself for the inevitable meeting.

From what Jenna knew, Dragon and Violet had barely spent any time together the last time he'd visited. Plus, Violet had been involved with Cliff. But maybe their meeting had been more significant than she realized.

About ten minutes later, her brother strolled back inside. Beth and Serenity were discussing the thrill of grandchildren versus the reality of getting old. Neither of them noticed Dragon's return nor his sudden stillness when he saw Violet.

Jenna saw his gaze lock on her friend's cheek. It traveled lower, to where she'd pulled her long sleeves up to her elbows, exposing more bruises. Violet self-consciously drew the shirtsleeves down to her wrists.

Dragon's expression darkened. Jenna moved closer to her friend, prepared to get between them if she had to. She wasn't sure what was going to happen, but she knew her friend didn't need to be any more hurt than she already was.

"The boyfriend?" he asked.

Violet met his gaze, then looked away. She nodded once.

"Where is he now?"

"Not with me. He's leaving town. I heard he was packed up and heading out in a couple of days."

Dragon was silent for a second. "Was this the first time?"

She returned her attention to him. "I wouldn't have given him a second chance."

"Good."

Dragon went back outside. Jenna glanced between them,

left with the feeling that something significant had just occurred, but she couldn't figure out what.

Dinner was a lively meal with plenty of overlapping conversation and laughter. Serenity claimed Beth's potato salad
for the vegan side and therefore won the bet of whose dishes
would be finished first.

Jenna looked at everyone around the table and realized
how quickly her definition of "family" had changed. Wolf
and Jasmine were missing, but they would be here next time.
With their baby. Beth would like that. She'd always wanted
more children and would love being a grandmother.

Jenna touched her own flat stomach and wondered what
it would be like to be pregnant. Longing filled her, surprising her with its intensity. She'd always wanted kids before,
but usually in a more intellectual way. This need burned hot
inside of her, almost making her ache.

With the pain came the realization that it was time for
her to move on to that stage of her life—motherhood. That
if things worked out with Ellington, then great. If not, she
would have a baby on her own. It wasn't as if she would be
raising it alone. She only had to look around to see all the
people who loved her and whom she loved.

"How's Jasmine feeling?" she asked Serenity.

"Wonderful. She's getting bigger every day. I'm hoping..."
She picked up her margarita. "We're all looking forward to
the baby being born."

Jenna might have imagined it, but she would have sworn
both Tom and Dragon shot her looks of concern.

Serenity turned to Beth. "Jasmine is using a midwife.
She'll have the baby at home."

Beth dropped her fork, then quickly picked it up. "That
sounds very, um, cozy."

Jenna laughed. "Don't pretend, Mom. I'm horrified, too." She turned back to Serenity. "Isn't it safer at a hospital, or in some kind of birthing center?"

"There's no reason to anticipate any problems," Serenity said calmly. "Childbirth is a natural process. The hospital is close by, but everything will go perfectly. She was considering underwater birth, but that would have meant using a birthing center."

Jenna nearly choked. "Who's under the water?"

"The baby," Beth told her, obviously trying not to laugh.

"What? The birth canal isn't traumatic enough? Hello, you're born, try not to drown?"

Serenity shook her head. "It's not like that, Jenna. Sometimes you can be very dramatic." She turned to Beth. "I believe she gets that from you."

There was a moment of silence, then everyone laughed. Beth grinned at Jenna. "I suspect she does."

Violet was aware of Dragon sitting next to her at the big table. Every time she glanced at him, he seemed to be looking at her. Watching. Waiting, although she couldn't say for what. It made her feel both uncomfortable and oddly protected.

When dinner was done, everyone helped clear the table. Violet was aware of the family reunion going on and wanted to excuse herself.

"I'm a little tired," she said, when the dishes were loaded into the dishwasher. "I'm going to head home."

There were plenty of hugs and good wishes. Marshall whispered that she was welcome to move back anytime she wanted. She collected her purse and walked to the door, only to find Dragon next to her.

"It was nice to see you," she said, feeling awkward.

"You can say good-night to me later," he told her. "I'm following you home."

"You don't have to."

"I want to."

"But..."

"Let him." Serenity had appeared at her side. "It's all right," the older woman added. "You can trust him, Violet. He won't hurt you."

"Good enough?" he asked.

Feeling nervous and ashamed but also a little relieved, Violet nodded.

He put his hand on the small of her back and urged her out the door.

"I'm perfectly fine," she said as she stepped into the night.

"Maybe this isn't about you," he told her. "Now drive."

Sure enough, Dragon followed her home. Violet expected him to walk her to the door, then leave. Instead, he followed her inside, then closed and locked the door.

He glanced around the small apartment, then set his keys and cell phone on the coffee table. He took her purse from her and put it next to his stuff. "How many nights have you been back in your apartment?"

"Three." She wasn't worried about his actions. More curious.

"Are you sleeping?"

She thought about the long nights, watching the hours pass by slowly. Painfully. It wasn't that she was afraid, it was the memories crowding into her mind that made it impossible to relax.

"I didn't think so," he told her. "You look exhausted. Go wash your face and get ready for bed."

"It's eight o'clock."

"So? Are you telling me you're not ready to drop on your feet?"

Until he'd said the words, she'd managed to fool herself. But when he spoke, she felt fatigue overwhelm her, and it was all she could do to stay standing.

"Okay," she said. "You're right. I'll go to bed. Thanks for seeing me home."

"Don't try throwing me out," he told her. "I'm not leaving."

She stared at him. "You can't stay here."

"Sure I can. Violet, you need to get some rest. The way I see it, the best way to do that is to make you feel safe. I may not be an obvious choice, but I'm still a good one. I'm perfectly trustworthy. Ask my mother. I'm going to stay here with you so you can relax. When we know Cliff has moved away, I'll disappear and you never have to see me again if you don't want to."

He was being nice to her. That was tough for her to take. Nice was fairly rare when it came to the men in her life. Cliff was proof of that.

She knew she could have thrown him out. All it would have taken was her to insist. She wasn't afraid of him…she just wasn't used to anyone taking care of her.

"Then I guess you should make yourself comfortable," she said, and went into the bathroom.

She carefully washed her face, then stared at the multicolored bruise on her cheek. No hiding it now. Her pj's from the previous night were hanging on the back of the door, so she slipped them on and went back into the living room.

While she'd been busy, Dragon had obviously returned to his car. A small suitcase stood by the door. His suit jacket and shirt were hung over the back of a kitchen chair, his black loafers tucked neatly by the refrigerator. He'd changed into sweats and a navy T-shirt. Even barefoot, he looked tall and powerful and just a little intimidating.

She didn't know what to do or where to look. It wasn't that he frightened her, it was that she was afraid if he was too nice, she might start to lose it.

Before she could figure out what to say or where to go, he crossed to her and took her hand. Then he led her into the bedroom and pulled back the covers.

"Get in," he said. "I'm going to sleep here tonight. On top of the covers. I'm not going to try anything. I'll be busy keeping the ghosts away."

She pulled free of his gentle touch and faced him. "Don't do this," she said, her eyes burning, her throat tight. "Don't be nice to me. Don't make it harder than it is."

"I don't want to make it harder. I want to help."

She thrust out her chin. "Maybe I deserved this."

He lightly touched her bruised cheek. "Violet, no one deserves this."

"You don't know. You don't know anything. I've been beat up before. Twice. It was common in my line of work." She squared her shoulders. "I'm not who you think, Dragon. I'm not a nice girl caught up in a bad situation. I never graduated high school. I was already selling myself before I was eighteen. I did it because it was an easy way to get money and get high. I did drugs and pretty much any guy with cash. It didn't matter when or where. I was a whore. I'm not like those other girls you know and I'm done trying to be something I'm not. This is me." Her voice rose with each word until she was nearly shouting.

When the first tear fell, she felt shame all the way to her bones. She turned her back, fighting for control.

"Just get out," she whispered.

There was only silence for the longest time. She brushed

away the moisture on her cheeks, not even wincing when her fingers pressed into the swelling.

Strong but gentle hands settled on her shoulders, turning her. Before she could stop him, he'd pulled her against him and was holding her.

"It's okay," he whispered.

"It's not," she mumbled into his T-shirt. He smelled of warm skin and fabric softener.

"It will be. I promise." He stroked her short hair. "You're not a whore, Violet. You're not bad and you don't deserve this. If you're trying to scare me away, you're going to have to work a whole lot harder than this."

Slowly, she raised her gaze to him. "Who are you?"

"Just a guy."

"Why aren't you running for the door?"

"There's nowhere else I want to be."

He spoke sincerely. She wanted to believe him, but her trust had been shattered one too many times.

He must have read that in her eyes. "Don't worry about it," he told her. "You can take all the time you need. I'm not going anywhere."

"You live in San Francisco."

One corner of his mouth turned up in a smile. "Okay, sure. Get picky. We'll figure it out."

She frowned. "I'm not dating you. I just got beat up by my boyfriend. Doesn't dating seem inappropriate?"

"No. Now come to bed."

Not knowing what else to do, she got into bed. He pulled up the covers, then circled around to the other side and climbed in next to her.

There were layers of sheet and blanket between them, but she still felt the warmth of his body and the gentle way he held her. He was careful not to jostle her ribs.

She lay with her head on his shoulder, his hand stroking her back. Every now and then he kissed the top of her head.

Eventually she started to relax.

"Aren't you going to turn the lights out?" she asked, her voice sounding sleepy.

"No. You'll worry if you can't see what's coming."

True, she thought, letting her eyes fall closed. But how did he know?

"Thank you," she whispered, right before she drifted off to sleep.

The arm around her tightened slightly, then released. "Everything is going to be okay now, Violet. Trust me."

Oddly enough, she thought she just might be able to do that.

Jenna glanced up as Violet walked into the store. The bruise on her face was fading, and for the first time since Cliff had attacked her, Violet looked relaxed and rested.

"Good night?" Jenna asked.

Violet hesitated, then nodded.

"I'm glad," Jenna told her. "This has all been rough for you."

"The memories are taking longer than I thought to go away," Violet admitted, then crossed to her. "Dragon stayed with me. Nothing happened. He wanted to help me sleep, so he spent the night. It helped me not be scared." She bit her lower lip. "Are you mad?"

Violet and Dragon? It made sense. He'd been asking about her when Jenna had visited Napa. As long as he wasn't moving too fast, she thought, knowing he was tough enough to press hard to get what he wanted.

"You're mad," Violet said. "It's okay. I won't see him again."

Jenna shook her head. "No. Don't. I'm not upset at all.

I think it's great. I can really see you two together. I was thinking that he could be pushy when he sees something he wants and I don't want him to push you."

"He didn't," Violet assured her. "Like I said, nothing happened. I don't know where this is going—if anywhere. I need some time to heal and I'm not even sure he's interested. I just wanted you to know where he was last night."

Jenna smiled. "I don't usually keep track of Dragon."

"I know, but this is different."

"I'm glad he helped. I'm glad you slept."

"Me, too."

Jenna studied the woman she'd hired. A few months ago, they'd been strangers. Now they were friends—much more so than the women she'd known in high school.

"Thank you for everything," Jenna told her. "For your help with the store and with my family. I couldn't have gotten through all this without you."

"I want to say the same thing," Violet said. "You've been so generous."

They hugged, then stepped back.

"I'm not going to cry," Jenna said, sniffing. "If I do, my mascara will run and I'll look like a raccoon."

"Not attractive."

They busied themselves with setting up. Serenity had another vegan cooking class that day and the sign-up sheet was full.

A little after ten, Beth came in.

"How is everyone?" she asked, sounding cheerful.

"Good," Jenna told her. "Are you here for the class?"

"Yes." Beth sounded defiant. "Serenity was telling me last night that if I went vegan, I wouldn't have to worry about my weight ever again. It sounds so healthy and I love all the food she's cooked."

Jenna raised her eyebrows. She had a feeling it wasn't a lifestyle her father would embrace.

"You know you have to give up all animal products. No meat, no eggs, no dairy."

"It's a little daunting," Beth admitted. "But worth a try. I'm going to sit in on today's class and see what I think."

"Good luck," Jenna murmured.

She and Violet cleared the space around the kitchen and set up the supplies. By eleven the store was filled with the students, but Serenity hadn't arrived.

"That's strange," Jenna murmured, looking at her watch. "She's always early."

"Maybe she got the time wrong," Violet said. "Do you want me to call her?"

"I'll do it," Jenna said, wondering what she was going to do if Serenity didn't show. She could probably follow the recipe, but she wouldn't have the same enthusiasm and charm as her mother. Serenity had a way of...

Her mind stalled, then rewound. The word reappeared. *Mother?* Had she thought that? Had she let down her defenses enough to let Serenity in that far?

Apparently, she thought, still not completely sure how she felt about all this. Beth was still the mother of her heart, but maybe, just maybe, there was room to love Serenity, as well.

Her cell phone rang, interrupting her. She grabbed it automatically and glanced at the screen. The 707 area code was familiar.

"It's Serenity," she said. "She's probably calling to say she's on her way." She put the phone to her ear. "Hello?"

"J-Jenna?"

The voice sounded thick and desperate. "Tom? What's wrong?"

"It's... Serenity can't make it to c-class." His word broke on a sob.

Fear came cold and fast, wrapping around her and making it hard to breathe. She held the phone tighter. "What's wrong? What happened?"

"She's in the hospital. She went in a couple of hours ago."

"I don't understand. Is she sick? Was there an accident?"

"She's dying."

Twenty

The drive to the hospital was a blur. Fortunately, Beth had taken charge and hustled Jenna into the car, leaving Violet to deal with the store.

Once they arrived, they found their way to the right wing, then the correct floor. Beth kept a firm hold of Jenna's arm, guiding her to where Tom stood, waiting for them.

It seemed to Jenna that her father had shrunk since the last time she'd seen him. His eyes were red, his face ashen. He looked as if he could have been admitted himself. When he saw her, he lunged for her, then wrapped his arms around her, holding on so tight, she couldn't breathe.

"She didn't want you to know," he said, crying loudly. "I said she should tell you, but she didn't want you to know."

Jenna felt mercifully numb. She wasn't an expert on shock but would guess she was experiencing it. Nothing made sense. Not the harsh overhead lighting, the uniformed nurses, the smells of lunch service and antiseptic.

Then Dragon was there, drawing his father back, giving Jenna a chance to catch her breath.

Her brother was in better shape than Tom, but not by much. He was pale, his expression grim.

"What the hell is going on?" Jenna demanded. "Where's Serenity?"

"She'll be back in a bit," Dragon told her. He glanced at Beth. "Could you be with him?"

"Of course."

Her mother wrapped her arm around Tom's waist and guided him to the chairs by the nurses' station.

Dragon took Jenna's hand in his. "Mom has stage-four pancreatic cancer. It's gone into nearly all her organs. She was diagnosed about four months ago. She was already pretty far gone. Aggressive treatment was an option, but she didn't want it. She said she refused to live her last few months vomiting while she was poisoned by medicine that wouldn't have a prayer of curing her."

Tears filled his eyes. "I'm sorry. This is what she wanted. To come see you. To give you a chance to know her before she went."

Jenna heard the words but couldn't absorb them. How could any of this make sense?

"No," she said slowly. "No. I don't believe it. Pancreatic cancer? That was the universe telling her to get in touch with me?"

"I'm sorry," Dragon said again.

She was aware that his pain was greater than hers. That she was losing someone she'd only known a few months while he was losing his mother. But she couldn't seem to get any of the information to stick. It was like swimming through thick water. Nothing sounded right, nothing felt right.

She pulled free of him and walked to the end of the corridor. As she turned, she saw him standing there, looking lost and broken. Quickly, she stepped into a waiting area and called Violet at the store.

"Shut it down," she told her friend. "Put up a sign saying there's a family emergency. Then please come here."

"Give me half an hour," Violet said before hanging up.

Jenna appreciated that she didn't ask a lot of questions. She wasn't sure what she could say.

As she moved out of the waiting room, she saw Serenity being wheeled back to her room.

"That's the last of it," Serenity was saying. "No more tests. No more probing. I may be ready to go, but I'm not going to let you make me feel even more miserable."

She turned and saw Jenna standing by the waiting room. Her mouth twisted.

"Tom called. I told him not to, but he said you had the right to know. I thought it would be better for you to find out after."

Jenna stared at her, not believing what she was hearing. After? As in after Serenity was dead?

Jenna turned and walked to the elevator. After pushing the down button, she waited impatiently for the doors to open. She jumped inside and pushed another floor. She didn't even know which one it was, nor did she care. It was only when the doors opened again that she realized she was on the main floor. She hurried through the lobby and stepped out into the late-morning light.

A thousand thoughts and sensations coursed through her. She hurt, she wanted to throw up, and she wanted to scream. This couldn't be happening. Not like this. Not with no warning. She turned slowly, unable to focus.

Then familiar arms steadied her. She hung on to her mother and let herself cry.

"I don't understand," she said between sobs.

"I know," Beth told her. "I'm so sorry, honey."

Jenna straightened. "Who does this? How dare she blow back into my life, make me care about her, then turn around and die? It's not right."

Beth's blue eyes were dark with unshed tears. "It's a unique path, but that's always what Serenity has chosen."

"Did you know?" Jenna demanded.

"No. How could I?"

"They knew," she snapped. "Dragon, Tom, Wolf. Even Jasmine. They all knew and kept it from me. I sat in their house, at their table as they showed me what their happy family was like and the whole time she was dying and no one told me."

"I'm sorry."

Jenna wished everyone would stop apologizing.

She pulled free of her mother's gentle hold and pulled out her cell phone. But who was there to call? What was she supposed to say?

"Why did they do this?" she asked desperately. "Why did they try so damn hard?"

"It's what Serenity wanted," Beth said quietly. "To know you before she died."

"Doesn't that strike you as monumentally selfish?"

"You were a missing part of her life."

Jenna shoved her cell back in her pocket and covered her face. Then she dropped her arms.

"Ellington knew," she breathed. "That's why she went to see him. That's why he was on her side. He knew what was happening." Her frustration grew. "I don't accept this."

Beth stood, watching her.

Jenna wiped away her tears. "I know why now. I know

why, so my new question is, why wait? Why did she have to wait so long?"

"People make choices for reasons we can never understand."

"I hate her."

"No, you don't. You love her. That's the problem."

Jenna looked at her mother. "I don't love her."

Beth smiled. "Yes, you do. A little. Not in the same way you love me, but there's a connection. It's okay," she added. "I'm nearly mature enough not to mind."

Dragon came out of the hospital. "She wants to talk to you."

Jenna marched up to him. "You should have told me," she yelled. "I had the right to know."

"That's what I told her," he admitted, anguish in his eyes. "She didn't want you to know because she knew it would change everything."

"Death has a way of doing that," Jenna snapped.

"Everyone gets a flaw."

She saw the pain in his expression. Her voice softened. "I'm sorry. She's your mother. This must be horrible for you."

"I'll get by."

"I called Violet to come take care of you."

His smile was weary. "She doesn't need to be here."

"I think she wants to be here." She turned back to the hospital. "I have to go inside, don't I?"

Her mother came up and put a hand on her back. "I'll be right here."

Jenna turned on her. "You're not hiding any big secrets, are you?"

"No, Jenna. Everything is fine." Beth drew in a breath. "We're going to have to be strong for Serenity."

Jenna looked at Dragon. "How long?"

He winced. "Days. Maybe weeks."

Jenna felt the sharp stab to her belly. "Okay," she whispered. "I can do this."

She led the way back inside and went upstairs. As she paused outside of Serenity's door, she told herself that everything would be all right. That she would be strong and support her family and have a small but tasteful breakdown later.

She walked into the hospital room.

Tom sat by Serenity, holding her hand. Serenity looked much as she had since Jenna had known her. Thin and pale, but still beautiful. When their eyes met, Serenity shook her head.

"You're thinking I should have told you."

"Yes," Jenna told her.

"In time you'll see that I was right."

Jenna doubted that but knew this wasn't the moment to have that argument. "How do you feel?" she asked instead.

"I'm in a little pain. They're going to give me some drugs to help with that. I hope they don't make me loopy."

Beth moved next to Jenna. "Are you going back to Napa?" she asked.

Serenity and Tom exchanged a glance. Serenity shook her head. "I don't want to die on the road."

"I understand," Beth told her. "You need to be around family and the people you love. Please, come back to my house. We'll set up a room downstairs. Your friends can come."

For the first time since Jenna had met her, Serenity looked surprised. "You don't have to do that."

Beth moved close and took the other woman's hand. "I

want to. You're Jenna's mother, too. We should all be together."

Serenity looked at Tom. His eyes were red and sad and helpless. He seemed to be disintegrating by the minute.

"Thank you," Serenity told Beth. "That's very kind of you." She turned to Jenna. "I'm sorry I did this to you, but I wanted you to know me. So you could be a part of us and we could be a part of you. I did it for you and maybe a little for myself."

Jenna nodded, as if she understood, even though she didn't.

In less time than Jenna would have thought possible, the "catchall" downstairs room at her parents' house had been cleaned out and repurposed as Serenity's private sanctuary. A hospital bed was brought in, along with a rolling table, but those were the only concessions to her illness. She insisted on comfortable chairs for her many visitors and that the window treatments be removed from the windows. She wanted to see everything, she declared. Large plants found their way into the corners of the room. Incense and candles burned on most flat surfaces.

Jenna was there when Serenity arrived from the hospital. She looked pale and frail. Tom helped her into bed and she slept for several hours. As she did so, Jenna sat by her, and he made phone calls, telling their friends what had happened. Beth had prepared a list of local hotels.

When Tom finished and returned to Serenity's side, Jenna went into the kitchen to see her mother.

"This is going to be difficult," she told Beth.

"Life often is." Beth pointed to the vegan cookbook she'd bought at the store. "I'm only going to try a few basic things, and I'll make sure I have most of the ingredients on hand. I have a feeling there are going to be a lot of people to feed."

"I think you're right."

Beth smiled at her. "Are you okay?"

"I think so. I'm still in shock."

"Not so angry?"

"Oh, the anger is there. I'm simply ignoring it."

"That's my girl," Beth said with a low laugh. "When in doubt, pretend it doesn't exist. I think you got that from my mother."

"I got it from someone." She glanced at her watch. "Wolf is flying in today. Jasmine isn't comfortable flying so far in her pregnancy. He said her mother would be staying with her until he gets back."

Beth nodded, then sighed. "I know Serenity would have loved to live to see her grandchild."

Jenna wanted to say she still could, but she knew that wasn't going to happen. The cancer had spread. There was no stopping it.

"I'm going to work this afternoon," she said, grabbing her purse. "I'll be back around five."

"We'll be here."

Over the next two days, more visitors arrived. The hospice nurse came by every morning to check on Serenity. There were others, as well. Wolf, of course, and about a dozen people Jenna had never met. Young and old, male and female. A guy in his twenties sat on a cushion in the corner and played what Jenna was pretty sure was a sitar. A tall, old woman in a magical-looking headdress stood over Serenity and chanted. Ellington visited daily, but Jenna didn't see him much and never alone.

She supposed she should be angry with him, too, for keeping the secret. She understood the ethics of his relationship with Serenity and knew he had, in his own way, tried to tell her the truth.

The ebb and flow of visitors provided a rhythm to the days. There were stories about Serenity's life, laughter and plenty of tears. Jenna found herself torn between wanting to be close to Serenity and wanting to get away.

Violet came when she could, spending the evenings holding Dragon. Marshall stood by the door, watching it all, then slipping away to his study where the world was still normal. For Jenna, time went both too quickly and too slowly. As always, Beth was there, strong in her support.

A week after Serenity had left the hospital, the hospice nurse walked into the kitchen.

"Very soon," she said. "I thought you'd want to know."

"Thank you," Beth said, watching Jenna.

Jenna nodded but found she couldn't speak. "I'll stay home today," she managed at last. "I'll tell Violet to close the store."

"Whatever you think is best."

A young guy walked in holding incense, asking for matches. Beth handed them over. When he was gone, she looked at Jenna.

"I'm never going to get that smell out of the carpet."

Jenna smiled, then started to laugh. After a few seconds, the humor turned to tears.

"I'm a wreck."

"You're preparing for someone important in your life to die. Give yourself a break."

Jenna looked at her mother. "I love you."

"I love you, too, hon. Now wipe your face. Serenity doesn't want to see you cry."

She returned to Serenity's room to the music playing and

the candles burning. Serenity lay on her bed, her eyes closed, her breathing slow.

Tom leaned over her and whispered something.

She opened her eyes.

"My children are all here," she said, her voice weak. "Move closer. I want to see you."

Jenna found herself between Dragon and Wolf. Tom stood on the other side of the bed. They joined hands. Serenity studied each of them.

"I've been very blessed," she whispered. "I couldn't ask for more."

She seemed to choke. Jenna started to move toward her only to realize her breathing had stopped. She waited, willing it to start again, but it never did. There was only silence.

Someone put out the candles.

Twenty-One

Jenna didn't wait for Serenity's body to be removed by the local funeral home. Instead, as soon as Beth had called the hospice center, Jenna ducked out, racing to her car and driving away. She'd gone about three miles before realizing she didn't know where to go or who to talk to. Everyone she knew and loved was back at the house.

She drove aimlessly through Georgetown, thought about heading to Dallas and from there... Where was there to go? She knew she couldn't outrun what had just happened—that she had to deal with it sometime. Just maybe not today.

After nearly an hour, she found herself parking in front of the healing center where Ellington worked. She walked inside and introduced herself to the receptionist.

The young woman looked at her. "You're Serenity's daughter?" she asked, her voice cracking slightly.

Jenna nodded.

"We just heard. I'm so sorry. I really loved your mom. She was very special."

Jenna didn't bother pointing out Serenity wasn't her mother. Somehow in the past few weeks, that had changed. She'd learned it was possible to have two mothers. Even if one of them had just died.

"I'll get Ellington," the girl said, grabbed a tissue and walked to the back.

A few minutes later, Ellington came up to the waiting area. Without saying anything, he took her hand and led her through the main hallway to a small patio next to his office. When they were alone in the dappled sunlight, he touched her cheek.

"How are you holding up?" he asked.

"I'm angry."

"At me?"

"Partly." She crossed her arms and turned her back on him. "It's not just you," she said dully. "It's that everyone knew. Tom and Dragon and Wolf and Jasmine. They all knew and no one said anything."

"She'd asked them not to."

"You'd think one of them would have taken me aside and whispered a hint." She spun back to him, remembering. "You hinted."

"No."

"You did. I remember. But I didn't get it. I wasn't expecting this."

Frustration built inside of her. She walked the length of the patio.

"It doesn't make sense," she told him. "I've been asking and asking, why now? Why did she choose this moment to get in touch with me? Now I know. She wanted to meet me before she died, which I get. She claimed that I was important to her. She talked about me to my brothers and celebrated my birthday, but she never bothered to pick up the phone. How am I supposed to believe her? She said she was waiting for me to get in touch with her. So this is my fault?"

Ellington didn't answer her. It was not as though he had any miracle information to share.

"If she wanted to know me, why did she wait so long? She could have contacted my parents years ago. Or me. I'm not that hard to find."

"Life takes different turns for different people," he said quietly. "I can't say what drove Serenity. Guilt maybe. I always wondered if she felt she didn't deserve to know you—not after giving you up."

Deserve? "That's crazy. She was a kid who got pregnant. She gave me to a warm, loving home. I don't have any regrets."

"But you're not the one who gave away your child. Serenity loved with her whole heart. She gave everything. Perhaps giving up a child made her look at herself in a way she didn't like. Maybe it wasn't about you so much as her."

"We'll never know," she said, feeling sick to her stomach. "I don't like this. Any of it. If I'd known, I would have asked different questions. I would have asked for the truth."

"If she'd wanted you to know, she would have told you."

She whirled to face him. "That's supposed to be good enough? I should believe that?"

"You don't have a choice."

She shook her head. "I don't accept that."

"Not accepting doesn't change what is."

"Don't you dare go all guru on me, Ellington. You've had your tongue in my mouth."

He gave her a smile. "That puts things in perspective."

There was a moment when she didn't feel quite so horrible, then the pain and anger descended, leaving her sad.

"I don't know what happens next," she said. "Do I stay in touch with my birth family? Do I not?"

"You don't have to decide today."

"I'm just so mad at her for dying like that. For not making things clear."

"Would you rather not have known her?"

A simple question, she thought, turning the words over in her mind. It would have made her life easier. She'd just been getting it all together when Serenity had shown up to mess it all up again.

"No," she whispered. "I don't wish that."

"Then take what you were given and treasure it. You knew her. She touched your life and you touched hers."

She glared at him. "I swear to God, if you start talking about ripples in a pond, I'll hit you."

"Sorry. Sometimes I get carried away."

"You need to stay away from the spiritual for a while. Get in touch with the real world. Go to Las Vegas for a weekend."

"I'll consider that." He moved close and drew her into his arms. "You're angry because she died. That's normal."

"The first stage of grief?"

"That, too. But in your case, you have legitimate reasons to be angry. My only concern is that you don't let that overshadow the relationship you had with Serenity. You can remember what was good or wallow in what has you so pissed. The choice is yours."

He smelled clean and masculine. Familiar. "I don't wallow."

"You were headed there."

"I have all these feelings and I don't know where to put them."

"Maybe they don't belong anywhere but where they are right now."

"Churning inside of me?"

"That's as good a place as any."

She sighed. "You always tell me the truth. I like that about you."

He kissed the top of her head. "At the risk of having you hit me, I can't regret having Serenity in either of our lives. Not only did I find her an amazing person, she brought us together."

"There is that."

He touched her chin, forcing her to meet his gaze. "I don't want to lose you over this," he said.

"You won't."

"I kept her secret."

"True, but I understand. Part of it because you're a medical professional and you had to, legally. Part of it is because she asked you to. Integrity can be infuriating, but it's important."

"Thank you."

"You're welcome."

Reluctantly she stepped away. "I need to get back to the house. There are going to be a lot of details to take care of. I'm guessing the funeral will be in Napa."

"Can I help?" he asked.

"I don't think so, but I'll let you know if that changes."

"Good. You'll call when you get back?"

She nodded. "Promise."

Beth stood with Tom in the small apartment he and Serenity had rented. There were signs of Serenity everywhere.

From the bright lavender sweater thrown over the back of a chair to the yoga mat rolled up in the corner. Flowers spilled out of several vases and a teacup still half-full of tea sat on the kitchen counter.

Beth guided him to the sofa and urged him to sit. She went and searched for coffee. When she didn't find any, she put water on to boil, then dug out some green tea bags. Quiet sobs drew her back.

Tom sat where she'd left him, his head in his hands. The tall broad-shouldered man looked broken. She moved toward him, then sat on the ottoman so she could face him.

He looked up at her, his face pale, his eyes dark with anguish. "I can't do this. I can't live without her. I've loved her my whole life."

She took both his hands in hers and squeezed. "You loved her and she loved you back. You had her complete heart. You made three beautiful children with her and now you have a grandchild on the way."

He dropped his head and began to cry. "I just want her back. She was too young, too full of life. I never wanted to believe this would happen. I told myself that she was different." He paused to catch his breath. "I didn't think she was going to die."

Beth swallowed her own tears. Tom's pain was as tangible as the floor and as big as the sky. She didn't bother trying to find the words to make it better. She knew they didn't exist.

The kettle began to whistle.

She got up and returned to the kitchen where she poured boiling water into two mugs and dunked in the bags. The smell of the green tea nearly made her gag, but she carried both mugs into the living room and handed him one.

"Thanks," he said, sounding grateful. Tears still poured from his eyes.

This time she settled next to him and put her mug on the coffee table.

"I'll get everything together here," she said. "What won't fit in the suitcases, I'll ship back in boxes." She hesitated. "Unless you want me to take care of her personal things."

He shuddered. "She has a few pieces of jewelry she wanted Jenna to have. They're back home. Everything here..." He swallowed, then ducked his head again.

"I'll take care of it," Beth said gently. She would get Dragon's address and ship everything to him. He could take Serenity's belongings over to his father when he was sure Tom could handle it.

She patted Tom on the shoulder and walked into the bedroom of their small rented apartment.

It only took a few minutes to pack up his clothes and toiletries. He and his sons were flying out that afternoon, with the funeral to follow in a few days. Marshall had arranged for their car to be delivered back to them using a moving service. It was already on its way.

When she returned to the living room, Tom was sitting exactly as she'd left him. His misery filled the room, making her ache in sympathy.

She sat with him until Wolf and Dragon arrived. Both young men looked as sad as their father.

"Thanks for all your help," Dragon said, giving her a quick hug. "We couldn't have gotten through all this without you."

"Of course," she said. She handed over the suitcase. "I'll send everything else back after the funeral." She looked at Dragon. "I thought I would send it to you."

He nodded. "Good idea." He pulled a business card out of his wallet. "Send it to the office."

"I will."

Wolf went to his father and drew him to his feet. "Jasmine called. She's in labor. We're hoping for a girl, Dad."

Tom walked unsteadily. "Serenity would have liked to see your baby born."

"She'll be there," Wolf told him, wiping his face. "I know she'll be in the room with us."

Tom nodded.

When he reached the doorway, he turned back to Beth. "I don't know what to say."

"You don't have to say anything. Jenna and I are flying in tomorrow morning. Let us know if you need anything."

"I'll pick you up at the airport," Dragon said.

"You stay with your family. We're renting a car. We'll call when we land in San Francisco."

"All right."

She smiled at Wolf. "Please tell Jasmine I wish her the best with the baby."

"Thanks. The midwife says it'll be a few hours yet. I should be home before the baby's born."

Life went on, Beth thought. No matter how much anyone suffered, life went on.

She walked them to Dragon's rental car. When they were gone, she returned to her SUV and pulled out the boxes she'd brought.

In less than an hour she'd packed up everything. When her car was loaded, she dropped off the keys with the landlord and drove to the post office to mail the boxes to Dragon. Then she returned home.

The hospice people had been by that morning to take back the hospital bed and table. The chairs and sofa had been returned to their usual places. Except for a few plants in the corners and the incense and half-burned candles on the windowsill, the room was empty.

Without having to close her eyes, Beth could hear the conversations, the laughter, the chanting, the tears. She remembered Serenity's last breath and willed her spirit to a peaceful place. Then she stepped out of the room and closed the door behind her.

She spent the rest of the afternoon getting ready for her trip to California. When Marshall arrived home a little after five, she had dinner mostly made and his favorite martinis waiting in a pitcher.

He smiled when he saw her, set his briefcase on one of the kitchen chairs, then crossed to her and kissed her.

"How are you holding up?" he asked.

"I'm okay. Getting through it." She looked into his face. "I don't tell you enough how much I love you. You're a wonderful man, Marshall Stevens, and I'm very fortunate to have you in my life."

"I'm the lucky one," he said.

She smiled. "I wish that were true, but it's not. You're everything to me. I want you to promise you'll never die."

"Sweet Beth."

He kissed her again, this time lingering in that special way of his. The one that always made her stomach flip and her insides tingle.

"I'm not going anywhere," he murmured.

Which wasn't exactly the same but would have to do, she told herself. "I'm not going anywhere, either."

Serenity's funeral was as unexpected as her arrival in Jenna's life had been. On a warm, early-summer afternoon, nearly three hundred people gathered in an old church to celebrate a life cut too short.

Jenna stood with Beth, just behind the row with Tom, Dragon, Wolf, Jasmine and baby Serenity. The infant had been born two hours after her daddy had arrived home and nearly forty-eight hours to the minute after her grandmother had died.

Friends and neighbors filled the church and spilled out onto the lawn where loudspeakers carried the service to those who wouldn't fit inside.

A minister spoke first, followed by a man in a robe. Jenna had a feeling many religions were represented as people spoke kindly of Serenity, telling stories that indicated she had known each of them. Dragon and Wolf talked about how much she had loved them and how she had been loved in return. Jenna had said she didn't want to say anything, and now, as she listened to other people talk about the woman she'd barely known, she was grateful to remain silent. She didn't regret having known her biological mother. She couldn't. She was a part of Serenity, and Serenity would always be a part of her. They were connected by more than biology. Serenity was her mother. How could she put those feelings into words?

After the funeral, everyone made their way to the family home. Jenna had already spent most of the morning cooking food from Serenity's stash of favorite recipes. She had made a lentil salad, sweet potatoes with curried beans, cookies and a whipped dessert called "Apricot Fluff."

She and Beth ducked into the kitchen to bring out what had been made only to find every inch of surface covered with casserole dishes. There were instructions on all of them, along with notes to Tom and his sons about how the cook had felt about Serenity.

"These are wonderful," Beth said. She dug around in a couple of drawers, then pulled out some paper and a pen. "I'm going to copy the notes and take them home with me. I can print them up in different fonts, then make a scrapbook for Tom."

"He would love that."

"Poor man." Beth read the nearest note, then started copying. "He's going to have a tough time."

"They all are."

Beth looked up at her. "Are you all right?"

Jenna nodded. "Thanks for coming with me, Mom. I couldn't have done this without you."

"I'm happy to be here. You know I'd do anything for you."

"I do."

From the living room came the sound of a guitar followed by a man singing. It took her a second to realize the song was "Amazing Grace."

Beth stopped writing and took Jenna's hand. Together they walked into the living room to join the others and finish the song.

Twenty-Two

The following Tuesday morning Jenna returned to the store. She found herself excited about getting back to the familiar routine of work. Violet had kept things running, which was a blessing. She was determined to give her new manager a week off as a gesture of thanks.

Stepping into her store was like coming home. She paused to enjoy the sight of full shelves, a crammed cooking class schedule and Violet sorting through food for the baskets they would sell.

"You're back!" Violet said, grinning at her. "I was hoping you'd come in today. People have been asking about you."

"I have returned and I'm not leaving again ever. Well, I might take a vacation in a year. How have things been?"

"Busy," Violet told her. "We're getting swamped with class requests."

"That's what I want to hear."

Although she'd spoken to Violet every day she'd been

gone, Jenna still had her friend take her through the highlights of what had been going on in the past ten days. While she was dealing with a lot of emotion, it felt good to be back at work, doing what she loved.

"The cast-iron cookware is doing great," Violet said, taking her to that section of the store. "Having it in so many colors helps, too, but it takes up a lot of room." She paused. "The landlord called while you were gone. The insurance company on the other side of us isn't going to be renewing its lease and he wondered if we wanted the space. He won't need an answer for about three weeks."

"There's a thought," Jenna murmured to herself. "We could put in an even bigger cooking area and let this part be all retail."

"That's what I was thinking," Violet said. "And I was thinking with the leftover space, we could have a little bistro that serves lunch. Maybe feature a different kind of cuisine each day. French on Monday, Italian on Tuesday, High Tea on Wednesday. That way the menu would be different and people would be comfortable coming back frequently."

"I hadn't thought of that," Jenna admitted, "but I like it. I know a lot of people at the culinary school both here and in Dallas. We could find a local chef who wants to work our lunch shift. Great idea."

"Thanks." Violet looked happy and excited as she spoke. "Only Ewe is a double space as well, so between us, we'd take up most of the block. Robyn and I have been talking about ways to do cross promotion. We're thinking of talking to the day spa one street over and see if they're interested, too. Our demographics all match."

Jenna heard an insistent tapping on the front door. She looked up and saw several women waiting to be let in. It was only five to ten, but who was she to argue with customers?

"We'll talk about this later," she promised. "I love all your ideas."

"That's what you pay me for."

When Jenna and Violet had come to terms on Violet's promotion to manager, they'd agreed on a small increase in salary along with a percentage of the profits. Apparently she was determined to make the most of the opportunity, which Jenna appreciated. Hiring Violet had been a good day.

Jenna unlocked the front door and held it open. She was immediately embraced by all the women waiting, a balancing act considering most of them were carrying covered dishes.

"We missed you."

"Such a loss. Serenity was wonderful."

"How you holding up, hon? Can I do anything?"

She greeted them all and returned the hugs, then pointed to the cooking area as a place to drop off their food.

But, unlike the people in Napa who had brought goodies for later, they quickly set out their food, as if they were having a party. It quickly became clear they were.

"I made Serenity's seven-layer dip," Virginia Heaton told Jenna, then wrinkled her nose. "Although I did use real sour cream and cheese."

Betty Vorse had brought several of the appetizers Jenna had taught early on, while Erica West carried in a Crock-Pot containing curried lentil soup.

By eleven there were over twenty women in the store, all eating and talking, telling stories about Serenity. Beth arrived with the last wave and moved toward Jenna.

"Violet called and said what was going on. I wanted to come join the fun."

"I'm glad you did," Jenna told her.

Beth tucked a loose strand of Jenna's hair behind her daughter's ear. "How are you holding up?"

"I'm okay. This is exactly what she would have wanted."

Beth eyed the table. "Without the chorizo dip."

Jenna grabbed a chip and dug in. "She might have tried it."

The women stayed well into the afternoon. About one, Robyn popped in from Only Ewe. She had a long, slim wrapped package in her hands.

"I heard there was a party," she said.

"A memorial for Serenity," Jenna told her. "There's plenty of food. Every time we start to get low, someone else shows up with something delicious."

"Serenity would say that was the universe at work," Beth said with a laugh. "In this case, she would be right."

Robyn handed Jenna the package. "She was making this for you. She died before it was done, so I finished it."

Jenna set down her glass of soda and took the gift. She set it on a table and carefully opened the plain gold paper. Inside was a knitted puppet of a chef with long red hair and green eyes. The puppet had on a tiny chef's jacket with "Jenna" stenciled on the left side.

Jenna felt tears fill her eyes. She didn't bother to fight them, instead giving in to both the loss and the happiness she felt.

"Thank you," she whispered. "It's perfect."

"She was amazing," Robyn said. "I barely knew her, but she touched my life. That's a special gift."

"The best gift," Beth added. "To love and be loved is our purpose. Serenity gave us all that treasure."

"And tofu," Jenna added with a half laugh, half sob.

Beth leaned against her, chuckling. "And tofu."

Violet raised her glass. "To Serenity. May you always travel with the wings of a butterfly."

"To Serenity."

Jenna drank to the unexpected gift that had been her birth mother. The woman who had brought each of them joy.

Violet arrived home happy and exhausted. The day had been emotional but also wonderful. She was excited about the plans for the store and happy to know that Jenna wanted to go along with all of them.

For once, she entered her apartment without thinking about Cliff. Her ribs were healing, as was her spirit. She wasn't whole yet, but she knew she soon would be.

After kicking off her shoes, she headed to the small kitchen. Thanks to Jenna, she was no longer content with a frozen dinner. Instead, she pulled out fresh tomatoes and the sea scallops she'd bought the previous day. She would sauté them in butter and garlic, serving them with pasta with fresh tomato and basil sauce along with a green salad. She'd had a long conversation with the wine expert at the Georgetown Winery and with her help had picked out two chardonnays and a merlot to try.

She'd barely pulled out a bowl to start the salad when someone knocked on her door.

Her first reaction was fear. Instinctive, powerful, it nearly made her knees buckle. Then she drew in a deep breath, despite the protest from her ribs, squared her shoulders and walked to the door. Cliff was back in Illinois. Marshall had confirmed that for her. She was safe. Better than that, she was stronger than she'd been before. Eventually, she would get her fight-or-flight response to realize that.

She peeked through the security hole and was surprised to see Dragon standing in front of her door. She quickly let him in.

"What are you doing here?" she asked. "Shouldn't you be in San Francisco?"

He looked tired and rumpled but still gorgeous. He had a garment bag in one hand and a briefcase in the other. When he saw her glance at them, he shook his head.

"I'm not moving in. I have a hotel a few miles away, but I wanted to see you. I needed to see you."

There was an intensity to his words, his gaze. They didn't frighten her at all, but they did leave her feeling confused.

"Why?" she asked.

He dropped his luggage onto the floor. "I miss you, Violet. I miss everything about you."

"You barely know me."

One corner of his mouth turned up. "Fair enough. I miss what I do know." He drew in a breath. "I'm here for a job interview. Actually, three."

She knew she should probably invite him to sit down or open a bottle of wine or something, but she couldn't seem to move. "I don't understand."

"I want to move here. I may have to work in Austin rather than Georgetown. Two of the interviews are there. But I'd still be close, right?"

"I don't understand."

The smile got bigger. "You just said that."

"I know, but it's still true. Why would you leave your other job?"

"Because I want to be with you and long-distance relationships suck."

She sank onto her sofa and tried to catch her breath. Dragon wanted to be with her? Was this a game?

He sat next to her. "Please don't tell me you don't understand."

"I don't. No one moves halfway across the country for a woman he's met three times."

"It's more than three times." He angled toward her. "I

want to get to know you better. I want to spend time with you. The only way I know how to do that is to be in the same town."

She heard the physical words. Individually they made sense, but when put into sentences, he might as well have been speaking Klingon.

"What if it doesn't work out?" she asked. "You will have turned your life upside down for nothing."

"A chance I'm willing to take."

He sounded as if he meant it. When she looked into his dark eyes, she saw sincerity and promise and a few other emotions she was scared to identify.

"This is nuts," she said, pushing to her feet and staring at him. "Did you listen when I told you about my past? I'm not kidding, Dragon. I was a prostitute. I have no idea how many men I've been with. I did drugs."

Despite all that, she'd escaped the life without any serious medical concerns and only a few broken bones. But the past was still there.

"You're a corporate lawyer," she continued. "I don't know how to do that."

"You probably don't want to get into the lawyer thing. What with not having passed the bar and all."

"You know what I mean. I can't be with those people. They'll know."

He stood. "They won't know unless you tell them and if they do, I don't care."

"You say that now, but you'll change your mind. I have tattoos."

The slow, sexy grin returned. "I know."

She wanted to believe him, wanted to go to him and do whatever he wanted, but she couldn't.

"Don't," she said, stepping back. "This is wrong. You're

playing a game and I'll be the one hurt. Cliff may have hurt me but you'd break my heart."

He crossed to her in two long strides, then cupped her face in his hands.

"It's not a game, Violet. I'm moving here because I need to be with you. If my mother's death taught me anything, it's that you have to seize the moment. To go after the people you love and make them important in your life."

He kissed her lightly. "You're everything I've been looking for. I know that sounds like a line, so I'm willing to go slow. But the second I saw you, I knew. Maybe it's destiny. All I can say for sure is I will do anything not to lose you."

She opened her mouth, then closed it. What was she supposed to say to that?

"You're not the only one at risk," he reminded her. "I'm putting myself on the line, too. But there's nowhere else I want to be."

The need to believe him burned hotter and brighter than any sun. She was desperate to give herself over to him but wasn't sure she had it in her to take a leap of faith.

He kissed her again, lingering this time, his mouth soft and warm.

"You have to heal," he said. "Not only on the outside, but on the inside. I'm a patient man. Just do me one favor. Don't go falling for anyone else while that's happening."

"Okay," she whispered, the word coming out involuntarily.

"Yeah?"

"You'd kind of be a hard act to follow."

He grinned. "I like hearing that." The smile faded. "Don't freak out, Violet, but I intend to marry you. You're the one."

The world jolted once. She stared at him, unable to speak.

Don't say it if you don't mean it.

She wasn't sure if she thought the words or said them out loud. Either way, he heard them.

"I mean it," he told her.

"I've never been the one before."

"You'd better get used to it. We Johnson men tend to bond for life."

He dropped his arms to her shoulders and drew her close. She stepped closer, willing to give him the chance he'd asked for, to maybe trust just a little.

"What if this takes longer than you think?" she asked suddenly.

"I'll be right here. I promise. I don't scare easily, nor do I give up."

"I won't give up, either," she promised, knowing it was as much as she had to pledge right now. But the promise of more filled her with a happiness she hadn't experienced in a long time. Maybe ever.

"What if he hates me?" Jenna asked nervously as she hovered in the living room of her parents' house.

"Why would he hate you?" Beth asked patiently.

"I'm dating his father. He might resent me."

"Just be yourself. Children respect that."

Probably good advice, Jenna thought, wishing her stomach would stop spinning and flipping. Advice she would take just as soon as the need to throw up went away.

It was a warm, sunny Sunday afternoon. Beth and Marshall were hosting a barbecue. Dragon and Violet were already in the back, as were other friends. Ellington and his son were due to arrive any second.

Life had gone on, Jenna thought. Toward the end of the week, Beth and Marshall would fly to California to spend a long weekend with Tom. Plans for expanding the store were well underway, and Jenna had already found a great chef to handle their new lunchtime service. Which was great, because she needed every spare moment to develop recipes for her new cookbook.

Dragon and Violet had started dating. They were both going slow, probably smart under the circumstances, but Jenna had a feeling they were going to make it.

Jenna and Ellington were also getting serious. She'd met his mother and mother-in-law and had apparently passed their inspection because she was now going to meet Isaiah.

Seven months ago, she'd felt broken. She would have said her life was a failure. Now everything was different. Not just her circumstances, but who she was on the inside.

The doorbell rang. Jenna jumped then hurried to open it.

Ellington stood on the wide covered porch, a small boy at his side. The child had dark hair and blue eyes, along with an open and engaging smile.

"Are you Jenna?" he asked eagerly. "I made you a picture."

He handed over a sheet of paper with a stick figure grouping of a man, a woman with red hair and a child at what looked like a picnic.

Jenna took it and smiled. "Wow. That's amazing. Is the lady with the red hair me?"

Isaiah nodded. "Daddy said you were real pretty. I'm not that good an artist, but I did my best."

"You did a great job. Come on in."

They stepped inside.

Beth introduced herself to Isaiah, then they all went out back and met the rest of the group. Isaiah gasped when he saw the big pool.

"Dad said we were going swimming, but I didn't know it would be this good." He walked up to Jenna and grinned. "Will you swim with me?"

"I would love to."

"Hey," Ellington said in mock annoyance. "That's *my* girl."

Isaiah giggled. "Daddy, you know you're always telling me to share. You have to share, too."

Everyone laughed.

Marshall took Isaiah aside and showed him how to make a fancy drink with grape juice, sparkling water and chunks of fresh fruit on a stick. Their neighbors, the Thomases, arrived, bringing Millie, their Golden Lab. Boy and dog bonded instantly and began chasing each other around the yard.

Jenna and Beth went into the kitchen to finish up the prep work.

Through the big windows, Jenna could see everyone having a great time. Dragon sat next to Violet, their hands entwined. Happiness radiated from both of them, which made Jenna feel all bubbly inside. Her dad was showing Isaiah how to throw the Frisbee to Millie. Ellington was in deep conversation with the Thomases, no doubt hearing about Mrs. Thomas's latest ache or pain.

"I've been thinking about my birthday," Beth said, leaning against the counter. "I know what I want."

"What?"

She smiled. "I want us to get matching butterfly tattoos. For Serenity."

Jenna laughed. "She would like that."

"I'm not telling your father," Beth admitted. "It's going to be a surprise."

"I'm not sure what he'll think."

Beth grinned. "That's half the fun."

Jenna felt a whisper of something against her arm. As if someone had touched her lightly. Affectionately. There was no one else in the room, but she knew who the touch had come from.

Love, it seemed, knew no barriers of space and time.

"I love you, Mom," Jenna whispered, speaking to both of the women who were responsible for her being here today. "Look."

Beth glanced to where Jenna pointed. A brightly colored butterfly fluttered next to the kitchen window, brushed against the glass, then flew away.

★ ★ ★ ★ ★

Book Club Guide

Suggested Menu:

Drink:
Margaritas

Appetizers:
Jalapeno Poppers

Meal:
Jenna's Mocha Chili (recipe follows)

Dessert:
Apricot Fluff

Jenna's Mocha Chili

1 onion, chopped

1 lb. hamburger

2 cloves garlic, minced

1 28-oz can of crushed tomatoes

1 15-oz can of whole, peeled tomatoes, undrained

2 15-oz cans of dark red kidney beans, undrained

2 T chili powder

1 t instant coffee granules

1 t cocoa powder

For mild chili: 1 green bell pepper, diced
For medium chili: 2 jalapeno peppers, seeds removed, chopped
For hot chili: 2-3 jalapeno peppers with seeds, chopped

Brown the hamburger in a heavy-bottomed pan, stirring frequently. Add onion and garlic and sauté until garlic is fragrant, about 30 seconds longer. Drain off the grease. Mix all ingredients together. Simmer for 1 hour on the stovetop or put into a slow cooker on high for 3 hours or low for 6 hours. To make this a vegetarian meal in honor of Serenity, omit the hamburger, sauté the onions and garlic in a little olive oil, and add 2 more cans of beans. You can use more kidney beans if you'd like, or you can use black beans or pinto beans for some variety.

Serve plain or top with onions, cheese, sour cream and/or avocado.

For more free recipes, join the Members Only area at www.susanmallery.com!

QUESTIONS FOR DISCUSSION

1. What are the major themes of this story? How does the title support these themes? Explain your thoughts.

2. Susan Mallery has often been praised for writing stories that pull at readers' emotions. Looking back on the story, discuss the moments that were the most emotional for you. What moments made you cry? What moments made you laugh?

3. What were the turning points? How and when did the characters change and grow? Who changed the most? Explain.

4. Which mother—Beth or Serenity—did you relate to the most, and why? Which father was the most like your father or husband, and why?

5. Discuss the ways the women in this story were different, and then talk about the traits they had in common.

6. Why do you think Serenity and Tom waited so long to find Jenna? Did they do the right thing? Why or why not? How should they have handled things differently? Under what circumstances do you think Jenna might have looked for her birth parents, if they hadn't come looking for her?

7. Discuss the turning points in Violet's subplot. How did this subplot support the major themes of the story? If you were Violet, how would you have reacted when Cliff

was rude to Jenna and Ellington? Have you ever missed warning signs in your own life?

8. Do you think things will work out between Jenna and Ellington? Violet and Dragon? Why or why not?

9. If you had to reinvent yourself the way Jenna did after her divorce, what would you do?

10. Under what circumstances could you see yourself giving up a child for adoption?

11. Do you believe that some people really are more in tune with the universe? Have you ever followed your intuition, your gut, even when logic said you shouldn't? What happened? How did the situation turn out? Were you right to listen to your gut, or should you have stuck with logic?

12. Beth struggled with weight all her life, but Jenna and Marshall thought she was beautiful as she was. Why do you think so many women feel dissatisfied with their bodies?

13. How will having known Serenity impact Jenna throughout her life? How has Jenna changed because Serenity entered her life? What do you think Jenna's life might've been like if she had been raised by her birth parents?